THE
ENEMY

CHARLIE HIGSON

Hyperion

New York

Text copyright © 2009 by Charlie Higson

First published in the U.K. by Puffin

All rights reserved. Published by Hyperion, an imprint of
Disney Book Group. No part of this book may be reproduced or
transmitted in any form or by any means, electronic or mechanical, including
photocopying, recording, or by any information storage and retrieval system,
without written permission from the publisher. For information address
Hyperion, 114 Fifth Avenue, New York, New York 10011-5690.

Printed in the United States of America
First Hyperion paperback edition, 2011
1 3 5 7 9 10 8 6 4 2

ISBN 978-1-4231-3312-4

Map illustration by Kayley Le Favier

Visit www.hyperionteens.com

For Sidney

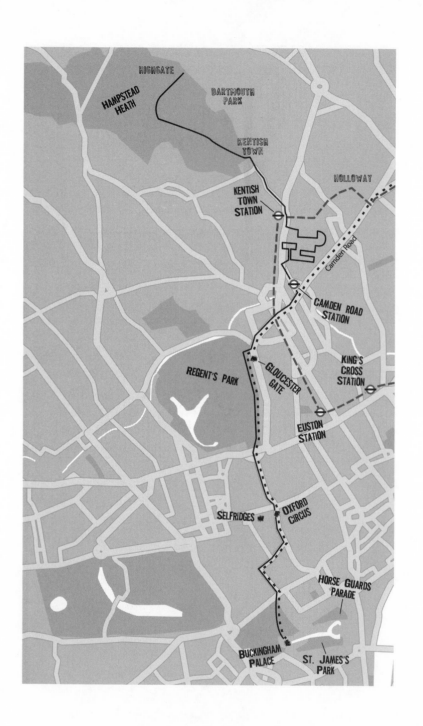

LONDON

THE MORRISONS/ · · · · · · · · ·
WAITROSE CREW

SMALL SAM — — — — — — —

SOPHIE'S CREW ————————

MORRISONS

WAITROSE ARSENAL
FOOTBALL
STADIUM

Holloway Road

ANGEL
STATION

OLD ST.
STATION

SPITALFIELDS

THE
GHERKIN

BANK
STATION

THE TOWER
OF LONDON

THE
ENEMY

Small Sam was playing in the parking lot behind the Waitrose supermarket when the grown-ups took him. He'd been with some of the little kids, having a battle with an odd assortment of action figures, when it happened. They weren't supposed to play outside without a guard, but it was a lovely sunny day and the little kids got bored indoors. Sam wasn't the youngest of the group, but he was the smallest. That's why they called him Small Sam. There had originally been two other Sams, Big Sam and Curly Sam, who had curly hair. Big Sam had been killed a few months ago, but Small Sam was stuck with the name.

It was probably because of his size that the grown-ups went for him. They were like that—they picked out the youngsters, the weaklings, the little ones. In the panic of the attack the rest of Sam's gang got back safely inside, but Sam was cut off and the roving pack of grown-ups trapped him in a corner.

They had come over the side wall, led by a big mother in a tracksuit that might once have been pink but was now so filthy and greasy it looked like gray plastic. She had a fat, egglike body on top of long skinny legs. Her back was bent and she ran stooped over, but surprisingly fast, her arms held wide like a scorpion's claws, her dirty blond hair hanging straight down. Her face blank and stupid. Breathing through her mouth.

Small Sam was too scared even to scream or call for help, and the grown-ups made no noise, so the whole scene was played out in horrible silence. The mother blocked off the route back toward the building while two lanky fathers ran at him from either side. Sam dodged them for a few seconds, but he knew they'd get hold of him in the end. By the time help came from inside, the grown-ups had gone back over the wall, with Sam stuffed inside a sack.

Maxie led a group of bigger kids out into the parking lot. Even though they were armed with spears and clubs and good throwing rocks, they moved cautiously, not knowing exactly what to expect.

"We're too late," said Callum, scanning the empty parking lot. "They've got him."

"Shame," said a stocky, dark-haired kid called Josh. "I liked him. He was funny."

"That's the second attack this week," said Maxie angrily. "What's going on? Either the grown-ups are closing in on us, or they're getting braver."

"They ain't brave," said Josh, spitting on the ground. "If they was still here I'd show them brave. I'd mash their ugly faces. Nothing scares me."

"So why were they here?" asked Maxie.

"They're just hungry," said Josh.

"We're all hungry," said Callum.

"We should have been here," said Maxie. "We should have been watching over them."

"We can't be everywhere at once," Callum pointed out. "There's not enough of us, not with Arran out with the scavs. Our job's to keep a lookout from the roof. The little kids knew they weren't supposed to be out here. Nobody should be out here. We should all stay inside."

"We can't stay inside all day," scoffed Josh. "We'd go crazy."

"It's good inside," said Callum.

"You're just scared to come outside," said Josh with a smirk.

"No I ain't," said Callum. "No more scared than you."

"Nothing scares me," said Josh.

"Then you're just stupid," said Callum.

"Nah," said Josh. "The thing about grown-ups is, some of them are strong, some of them can run fast, and some of them are clever, but the strong ones are slow, the fast ones are stupid, and the smart ones are weak."

"Tell that to Small Sam," said Maxie angrily, "and to Big Sam and Johnno, and Eve and Mohammed and all the other kids we've lost."

"Grown-ups won't get me," said Josh.

"What?" said Callum. "So it was their fault they got taken? Is that what you're saying?"

"Yeah, I am," said Josh.

"Shut up," Maxie snapped at the two of them. Then she said the thing that nobody wanted to admit. "We can't go on like this." Her voice was heavy with bitterness. "Soon we're all going to be dead. I can't stand it anymore."

She threw down the spear she had been carrying and sat on the ground, resting her head in her hands.

It was her fault. That was all she could think. It was all her fault.

When Arran was away she was supposed to be in charge. She couldn't remember when it had been decided—Arran was the leader, she was second in command—it must have happened early on, when most of the kids had been too frightened and confused to do anything for themselves. Arran and Maxie had just got on with it, organizing everyone, keeping their spirits up. Arran was clever and likeable. Right from the start he'd kept his head and not panicked. He'd been captain of the soccer team at William Ellis School, and nothing ever seemed to freak him out. The two of them had worked together. A team. Maxie had always been good at getting other children to help out. There were better fighters than her, true, but they were happy for her to tell them what to do. They didn't want the responsibility. And when Arran wasn't there, she was the leader.

So, it was all her fault. Another kid gone. She shut down part of her mind. She didn't want to think about what the grown-ups would do to Small Sam.

She started to cry. She didn't care who saw it. Callum looked at Josh. They both felt awkward. In the end it was Josh who squatted down next to her and put an arm around her shoulders.

"It's all right, Max," he said quietly. "We'll be all right. Something'll happen, someone will come. Something's gonna change. When Arran and the others get back we'll talk about it maybe, yeah? Make a plan?"

"What's the point?" said Maxie.

"When Arran gets back, yeah?"

Maxie looked up into Josh's concerned, grubby face. "Sorry," she said.

"Come on," said Callum. "Let's try and find out how they got over the wall. Then we should get back inside."

"Yeah." Maxie jumped up. It was okay as long as you were doing something, as long as you didn't stop and think.

She wished Arran were here, though. She always felt safer when he was around.

It was just . . . What was he going to think?

Another kid gone.

All her fault.

2

A burster was lying in the middle of the road. A father by the looks of it, though it was hard to tell. He had the familiar look of a vegetable, or a piece of fruit, left too long in the sun. The skin blackened, shriveled and split, the overripe flesh inside squeezing out. His insides had turned to mush. This was what happened if any grown-up lived long enough to let the disease run its full course. They literally burst.

Arran prodded the body with his sneaker. As he did so, the skin popped, and a stream of pus oozed out, followed by a bright pink blossom of soft fat.

Arran was leading the scavenger party. Tall, fair-haired, and athletic, he had a knife in his belt and carried a pickax handle as a club.

"Gross," sniggered the boy at his side, who had a shock of curly hair bleached almost white.

"Come on. We don't have time for this." Arran turned his back on the corpse and continued up Holloway Road. When the disaster first happened the kids had been appalled and fascinated by dead bodies. Now they were used to them. They hardly even noticed them. A burster, though, was still a little special.

The scavenger party took up their positions with Arran and trudged on. They hadn't gone another hundred yards, however, before the bleach-haired boy, Deke, slowed down.

"What's that?"

They stopped and listened.

"Dogs," said another boy, and he moved to the front. He was shorter than Arran and not as strong. He had proved time and time again, though, that fighting was not all about strength. Arran was the leader, but Achilleus was the best fighter of them all, with a wiry build, dark eyes, and olive skin. He spent most of his spare time shaving elaborate patterns into his short hair. He could be moody and sarcastic and quick to lose his temper, but nobody much minded because he'd saved them all many times with his combat skills. He moved fast, used his brain, and was utterly ruthless in a fight.

They waited. They could hear the dogs long before they saw them. A cacophony of howling, yelping, and barking. All jumbled together, it sounded like a single mad beast.

Achilleus leveled his spear, pointing it toward the noise. It was made from a metal spike he'd found on a building site. It had a heavy lump at one end, and he'd sharpened the other into a vicious point. It was perfect for keeping grown-ups at bay. He could stab with the front and use the back end to batter them. It was definitely not for throwing. Too precious for that.

Arran took up a defensive position behind him, next to Freak and Deke. Freak and Deke were a team, best mates. Before the disaster they'd taken to the streets armed only with spray cans. Their tag was "Freaky-Deaky," and it could be seen all over Tufnell Park and Camden Town, sprayed on walls and shutters, stenciled on to the sidewalks, scratched on the glass in bus shelters. They knew all the back ways, all the alleys and shortcuts. Freak, whose real name was David, had close-cropped hair and a thin, pinched face. He was always sniffing. Deke was the bigger of the two. He was good looking and would have been popular with the girls if he hadn't spent all his time with Freak. The two were inseparable, always finishing each other's sentences and laughing at each other's jokes. Freak carried an ax and Deke a sledgehammer. They were mainly for knocking down doors and opening windows, although, if needed, they could be used as weapons.

The last in the group was Ollie. Small and red haired, the cleverest of them all. He had sharp eyes and could think quickly. He kept himself to himself, and most of the time he kept quiet. But when he did speak, people listened. Arran would often ask Ollie for advice, and it was never seen as a weakness. Ollie always knew the best thing to do.

As the barking of the dogs grew louder, Ollie stepped back and to one side, keeping a clear line of sight. His weapon was a slingshot that he had taken from a sports shop. It was a powerful hunter's model, with a pistol grip and a metal brace that fitted over his forearm. He drew the rubber band back and tucked a heavy steel ball into the worn leather pouch.

Whenever the kids were outside of camp, they traveled in groups of at least four. One to look ahead and lead the way, two to check the sides, and one to watch their backs. But, as Freak and Deke always worked together, there were five of them today. They had learned early on to move down the middle of the roads, rather than to stay out of sight among the buildings along the sides. Grown-ups could hide in the shadows and grab you from the darkness. They weren't such a threat in the open, because on the whole they didn't move fast enough. The biggest danger was if you got surrounded.

In a mass the grown-ups were a real threat, bigger and heavier than the kids, and diseased. Grown-ups were rarely organized enough to plan any real strategy, though, and for the most part they came lumbering out in a pack from the side. Then the best thing to do was run.

Anything to avoid a fight.

Dogs were different, however. Unpredictable. Dangerous.

"Are they coming our way?" said Freak, scratching his stubbly head.

"Think so," said Ollie, his slingshot creaking.

"Let them," said Achilleus. "I'm ready."

"It gets more dangerous every time we come out," said Arran.

"Tell me about it," said Deke, nervously twisting his sledgehammer in his hand.

Then the first of the dogs appeared, a skinny mongrel with one eye. It bowled out into the street, fell over, wriggled on the ground, then lay on its back in surrender. A second dog was hard on its tail, a dirty pit bull. It had evidently been chasing the mongrel, because it came at him with teeth bared and hackles raised.

There was an almost comical moment when the two dogs realized that they had an audience. They both did a double take and looked at the boys in surprise. The rest of the pack came into view at almost the same time, howling and barking.

They skidded to a halt and a couple of them knocked into the pit bull, who turned and snapped at them.

The little mongrel saw its moment and scurried off. The pit bull stood there, sniffing the air. The other dogs were a mismatched mob, with missing fur and diseased eyes caked with pus. Some were limping, some wounded. One sat down in the road and vigorously scratched its ear, until another dog bit it and it scampered away.

The pit bull strutted forward, growling, then it started to bark at the boys, and the rest of the pack joined in. Instantly the street was filled with their racket.

"Will they attack, do you think?" asked Freak.

"Depends how hungry they are," said Arran.

"They look pretty hungry to me," said Deke, and he gripped his sledgehammer tighter.

"Try and scare them off," said Arran, and the boys now made a racket of their own, yelling and screaming and waving their arms. Some of the dogs backed off, but the bolder ones were soon inching closer.

The big pit bull shook his head and nosed ahead, his claws scratching on the asphalt.

"Take him out," said Arran. "He's the boss. Maybe the others will get the message."

Ollie loosed his shot. The steel ball hit the dog squarely in the forehead, his legs crumpled, and he went down without a sound. The other dogs sniffed him, and one or two set up howling. Then a big German shepherd ran from the back of the pack, leading three other hounds with him. Achilleus went down on one knee, and as the dog pounced, he stuck him through the chest with his spear. The followers veered off to the side, and Ollie hit one more with a steel ball, breaking its leg. It yelped and turned tail, dragging its leg behind.

With a great war cry, the boys charged, and the rest of the dogs scattered.

Ollie quickly searched the area for his ammunition. He found his second ball lying in the gutter. The first one was stuck in the pit bull's head in a neat crease of broken bone.

The five of them knelt by the dead body.

"Can we risk eating it?" said Freak. "What's that parasite Maeve's always going on about? That worm thing you can catch from eating dog? Tricky something."

"Trichinosis," said Arran. "He'll be all right if he's well cooked."

"Yeah," said Deke. "We'll deep-fry him in batter, with some fries and a nice glass of wine. Delicious."

Freak giggled. "I know a gourmet recipe for fried dog."

"We can't waste any food," said Arran. "Some of the kids are getting really thin. Leave the German shepherd, though. He's too big to carry and his carcass might keep the pack busy."

Achilleus took out his knife and gutted the dead animal, leaving the purple-gray entrails in the road to further distract the other dogs.

He then tied the dog's legs together with some nylon cord and slung it over Arran's shoulder.

"Should we go back?" said Freak.

"We need to find as much food as we can," said Arran. "It's always a risk leaving camp, and it gets riskier every time. The dog's not enough for twenty of us."

Every day a scavenging party left the camp to look for

supplies. They searched among the empty houses and apartments for any abandoned cans, packages, and bottles. Each time they had to start their search farther from Waitrose. All the buildings close by had long since been picked clean. Most days they found nothing, but a lucky discovery could last them a long time.

They knew it couldn't last, though. They had already been through every accessible building within a mile of Waitrose, except around Crouch End, which had been destroyed in a fire, and up around the Arsenal soccer stadium, where there was a large nest of grown-ups.

Sooner or later they would have to move camp.

But where would they go?

Arran pushed his hair out of his eyes. His guts hurt. He didn't really feel hungry anymore, just sick and tired. He'd grown to hate these streets. The smell of them, the filth everywhere, the grass and weeds pushing out of every crack, the constant fear chewing away at him. He had been happy at first when they'd made him leader, but then it slowly dawned on him that he was responsible for everyone else. If anything went wrong he had to take the blame. That was why someone like Achilleus, who could easily beat him in a fight, was happy not to be in charge. He could show off and suck up the praise, but when a tough decision had to be made, he would sit back, hold up his hands, and let Arran sweat it out.

It was a warm and sunny spring day. There was a real sense that summer wasn't far off. Normally Arran would have enjoyed the sunshine and warmth. In the past he had always loved seeing the first green leaves come out on the trees, as if the world were waking up. Now it just meant that the grown-ups were getting bolder. In the winter they'd been too cold and feeble to be much danger, but the change in the weather seemed to give them new courage and strength. Their attacks were becoming more frequent.

They were hungrier than ever.

The kids trudged up Holloway Road. It was full of memories for Arran—eating at McDonald's, shopping with his mom, going to the movies. . . .

He tried to shut the memories out. They only made him feel worse.

When they came to Archway they moved more cautiously.

There was a tube station here, a perfect hiding place for grown-ups.

"Which way?" said Deke.

"Highgate Road," said Arran. "We'll work our way toward the Whittington."

"Ain't going in no hospital," said Achilleus.

"What's the problem?"

"There won't be nothing in there," said Achilleus.

"Maybe drugs?" said Ollie. "Paracetamol and antibiotics and that."

"Doubt it," said Deke. "When everything kicked off, it would have been the first place to be looted."

"We'll take a look anyway," said Arran. "Just in case. But let's try the houses around here first."

"Ain't going in no hospital," Achilleus repeated.

"What about the swimming pool, then?" said Freak.

"What about it?" said Achilleus.

"Worth a look, eh?"

"Why?" said Achilleus. "You feel like taking a swim?"

"Nah," said Freak, "but there was always a vending machine in there."

"Never worked," said Achilleus. "Always stole your money."

"Worth a look," said Freak. "Think about it . . . Mars Bars, chips, chewing gum . . ."

"Won't be nothing in there," said Achilleus. "Not after all this time."

"Listen," Freak insisted. "Far as we know, us and the Morrisons crew are the only kids around. And they never come up here. All I'm saying is we should look. Okay? If we're looking in the Whittington we should look in the pool as well. We search everywhere, in't that right, Arran?"

"Suppose so," said Arran.

"Waste of time," said Ollie. "When have we ever found a vending machine with anything in it?"

"You agree with me, don't you, Deke?" said Freak.

"He agrees with everything you say," Achilleus scoffed.

"Try me," said Deke.

"The world is flat," said Freak.

"Yes it is," said Deke.

"Penguins can fly," said Freak.

"Yes they can," said Deke.

"I am the greatest kid that ever walked the earth," said Freak.

"Yes you are," said Deke.

"Ha-ha, very funny," said Achilleus.

"Akkie is a jerk," said Freak.

"Yes he is," said Deke.

"I think you've made your point," said Arran, trying not to smile. "We'll take a look."

Ollie sighed. This was a waste of time. What they needed was proper food, not junk. But Arran had spoken, and he was their leader.

Ollie shoved a hand into his jacket and rolled the heavy steel shot between his fingers. The cold hardness comforted him.

He didn't like the idea of exploring the swimming pool. He was always scared on these hunts, and going into the unknown like this just made his heart race faster.

"Come on," said Arran. "Let's go."

"Searching the swimming pool is a genius idea," said Freak.

"Yes it is," said Deke.

3

The glass doors of the swimming pool were cracked and so covered with dust on the inside that it was impossible to see anything through them. Deke hefted his sledgehammer and took a swing, aiming for a spot next to the handles. The glass exploded with a bang and fell out of the frame in sparkling nuggets.

"Cool," said Freak.

"Yes it is," said Deke, who loved destroying things. In the early days, just after the disaster had happened, and before he understood the dangers, Deke had wandered the streets in delight—breaking, burning, smashing—hardly able to believe that there was nobody around to stop him, and that he could do whatever he wanted.

That crazy, joyous freedom had been cut short when he'd discovered that not all the adults had died. And those who had survived would treat you far worse than any parent, teacher, or policeman, if they ever caught you. A parent might have grounded you, a teacher might have kept you in after school, and the police might have arrested you, but none of them would have tried to eat you, like the grown-ups who wandered the streets these days.

He still got a kick out of destroying things, though, when he got the chance, which was why he often volunteered to join a scavenging party.

He stood back from the shattered door to let Achilleus see inside.

Achilleus leaned in and looked around.

"We'll need the flashlights."

They all carried hand-powered LED dynamo flashlights that didn't need batteries. They quickly fired them up by pumping the triggers that spun the flywheels inside. After thirty seconds the flashlights were charged enough to give a good three minutes of light.

They stepped into the entrance lobby and shone their beams across the dirty floor and walls. Ahead of them was the reception desk. To the right, past a turnstile and low barrier, was a small seating area that opened out on to the pool. A wide passage led the other way to the changing rooms.

The reception desk was covered with cobwebs, and the faded, peeling posters on the walls were from a different world. They showed smiling, happy children and talked of health and fitness and community activities. There were a few animal trails in the dust, and debris on the floor, but no sign of any recent human activity.

"Vending machines used to be through there," said Freak, nodding toward the fixed tables and chairs in the seating area.

"We'll take a quick look," said Arran, and without having

to be told, Achilleus led the way. He climbed over the turn-stile and dropped into a crouch on the other side, spear at the ready.

"All clear."

One by one the others followed, Ollie bringing up the rear, flashlight in one hand, slingshot in the other.

They walked cautiously forward. As they moved closer to the pool, they noticed a smell. The choking, rotten stink of stagnant water.

"Aw, who farted?" said Deke, holding his nose. Freak sniggered, but nobody else laughed. The pair of them liked to joke around to keep the fear away, but the others had their own ways of dealing with their nerves.

Achilleus was tensed and alert, ready for action, almost willing a grown-up to jump out at him. Arran tried to stand tall and appear unafraid, imagining he was casting a protective shield around his little group. Ollie kept glancing back over his shoulder. He was so used to watching the rear that he almost found it easier walking backward.

"That is an evil smell," said Freak.

"Keep it down," said Achilleus.

"Come off it, Akkie," said Deke. "If there was anyone here, I think they just might have heard that bloody big bang as I took out the door."

"Shut up so's we can listen, Deke."

"Okay, okay."

They shone their flashlights around the seating area where the vending machines had once stood.

Nothing. Empty.

"They're gone," said Arran.

"What a surprise," said Achilleus.

"Told you this was a waste of time," said Ollie. "Now can we go?"

Arran carried on toward the pool. A dim light was glowing green through the windows around the high ceiling. The air felt hot and moist. He used to come here nearly every week in the summer. There was a waterslide that snaked out of the building and back again. It had always been noisy here, busy with kids. There had been a wave machine and all sorts of fountains, waterfalls, and jets. Now it was absolutely quiet and still and stank like a sewer. Stringy weeds hung from the waterslide that stood on rusting supports.

Arran was aware of his heart thumping against his ribs. He didn't like being here.

"We should take a proper look around," said Freak, joining him by the pool and shining his flashlight around the cavernous space.

There was still water in the pool, but it was a soupy greenish-brown color. Clumps of algae and weed floated on the surface, and odd pieces of furniture had been dumped in it. Arran could see chairs and tables, a filing cabinet, and what looked like a treadmill, probably from the gym upstairs.

More algae and mold made its way up the walls, covering the windows—this was what was turning the light that weird ghostly green.

The others came through.

"We should go," said Ollie, nervously glancing back toward the entrance.

"Scared, are you?" said Deke.

"'Course I'm scared," said Ollie simply. "I'm always scared

when we go somewhere we've never been before. It's good to be scared. Keeps you alive."

"Check this out," Freak hissed, interrupting them. He was shining his flashlight across the pool.

A vending machine stood there, half submerged in the water, but they could see that it was still stocked with chocolate bars and candy and chips.

"We've struck the jackpot," Deke whispered.

They moved closer to the water's edge, marveling at the treasure trove in the stagnant pool. The side of the pool sloped gradually into the water, giving the effect of a beach. The smell was appalling, and the floor was slippery beneath their feet.

"What's it doing in the water?" said Achilleus.

"Who cares?" Freak and Deke said in unison.

Arran shone his flashlight on a sign; it was still just about readable beneath the fungal growth on its surface.

NO RUNNING. NO DIVING.

"See that?" he said. "No diving."

The others sniggered. The thought of diving into the dark, stinking water was disgusting, but nevertheless somebody was going to have to wade in if they wanted to get to the vending machine.

"I don't like it," said Ollie. "It's not right."

Once again he glanced back toward the entrance, making sure that their way out was clear.

"There's nothing here, man," said Deke. "No one. The place is deserted. Look at all that crap in the water. The vending machine must have been dumped there ages ago, and forgotten about."

"Come on," said Ollie. "I'm leaving."

He jumped as Freak suddenly shouted, his voice startlingly loud. "HELLO? ANYBODY HOME?"

The sound echoed off the hard walls.

"See? Nothing."

"You're an idiot," said Achilleus.

"Yeah? And who are you, then—Brainiac, the world's brainiest kid?"

"Don't start arguing," said Arran wearily.

"Look," said Deke, "we've been here long enough. If anything was going to happen it would've happened by now. This place is dead, like the rest of London. Like the rest of the world, for all we know. Dead."

"We're not dead," said Arran, "and I want to keep it that way."

"Then let's get the stuff from the machine," said Deke. "Food, yeah? To eat? You remember food, don't you?"

"I'm not sure about this."

"Oh, for God's sake, this is a waste of time." Freak walked to the water's edge, holding his nose. Deke groaned as he watched his friend wade in. Soon the slime was up to Freak's knees, then his thighs. He kept going until he reached the machine. Turned to wave, then peered inside.

"Sick!" he said, grinning. "You should see this."

"Freak! No!" Deke screamed.

The whole surface of the water around Freak had come alive, as if some huge beast were rising from the depths.

Deke splashed into the pool, yelling.

"Idiot," said Achilleus.

There were shapes emerging everywhere now, seemingly

made from the same green slime as the water itself. They pushed up out of the bubbling pool.

People. Men and women. Blanket weed hanging off them and tangled between their outstretched fingers like webs.

"GROWN-UPS!" Arran shouted.

Ollie grabbed a steel ball, slipped it into the pouch of his slingshot, and pulled back the rubber band. . . .

There were too many of them. In his panic he wasn't sure where to aim.

Freak was swinging his ax around wildly at the weed-covered grown-ups nearest to him. He got one in the fore-arm, shattering it, and on his return swing took another in the side of the head, but their numbers quickly overwhelmed him, and as the grown-ups closed in on him, there was no longer room to use his weapon effectively. On his next strike the ax head sunk deep into a big father's ribs and stuck there. The father twisted and writhed, churning the water and tearing the ax from Freak's grasp. Freak was defenseless. Wet, slimy hands closed around his neck. He struggled to throw them off, swearing at the grown-ups.

Ollie couldn't risk a shot that might hit Freak, so instead he aimed at one of the grown-ups on the edge of the attacking group. A mother. He loosed a shot and struck her in the tem-ple. She toppled over and was swallowed by the water. Then a noise made Ollie turn—more grown-ups had moved into the seating area to block their exit.

"We're surrounded!" he shouted, swinging his slingshot around toward them.

Arran could do nothing to help. Grown-ups were swarm-ing to the edge of the pool and slithering onto the tiles. He gripped his pickax handle and lashed out at them two-handed. A fat little father with useless legs hobbled out in a crouch, like some horrible, ungainly frog. Arran caught him under his chin with an uppercut, and he somersaulted backward into the water.

Deke had been trying to get to his friend, but the water was thick with wallowing grown-ups. He was forcing his way onward, using the tip of the sledgehammer's handle as a butt. Driving it into anybody that got too close.

Achilleus was waiting on the edge. He knew that he wouldn't be able to fight effectively in the water. He darted backward and forward, picking off stray grown-ups and watching Deke's progress.

"Go on!" he urged him.

It looked like Deke was going to make it to Freak, but just before he got there, three big grown-ups pulled Freak over, and he sank beneath the surface.

"Hold on, Freak!"

Deke powered the last few feet and dived in after his friend.

"Idiot," Achilleus said again. There was nothing for it. He was going to have to go and help. He gave a war cry and surged in, high-stepping, spear flashing in quick hard thrusts, teeth bared.

The grown-ups seemed to sense that he was dangerous, and fell back. There was no sign of Freak and Deke, though.

Over by the seating area, Ollie was ducked down onto one knee to steady his aim, and was launching a barrage of shots toward the grown-ups blocking the way out. He couldn't take his eyes off them for even a split second, so he had no idea what was going on behind him. He prayed that the others would join him soon, because he couldn't keep the grown-ups at bay forever.

"Help me, someone!"

Arran looked over and saw what was happening.

"Achilleus!" he shouted. "You get Freak and Deke. I need to help Ollie."

He had no idea if Achilleus had heard him, and he couldn't wait to make sure. A group of grown-ups was rushing Ollie, who couldn't reload fast enough to hold them back. Arran raced over and plowed in, his club flying. The wood cracked against a father's skull. He howled and toppled sideways. Arran was finding it difficult to fight with the dog slung across his shoulders, but he swung again, this time aiming for a grown-up's knee. There was a snap of breaking bone, and the grown-up was out of action.

"Got to push them back!" he yelled, and surged forward, driving the grown-ups over the seats and tables.

Achilleus reached the vending machine. Oblivious to the stink and the slime, he plunged a hand under the water roughly where he had last seen Deke. He grabbed hold of sodden material and tugged hard. It was a grown-up. He stuck his spear into it, twisted, and pulled it out. The next moment the water boiled and erupted as Deke broke the surface, bringing Freak up with him. Freak looked confused and limp.

"Got him," Deke spluttered. His face was glowing white in the gloom so that it looked almost luminous.

"Come on," said Achilleus. "Let's go."

But the attack wasn't over. An enraged father bundled

into them, knocking Deke hard into the vending machine and smashing the glass. Deke grunted, winded.

Achilleus dealt swiftly with the father, striking him in the mouth, and with that the remaining grown-ups gave up. They fell back as Achilleus and the other two waded toward the edge. Achilleus started taunting them, cursing and swearing and calling them all the names he could think of, daring them to attack.

"Come on, you lazy sods! Attack me, you cowards, come on!"

But the grown-ups were melting away, slipping back under the murky surface of the pool. Achilleus felt a surge of relief; his bravado had been all show. He was exhausted, Freak and Deke had lost their weapons, and if the grown-ups did mount a full-scale attack, the boys would stand little chance. He looked back. The other two were still stumbling through the water. Deke looked like he was on his last legs. Achilleus went to him, grabbed hold of Freak around the waist, and pulled the two of them along until, spluttering and slipping and stumbling, they staggered to the poolside.

"What kept you?" said Arran as they joined him and Ollie, who had secured the seating area.

"I had to rescue the Chuckle Brothers," said Achilleus.

"We couldn't leave without having a swim," said Deke, his voice hoarse and cracked. He coughed and doubled up in pain.

"Is he all right?" Arran asked Achilleus.

"Think so. Come on, what's the holdup? Let's get out of here."

"Easier said than done." Ollie loosed a shot at a black silhouette in the reception area. "They're blocking the exit."

Achilleus swore. "I've never seen anything like this before. These are some clever bastards. They set a trap for us."

"These guys are getting scary," said Ollie.

"We'll get our breath back and take them," said Achilleus. "They don't scare me."

Deke was coughing again and shivering. He moaned. He looked whiter than ever. Freak seemed to be coming out of his daze, though. He shook his head and rubbed his temple with the heel of one hand.

"My ax?" he said.

"It's gone, Superman," said Achilleus. "Forget it. We'll find you another one. For now we've just got to get clear of this dump. You reckon you can walk now?"

"I'm fine," said Freak.

"Deke don't look so hot."

Freak turned to his friend.

"Thanks for getting me out of that, bro," he said.

Deke nodded. "No probs." But his breathing was fast and shallow, and there was a bubble of blood on his lips.

"You hurt?"

Deke forced a feeble grin. "I think I'm poisoned."

"You was under the water for a long time, man, a long time," said Achilleus.

"I feel sick." Deke swayed to one side, and Freak caught him.

"You're bleeding," said Freak, putting a hand to Deke's side. His clothes were stained black by blood. Achilleus lifted his arm; a large shard of jagged glass was sticking out of his side.

"Oh no," said Freak.

"I'm all right," said Deke. "It's nothing." But then he coughed again and there was blood in his spit.

"It's in your lung, man," said Achilleus. "The glass."

Deke's eyes were rolling up in his head.

"Hold on, bro," said Freak.

"I think I'm going to . . ."

"Don't faint, bro," Freak shouted, and shook his friend as he fell into unconsciousness. "Arran! We got to get him out of here."

Almost as Freak spoke, the grown-ups attacked again. At least ten of them blundered up from the pool.

Arran was filled with a blind rage. He couldn't stand it that another kid was wounded. They didn't have the drugs to deal with it, and the water in the pool must have been swarming with filth and germs. With a great roar he lashed out to right and left, smashing his club into the grown-ups, shattering bones, breaking noses, loosening teeth, closing eyes. He was hardly aware of what was going on around him, only that Achilleus was at his back, cold-bloodedly dealing with the grown-ups in his own way.

When a mother came at Arran, long hair flying, he gripped her by the throat and squeezed. Her head thrashed from side to side, her scabby hands flapped at him. Her hair whipped out of her face so that for a moment he saw her clearly.

Her nose was half rotted away by disease. There were boils and sores covering every inch of skin. Her lips were pulled back from broken teeth, showing black shrunken gums.

Everything about her was disgusting, inhuman, degraded —apart from her eyes. Her eyes were beautiful.

Arran looked into them, and for a moment he saw a flash of intelligence.

He froze. Time seemed to stop. He had the sudden vivid notion that this was all a stupid dream. He had imagined the whole thing: the collapse of society, the fear and confusion, the months spent hiding out in Waitrose. It wasn't possible, after all. It wasn't possible that the world had changed so much. So quickly. It wasn't possible that he had become a savage. A killer.

The mother tried to speak, her lips formed in a ghastly pucker, and a single syllable came out.

"Mwuhh . . ."

Tears came to Arran's eyes. He couldn't do it anymore.

He loosened his grip.

The mother wriggled free and sunk her teeth into his neck. Then Achilleus must have stabbed her, because a bright spray of blood hosed out from a wound in her chest. The next moment she was gone and Ollie was pulling him toward the turnstiles.

"Move it, Arran!" he shouted, and Arran slithered over the turnstiles in a daze.

"Where's Freak?"

Freak had been fending off the grown-ups with his bare fists, punching, kicking, butting, trying to protect Deke. But he was losing the fight. The grown-ups had sensed that Deke was wounded. They had given up trying to block the exit and were concentrating their efforts on getting at him. Two of them had taken hold of his legs, and Freak was engaged in a ghastly tug-of-war.

"Leave him!" Ollie screamed.

"I can't!"

A grown-up lurched into Freak from the side, knocking Deke out of his hands.

"Deke!"

The name stuck in Freak's throat as he watched Deke being dragged quickly away, face down on the hard tiles, leaving a long, bloody smear. Freak chased after them, sobbing and screaming insults, but it was no good. There was nothing he could do.

The grown-ups pulled Deke under the water, and he was gone. The last Freak ever saw of his friend—the boy he had grown up with, shared six years of school with, played soccer with, watched TV with, laughed with, argued with—the last he ever saw, was his bright yellow hair sliding into the sludge.

"Get out of there, now!" shouted Achilleus. "I'm not coming back for you this time."

No . . .

Freak was going to go after his friend. He knew it would be suicide, but he hated to leave poor Deke at the mercy of the grown-ups.

There was a reason these boys were still alive, though. Something made them stronger than the other kids, the ones who had died in the early days, who had simply lain down and given up, unable to cope with the terrible things that were happening in the world. These boys were survivors. The will to live was stronger than any other feelings.

Freak turned on his heels and sprinted out of there.

Callum was in the crow's nest. He loved it up on the roof; it was his favorite place. He couldn't wait for it to be warm enough to sleep out here. You could see the whole of Holloway spread out beneath you. Like Google Earth. The kids had built the crow's nest around the dome that stuck up from one corner of Waitrose. They had used scaffolding poles and planks and ropes and any useful bits and pieces they could find. A ladder at the back led to the sloping roof of the supermarket. From there you could climb down across the tiles to a small tower they had constructed at the edge of the courtyard. The courtyard was a rooftop terrace in the center of the building, enclosed on four sides but open to the sky.

The lookouts could communicate with other kids in the courtyard through a speaking tube. More speaking tubes linked the courtyard with other parts of the supermarket. The system was based on what they used to use on ships to communicate between the bridge and the engine room. It wasn't much more than a series of long metal pipes that had been slotted and bent through the ventilation and cabling ducts of the building, but it was surprisingly effective.

Callum felt safe up here. He and Josh were the main lookouts and could normally tell if there were any grown-ups around. The only blind spot was the parking lot at the rear of the building from where Small Sam had been snatched. Those kids should never have been out there without a guard. Callum was ticked off that he had missed the grown-ups sneaking through the gardens, and since the attack he had spotted loads more of them about. He kept a pile of ammo on a specially built ledge—rocks and stones to use as missiles, mainly—and he was itching to have a go at any grown-ups stupid enough to get too close.

He was keeping a lookout for Arran's scav party. They needed Arran back. Everyone was on edge since Small Sam had been taken. Arran would calm everyone down, sort things out. Stop the little ones from being scared.

Callum never went scavenging. He had convinced the others that he was more use to them on the roof. In fact, he hadn't been out of Waitrose, except to come up here, for nearly a year. There was an invisible rope attaching him to it. In his mind he wandered the streets below, like a character moving around a game, but in real life he never wanted to go out there again. Waitrose was safe. He had everything he needed here. He was happy. Almost happier than he had been before the disaster.

The one thing he longed for, though, was peace and quiet. To be alone, really alone. That would be bliss. To just sit there, in all the space of the shop, without it being full of other kids. Sitting here in the crow's nest was as good as it got.

He put his binoculars to his eyes and scanned the Holloway Road.

"Come on, Arran, we need you. . . ."

5

hey were limping along. Ollie and Achilleus were walking ahead of Arran and Freak, who were both silent, lost in private thoughts. Ollie knew well enough not to push it. If the other two didn't want to talk about what had gone down, then he wasn't going to try to make them. Freak had lost his best friend, and Arran had been badly bitten. Ollie hadn't expected him to take it so badly, though. Arran was tough. Hated showing any weakness in front of anyone else. Something had happened to him back at the pool. He had the look of someone who had stared at something nasty. Stared for too long.

Arran's skin had been punctured. There would be a big danger of infection. The grown-ups were filthy and riddled with germs and disease. Luckily, Arran hadn't been in the water, but the mother who had attacked him had looked pretty foul.

Why had Arran frozen like that? All the fight went out of him. One minute he was cracking skulls with his club, and the next he was just standing there, in a dream. Had he lost his nerve?

Arran had to know that nobody would blame him for what had happened to Deke. It had been Freak's stupid idea to go into the pool. How could they have prepared for the ambush? It wasn't like grown-ups—usually they were stupid and slow and confused. Not much different from the pack of dogs the gang had dealt with earlier. This bunch had acted together. Organized. A team.

How many of the adults had they killed? he wondered. He knew for sure he had hit seven of them, but it didn't mean that each shot was a killing shot. When they'd bundled out through the reception area he'd seen two of his targets lying still on the floor. He must have fired thirty pellets, maybe more. It had been too dangerous to try to collect them afterward. He had a pile back at the camp, but it was a lot to lose in one day. At this rate it would be sooner rather than later that he ran out altogether. He'd have to find some more, or start collecting pebbles.

Damn. He loved those heavy steel ball bearings.

His ankle was sore; he had landed wrong leaping over the turnstiles. They made a sorry bunch. Freak had been pretty badly mauled. He was covered with filth and there was blood on him, but as far as it was possible to tell, it didn't look like his own blood. At least Achilleus looked unharmed. He swore that boy had iron underpants.

Achilleus wasn't particularly a friend of Ollie's. He was always having a go at him for being too rich, too clever, too quiet. But Ollie didn't let it get to him. The two of them had a sort of grudging respect for each other. When it came down to it, Ollie valued Achilleus's fighting skills, and Achilleus valued Ollie's brains. They usually kept out of each other's way. Ollie wasn't used to being up front. It felt weird.

He remembered driving in the family car. Him and his mom and dad and three brothers. Ollie had always sat in the back, staring out of the side window, trying to keep out of their arguments and fights. He remembered the few occasions when it had been just him and his dad, and he'd gotten to ride up front in the passenger seat. How different it had felt, like they were equals. And how nice it had been to get his dad all to himself. His dad had been like Ollie. Quiet, distant, always thinking about something.

They were all dead now. All five of them.

His dad had been the first to go. One of the very first to die when the illness struck. He had even been on the news; the headline had said something like "Another Death from Mystery Illness Sweeping Europe." Then there had been more and more deaths, and not just in Europe—all around the world. They'd stopped mentioning individuals; it had been whole streets, then whole towns. It had all happened so fast, people had been stunned and hadn't really had time to panic. The whole world had sort of gone into shock. His mother had been frantic after Dad died. She'd packed the house up, ready to try to escape to the countryside and stay with Auntie Susan. But she'd fallen ill before they could get away. Then it was just Ollie and his brothers. They'd tried to leave London by themselves. His oldest brother, Dan, got sick next. He'd been eighteen. Then Will, sixteen.

His younger brother, Luke, hadn't been old enough to get sick. He'd been killed in a riot up near Finsbury Park. That must have been over a year ago. It felt more like a century. By then, Ollie had had no more tears left to cry; the catastrophe had been so immense, so overwhelming, that he had just pushed it out of his mind and concentrated on trying to stay alive. He owed it to his family, as the last one left, not to die.

"We should have never gone into there in the first place," said Achilleus. "Freak's an idiot."

"Leave it," said Ollie. "We couldn't have known."

"All for a bloody vending machine," said Achilleus. "Chips and candy! We're not babies."

"Would have been nice, though," said Ollie. "I could really do with a Mars Bar right now, and a can of Coke."

"Yeah." Achilleus smiled. "You know what I used to really like? Jaffa Cakes. I could eat a whole pack in one go. But all we've got to look forward to when we get back is roast dog."

"Better than nothing," said Ollie. "We haven't had meat in ages."

"Hold up. . . ."

Achilleus raised a hand and they all stopped. They had come to the part of Holloway Road where they had had the fight with the dogs. A group of people was up ahead, clustered around the carcass of the dead German shepherd.

"Can you make out who it is?" said Achilleus.

Ollie had the keenest eyesight of all of them. He shaded his eyes and squinted.

"They're kids," he said.

"Ours?"

"Nah. Morrisons."

When everything had fallen apart, one group of local kids had ended up taking shelter in Waitrose, and another group had taken up Morrisons, the cheaper supermarket in the nearby Nag's Head shopping center. Kids had mostly ended up in the place where their moms and dads had gone shopping. Not all, though. Ollie guessed Achilleus was more of a Morrisons kid.

In the struggle to survive, where every scrap of food was fought over, the two groups of kids led totally separate lives. There was even the occasional skirmish in the street.

Achilleus turned to Arran.

"What do we do? There's more of them than us. Should we go around the back way?"

Arran looked at the other gang, then at his feet, then up at the sky.

"I don't know," he said eventually.

"I'm wiped," said Achilleus. "I can't face another fight, and I can't face going the long way around, looking out for grown-ups every step of the way."

Arran sighed, pushed past him, and kept walking.

"If they want to have a go at us, let them," he said. "I don't care anymore."

Achilleus watched him go, then shared a look with Ollie. "Come on."

They made sure that Freak was still with them, and hurried to catch up with Arran.

The Morrisons crew soon spotted them, and they took up a defensive stance in the middle of the road.

Arran carried on walking toward them. He wasn't going to stop. Achilleus ran past him.

"We don't want no trouble," Achilleus called out to the other gang. "We've had enough for one day. We just want to get back. We ain't got nothing you want."

The Morrisons crew stood their ground, sullenly watching

them as they approached. They were armed with an assortment of knives, sticks, and spears. Ollie spotted their leader, Blue, a muscley kid with close-cropped hair. Ollie smiled at him, being as open as he could, showing that they meant no harm. A couple of the Morrisons crew nodded at them as they arrived, showing no expression. Blue noticed the dog, still strung across Arran's back.

He looked from the dead pit bull down to the German shepherd.

"You do this?"

"Earlier."

Arran snapped out of his weird mood. He knew he had to put on a brave face. It was important not to show any weakness. They had nothing in their camp the Morrisons crew could want, but there was always a danger that they might lose some good fighters if the Morrisons thought they'd have a better life in the rival supermarket.

"You look pretty messed up, man," said Blue, staring at Arran and then at Freak. "Was it the dogs?"

"No," said Arran. "Grown-ups. At the pool. Don't go up that way."

"Never do," said a big, slightly stooped kid who looked almost like a grown-up. He was Mick, the Morrisons equivalent of Achilleus. Their top fighter.

"There's been a lot of attacks lately," said Blue.

"Too right," said Arran. "They're getting desperate."

Blue looked at him. "There's been some trouble up at Waitrose," he said.

Ollie's heart caught in his chest. His stomach flooded with acid. Now what?

"What sort of trouble?" said Arran.

"Some sort of an attack. There's been grown-ups hanging around all day."

"Oh crap," said Arran, and he ran off down the road, the rest of his group struggling to keep up.

The Morrisons crew had been unusually friendly and helpful, Ollie thought. Which probably meant that they were getting scared. When it came down to it, the kids had to stick together.

The grown-ups were the real enemy.

"T hey're back!" Josh ran up to Maxie.

Maxie's heart thumped against her ribs. She had been desperate for Arran to get back, but she was also terrified of what he would think. He had left her in charge and she had mucked up.

She didn't want to show how she was feeling in front of everybody. She couldn't lose it twice in one day.

"Get the gates open," she said, pleased that her voice sounded strong and clear. "Who's on lookout now?"

"Callum," said Josh.

"I didn't really need to ask, did I?"

"He practically lives up there."

"Get someone to ring the bell," said Maxie.

"I'll do it." Josh hurried off. In a moment Maxie heard the clang of the bell that told everyone to get ready to open the gate.

Maxie went over to the speaking tube. She banged on it to alert Callum, then called into it.

"Callum?"

"Yeah."

"Can you still see Arran and the scavs?"

"They're nearly here."

"Is it safe to open the gates?"

"Yeah."

There was a pause and then a shrill whistle.

All clear.

Soon afterward there came the sound of the steel shutter being cranked up. The shutter was the old security gate that blocked off the main entrance to the store. It was operated by turning a big wheel set into the wall.

Maxie stood there, listening, but not daring to look. Trying to slow her breathing and take control of herself. Once the shutter was up the gate crew could move out into the mall and open the barricade.

The barricade was a huge fortified gate that opened on to the street. It had been built by Bernie and Ben in the early days. Bernie and Ben were two emos who looked identical, even though Bernie was a girl. They had straight black hair and wore black combat trousers, black T-shirts, and black sweatshirts. Both of them were into robotics and used to watch programs like *Scrapheap Challenge* on TV. They had built loads of modifications around the shop, including the speaking tubes. They were also in charge of opening and closing the barricade.

In a moment there was a flood of light and then the hubbub of voices from the street. Maxie tensed. The last two hours had been hell. An eternity of fear and apprehension. She had a horrible sick feeling in her gut.

At last, there he was.

She gasped, despite herself. He looked awful. There had been trouble. It wasn't just the wound in his neck and the blood on his clothes—he was horribly pale, and there was a look in his eyes. A look of despair she had never seen before.

It was a moment before she realized there were only three others with him.

Oh no.

She wanted to run to Arran and throw her arms around him. To comfort him, to comfort herself, to hold on to something.

He would hate it, though. He had no idea how she felt about him. She mustn't let him find out. She wasn't one of the pretty ones. She had a plain, square face and mousy curly hair that tangled into knots so that she had to hack away at it with scissors. To Arran she was just his second in command. That was all. She was tough. There was nothing girly or pink about her. If he knew that she'd always fancied him, he'd run a mile.

Fancy?

What a stupid word that was. It was more than fancy. She loved him. Another stupid word. Love. What did it really mean? She knew how it felt. Good and bad at the same time. There was no one else. No mom and dad. No brothers or sisters. There was just Arran.

But he was hurt.

They both spoke at the same time. The same words—
"What's happened?"

So he knew it, too. He could read it in her face. She had screwed up.

Who was going to explain first?

Arran sniffed and cleared his throat.

"We lost Deke," he said flatly.

"Oh no . . ."

Arran shrugged. "There were too many of them."

Maxie didn't know what to say. She was glad that Arran had told his news first. It didn't make hers sound so bad. But it was bad.

Arran looked at her. "We saw Blue and the Morrisons crew," he said. "Told us there'd been trouble."

"Some grown-ups got over the wall at the back," said Maxie.

"How many?"

"Not sure. Four or five . . ."

"They get anyone?"

Maxie nodded.

Arran looked around, trying to see who was missing.

"It was Sam," said Maxie. "Small Sam."

"Poor little bugger," said Arran. "This hasn't been a good day."

"No. There's been grown-ups hanging around since you left. I keep expecting them to attack again."

"They won't attack Waitrose," said Arran, taking his club over to the rack where they kept their weapons. "They never have."

"They might," said Achilleus, who was already at the rack with Freak and Ollie. "They're changing. It's getting tough, man."

"It's all over for us," said Freak, looking utterly miserable and defeated.

Achilleus grabbed him and slammed him into the rack, spilling weapons onto the floor.

"That was your bright idea, Freak," he snarled. "None of this would have happened if it wasn't for you. Don't never forget that. Deke's blood is on your hands, man."

Arran pulled him off.

"Don't be an ass, Akkie," he said.

Achilleus turned away and let his breath out in a dismissive huff, before sinking into sullen blankness.

"We're not going to start blaming each other," said Arran. "It won't get us anywhere. We're all in this together. If we start fighting among ourselves it really is all over. Okay?"

"Yeah, whatever." Achilleus wandered off.

Arran put a hand on Freak's shoulder.

"You all right?"

Freak looked at his hands. Stained red. He wiped them on his shirt and shrugged.

Ollie took the dead dog off Arran, who seemed to have forgotten he was still carrying it.

"Come on, Freak," he said. "Let's see what we can do with this."

In a moment Maxie was alone with Arran. She was desperate to explain herself.

"They came into the parking lot," she said. "We'd told the little kids not to go out there."

"Not your fault," said Arran.

"I thought you were going to be so mad at me," said Maxie quietly.

"Not your fault," Arran repeated.

"I know, but . . ."

"In case you hadn't noticed, Maxie, I didn't do so good either."

Maxie almost burst into tears.

"We can't go on like this, Arran."

"Yeah?" Arran stared at her, that bleak look still in his eyes. "So what are we supposed to do, then?"

"I don't know, do I?" said Maxie, trying to control her voice.

Arran sighed and ran his fingers through his hair. "Sorry," he said. "It's been a tough day. I'm the leader. I'm supposed to know what to do, aren't I?"

"You can't know everything. You can't always be expected to know the best way to . . ." Maxie stopped herself. It wasn't helping. "We should call a meeting. Talk about it."

"Later," said Arran. "I'm tired." He closed his eyes for a moment. Maxie took the opportunity to study his wound. It looked nasty, a row of weeping black holes surrounded by yellow and purple bruising. She touched him gently with her fingertips.

"Does that hurt?"

Arran winced, then nodded.

"You need to have it looked at," said Maxie. "Come on."

They went upstairs. The floor above the shop was mostly a storage area, but there were offices here, the canteen, and access to the roof terrace. One of the offices had been turned into a sick bay, and they kept a basic medical kit there. Antiseptic, painkillers, and bandages. They found Maeve sitting at a desk, staring out of the window. Maeve acted as nurse and doctor. Her parents had both been doctors and she'd picked up bits and pieces from them. She knew more than any of the other kids, so in their world she was an expert.

Arran showed her the damage and she went to work.

She cleaned the cuts, put on some disinfectant, and taped a bandage over it, then gave him something for the pain. She said nothing. They all three knew that it was serious. There would be an anxious wait to see whether the wound got infected. Three kids had died from infections since they'd been holed up here. To lose Arran in the same way would be a catastrophe.

Maxie didn't know what she'd do without him.

That evening the kids held a meeting in the courtyard on the roof. They had made the area as civilized as they could manage, adding to what was already here with stuff they'd scrounged from nearby buildings. There were plants in raised beds and pots, garden furniture to sit on, some tables, and two big barbecues where they did most of their cooking.

They had a few solar-powered lamps, and candles in jars, and they had lit a fire in the barrel from inside a washing machine that Ben and Bernie had turned into a brazier.

Small Sam's sister, Ella, was sobbing quietly in a corner. Maeve had an arm around her, but most of the others just ignored her. They had all lost someone. They didn't want to be reminded.

Maxie tried hard. Tried not to glance over at the little girl. Tried not to think about how awful she must be feeling. And it wasn't only Ella. Freak was lurking in the shadows in another corner. He hadn't said a word since they'd got back.

"As you all know, we lost two kids today," said Arran. "It's getting bad. I don't know how much longer we can hold on here."

Instantly there was a chorus of distressed voices.

"But where would we go. . . ?"

"We're safe here. . . ."

"We can't go out there. . . ."

"We'll be all right. You'll find food."

"You'll kill all the grown-ups."

"I won't!" Arran shouted, his voice breaking. This shocked everyone into silence. They weren't used to seeing Arran lose his temper.

"I can't," he went on. "There's too many of them. I can't kill them all. We can't go on like this. We're getting weaker every day."

There was a long silence. The little kids looked terrified. They couldn't handle this. None of them wanted to face up to the reality of their situation.

A fair-haired kid with a wide mouth they'd nicknamed Monkey Boy, because he loved to climb things, broke the silence.

"We're doing all right, Arran. We're not starving or nothing. You brought us back the dog today."

"Yeah, right," Arran said bitterly. "And how long can we go on like this? Eating dogs? Being taken by the grown-ups? One by one. Huh? How long? We bumped into Blue and the Morrisons crew before. They agree. They reckon the grown-ups are getting worse. They're wearing us down."

Callum stood up and stepped into the flickering light of the fire.

"Listen, Arran," he said. "You're scaring the little ones.

We know it was tough today. We know you got hurt and you lost Deke and all that. We know why you're angry, but . . . well, go easy, yeah?"

"Yeah, sorry," said Arran, and he wiped sweat from his forehead.

Callum stayed standing.

"Can I say something else?"

Arran nodded.

"We mustn't ever leave here."

"Didn't you listen to anything I said?" asked Arran.

"This is our home now," Callum went on. "It was bad luck today. That's all. We'll just have to be more careful, yeah? We've made this place safe. We're learning all the time. We've survived this far. Why shouldn't we carry on? I been on the roof nearly all day, and I can tell you, I seen it out there. It's not safe, yeah? Not safe at all. . . ."

Almost as if to illustrate Callum's point, there was a crash and a yell from the street below, followed by a hideous scream.

Josh scuttled over the roof from the crow's nest and shouted down to them.

"There's something out there!"

Arran could see the fear in the faces of the smaller kids. Callum was right. All he had succeeded in doing was to frighten them. He should have been more careful about what he said in the meeting. Should have kept his temper. The kids looked up to him. They expected him to never show any doubt.

But he felt rotten and he couldn't pretend anymore. He was scared too. He was scared twenty-four hours a day, and he was sick of having to spend all his time feeling tense and fearful, like a wild animal.

And now it had happened. The thing he had feared most. He was wounded. Already he could feel a twitching, scratchy heat clawing at his neck. He put his hand to the bandage. His head was swimming, like he had a bad cold.

It wasn't the wound that had changed him, though. It was the grown-up back at the pool. The mother. He had looked into her eyes and he had recognized something.

He shook his head. He had imagined it. It couldn't be.

Someone was shouting.

He shook his head again.

"Arran, what's going on?" It was Callum. He looked panicked. "Are they attacking us?"

He was surrounded by them, all these kids who depended on him. They needed him to tell them what to do. Even if he was wrong, he had to look like he was in control. His feelings didn't matter right now.

"No," he said, standing up. "They've never attacked before."

"But you said they were changing. . . ."

"They can't change that fast."

He moved in through the sliding glass doors to the canteen, which was off to one side of the terrace. There was another thud from below. A scraping sound as if something was trying to get in. Would the grown-ups really attack Waitrose?

The canteen was in the corner of the building, directly below the dome. Windows looked out onto balconies that ran the length of the two outer walls. From there you had a perfect view of Holloway Road at the front and Tollington Road at the side. Arran opened a door and went out onto the front balcony.

The sky was clouded, so no moon or stars shone down. And the streetlamps hadn't worked in over a year. Arran could just make out figures moving below.

"Get some light!" he shouted.

"What is it?" said a voice from inside. "What's happening out there?"

"Keep quiet."

Monkey Boy brought him a dynamo flashlight. A bigger,

more powerful version of the one he carried. It was already charged. He switched it on and moved the beam around until he saw something.

A father with a purple bloated face, his eyes weeping pus. He looked up at Arran and bared his broken teeth in a snarl.

"Grown-ups."

"But you said—"

"It doesn't matter what I said," Arran snapped.

As Arran raked the beam across the ground, another figure appeared. It was a boy of about sixteen, dressed in a patchwork of colorful rags and mismatched cloth, with an old leather satchel over one shoulder.

"Let me in!"

"Don't let him in! Don't let him in!"

A group of grown-ups ran at the boy, and he disappeared from view. Arran desperately tried to catch him in the beam.

More kids were crowding on to the balcony, trying to see what was happening. Panicked. Shouting and screaming.

"Arran, what do we do?"

"Who is he?"

"Are they attacking us?"

"Can you see anything?"

Arran couldn't think straight. They had fallen into a trap earlier. He wasn't going to let it happen again. He had to make the right decision. But his head was throbbing and the noise in his ears . . .

"Shut up!" he roared. "All of you be quiet!"

There was silence.

Arran gave the flashlight to Maeve, who had pushed through the jostling kids to be at his side.

"Keep this aimed at the road," he said.

"What are you . . . ?"

But Arran was already going.

He found Callum inside the canteen.

"Get on the roof," he said, giving orders on the move. "I need some decent light out there, throw down some burning torches. And stay up where you can see what's happening. I need you to be my eyes!"

They could just hear a thin pitiful scream from outside. The ragged boy.

"Please. Help me!"

"Let him in," Maxie yelled, running over to Arran. "He's a kid."

"No, no, it's not safe!" shouted Callum. "We don't let anyone in. This is our place."

"He'll be killed—he's just a kid."

A wave of sickness hit Arran. He held his head in his hands, closed his eyes and gritted his teeth. He kept seeing that other face—the mother from the pool. He rubbed his temples.

"Arran . . . ?" It was Callum, tugging at his elbow.

Arran exploded.

"I thought I told you to get up on the roof!"

"Yes, but—"

"Get up there now! I'm going out. If it gets bad, use a bomb."

"A bomb? They're for emergencies."

"And what does this look like to you?"

"Okay, okay."

Callum turned and ran off.

"Ollie?" Arran called out. "Where's Ollie?"

"Here."

"Clear the balcony and get out there with your sling—take anyone else who's a halfway decent shot. I need covering fire."

"Okay."

"Achilleus?"

"Here."

"Get a war party together—our five best fighters—and get some weapons. Maxie, I need a back-up team. Anyone else who can fight. Bernie and Ben on the doors."

"No way, Arran," said Ben. "You can't open them. You don't know how many grown-ups are on the street. If they get inside . . ."

"If I say we open them, we open them. There's a kid out there."

"You can't let him in. We don't know who he is. What if we lose more of our own?"

"Every kid in London is one of our own, Ben. Okay? Now stop questioning me."

"Sorry."

Arran strode across the canteen, now crowded with little kids. They moved around in a frightened pack, like a flock of chicks. As Arran and the other fighters moved through them, they hurried to get out of the way, shrieking.

"For God's sake, somebody get this lot to the storage room!" Arran shouted. The storage room was the safest place in the supermarket, and it was where most of the kids slept.

Arran took a side staircase that came out near the main entrance.

Bernie and Ben were waiting to wind up the steel shutters.

Arran nodded to them and went over to the weapons rack. Achilleus was already there with five others, including Josh, their eyes glinting in the half-light.

There was a bang from the front of the shop. A cracking sound. Arran grabbed his club and went over to the windows. He pulled aside a steel shelving unit that had been jammed up against them for safety. At first it was too dark to see anything through the filth and grime. He leaned forward, pressing his face against the cool glass. Suddenly he jumped back as a body flung itself at the window with a loud thud.

It was a grown-up. A father. Arran watched as he smeared his ruined face along the glass, like some grotesque child's prank. It left a long snail's trail of pus and snot and saliva as it continued to the side and downward before flopping to the ground. It looked dead.

The windows were made of reinforced glass, but if someone really wanted to they could probably break their way through.

Achilleus had followed Arran over.

"You really going out there, man?"

"Yes."

"I hope you know what you're doing."

Arran looked at Achilleus, but said nothing.

When he got back to the entrance, the shutters were nearly up and Maxie was speaking to Callum on the roof through the speaking tube. Arran pushed her aside and barked into the mouthpiece.

"Have you thrown down the torches yet, Callum?"

"Just lighting them now."

"Can you see anything at all?"

"Hard to make out what's going on. There's a whole bunch of grown-ups. Some are attacking the shop, the rest seem to be attacking a kid. He keeps getting away from them. He's running around like a nutcase. Don't know how much longer he can hold on."

"How many grown-ups?"

"Can't tell. They don't seem very organized."

"Is the kid armed?"

"Don't think so. Wait, they've got him. He's surrounded."

Arran swore and ducked under the shutter into the mall.

What they called the mall was little more than a covered walkway that ran down the side of the shop from the street at the front to the parking lot at the rear. Arran looked quickly in both directions. Apart from a couple of dead palm trees in pots, it was empty.

"Clear!" he yelled, and Achilleus brought the others out behind him.

"Bernie and Ben! We need the street doors open."

The emos came out. They weren't fighters, they were engineers. They both looked terrified.

"Can't you open the barricade?" said Bernie, her eyes darting about anxiously.

"No," said Arran. "We need all the fighters ready for action. Now hurry."

"But there's grown-ups out there."

"We'll kill them if we have to," said Arran.

"Yeah, you wimps," scoffed Josh. "They don't scare me. I can't wait to get out there. It's gonna be a massacre."

"It's too risky," said Bernie.

"Whoever that kid is, he's in trouble," said Arran.

"What if he's one of them?" said Ben. "What if it's a trap?"

"Then we'll kill him as well."

There was movement from the shop as Maxie brought her back-up squad out. They had longer defensive pikes designed to keep attackers at bay.

"You stay back here," said Arran. "Defend the mall. If anyone gets past us, you'll need to stop them from getting inside."

"You sure about this?"

Arran tried not to sound too angry.

"Yes," he lied.

Then Freak appeared, looking pale-faced and wild-eyed. He was holding a short spear.

"I'm coming with you," he said.

Nobody argued.

Bernie and Ben reluctantly moved over to the barricade and prepared to pull it back. They had rigged a system of two great gates on wheels made from bits of metal they had laboriously cut up and bolted together by hand. The metal was mostly from old cars.

They undid the padlock, pulled the chains loose, and slid the heavy iron bars aside. Then they slowly rolled back the gates with a terrific squealing of metal against metal.

As soon as the gap was wide enough, Arran hurled himself through. A startled grown-up was standing nearby. Arran clubbed it on the head, and it hit the pavement with a crunch.

Next out was Freak, itching for a fight, with the others behind him.

"Come on," said Achilleus, and his fighters fanned out in the road. With Arran and Freak at the front, they marched over to where at least twenty grown-ups had formed into a crude circle.

There was a shout from above, and a flaming torch arced out into the night, turning end over end and landing in a shower of sparks near the restless circle.

The grown-ups were thrown into a mad panic, and Arran started to run, charging into them, barging through the mass of bodies to get to the center, smashing skulls to left and right as he went.

Achilleus came behind, jabbing with his spear. Making sure none of the grown-ups closed the gap.

Josh was shouting at the grown-ups.

"Come on, you ugly freaks, come and get it!"

The boy in the patchwork coat was on the ground, clutching a piece of sharp wood. Arran grabbed him by the arm.

"Move it!" he shouted, dragging him to his feet. He pushed him toward Achilleus's team, who formed a protective ring around him. The circle of grown-ups had broken apart and formed into a loose milling mob. Arran realized that the way back to the shop was blocked. But then he saw a crazed flurry of activity, and the grown-ups bolted to one side like a disturbed shoal of fish.

It was Freak. He'd gone berserk. Yelling and screaming, lashing out with his spear with no regard for his own safety.

"Leg it!" Arran shouted to Achilleus. "Get him inside!"

Achilleus's team made it back to the shop and pushed the

patchwork kid through the barricade to where Maxie's group was waiting.

"Take him into the shop," Achilleus said. "Watch him."

Arran was looking for Freak. He had lost sight of him in the chaos.

There he was.

He'd fallen; a grown-up was on him, his hands at his throat.

"Achilleus! With me!"

Arran was running. His lungs on fire. He wasn't going to make it in time.

There came a sharp crack and the grown-up toppled over, felled by one of Ollie's slingshots. Then Arran and Achilleus and the others were there, weapons a blur, and Freak was on his feet.

He pointed down the road, too tired to speak. Arran looked where he was pointing. He could just make out a fresh mob of grown-ups charging toward them from the crossroads.

Arran stood his ground, ready for anything. All his doubts were forgotten. He was focused on trying to stay alive and protect his friends. Achilleus's fighters were with him, spears bristling as the grown-ups came on like a wave surging on a beach. But at the last moment the grown-ups parted and ran past the little knot of kids. They had no appetite for a fight. Arran quickly saw why. They weren't attacking, they were retreating.

Blue and a squad from Morrisons were thundering down Holloway Road after them, throwing rocks and yelling.

Blue spotted Arran and ran over.

"What's going on?" he said.

"You tell me."

"There was some idiot," said Blue, panting, resting his hands on his knees. "He was trying to get in. We chased him away, then found this lot. Never seen so many grown-ups together before."

As they were talking, the fleeing grown-ups slowed, stopped, and turned. Other grown-ups emerged from the darkness on all sides. The way back to Morrisons was cut off.

"You better get in the shop with us," said Arran, and without another word the two groups ran back over to the barricades.

Arran was last in. Screaming at Bernie and Ben to close the doors, he squeezed through the gap, an enraged group of fathers hot on his tail.

Maxie was waiting with her own team, armed with their pikes. They poked them into the faces of the lumbering grown-ups, who squealed and shied away. The gates trundled shut and the kids could hear the grown-ups throwing themselves against the metal in rage.

Arran tried to say something, but an explosion from outside drowned him out. A burst of leaping flames filled the street. Callum must have launched a bomb from the roof. Bernie and Ben had made the bombs out of fireworks that they'd dismantled and bundled tightly together.

The initial boom was followed by a cacophony of bangs and screeches, whines and whistles, as colored bolts and burning embers shot in every direction.

It lasted no more than thirty seconds, but when it was over, Holloway Road was quiet. Bernie and Ben secured the door, shunting the bars across, rattling the chains into place, snapping the padlock shut. Their hands were shaking, but they worked carefully and methodically, trying not to panic, making sure that everything was properly done. Arran and Achilleus stayed to make sure it was okay, then took the emos back into the shop, where they helped wind down the shutter.

At last they walked over to where Maxie and three of her team had the patchwork boy pinned down on the floor, his satchel by his side.

Arran stood over him, breathing heavily, exhausted. He hoped it had all been worthwhile.

"Who are you?" he asked.

The boy smiled. He had a shock of stiff, matted hair, a wide mouth set in a thin, clever face with a nose that was slightly too large for it.

"I'm glad I found you."

"Who are you, I said."

"What difference does it make what my name is?"

Achilleus kicked him. "Who are you?" he grunted.

"Let me up and I'll tell you."

"Why should I?" Arran demanded.

"You went to all that trouble rescuing me, don't you want to know what I've got to say?"

"What have you got to say?"

"Let me up and I'll tell you."

"No. Tell me now. We can't trust anyone. We've already lost two kids today."

"And what am I going to do? Eh?" said the boy.

"I don't know," said Arran. "It's been a day full of surprises. I don't want to be surprised again."

"I think you'll find what I'm going to tell you surprising."

"Try me."

Arran nodded to Maxie's team, and they backed off slightly. The boy sat up, smiling, and scratched his hair.

"I know a place that's safe," he said. "You don't have to live like this."

"Safe?" said Arran. "How safe?"

"Food. Water. Clean beds. Medicine. No grown-ups. Does that sound safe enough for you?"

"Where is this place?"

The boy grinned, his face all teeth.

"I thought you'd never ask."

"'ve traveled all the way across London to find you."

"Bull. How did you know we were even here?"

"I didn't. That's the whole point. My job was to find other people, kids like you."

"What do you mean, your job?"

"I was sent."

"Yeah?" said Ollie. "By who? God?"

"Why don't you let me tell you? Eh?"

They were on the roof, crowded into the little courtyard. Blue and his fighters were in a huddle to one side. Once they were sure it was safe, two of them had gone back to Morrisons to fetch a girl called Whitney, who seemed to be second in command to Blue, just as Maxie was to Arran. Whitney was big for her age and sat there hard-faced, waiting to be impressed. Her hair was knotted into tight braids, and she wore an immaculate white tracksuit that must have been the devil to keep clean. Blue's fighters seemed to be wary of her and quite respectful. It was easy to see why: Whitney had the look of a girl who had never taken any nonsense from anyone.

Achilleus and his fighters were sitting opposite the Morrisons crew, each side trying to outdo the other in toughness.

Arran sat in a big plastic-covered armchair set back from the fire, his face in shadow. He was happy for Ollie to take charge. Ollie was the best speaker and pretty sharp. He'd see through any lies.

Everyone who had taken part in the battle was shattered, so nobody questioned Arran. If he wanted to let someone else do the talking, that was cool. Truth was, though, he was feeling awful. The whole side of his head was hot, and his ear was blocked and throbbing. He ground his teeth together, let his eyelids fall shut, and tried to concentrate.

It didn't help.

Whenever he closed his eyes he could see the grown-up back at the pool. Those eyes. That intelligent look . . . that sound. Had it been trying to speak?

"Mwuh . . ."

And then it lunged at him, teeth bared, and he jerked his eyes open.

Tried to work out what was going on.

The patchwork boy was speaking.

"Sixteen years ago, something happened," he said to no one in particular. "As far as we know, everybody on the planet got diseased, but it's taken all this time for the symptoms to show. Sixteen years."

"Or else something stopped happening," said Ollie.

"What do you mean?"

"Either something happened sixteen years ago that made everyone ill," Ollie went on slowly, "or something stopped happening that had been making people ill. So that anyone born after then was all right."

"I suppose so," said the patchwork kid.

"It's not sixteen years." Everyone looked at Whitney. "I ain't been counting the days, but it's been a year—year and a half—since the disease first showed."

"Doesn't make any difference," said Patchwork. "Basically the adults are all either dead or diseased, and us kids have got to look after ourselves."

"We don't know that," said Small Sam's little sister, Ella. "We don't know if the whole world's like this, do we?"

"There must be some grown-ups around who aren't sick," said Monkey Boy. "They'll rescue us."

"Like Whitney said, it's been over a year," said Freak, his voice sounding like it was coming from a million miles away. "If anyone was coming to save us, I think they'd have showed up by now, don't you? Instead, all we've got is this guy. Joseph and his coat of mangy colors."

"No one's going to help us," said Patchwork. "I can promise you that. Everyone over the age of sixteen got sick and died."

"Not everyone," said Whitney.

Patchwork shrugged. "Some of the adults are just taking longer to die than others, that's all. They've become Strangers."

"What are you talking about now?" said Blue.

"I guess you call them something different. The adults who are diseased but not dead yet. Like that lot outside earlier."

"We call them grown-ups," said Blue. "Cuz that's what they are."

"To us they're Strangers. We were always told about 'stranger danger.' And this lot truly is dangerous. God must really have it in for us."

"I don't think God would do something like this," said Ella.

"Maybe it was God," said Patchwork. "Maybe it was something else."

"Like a meteor from space or something," Ella suggested.

"I think it was to do with global warming," said Bernie. "I think it was an ecological disaster."

"I think it was a disease, like AIDS," said Maeve.

"Could be," said Patchwork. "But we have a theory that it was terrorists or something."

"Yeah," said Achilleus. "Like a bomb, man. A chemical bomb, or some new biological weapon that went wrong."

"Nah. It was the scientists," said Blue. "Mucking about with stuff, genetically modified crops and all that. Nano-technology."

"That's just stupid," said Bernie. "Scientists did a lot of good for mankind."

"Who you calling stupid, you emo loser?"

A rumble of voices broke out, and Maxie had to shout over it.

"Let's not fight." She sounded like a tired and fed-up parent.

Arran smiled. Maxie was right. With so much bad stuff going down, it was ridiculous to be squabbling among themselves. He liked Maxie. He had from the start. She was the type of girl he used to hang out with, before all this kicked off. Now he was so stressed all the time he had no energy left to think about that sort of thing. He could tell she wasn't interested in him anyway. To her he was just the guy in charge. She probably resented him for being number one. If he hadn't been around maybe she would have been top dog.

He closed his eyes.

He shouldn't think like that. He really had no idea what Maxie might feel about anything. The poison in his system was messing with his mind.

Earlier, when Maxie had touched his neck, he'd felt a little jolt. It was so long since he'd been touched like that. It was kind and soft and gentle. Maybe he'd blushed. He hoped she hadn't noticed anything.

He tried to imagine what it would have been like if he'd met her before. Putting on his best clothes, going on a date, maybe to see a film or a band.

He imagined kissing her.

Don't go there, Arran, you'll only make yourself sad.

The noise died down and Whitney took charge. "Let's hear what the scarecrow's got to say," she said, turning her hard stare on the patchwork boy.

"Thank you," he said.

"So, for all your clever talk, you don't know what caused it, then?" Whitney asked. "The sickness."

Patchwork shook his head. "No one knows. How could we? We're just kids. Adults used to tell us things, in newspapers, on TV, at school. But now there's no adults left to tell us anything. And you can look at that as a good thing or a bad thing."

"It's a disaster," said Maxie.

"Is it? This is our world now."

"It's a crap world," said Callum, and a few of the kids laughed.

"Not where I've come from," said Patchwork.

"So where have you come from?" said Ollie.

"Buckingham Palace."

There was a snort of laughter followed by a chorus of jeering and mocking from the assembled kids. Patchwork just smiled.

"It's true," he said. "Why not? The Queen's dead, all the people that looked after her, all the guards in their bearskin hats, the police, the tourists . . . No more adults telling us what to do. There's just us kids. And we can do what we like."

10

"You really trying to tell us you live in Buckingham Palace?" said Whitney, her deep brown eyes softening into a smile.

"Yeah. It's cool. It's got a lake and a garden with a big wall around it with spikes on the top. It's safe. We grow food in the garden, we drink water from the lake, we sleep in the Queen's beds. Nobody can get in and there's enough of us to keep the place secure. We got our own guards now. We're making a fresh start."

"So what are you doing here, then?" said Ollie.

"We figured there must be other kids like us out there," said Patchwork. "Kids who survived. And the more of us we can get together, the better it'll be. It'll be safer. We can grow more food and work together to gradually rebuild the city. We can start to make London new again. Next to the palace is St. James's Park; there's enough space there to plant fields, if we've only got enough people. So I was sent to find other kids, tell them about what we're doing, and bring them back."

"Yeah, well, we've got news for you," said Callum. "We ain't going. Why would we ever leave this place? We don't need your Buckingham Palace, thank you very much. We got Waitrose."

"Shut up, Callum," said Achilleus. "Let's listen to the man."

"You've come all the way across town by yourself?" said Ollie, not convinced.

Patchwork's face clouded over.

"There was five of us to start with," he said. "We thought all of London would be like where we come from—organized. We didn't realize how dangerous it was out here. How many Strangers there are."

"Why?" said Ella. "What's it like where you come from?"

"I told you. It's safe. Most of the Strangers have disappeared from the center of town. We killed loads of them early on. Those that are left keep out of our way. They're beaten. But it was mad getting here. We had to come through the badlands. They picked us off one by one. I lost Alfie just today. He was the last one. There's only me left."

He swallowed hard. It was obvious he was trying not to cry. Nobody spoke for a while. In the end Ollie broke the silence. He squatted down and spoke gently to Patchwork.

"How many other kids have you found on the way?" he said. "How many have you sent back?"

Patchwork sniffed. "None. You're the first. The original plan was to keep going around London recruiting all the kids that were left. But it's too dangerous for that." He smiled and looked up at Ollie. "You lot, though, you could really make a difference. Together we could get back easy. You know how to look after yourselves. You're good fighters. The best I've ever seen. I can take you there. I can take you to safety."

"Let me ask you a question," said Arran, his voice sounding hoarse and croaky. Everyone turned to him; it was the first thing he'd said since the meeting began.

"What?"

"Why should we go into the center of town? Why shouldn't we just leave London? Go to the countryside? Surely we've got a better chance of surviving out there. That's where all the grown-ups were trying to get to when they started dying."

"Exactly," said Patchwork. "And I reckon that's where they all went. The center of London is empty, there's none of them around, but the further out we got, the more of them we found. I reckon if you tried to get out of town you'd just come across more and more of them. It's miles before you hit any proper countryside, but into town from here, how far is it? Five or six miles at the most. You could walk it in two hours if you didn't have to fight any Strangers. Who knows what you'd find out there if you did manage to leave London. But in the center, where I've come from, I can tell you what it's like—it's safe."

"How do we know you're not lying?" said Ollie.

"What would I gain by that?"

"Dunno. Don't really know anything about you."

"Yeah," said Blue. "What's your name?"

"Some people call me Jester, some call me Magic Man. . . ."

"Some call him jerk," said Achilleus, and there was a fresh round of laughter.

Jester nodded. "Yeah, some might call me that. I've been

called worse. You can laugh at me if you want, or you can listen."

"We'd need proof before we left this place and went marching off across London," said Ollie.

"I've got proof."

"Yeah?"

"I've got pictures."

"What sort of pictures?"

"From an old Polaroid camera. Photographs."

"Show us."

Jester took his satchel off his shoulder and opened it. He rummaged around, then produced a cardboard folder. From inside it he took out a handful of square, glossy photos. He passed them to Ollie, who flicked through them, a smile slowly spreading across his face. He brought them over to Arran, who had to lean forward into the light to see them properly.

They weren't faked. You couldn't fake a Polaroid. It wasn't like the old days when you could use a computer to do anything you liked. There was no Photoshop anymore, not without electricity to power the computers. Photoshop was just one more thing that had seemed really important at the time, but now was completely irrelevant. Useless.

These pictures were the real thing. They showed Buckingham Palace and a group of happy, healthy-looking kids—posing at the front in the parade ground, inside eating lunch around a big grand table, working in the gardens, swimming in the lake, playing soccer. It looked like an impossible paradise. A glimpse into another world.

Arran felt a lump in his throat. His hands were shaking. He gave the photos back to Ollie, who gave them in turn to Blue. Soon they were being passed from one excited kid to another, all grinning and shaking their heads and starting up a happy murmur of approval. The only one of them who scoffed was Callum. He looked at the pictures in disgust and sneered at the people in them.

Arran's eyes were misting up. What he had been shown was Unimaginable. It was hope. If what this guy was saying was true, then maybe things would be different in the future. Maybe he and Maxie would have a chance. Earlier it had seemed that there was no way out, that they would all slowly die here in this miserable empty supermarket. Picked off one by one, killed by disease, grown-ups or dogs, or each other.

Was there really a way out?

He barely listened as Ollie questioned Jester further, getting more details.

He was remembering what life had been like before. In his parents' big house in Dartmouth Park. Playing on the Heath with his mates. Going into Camden to walk around the market. Hanging out on the streets, chatting. Eating Sunday lunch with his mom and dad.

His mom and dad . . .

He couldn't picture exactly what his dad had looked like. He had been a busy man and was hardly ever at home. But Mom . . .

He could never forget her face.

It was the face he had seen at the pool.

His mother.

No.

It wasn't true. He'd imagined it. No way that—thing— could have been his mother. It was a trick of the light.

He realized there were tears streaming down his face. He was glad that nobody could see him. He had turned into a little kid again and just wanted his mom to wrap her arms around him. Speak softly to him. Sing him to sleep.

The thing at the pool, though, if it had been his mother, had tried to kill him.

"Mwuh . . ."

He wiped his face, dried the tears. If his eyes looked red, they would assume it was because of his wound.

"We're going," he said firmly, and everyone looked at him. "I don't care if Jester is making it up. I don't care if there's nothing at the other end. We can't stay here any longer. In the morning we pack up everything and we go."

"Wait a minute," said Maeve. She wasn't like the other kids. She wasn't a Londoner. She'd been visiting friends in Camden when everything had kicked off, and had been stuck here ever since. "Shouldn't we discuss this a bit more?"

"What's to discuss?" said Arran.

"Well, I just think it's crazy," said Maeve.

"Maybe," said Arran. "But I'm not staying here."

"What you said before. About going to the countryside. Surely, if we're going anywhere, that's what we should do. The city's crawling with grown-ups. The only food we can find is cans and dried packets and the half-rotten crap we find in abandoned houses. This is no kind of life."

"I told you," said Jester, sounding exasperated. "We're growing food at the palace. It's all organized. You go any-where else, you're going into the unknown."

"I grew up in the country," said Maeve. "I know it. We need to get away from the city and go where we can properly farm things and keep animals. We need space and clean air. We need to get out of London."

"One day, maybe," said Arran. "But we have to take it one step at a time. If Jester's right, and it's safe in the center, if we can make camp at the palace and get strong, then we can prepare. I don't know—send out scouts, like Jester, only better armed—find the best route. . . ."

"Why wait?" said Maeve. "If we head into the center of London we're going the wrong way. Can't you see that?"

"It's what we're doing," said Arran, who felt exhausted and had had enough talking for one night.

"Maeve's got a point, though," said Maxie. "If we link up with the Morrisons crew we'll be strong. We'd have a good chance of getting out. It might be our only chance. To properly start a new life."

"We should vote on it," said Maeve.

"Okay, okay," said Arran, who just wanted to go to sleep. "But these are city kids, Maeve. All they know is London. Some of them have never even been out of the city."

"Well I have," said Maeve, "and take it from me, London's not the center of the world. Our only chance for a decent future is to get out. I've been arguing for this since we set up camp here. Now's our chance to do it properly. If we head north up the A1 and then follow the M1, in two or three days we'd be clear of the city."

"All right," said Arran. "You've made your point. All those in favor of going to the palace with Jester, put up your hands."

Ollie carefully counted the show of hands.

"And anyone in favor of Maeve's plan, put your hands up."

Arran was surprised at the number of hands going up in support of Maeve. Once again Ollie counted. But it wasn't enough. The vote had gone Arran's way.

"That's it, then," he said. "It's decided." He hauled himself up out of his chair and walked over to Blue.

"What do you reckon?" he asked. "You coming with us, or do you need to take a vote as well?"

"We don't need no vote. We ain't no democracy, man. I'm in charge. End of story."

"And?"

Blue stood up and looked Arran in the eye.

"We're coming."

They gripped each other's hands. It felt good to be doing something for themselves. Then Blue turned to Jester and the light went out of his eyes.

"If you are lying to us, though, *Magic Man*, you are dead."

11

Small Sam wasn't dead. That thought was firmly lodged in the back of his mind. He wasn't dead. When they'd put him in the sack he'd thought that that was it. All over. He'd fainted, and when he'd woken up he was being jostled along on one of the grown-ups' shoulders. The grown-up stank, but the sack smelled worse. Of grease and rotting meat and poop. Sam didn't like it in the sack. He couldn't see anything. He'd wet himself.

They'd brought him to this place and dumped him on the floor. He had no idea where it was. He was still in the sack. It had taken them about ten minutes to get here. They'd carried him up stairs. Lots of stairs. They must be somewhere high.

At first, whenever he moved, one of the grown-ups would kick him, and if he whimpered they'd kick him again. Then someone had sat on him for a while, but once he'd stopped struggling, they got off him. He'd lain very still after that, as still as if he'd been dead, and they finally left him alone.

So he was still alive. For now. He knew, though, that un-less he was very lucky he probably wouldn't make it through the night. He had no doubt at all that the grown-ups were planning to eat him. That's what they did to the kids they captured. The only reason they hadn't already eaten him was that they were too full.

While he'd been lying there in the sack, quiet as a mouse, still as a corpse, he'd heard them eating. They must have caught another kid before him.

The grown-ups moaned with delight as they fed. Chewing loudly, slurping and belching. Sometimes there was a crunch, or one of them would spit. Once there had been some sort of fight.

Sam was glad that they had something else to eat, but felt awful that it was another kid.

And he was glad, so glad, that he couldn't see anything. The smell of blood was bad enough. It made him want to throw up.

It was quiet now. He could almost imagine that he was alone.

He'd been so scared, more scared than he'd ever been before in his life, and although his life had so far been quite short, there had been a lot of scary moments in it. Like when his mom and dad had left him. It had happened one night. His mom had come into the room he shared with his little sister, Ella. Mom had looked bad. Tired and sweaty and ill, with yellow skin and big black rings under her eyes. Gray lumps around her nose. Zits like a teenager. She had been shaking, her teeth chattering so loudly he could hear them, rattle, rattle, rattle. She'd woken him up and hugged him, and he'd felt her tears on his neck. She'd told him that she and Dad were going away. She said there was nothing she could do to help him and his sister, and if she stayed it would be dangerous for them.

Mom had told him to look after Ella, and he had tried. He had really tried. But he was only small. And now he'd left Ella all alone. She would be sad without him there. He hoped his mom and dad would understand. The thing was, though, he was too small to look after anyone, really. He was only nine.

At least he hadn't seen his mom and dad die. Sometimes, when he felt sad and lonely, he would picture them alive. Happy. He saw them on a sunny island, like when they'd gone to the Canary Islands. He told himself that they'd just gone away on a long holiday to somewhere where the disease hadn't happened. They were on a beach in their swimsuits and sunglasses, drinking cocktails with umbrellas in them. That always cheered him up, imagining they were safe somewhere and that they were maybe thinking about him and Ella. They were probably planning to come back and rescue them.

Deep down, though, he knew that really they would never be coming back. They must have died just like all the other grown-ups. Because if they hadn't died . . .

They'd be like the others.

These grown-ups, the ones who had captured him, weren't people anymore. They couldn't speak, only grunt and hiss at each other. They were mad things. All they thought about was food.

Oh, Mom, I wish you were here now. . . .

He wasn't really scared anymore. At first it had been almost too much to bear. He had gone stiff with terror. But it was tiring being scared, and it had slowly worn off, so that now he felt numb. And he was bored.

How long had he been lying here? A tiny bit of light could

get in through holes in the sack, and he could see enough to know that it was dark now. Grown-ups were too stupid to light fires or use solar lamps or even flashlights. They had forgotten everything.

He hoped that they were asleep, because then maybe he could try to get away. He wasn't tied up or anything. All he had to do was slip the sack off and make a run for it.

Once he had gone on a school trip to a farm. He had seen sheep and cows and pigs and chickens and he had wondered why they didn't try to escape. It looked easy. But the thing was, back then the animals were stupid and the humans were clever.

This was different. These grown-ups were stupid and he was clever. Yes, he was only small, but he was cleverer than they were.

He smiled.

He was going to escape.

He would wait a bit longer, though, until he was really sure it was safe.

He started to count, not too fast and not too slow. He reckoned that when he got to a thousand, if he hadn't heard any movement, he would take the sack off and have a look.

One, two, three, four, five . . .

Twenty-five, thirty, thirty-five, forty . . .

Counting to a thousand was taking much longer than he had thought; it seemed to go on forever. He got fed up at 420 and stopped.

It had been ages since the grown-ups had made any noise. They must be asleep. Or maybe they had gone out hunting again and left him alone?

Slowly, ever so slowly, he started to wriggle out of the sack, trying to make tiny movements. Every few seconds he would stop and listen, and once he was sure it was okay, he would go on.

Little by little the sack came off, until it cleared his head. Now he was lying on his side on a sticky, stinking carpet.

He looked around without moving his head. At first it was too dark to see anything properly. He could just make out that he was in a long room with windows all down one side. There was a pale stripe of bluish gray against the black.

He waited, unmoving, as his eyes got used to the light, and gradually bits and pieces of the room came into view.

He could see six grown-ups nearby. The mother and the others who had captured him, as well as two others—a fat old father with a bald head, and a younger one with a straggly beard. They were all fast asleep and snoring and snuffling.

The room was filthy. There were broken bones on the floor. There were a few greasy chairs, a pile of old rags in the middle, and in one corner was the grown-ups' toilet. They had done their business on the carpet and there were flies buzzing around it.

He retched. He wanted to use a swearword. He thought of the worst thing he knew and said it loudly in his head.

Bastards.

They didn't know better than to poop on the floor.

The dirty bastards.

Back at Waitrose they had a system. They used buckets as toilets, and every day they took turns to empty them into the drains outside.

Not this lot.

He hated them.

The nearest one, a father, let off a long slow fart and rolled over in his sleep. A shaft of moonlight fell across his face. Sam looked at him. He had never seen a diseased grown-up so close before. He had only seen them lumbering past in the street from a safe distance.

This father was dirty and very ugly. His hair was all stuck together and it didn't really look like hair. His skin was orangey-yellow and hanging loose in flaps, covered in sores and blisters and boils. It had cracked open in places, showing a gooey blackness underneath. He yawned and Sam saw that there was a big hole in his cheek. Through it he could see broken rotten teeth.

Sam got into a crouch and backed away from him.

His heels dug into something soft. He hadn't noticed a seventh grown-up curled against the wall. It shuddered in its sleep and shifted restlessly. Sam held his breath. It was a mother. She wrapped her arms around one of his legs, nuzzled against him, and relaxed.

She was younger than the other mother, with a tangle of black hair. There was a silver butterfly pin stuck in it. Sam thought it might be a good weapon. He carefully slid it out and held on to it tightly. It was like a long needle, with the silly, jeweled insect perched at one end. If any of these filthy bastards came near him he would stick it in. Yes he would. Just you watch him. He would stick it in good.

Dirty bastards.

Bastards, bastards, bastards . . .

It felt good to swear. Even if it was only in his mind.

He tried to pull his leg free, but the mother had too strong a grip on it. If he tugged too hard she might wake up. He studied her. She looked quite nice, quite pretty. Then she turned her head and he saw the other side of her face: it was a nest of boils. Great round lumps covered the whole of her cheek, her neck, her ear, even her eyelid. The skin was stretched tight, and it looked like the lumps might burst at any moment.

Sam had a terrible urge to pop one with the butterfly pin. Instead he leaned over and used the tip of it to tickle her skin. Soon she started to twitch and then let go of his leg to scratch the spot. With a sigh of relief he managed to step clear.

He would have to be much more careful. The more he took in of his surroundings, the more he realized that there were grown-ups everywhere. The floor was covered in them. If he took one wrong step he would tread on one. He remembered when his dad had taken him to the zoo in Regent's Park. In the reptile house they tried to spot lizards or snakes in their glass cages. When you first looked you couldn't see any, but if you were patient, you spotted them. Lying in clumps, on top of each other, under rocks, half buried, lazy and bloated.

He had to get out of here.

He moved cautiously to the window. To try to get some idea of where he was.

To begin with, he could make no sense of what he saw. It was a huge alien space. Not inside but not outside. It reminded him of something.

Yes. The amphitheater in a gladiator film.

Of course.

It was the Arsenal soccer stadium. He was in a hospitality box, looking across the rows and rows of red seats toward the field. There were grown-ups out there, some sleeping in the seats, some lying on the floor, some wandering aimlessly about.

Maybe they'd come back here because it was familiar; it meant something to them. There was certainly not going to be any more soccer played here for a long time. Far below, the grass on the field had grown high. A father was standing there, very still, like a statue. Grass up to his knees. He was fat and, like a lot of grown-ups, looked completely bald. He wore a white vest with a red cross of Saint George on it. Sam had the unnerving feeling that he was looking straight at him.

Sam felt sad. Dad had brought him here once. He remembered how full of life and sound and color it had been. He'd been scared at first, all those people shouting and singing and swearing and jumping up and down. But he'd gotten into it and had ended up shouting along with them, even though he wasn't really a soccer fan.

Now look at it. . . .

There were sliding glass doors here that opened onto the terraces, but even if they weren't locked, the noise of trying to open them would most likely wake the sleeping grown-ups. Besides, there were more grown-ups out there. If they spotted him it would be impossible to get away from them in such a wide-open space. No. There had to be another way out, a back way. There must be some stairs down behind the stands.

He crept across the carpet. The room was very big; it opened up at the back into a sort of dining area with broken tables and chairs in it. There were still more grown-ups sleeping here, and Sam had to look away as he glimpsed a half-eaten body lying under one of the tables.

Don't look. Don't look. Don't look.

He tried to pretend that he was in a film. He'd always had a good imagination; he could lose himself in a game for hours and hours. The film was *The Lord of the Rings*, and he was a hobbit in an orc castle. His dad had been reading him the book at night before he got sick, but it had been a bit old for him. He preferred the movies.

He wasn't just any old hobbit. He was Sam. Samwise Gamgee, the bravest of them all, and the butterfly pin in his hand was an elf sword.

That's right, keep thinking about something else.

It was darker back here away from the windows, and the smell was even worse. He remembered the time he lost his lunch box. He thought he'd left it at school. It turned up weeks later under a seat in the car. When Sam opened it, it was full of stale air and rotting food and horrible green fungus that sent up a cloud of spores when it was disturbed. He actually had been sick then, the smell had been so bad.

This was worse. His eyes were stinging.

Dirty bastards . . .

He edged his way forward, scanning the floor for any sleeping bodies, feeling gently with his toes, holding his nose with his fingers and breathing through his mouth. This place must be full of germs. Was it bad to breathe them in?

He spotted what looked like a door, on the far side of the room, past a bar. He headed for it, speeding up slightly. Halfway there a figure loomed up in front of him, and his heart caught in his ribs.

One of the grown-ups had woken.

Sam dropped to the floor and flattened himself against

the sticky carpet, pressing his face down so that he would be hard to spot. Sometimes it was good to be small.

The grown-up shuffled past a few inches from where Sam was lying. As soon as he had gone, Sam scuttled over to the bar and crouched down behind it.

He could sense that the grown-up had heard something, though. It made a strangled sound and began to move about in the dark.

Sam was still clutching the butterfly pin. It wasn't enough. He needed to find something else he could use as a weapon. With his other hand he felt around on the shelves behind the bar. There must be something. A corkscrew maybe, or even a knife. His hands closed over a hard plastic object. He ran his fingers over it, trying to work out what it was.

A cigarette lighter.

Better than nothing. It might help him to see where he was going, if he ever got out of here. He slipped it into his pocket and kept on searching.

He found nothing else and eventually the grown-up stopped moving about. Sam left it as long as he could—he was so close to getting out he couldn't stand waiting here any longer.

He peered around the end of the bar. Nothing. No movement. Only those dark shapes on the floor. He tiptoed to the door, passing through a wet patch. He didn't like to think what it might be, but it made his feet suck and squelch.

It sounded horribly loud to him, but he couldn't stop.

Keep moving, Sam. Just get out of here.

He was at the door. It was open.

Thank God.

He'd made it.

So long, you dirty bastards.

He went through. It was pitch-black out here; he couldn't see his hand in front of his face. He told himself that it was all right. Nothing would jump out at him, because nothing could see him.

It didn't help.

He was petrified. If he hadn't peed himself earlier, he would have done it now. His heart was beating so hard he could feel his whole body shaking, and in the dead silence the blood surging in his ears was deafening. He'd always been scared of the dark. His mom had told him not to worry.

"If you can't see the monsters, they can't see you."

Back then there had been no monsters. Not real ones. Only imaginary.

Now . . .

He held his breath and inched forward, his hands stretched out in front of him, feeling the floor with his feet.

He came to a step.

Stairs.

Good. They would take him down, away from this awful place.

One step . . . two steps . . .

It would be a long climb, but maybe there would be windows soon.

Step followed step followed step. He started to move quicker as he grew more confident. Finding a rhythm.

He came to a wall and was confused for a moment until he realized that the stairs turned a corner. He reached out his hands, groping in the darkness.

They touched something warm and soft.

What was it?

It moved.

No . . .

He turned around. He had to get away. There was only one thing it could be—a grown-up.

He started to cry. He couldn't run, not in the dark. He fell to his hands and knees and crawled like a dog. His eyes screwed shut. The grown-up was coming after him; he could hear its feet scraping, its breath rasping.

Sam felt strong hands grip his ankle. He kicked out. Got away. Sped up.

But where could he go? Upstairs there were only more grown-ups.

If he moved to the side and kept still, maybe this one would go past him. He tried it. But the grown-up was already there, on the step next to him.

Sam shouted in panic and scurried up the steps as fast as he could. He was back at the door to the directors' box. There was movement on the other side. The grown-ups were waking up.

It was all over. He should never have shouted.

He blundered into the room, the weak light seeming suddenly bright after the inky blackness of the stairwell.

There was a wet slurp behind him. He turned. The grown-up was filling the whole doorway. He was huge, a tall father, well over six feet. He was wearing a long, soiled overcoat and had a huge black beard and no teeth. He opened his mouth in a silent howl and grabbed Sam, clutching him to his chest.

Another father blundered across the room and tried to snatch Sam back. The giant swatted him away.

More grown-ups came on now, with hunched backs and bent legs too feeble to hold their weight.

The giant must be an intruder, come to steal food. The group in the directors' box didn't like it. They swarmed around him, their strength in numbers, as he pushed them away and lashed out at them. Sam was being crushed against his hot damp chest. The mother who had first snatched him got hold of an arm and tugged. Sam felt like he was going to be torn in half.

"Get off me! Get off!" he shouted, but the sound of his voice only seemed to send the grown-ups into a frenzy. Sam was surrounded by a stinking, fetid mass of bodies, hands clawing at him, faces looming close. But nothing could make the giant let go.

Sam's hand holding the butterfly pin was clamped in the fold of the giant's arm. Then he remembered the lighter. With his free hand he groped in his pocket until he found it. He prayed that it would work.

He pressed the button. Nothing. He pressed again. Still nothing.

Again . . . *Click–click–click* . . .

A spark.

Come on. Come on.

There were spots dancing in front of Sam's eyes. His ears were singing. He couldn't breathe. Any moment now he was going to pass out.

Again he pressed, and this time a small orange flame sprang into life.

He raised his hand and put the flame to the giant's beard.

The effect was spectacular. There was a blinding, scorching flare as the beard crackled and sizzled. The giant yelped and dropped Sam, batting at the flames and sparks with his huge, grubby hands.

Sam was in danger of being trampled underfoot. The giant was hopping and dancing around. Sam flinched clear as hands reached out for him. He realized he still had the lighter clutched in his hand, with the flame lit. He held tight to the bottom of the giant's coat and put the flame to it. In a few seconds it was alight.

The giant stumbled across the room as the flames spread up his coat. Some of the other grown-ups kept a fearful distance, others jumped on his back. Soon a full-scale battle was raging, the remaining bits of furniture were being smashed to pieces and set alight. A fat mother seemed to actually explode as if her clothing had been trapping flammable gases.

Flaming bodies ran in panic. The giant was a living fireball. The room was lit up bright as day, and Sam could see the full horror of it. The blood and filth and bits of dead bodies.

It was like a vision of hell.

He didn't stay to watch.

"Die, you dirty bastards!" he yelled, and in a moment he was back on the stairs, holding his lighter up to see where he was going. Its feeble light slowly dimmed as the last of the fuel ran out, but he was hurrying down, three steps at a time.

There was a shriek behind him. He looked around. Flames were leaping down the stairwell, and burning grown-ups were coming after him.

Run, Sam, run. . . .

12

'm not coming."

"What do you mean you're not coming?"

"I'm not leaving this place, Arran. It's home. It's safe. I like it here. I'm not leaving and you can't make me."

"Callum, you can't stay here by yourself."

"I won't be by myself. Others will want to stay, just you see. I won't be alone. Not everyone wants to go."

"But they're all outside, waiting. It's arranged."

"Ask them," said Callum. "Ask them if they really want to go, or if they'd rather stay here with me."

"We took a vote on it," said Arran wearily.

"No we didn't. We voted on whether to go into the center of town or into the countryside. You never asked them if they'd all rather just stay here. So ask them."

"You ask them," said Arran.

"No," said Callum. "I'm not going out there. I'm happy here." He sat down and folded his arms.

"Well, what if one or two did want to stay?" said Arran. "How would you survive, Callum? It's crazy."

"I'll tell you what's crazy," said Callum angrily. "You lot, going off out there, just because some weird kid in a patchwork suit turns up. It's like that fairy story The Pied Piper of Hamelin, where he takes the kids away and, I don't know, eats them, or something."

"That's not what happens."

"Yeah, well, whatever, it hasn't got a happy ending. Why did you listen to that idiot? Hmm? Why did you believe him? He's obviously lying."

Arran looked around the supermarket, where he had spent the last year of his life. They were on the shop floor, surrounded by row upon row of empty shelving. He was sick of the sight of the place.

"Callum," he said steadily, "anything's better than staying here and dying one by one."

"It doesn't have to be like that. You do what you want, Arran, but I'm staying."

"You can't."

"Why not?"

"Why not?" The thought of getting out of here filled Arran with a light, airy feeling. He'd had a bad night. The pain in his neck had steadily grown worse. He didn't know if he'd slept at all. Now his head was throbbing, his eyes were dry and sore, and he was sweating heavily. The last thing he wanted to do was hang around here worrying about himself.

He looked at Callum, sitting stubbornly in an old armchair, as if nothing in the world could shift him.

"What if the grown-ups get in?" he said.

"They won't try and get in if they think there's no one here."

"They're bound to try, though, and I mean . . . Jesus, Callum, come on, what will you eat?"

"I can scavenge just like you did. If there's less of us, there's less mouths to feed. It'll be easier, actually."

"Yes, and what if it's just you? What then?"

"It won't be. Loads of other kids will want to stay. You're forcing us out and we don't like it."

Arran sighed.

"All right. I'll ask them," he said.

He walked outside into the sunshine. All the Waitrose kids and the Morrisons crew were assembled there—fifty-seven of them in all. Carrying sleeping bags and backpacks, food, water, and weapons.

"Callum says he's not coming," Arran announced. There were groans from the kids.

"Typical."

"He only ever thinks about himself."

"Leave him. He's not a fighter. We can live without him."

"We can't just leave him here, though," said Maxie. "He'll die."

"So what?" said Achilleus. "Let's get going."

Arran shouted them down. "Does anyone else want to stay?"

No one.

The kids stood in silence, shaking their heads.

"You sure?" said Arran. "You don't have to go if you don't want. Who'd rather stay here with Callum?"

Still no one.

Arran closed his eyes and rubbed his forehead. There

was nothing for it: he would just have to persuade Callum to come. He strode back inside.

Bernie turned to Ben. They looked very pale out here. Their black clothes accentuated the whiteness of their skin. They hardly ever went outside.

"Shame to be leaving it all," said Bernie. "Everything we built."

"We can build more," said Ben. "If Jester's telling the truth, we can make loads of cool stuff in the palace. We can rebuild the whole of London. We'll be famous. They'll put up statues of us."

"Yeah, but . . . the speaking tubes, the barriers, the stoves we rigged up in the canteen, the new signaling system we were working on. It took us ages."

"You want to stay?" said Ben.

Bernie looked wistfully over toward the supermarket.

"No," she said. "I want to be a million miles from here. It reminds me too much of everything we've lost. All the friends who've died. All the bad times."

"It's a fresh start," said Ben. "We'll build newer and better stuff."

"Yeah." Bernie smiled and put an arm around Ben.

Nearby, a group of little kids was clustered around one of the Morrisons crew. A tiny six-year-old called Joel, who had an even tinier puppy wrapped in an old jacket in his arms.

"Oh, he's so cute."

"Look at him, he's licking my hand."

"What's his name?"

"Godzilla," said Joel, and they all laughed.

Maxie looked on and smiled. They'd kept dogs in Waitrose

at first, as guard dogs and companions, but it had gotten too difficult to feed them, and they'd become semi wild. In the end they'd had to turn them loose. They were probably dead now, along with most of the other pets that had relied on humans.

Maxie noticed a kid on the edge of the group, not joining in. He just stood there, wide-eyed, molding a big lump of Blu Tack putty in his hands. She went over to him and crouched down.

"What's your name?" she asked. The boy stared at her but didn't speak. Instead he rolled the Blu Tack out into a long rope between his fingers.

"He don't speak," said Blue, walking up. "Not since his mom and dad died."

"Poor little guy."

"He's not deaf or nothing."

"No."

"We call him Blu-Tack Bill. He's always playing with the stuff. Only thing that keeps him happy."

Maxie smiled at Bill and noticed that he had formed the Blu Tack into a letter *B*. *B* for Bill.

"I suppose we're all going to have to get to know each other," Maxie said to Blue.

"Guess so."

"I'm Maxie, by the way."

"S'all right, girl. I know who you are."

Maxie smiled awkwardly, not sure how to take this. Blue scared her slightly. He reminded her of boys from before, the ones that shouted at you in the street and laughed with their friends when you tried to ignore them.

"Are you, like, Arran's girlfriend?" Blue asked.

"No," said Maxie, a little too quickly and a little too indignantly. "Why would you think that?"

"Dunno. You're, like, his second in command."

"Is Whitney your girlfriend?"

"Whitney? No way." Blue laughed.

Maxie made a face that said "Well, then."

Arran came out of the shop, a dark look on his face.

Maxie went over to him. "No luck?" she asked.

"He won't budge."

"We could force him."

"What's the point? If he doesn't want to come, he doesn't have to."

"We can't leave him."

"I don't think we've got any choice."

"Maybe I should speak to him," said Maxie.

"Waste of time." Arran approached Blue. "Any of your lot want to stay?"

"Nah. We've had enough of Holloway. We're going to the palace."

He grinned, and Arran couldn't help grinning back.

It was hard to believe. They really were going to Buckingham Palace.

One of Blue's deputies ambled over in a loose shuffle. He was tall and bony with a messy Afro and a sleepy look about him. He scratched an armpit.

"You ready?" he drawled.

"Yeah." Blue nodded to Maxie. "Lewis, this is Maxie. Maxie—Lewis. He looks dopey, but don't be fooled for a moment. He's a killer. He'll be protecting the left-hand side."

Lewis smiled sleepily and lifted a hand in greeting to Maxie.

"Okay," said Maxie. "I guess if Callum's not coming, then we're ready to go."

Blue, Arran, and Jester had spent the morning working out a plan of action. As usual they would stick to main roads and stay in the middle, keeping well away from the buildings on either side. Arran and Blue were to lead the group along with Jester and the best fighters from each crew. Maxie was taking the right flank with a smaller gang, Lewis the left. Ollie was in charge of bringing up the rear with a motley crew of skirmishers. The remaining older kids would be in the middle, surrounding the little kids, who were being looked after by Whitney, Maeve, and some of the more responsible girls. Two of the kids had been assigned to take attendance, one for each crew. Josh was keeping it for Waitrose, and Whitney for Morrisons. It was their job to keep track of everyone, so that nobody got left behind. Josh took out his list and carefully drew a line through Callum's name. He felt a bit bad about it. He had spent a lot of time with Callum up on the roof. They were friends. But Callum had been weird lately and, in a way, Josh was glad to be rid of him.

He was itching to be off.

Ella was in tears. She pushed her way through the big kids to Arran.

"I want to stay," she said.

"What? You can't, Ella." Arran got down on his haunches so that he was at her level.

"I have to."

"Why? What's the matter, darling?"

"It's Sam," Ella sobbed. "What if he comes back and I'm not here?"

Arran put his arms around the little girl and gave her a hug.

"Oh, Ella," he said. "He won't be coming back, I'm afraid. He's gone forever. You have to accept that."

"No!" said Ella angrily. "He's not dead. He'll come back to me. He's my brother, and I just know it."

"Ella, if I thought for one moment that Sam was coming back, I'd wait here for him. We'd all wait. You know that. But he's gone. Like all the other kids we've lost. We have to think about ourselves now. Think about the future. Sam would want you to be happy, wouldn't he?"

"Yes."

"He'd want you to be safe?"

"Yes."

"So, for his sake we have to go. All right?"

Ella sniffed and nodded. "You'll look after me, won't you?" she said.

"'Course I will. Tonight you'll be safe in the palace, like a princess."

Arran stood up, then closed his eyes as a fresh knot of sickness worked its way through his guts. He had wanted to get away hours ago. They had planned to leave early. But getting the kids organized had been a nightmare. He felt like a dad getting his kids ready to go on vacation: dealing with squabbles and complaints and questions, nagging at them to get packed, shouting at them when they forgot things. And then there had been the holdup with Callum.

Now it looked like they were at last ready to get moving.

They were going to follow the main road down to Camden, cut through Regent's Park to the Marylebone Road, and then cross over to Portland Place. Portland Place would take them to Oxford Circus, from where they would head down Regent's Street to Piccadilly Circus and cut through to St. James's Park. From there it was a straight run along the Mall to the palace. Walking fast they could do it in two hours. But the little kids would slow them down, and if they came across any grown-ups, which they were bound to do, that would slow them down further. They should still make it before the end of the day, though. So there was no panic. It had taken Jester and his friends much longer to get up here, as they had made the mistake of taking back roads and side streets, assuming they would be safer. They had wasted a great deal of time dodging grown-ups, running, hiding, and fighting.

Arran hoped that the sheer force of their numbers today would deter any grown-ups from attacking. And if they did attack, well then—they were ready for them.

They were an army.

He watched the kids as they got into formation. There was an excited, slightly dizzy atmosphere, like at the start of a school trip. The little kids in particular were in very high spirits. They hated being cooped up indoors all day and were happily getting to know each other. The older kids were a little more wary. Some of them had fought each other in the past. Arran and Blue had been working hard to make sure nobody started fighting again. A shared goal and a shared enemy were helping, and the mood was positive for the time being, but Arran knew that if anything went wrong it would quickly lead to arguments and infighting.

"Come on, then," he said, throwing one last quick glance back toward Waitrose. "Let's go."

He raised an arm, held it above his head until he was sure that everyone had seen it, and then let it drop toward the center of town.

A cheer went up. Arran started walking. The rest of the kids fell in behind him.

They were marching to a new life.

13

Small Sam was curled up in a ball. He had made himself as teeny as he could. He was inside an empty water tank in the attic of a house somewhere near Finsbury Park. He was sharing the space with several dead and rotting pigeons. They gave off a choking smell that caught in his throat and made his eyes sting, but he hoped the smell would hide his own smell. Hoped it would keep the grown-ups away. So far it was working. He had been here all night. Waiting. Listening. It was almost like being back in the sack again.

The last few hours had been a blur, and he was exhausted. He'd been chased down the stairs at the stadium by three grown-ups. Two of them had been on fire. They hadn't made it to the bottom of the stairs, and Sam had managed to lose the third one in the maze of concrete corridors and walkways behind the stands. But he had also got lost himself. At one point he found himself running across the field, with several bewildered grown-ups watching from the seats.

Eventually, though, he had found a way out, and as he ran off he'd looked back to see the whole of the top of the stadium on fire. A tower of flames reached up into the night sky.

He wondered how many of the grown-ups would burn, and it made him happy. His happiness had been short-lived, however, because he realized that he didn't really know where he was or how to get back to Holloway Road. He had wandered the streets for ages and had somehow ended up in Finsbury Park. He had heard the older kids talking about Finsbury Park. They never came up this way. It was too dangerous. There were too many grown-ups, and lots of the buildings had been damaged by fire. He had an idea that the Seven Sisters Road would take him back to Holloway, but he wasn't sure which way he should go.

While he had been standing there, trying to decide, he'd been ambushed by another bunch of grown-ups. Luckily he heard them coming as they stumbled about clumsily in the dark, and he'd gotten away, ducking and scurrying and crawling through derelict gardens. At one point one of them grabbed hold of him in the dark, but he stabbed the butterfly pin hard into its hand, and it dropped him like a burning coal. In the end, tired of running, he had broken into a house and made his way up into the attic, where he had found the empty water tank.

As he lay there through the long hours of darkness, he cheered himself up by imagining what the others would say when he got back to Waitrose.

"Sam, you're alive!"

"Nobody's ever done that before."

"You're a hero!"

"Tell us all about it!"

"How many did you kill?"

He pictured them all crowded around him, asking questions, patting him on the back, smiling. The kids at the supermarket were his new family now. The biggest family a boy could hope for. Maybe they would even break out some of the candy they kept for emergencies, as a special treat. Sam loved candy. It was the thing he missed most in the whole world.

So he had drifted in and out of sleep and in and out of dreams, curled up in the bottom of the water tank, surrounded by dead pigeons.

It was light now. It had been light for some time. He had watched the bright sun wake up and peep through the cracks in the roof where the tiles were missing or broken. Somewhere nearby a live pigeon was cooing, and he found the sound comforting.

But he was hungry and he was thirsty and he longed to be safely back at Waitrose.

He uncurled himself and shifted into a crouch, his leg muscles shaking and weak. His knees and back stiff.

He peered over the edge of the tank, not knowing what he might see.

Just an attic. Full of dust and cobwebs and a few sagging cardboard boxes.

No grown-ups.

It was safe to leave. He would have to check every step of the way from now on, though. He couldn't afford to make any more mistakes. He'd been lucky to get away twice. He doubted that his luck would hold much longer. And it was easier at night. There would be more grown-ups about now that it was daytime.

He told himself that it was just a game. He'd always been

good at hiding. Hide-and-seek had been one of his favorite things to play. It had been scary when he'd played with his dad. His dad was big and would make monster noises.

These grown-ups were just the same. They were like his dad. All he had to do was keep out of their way.

He went to the opening in the attic floor that he had climbed up through earlier, lay down on his belly and lowered his head until he could properly see the landing below.

It was all quiet.

He slid down the ladder and crept along the landing to the window at the end. It led out onto a small flat roof. The street looked empty. He opened the window and crawled out, keeping low, keeping small.

He had a pretty good view of the street from here. He looked to left and right. There was no movement at all. No wind in the trees, no birds flying, no animals moving about.

No grown-ups.

He climbed down off the roof.

It was then that he saw the bicycle. Leaning against a row of trash cans in the front garden. It looked undamaged. He knelt down and checked it out. The chain was still in one piece, but the tires were nearly flat.

There was just enough air in them, though, to be able to ride it. It would get him as far as Waitrose at least.

He pushed it out of the garden and into the road. There was still nobody around. He climbed onto the seat and started to pedal. It was hard work. The bike seemed to be stuck in a high gear. It was moving, though. He pedaled harder, building up speed. The bike creaked and groaned and complained, but he kept at it, wobbling along like he was drunk.

He'd been confused last night, but finding the bike had given him fresh confidence. All he had to do was follow the road signs to Holloway and he'd be all right.

He turned left into the Seven Sisters Road and cycled on. The squashy tires made the bike unsteady and difficult to steer, but he was still going much faster than he would be if he was walking.

For the first time in twenty-four hours he smiled. It was a sunny day. The streets were clear, he was zooming along on his new bike. Well, not quite zooming. More wobbling, perhaps. But it didn't matter. He was going home.

Once again he imagined the look of amazement on the faces of his friends.

"A bike, Sam? You found a bike!"

"Well done—you're the coolest."

"King of the streets!"

Then he heard footsteps behind him.

He looked back. There was a grown-up following him. A lone father. Loping along on stiff legs, panting with the effort. As Sam watched, another grown-up joined him, a mother this time, her hair tied up in a big untidy knot on top of her head.

Then another and another. They were coming out of the streets on either side. Sam had to keep glancing back and then looking ahead to make sure he didn't hit something. There were cars abandoned all over the roads, and you had to be careful or you would crash into one.

More and more grown-ups were pouring into the road, half running, half walking. Sam skidded around a van and saw two ugly fathers coming at him from the front, one on either side, in a pincer movement. He sped up even more and just managed to squeeze between them as they made a lunge for him. He careened all over the road, out of control, then stood up on the pedals and pumped them as hard as he could. It was about as fast as the bike would go on these junk tires, and he was scared it wasn't fast enough.

He had never cycled so hard in his life: his lungs were on fire, his heart trying to punch its way out through his rib cage. Before, he had thought that he was flying along, but now he seemed to be moving in slow motion.

Come on. Come on.

He realized there were tears streaming down his face.

His happy dream of being welcomed home as a hero was in tatters. Nobody would ever know what he had gone through last night. Nobody would know about the battle at the stadium. The giant's beard on fire. His escape across the field. Hiding in the water tank. It had all been for nothing.

Nothing . . .

No. Damn them. He wasn't going to let them catch him. He was Sam the Giant Slayer. He was going to escape.

Then, as if in answer to an unspoken prayer, the road began to slope gently downward, and he picked up speed, still pedaling furiously. When he next looked back, the grown-ups had fallen behind. Yes. He was getting away.

See you, losers!

On he went. His legs like Jell-O. And each time he looked behind him, the grown-ups were farther away.

He whooped.

He screamed.

He was Sam the hero again.

By the time he hit Holloway Road he was alone. He had lost sight of the shambling idiots. Ah, they were probably still following him, but they'd take ages to get here—he had plenty of time to get inside.

There it was. Waitrose. His home. The lookouts on the roof would have spotted him already. He waved, but couldn't see anyone. Maybe they were already at the speaking tube, sending orders to the kids below.

"You'll never believe it! It's Sam, riding a wonky bike like a crazy kid!"

Maybe the doors would open up for him as he arrived.

He cycled up to the front of the shop and jumped off his bike. He couldn't hear anyone inside.

"Hey!"

He pulled the chain that rang a big bell above the shop floor. Pulling and pulling and pulling.

"Open up!" he yelled. "It's me, Sam. I'm back!"

Nothing. What was taking them so long?

"Hey! You lot. It's me. Let me in. . . ."

He stopped shouting and listened. He couldn't hear anything. He pulled the chain again. Maybe it was broken? No. He was sure he could hear the bell ringing in the shop. So why was nobody coming?

He stepped back and went over to the window to try to see inside, but all the shutters and barricades were up. He banged on the glass. Shouted again.

He huffed. This wasn't how he'd pictured it at all.

Something caught his eye and he turned to look back the way he had come. Bodies walking. His heart lifted for a brief moment. It must be a scav party returning. They'd get him in.

They were too big, though, too slow.

And there were too many of them.

Tears sprang back into his eyes

Why had he lied to himself?

It was the grown-ups who had chased him down Seven Sisters Road. They must have carried on, doggedly following his trail, and now they were shuffling nearer.

He ran back to the door and tugged at the bellpull, screaming at the top of his voice.

"Let me in let me in let me in!"

The grown-ups heard him and broke into a lazy jog. They weren't exactly hurrying, though. Why would they need to? They'd catch up with him in the end.

14

Callum could hear someone outside. Ringing the bell, banging on the windows, shouting. He stayed in his chair, unmoving. If he sat here long enough they would go away. For the first time in a year he was alone. Properly alone. He truly believed that if he was careful, if he stayed hidden and kept quiet, the grown-ups would ignore the shop, leave him be. Arran had left him some food and water, without telling the others. That was a cool thing to do. But what Arran couldn't have known was that Callum already had loads of stuff stashed away. He had been hoarding since they first came here. In secret places. Above loose ceiling panels, in the wall spaces behind cabinets, in forgotten storage areas. It had been obvious to him from the start—if he didn't look after himself, he was going to wind up dead. Let the others share, let them ration everything, divide food into portions—when everything ran out they'd quickly start fighting over what was left.

There was only one of him. This was his kingdom now. He was Arran, Achilleus, Freak, and Ollie all rolled into one.

He hadn't been making it up when he'd told Arran he thought that some other kids would want to stay, though. He'd half hoped they would, but after the initial surprise that nobody did, he'd soon discovered that it was much better this way.

There was nobody to get on his nerves. Just him and his stash. Alone. Peaceful. Bliss. No more arguments. No more petty fights. No more needling or bullying. Most of the time, being here had felt like being in the *Big Brother* house. Everyone living on top of each other, with nothing to do except moan and bitch. Occasionally a scav party had brought back books they'd looted, or games and puzzles, anything to lift the boredom, but it had never been enough.

Now there was nobody to tell him what to do. What was the point, if the adults had all died, of simply getting jumped-up kids to boss you about? Oh, sure, he liked Arran, but he didn't ever remember voting that he should be in charge.

It would be different now. Callum could do whatever he wanted. He even had a portable CD player. He'd kept it hidden in his most secret stash, along with some CDs and, most important of all, batteries. Batteries were more precious than gold. They'd found stacks of them in the shop when they first arrived, and they'd thought that they would last forever. Callum had been the first to realize just how quickly they would run out, though, and had set about hoarding them. Now he didn't have to hide them anymore.

He was looking forward to putting on some music. He hadn't listened to any music for about six months. A lot of the kids had had iPods and other MP3 players, but they were completely useless as there was no way to charge them. Deke had once found a solar charger in a shop, but it never worked properly and it eventually broke. And that was the end of that.

Until now.

Sweet.

Callum was nicely set up.

But now someone was trying to spoil it. Making a racket outside, drawing the attention of any grown-ups who happened to be in the area.

Well, they could make as much noise as they wanted. He wasn't about to let them in. This was his crib now. It was not for sharing.

He closed his eyes. Soon, whoever was outside would go away, and he could have some more peace and quiet.

15

The grown-ups hobbled down the road on bent legs. Some were dribbling. Some were clacking their teeth together and making a sort of humming, buzzing sound. Some scratched at their sores and rashes. Some were shaking all over and whipping their heads from side to side. One was missing a hand, and his forearm was green and gangrenous. All of them were hungry and crazy and in pain. The creature by the shop was food. They would catch it and rip it open and feed on it. That was all that mattered to them.

Sam reckoned he had about thirty seconds before they got to him.

He studied the barriers, his eyes darting about wildly. He knew they couldn't be forced, but they were built to keep out grown-ups, and he was small—maybe he could find a way. . . ?

He frowned. There was a small gap at the top. The barriers hadn't been closed properly. If he could climb up he just might be able to squeeze through. He jumped up and grabbed hold of the top of a metal sheet. It bit into his hands, but he ignored the pain.

He glanced down the road. The grown-ups were nearly upon him.

His feet scrabbled on the metal, trying to get a grip. His sneakers squeaked. He found a little bump and his foot held fast. Now he pulled and wriggled and kicked, and then he was up. On his belly. He was right. He could just fit through the space at the top. It was tight, though, and he could hardly breathe as he forced his small body into the narrow gap, scraping his skin on the edges, his feet kicking out behind him like a mad frog.

He could hear the grown-ups. They had finally gotten here. He felt hands trying to take hold of his ankles. He kicked harder, and with a mighty effort he wrenched his hips through and then slithered and tumbled down the other side into the covered mall.

Outside, the grown-ups whined and moaned. He hoped they couldn't get in. The barrier was usually bolted shut, but the bars weren't in place and the chain was hanging loose. Why hadn't it been done properly?

Awful thoughts came into his head. What if there had been an attack while he was gone? What if everyone was dead?

He ran over to the shutter. It hadn't been wound down all the way. Again, a grown-up wouldn't fit through. But he was Small Sam.

He wormed his way under on his belly and stood up. Slowly he walked farther into the shop, fearful of what he might find.

It all looked the same as ever—except that it was deserted.

"Hello?"

His voice sounded feeble and tiny.

He walked deeper inside.

Somebody was in an armchair. In the area at the back, where they had cleared a space and moved in some furniture. Just sitting there. Doing nothing. He wasn't dead, though. He blinked.

It was Callum.

"Hello?" said Sam, walking closer. "Are you all right?"

Callum nodded slowly, watchful. "How did you get in?" was all he asked. No surprise or joy at seeing Sam back from the dead.

"The barriers weren't properly shut."

"I must have not closed them right when they left."

"What do you mean?" said Sam. "When who left?"

Callum told Sam everything that had happened. Sam slumped down on a sofa, exhausted.

"They can't have gone," he said.

"Well, they have. All of them."

"Except you."

"Except me."

"Why didn't you go with them?"

Callum shrugged. "I like it here."

"Didn't you hear me, though?" said Sam. "When I was trying to get in? I rang the bell."

"I didn't know it was you, did I? How could I? I thought it was one of them, a grown-up."

"It was me," said Sam, and he started to cry. He was so

tired. All he wanted to do was lie down on the sofa and go to sleep, but Callum was looking at him in an odd way. Sam was so confused. He wasn't sure he trusted Callum. Wasn't even sure that he was telling the truth. Had a raggedy boy really turned up and led everyone away?

"My sister Ella," he said quietly. "I promised to look after her, and now she's gone."

"They didn't leave that long ago," said Callum. "You could catch up with them easy."

"I'd have to go back out there."

"Yeah." Callum nodded his head slowly, watching Sam with glittering black eyes.

Sam stood up. "Is there a bicycle pump here?" he said.

16

Arran's head was spinning. Walking in the hot sun was boiling his already feverish brain. He felt faint and found breathing difficult. He was trying hard not to show it, but every now and then he would sway and stumble sideways across the road. He took another sip of water. His hundredth since they'd left, it seemed like. At this rate he'd finish his supply before they even got to Camden.

The truth was, he felt awful, and he knew it was serious. Germs had got in through his broken skin and they were breeding in his blood.

He could have wept. If Jester had only showed up a few hours earlier, then Arran would never have gone up to the pool with the scav party. Deke would still be alive, and Small Sam too, probably. Then Arran wouldn't have this bloody bite in his neck. It was typical to be shown a way out, to be offered a place of safety, to have hope dangled in front of you, only to have it snatched away like this.

It just wasn't fair. He might make it to the palace only to drop dead.

Whatever happened, he was going to make sure that they all got there safely, though. His kids. Even if it was the last thing he did. He had to focus on that and not brood over anything else. He was responsible for this lot and he wasn't going to let them down.

He needed to take his mind off his injury. He saw Freak, trudging along, head down, staring at the ground, his hood pulled forward to cover as much of his face as possible.

"You all right, mate?" he asked.

Freak grunted. Could have been yes or no.

"D'you mind leaving the shop?"

Freak shrugged. Since he'd gone crazy in the battle last night he'd slipped back to being silent and moody.

"There wasn't anything more you could have done," said Arran kindly. "Even if we had got Deke away from there. He had glass in his side. His lung was punctured."

"I know," said Freak. "I just miss him, is all. He used to make me laugh. Nothing else did. He made me forget all this."

"If I knew any jokes I'd tell you one," said Arran.

"Don't bother, mate. You're terrible at telling jokes."

"Yeah, I know," said Arran. "Always have been. Luckily I was good at soccer, so it didn't matter. That's what I'd really like to do, you know, play soccer again. First thing when we get there, I'm going to set up a game. You'll play, won't you?"

"If we get there."

"We'll get there," said Arran.

"I wish I had your confidence," said Freak bitterly.

Arran said nothing. He might have fooled Freak, but he wasn't fooling himself. So far they'd seen no signs of any life at all, but he doubted it would stay that way. They'd definitely have to deal with grown-ups somewhere along the way. The image of the mother at the pool—his mother?—came unwanted into his head again.

"It's not my mother," he said without meaning to.

"You what?" Freak gave him a puzzled look.

"Nothing," said Arran, and he pressed a palm against his hot temple.

"Listen, Freak," he went on. "This might be tough, getting there and all, and we're going to need all the help we can get. You walking along like that, looking like crap, it's going to make the little kids scared. Be tough for them, yeah?"

Freak raised his head and stared at Arran.

"How did it end up like this?" he said. "We're just kids ourselves."

"It just happened," said Arran. "Let's not try to figure it out, eh, Freak?"

"I dunno."

Arran unslung his backpack and opened it.

"Here," he said. "I got something for you. I was waiting for the right moment. I guess this moment is as good as any." He pulled out a can of spray paint. Freak's eyes went wide.

"Where'd you get that?" he said.

"I found it when I was clearing out Waitrose, getting ready to leave. It was packed away in the back of a cupboard. Dunno who put it there."

"You got any more?"

"I got five, mate. Black, white, red, yellow, and silver." He passed one to Freak, who rattled it.

"Still half full."

Arran handed over the other four cans, and Freak stashed them in his own backpack.

"Maybe if you can spray your tag somewhere—Freaky-Deaky—it'll sort of keep Deke alive. Write in big letters 'Deke lives,' or something. Don't let them win. The grown-ups."

Freak pushed his hood back off his head and walked straighter and taller. "Arran?"

"Yeah?"

"Don't worry." Freak put a hand on Arran's shoulder. "I'm with you all the way, man."

"Thanks."

Jester came over, his big mouth stretched into a tooth-filled grin.

"This is going to be so much easier than getting to Waitrose," he said.

"I hope so," said Arran.

"It will be, you'll see. You guys know how to look after yourselves."

Arran's stomach clenched and he felt suddenly sick. He couldn't speak for a moment, but Jester filled the silence.

"Something I want to know," he said. "How come you all ended up living in Waitrose?"

"It just sort of happened," said Arran. "I don't know who got there first. But we all turned up looking for food."

"And was there any?"

"Some. Amazingly. I think they'd stored up emergency supplies. There was stuff out of the way in freezers and up-stairs in the storerooms. We had to break some locks, but we got to it all in the end. Same thing happened in Morrisons.

There was nothing fresh, of course, no fruit or vegetables or fresh meat, but there was canned stuff, and other useful things like candles and string and knives and batteries and I don't know. . . ."

"No soap," said Jester.

"Yeah, there was soap."

"Shame you didn't use any of it."

Arran looked at Jester; his smile was even wider than before.

"What are you saying?"

"No offense and all," said Jester, "but you lot stink. You probably don't notice it, living there all the time, but I'm telling you, it's a relief to get out of that shop." He held his nose theatrically and screwed up his face.

"We wash when we can," said Arran. "There were bathrooms there. Ben and Bernie rigged up a way to heat rainwater, but we weren't going to waste too much of the stuff on washing. And, I mean, you're right—after a while you don't notice the smell."

"What about your clothes?"

"We wash them now and then if we have to, but mostly we find new stuff in the shops. It's easier."

"You had it all worked out, didn't you?" said Jester appreciatively. "That place looked like a fortress."

"Yeah, we made it safe," said Arran. "And once we were there, well, where else could we go? We've been living on what we could find in the houses around here, but it was getting harder and harder. We'd have starved soon enough if you hadn't shown up."

"You're going to make a real difference," said Jester. "We

can properly start getting ourselves sorted out at the palace."

"It's in Babylon," said Arran.

"What is?" said Jester. "What do you mean?"

Arran laughed. "Sorry. I was thinking about something else. The words just came out."

"You sure you're feeling okay?" said Jester. "You look kind of hot and sweaty."

"It's nothing," Arran lied. "I'm just reacting to this bite. It's not serious."

"We got medical books at the palace," said Jester, "and lots of drugs. A girl called Rose looks after us. She knows her stuff. We'll fix you up. We've even got antibiotics."

"I think that's what I need."

"Yeah."

Arran took some more water, felt it trickling down his throat. He pictured it like a stream of mercury. It hit his stomach, and another wave of sickness came over him. The sun seemed very bright all of a sudden, sparking off the cars and breaking up into fierce colored shards. He closed his eyes and instantly snapped them back open.

That face. Every time. His mother's face. He couldn't get rid of it.

"Don't go to sleep," said Jester.

"What? No . . ."

"Not while you're walking. Do you want to stop for a rest?"

"No way," Arran protested. "We've got to keep moving."

Achilleus ran up with Big Mick, Blue's best fighter. They'd been scouting ahead.

"It's all clear as far as the tube station," said Achilleus.

"Far as we can see, there's no one around."

"Did you look inside the cupboards?" said Arran.

"Inside what cupboards?"

"Ignore him," said Jester, comically twirling a finger around his temple. "He's rambling."

Arran tried to laugh it off again. "Sorry," he said. "I'm just tired. Didn't sleep last night. You know what it's like when you think you're only thinking something and you say it out loud."

"Yeah," said Achilleus, but he didn't look convinced. He let Arran walk on a bit and went over to find Maxie on the left flank.

She was walking along, grim-faced and alert. She nodded when she saw Achilleus.

"I'm worried about Arran, man," he said.

Maxie looked concerned. "What's the matter with him?"

"He don't look well. He's saying odd things."

Maxie sighed. "Can you take over here? I'll go and talk to him."

"Sure."

Maxie jogged to the front of the group and found Arran. He looked pale and red-eyed. Her heart started beating faster. He had to be well. He had to be. They couldn't do this without him.

She slipped her arm through his, and he turned slowly. For a second he looked vague and tense, as if he didn't recognize her, and then his face relaxed.

"Maxie."

"Achilleus says you're not feeling very well."

"I'm feeling fine. I'm fine. Don't worry about me."

"You look awful."

"I'm just hot." Arran put a hand to his forehead and swayed. Maxie had to catch him to stop him from falling.

"Blue! Wait!" she shouted, and Blue held up his hand for the group to halt. Maxie took Arran to the side of the road and sat him down on the curb. He slumped forward, his head hanging down between his knees, and was sick on the street, throwing up a thin, watery stream.

"You're not good," said Maxie.

"I feel better for that," said Arran. "I'll be okay now."

"We'll rest for a while."

"No. We've hardly gone any distance at all, Maxie. We've a long way to go today."

"You can't go on in this state."

"I just needed to be sick," said Arran. "I'm fine now." He stood up and immediately staggered sideways into a car.

He muttered something unintelligible.

"What was that?" said Maxie.

"I need to put my Playmobil away."

Maxie exchanged a worried look with Blue and Jester, who were standing watching.

"This is serious," she said.

17

"When I'm gone," said Sam, "you'll have to properly close the doors."

"I will, yeah, I will," said Callum. "I should have done it before, but I wasn't sure exactly how. I should have paid more attention to the emos."

They had found a pump and two more bikes in the back by the loading bay. Sam vaguely remembered some of the older kids using the bikes in the early days, before it got too dangerous out on the streets. These bikes were too big for him, though, so he was going to stick with his lucky bike.

After finding the pump, the two of them had gone out on to the balcony and watched the grown-ups below. They half-heartedly pawed at the doors for a while, and threw things at them—one of them tried to force the doors open with a long stick. At one point a fight broke out and a mother was knocked down, unconscious or dead. Eventually they all gave up and wandered off. Sam's bike lay untouched in the street.

Callum guarded the door while Sam got the bike back inside. Then he pumped up the tires, mended a couple of punctures, and straightened out a bent wheel. Now that he knew Sam wasn't going to be staying, Callum seemed to be behaving more normally, although maybe he was being just a little bit too helpful. As if he were anxious to get rid of Sam.

For his part, Sam was dead on his feet, but he knew he had to keep going until he caught up with the others, or he might never be able to find them again. There was no way he would be able to get to the palace all by himself.

He had a quick snack of stale biscuits and water before taking the bike back outside.

Callum was hovering in the open doorway now, looking nervously up and down the street. It was obvious he didn't want to leave the building at all.

Sam climbed into the saddle, checked once more that the road was clear, and pushed off.

This was more like it. The bike went fast and straight. He whizzed along to the junction and turned onto Camden Road. Soon he was climbing the hill past the prison. It was heavy going, and halfway up he had to get off and push. All the while keeping a lookout for any grown-ups. Once he got to the top, it was downhill all the way to Camden.

He got on the bike and took one last look back.

Good-bye.

A few seconds later he was sailing down the hill, the wind in his hair, dodging in and out of the cars in the road. The kids had given up checking cars long ago. Most were out of gas, and nobody knew how to start them, or unlock the steering, without the keys. Besides, a lot of the roads were blocked by abandoned and burned-out vehicles.

Sam almost didn't spot the group of people up ahead before

it was too late. They were moving down the hill between the cars in the same direction as him. Sam had had too many disappointments today to let his guard down and hope that this could be his friends. He was right not to be too optimistic. They were grown-ups, walking slowly but purposefully.

He would have to go around them. He cut off down a street to the right. He didn't really know the area around here. His mom and dad had never let him ride his bike on the roads. They said it was too dangerous. He'd only ever ridden in the park before, or on special trips to Epping Forest.

He told himself that he'd find his way. If he just kept heading downhill he was sure he'd hit Camden Town.

There was a dark thought scraping at the back of his mind, though.

What was it? What was wrong?

Something to do with the grown-ups.

No. He wasn't going to worry about them. They hadn't seen him. He could get around them all right.

They weren't after him.

What were they after, though?

18

Maxie was sitting with Arran under the blue-painted railway bridge by Camden Road station. She had moved him here to be out of the sun. He was shivering, but she didn't think it was from cold.

"You've got to keep everyone together," he muttered.

"Don't worry about that," said Maxie.

"I wish I didn't have to."

"Didn't have to what?"

"Worry."

"You don't, Arran. You've been cut. You're sick."

Arran grabbed Maxie's arm. "That doesn't make any difference," he said. "It's like I was saying to Freak—" He broke off, confused. "Was I saying it to him? Did I say it? I don't remember. . . ."

"What? What were you saying?"

"We shouldn't have to deal with all this crap, Maxie. We're just kids. I never realized before. Our moms and dads used to deal with crap so that we didn't have to. They worried about things for us, and they did difficult things for us, so that we could just keep on being kids. We used to laugh at them and call them boring and pointless, but they protected us, they made the world safe for us so that we could play. I don't want to be an adult, Maxie. I want to go back to being just a kid again. But I can't. It's not an option. I've got to be a father to these little kids, and you've got to be a mother. They need us. I wish they didn't. I wish I wasn't needed. Look around. I sit down for a rest and everything falls apart."

Maxie stood up. Arran was right. The excitement of being outside was making everyone careless. There was still a party mood. Kids were perched on cars, chatting, or sitting on the curb in the sun.

Maxie shouted to Blue. He strolled over, trying to look cool.

"What's up?"

"We need to keep alert," she said. "We need to keep organized. We have to be ready at all times."

Blue shrugged. "We're ready."

"We're not."

Blue gave her a look. "The only one not at their post is you, girl."

"I'm making sure Arran's all right."

"Ain't you got someone else can do that?"

"Yeah." Maxie went to find Maeve.

Ollie was at the rear of the group, nervously looking back the way they had come. The other skirmishers, armed with javelins, slings, and rocks, were squatting in the shade of a van, talking about soccer. Ollie wished they were taking this more seriously.

"It's not right," he said, trying to get their attention.

"Chill out," said one of the Morrisons crew. "There's no one around."

"Yeah, but there *should* be people around," said Ollie, squinting up the road toward the top of the hill. "We haven't come down this way for ages because it's always been too dangerous. So where are all the grown-ups now?"

"They're hiding from us, man," said the other boy. "Anyone tries to attack, they'll be massacred."

Ollie looked around at the scattered group.

"Everyone's relaxed too much," he said.

"Except you," said the boy, and the others laughed.

"Be quiet a minute!" Ollie put a finger to his lips.

"What?"

"You hear anything?"

"No . . . No, wait. Now I hear something."

There was a swooshing sound, like waves rolling pebbles across a beach, and a murmur like the wind.

"Something's coming," said Ollie.

Josh was moving among the kids, trying to keep them alert. Most grumbled at him, and when he got to the Morrisons team, who were supposed to be guarding the right flank, they looked half asleep. Josh struggled to remember the name of the tall, dozy-looking kid with the Afro who was meant to be in charge. Lewis. That was it. He was sitting slumped against a storefront, his eyes closed.

"We should be ready in case anything happens," said Josh, worried that he was sounding like some anxious teacher on a school trip.

"I'm conserving my energy," said Lewis, and he yawned.

"You should be watching the flank. In case any grown-ups come in from the side."

"I'm listening," said Lewis. "I've got bat ears."

"I don't want to be a pain in the ass," said Josh. "You might think this is all a joke but—"

"It's cool," said Lewis.

"What's cool?"

"You're cool, I'm cool, everything's cool."

"If we lose any kids . . ."

"I won't lose you no kids, bro. I'm cool. You got nothing to fear, Lewis is here."

"You think I'm scared?" said Josh. "I ain't scared. Nothing scares me, man."

"If you say so, bro."

"Yeah, well, just tell me if your bat ears pick anything up."

Lewis slowly opened his eyes. "I'm hearing something now, man." He jumped to his feet surprisingly quickly, and Josh could see that his whole body was tensed. What had he heard?

"Up, up, up!" Lewis yelled at his team, and in a moment they were all ready.

Arran was aware of shouting. Coming from the rear of the group. He'd been lost in his thoughts, trying to regain his strength so that they could get moving again.

"What's going on?" he said.

"Dunno," said Maeve, who was sitting with him, unable to do much more than offer sympathy.

"Help me up."

"Arran . . ."

"Help me up, Maeve!" Arran snapped, and Maeve hauled him to his feet.

"Where's my club?"

Maeve fetched Arran's pickax handle and gave it to him.

Lazy. He'd been lazy. He was supposed to be in charge, a leader. He pushed his way through the milling kids to the rear of the group, where the commotion was. He saw Ollie. Ollie would know what was going on. He was sensible.

"We heard something," Ollie explained.

Before Arran could say anything, someone shouted.

"Look!"

People were coming over the brow of the hill. A solid line of grown-ups, their shuffling feet scraping on the street, a low moan rising from the herd.

Sounds like the seaside, Arran thought, and closed his eyes for a moment. He was back in Portugal with his mom and dad. Lying on his back, sunbathing.

"Have you got your lotion on?"

"Yes, Mom . . ."

She leaned over him. Smiled. Arran liked it when she was happy. Then her smile grew wide so that her mouth was a gaping hole surrounded by jagged teeth. She lunged at him—

"I've got my lotion on!" Arran shouted.

"What?"

"Nothing." Arran wiped sweat from his face.

"Jesus," said Ollie. "There's loads of them."

"Get into place!" Arran yelled, just as Blue ran up with Jester and the rest of the fighters.

Arran was pleased to see how fast the kids got themselves together and back into battle formation.

The front line of grown-ups stopped about a hundred yards away, and the two groups stood looking at each other.

"What are they doing?" said Blue.

"God knows."

Jester whistled. "They're like a bloody army," he said. "Can you take them, d'you think?"

"Don't know," said Blue. "I've never seen so many in one place before. They ain't usually this organized."

A smaller group of grown-ups pushed to the front and stepped clear of the pack. Almost as if they were in charge. At the vanguard of this new group was a huge fat father whose neck didn't seem able to support the great cannonball of a head that lolled over his chest. Random tufts of hair sprouted from his otherwise bald scalp. He was wearing shorts and an England vest with the cross of Saint George on it. A pair of wire-framed glasses with no lenses in them perched on his squashed and rotting nose. He rolled his head back and stared at Arran. It looked like he was laughing.

"They must have been following us," said Arran, his head clearing as his system was pumped full of adrenalin. "We need to avoid a fight if we can."

"How we gonna do that?" said Blue. "Look at 'em. They're not going to go away."

"We'll back off," said Arran. "See what happens. Maybe get to somewhere safer. Somewhere we can defend. Where's Ollie?"

"Here."

"Stay with us. We'll need your firepower."

He and Blue shouted orders, and the kids began to retreat from the grown-ups. Arran and the best fighters stayed at the back, facing the enemy. The road in the other direction was still clear. Maxie and Lewis kept with their teams on the flanks. The little kids had formed into a tight, frightened bunch in the middle. They were huddled so closely together that it was difficult to keep them moving. They kept bumping into each other and anxiously looking back. Maeve and Whitney goaded them, shoving them along, encouraging them, telling them not to worry, but there was a mounting sense of panic.

Staying indoors all the time, the little kids had been sheltered from the worst of the fighting. They weren't used to this. Some of the older kids, too. They weren't all fighters.

The grown-ups kept pace with them, advancing down the hill. Creeping closer. The father in the Saint George vest still at their head.

"Stay together!" Arran shouted.

Then three emaciated grown-ups blundered out from a side street, so starved they might as well have been skeletons. They made a dash toward the little kids to try to separate them from the group, but were swiftly knocked down by Lewis and the Morrisons fighters on that flank. Maxie watched them go into action and was impressed by their skill. Blue had been right: frizzy-haired Lewis might have looked dozy, but he moved fast when he had to, and dealt with the grown-ups ruthlessly and efficiently.

The sudden attack, though, had spooked the little kids. A bunch of them broke away and started to run.

"Stop them!" Maxie yelled, but there was nothing Maeve, Whitney, and the others could do. In a moment the little kids were darting in all directions, and even some of the older kids were starting to run. A bunch barged right past Maxie, who screamed at them to get back, but it was no good.

"Come on," said Lewis, and he and his team ran after the fleeing kids. "We'll get 'em."

As the orderly group broke up, it seemed to give encouragement to the grown-ups. The fat father in the Saint George vest raised his arms above his head, bellowed, and at last they attacked, coming as fast as they were able down the hill.

"Hold the line!" Arran shouted, and the fighters got into position, spears bristling.

Nothing was going to stop the grown-ups; they waddled and limped and scurried onward. The kids watched them getting closer—a hideous row of smashed and diseased faces.

Arran stood fast, Achilleus on one side, Blue on the other, more fighters spread out across the road. Behind them in a shorter line were Ollie and the skirmishers. Silent. Waiting.

19

Closer and closer the grown-ups came until at last Arran gave the order.

"Fire!"

A hail of pellets, stones, and javelins flew at the grown-ups, and as they went down, Arran moved the fighters forward. The first wave of attackers was almost immediately smashed to the ground, and this hampered the rest from getting forward.

Arran spotted Saint George clambering over a body. He took a swing at him, but the fat father ducked just in time.

"Maxie!" Arran shouted. "We need support!"

Even as he said it, Arran looked around to see Maxie arriving with her flanking squad. Their eyes met. They must have both been thinking the same thing at the same time. They were linked. For a moment it was as if nobody else existed. Arran was so proud of her. She was brave and strong and clever. She smiled at him and he smiled back. He knew at last. He knew that she felt the same way about him as he did about her. He just knew. He couldn't say how. And she understood. He felt a great force of happiness well up inside him.

He was ten feet tall. Knowing that somebody cared about him made all the difference. It gave him fresh strength. He could cope with anything now.

He turned and slammed his club into the face of a father who had managed to get past the fallen bodies.

With Whitney and Maeve's help, Lewis's team had managed to take control of the little kids. They had herded them off to the side, where a paved pathway ran above the Regent's Canal. It looked easy to defend. There were tall walls on one side and railings on the other. Past the railings was a fifteen-foot drop to the canal towpath. The older kids had to push and shove and yell at the younger ones to stop them from running again. Whitney stayed at the center, gathering them in, towering above the smaller kids, pulling them to her, calming them.

While the main group of grown-ups had been waiting, a splinter group had come around the side, trying to get at the smaller, weaker kids. A gang of them blundered across the road toward the pathway, and a father charged, breaking through the bigger kids at the end and taking hold of a screaming girl. His face was so swollen with boils he looked like some ghastly sea creature, a puffer fish.

"No you don't!" Whitney bellowed, and she punched him so hard that his boils exploded and half his face fell away as he let go of the girl and flipped over backward.

Maeve, Ben, and Whitney picked up the stunned father and dropped him over the railing, where he landed with a smack on the pavement below. Meanwhile, Lewis shoved his way through the crowded kids and back out into the road, yelling at the other grown-ups.

"Stay back!"

The grown-ups froze.

Lewis would keep them away for as long as he could. He prayed that the main fighting force would hold out, or else the chances of any of them getting to the palace alive would be very, very slim.

Maxie was next to Arran now, fighting almost back-to-back. The kids kept in a tight pack, and it was hard for the mostly unarmed grown-ups to get at them. Some were breaking through, though. Arran saw two of his fighters go down, swamped by numbers. Then one of the Morrisons crew screamed as three big mothers grabbed hold of him and dragged him off. The grown-ups were chipping away at them. At this rate it wouldn't be long before they were overwhelmed.

Arran looked around. Jester was nowhere to be seen. And where the hell was Blue? When the fighting kicked off he'd disappeared.

Had he run or had he been taken out?

Arran hated grown-ups.

His neck was throbbing, and it reminded him of what they had done to him. Anger bubbled up inside, almost like a physical thing, something hot and writhing, waking up and struggling to get out. His blood sang in his ears and boiled in his veins. He wasn't going to let any more kids die.

He gripped his club tightly in his hands, swatted a mother out of his way, and stepped forward.

"We've got to break them!" he shouted. "Take the fight to them!"

"I'm with you, boss," said Josh. "They don't scare me!"

One by one the other fighters joined him, hacking through the massed ranks of the grown-ups.

Ollie was still behind the fighters, loosing off a shot whenever he got the chance. He had lost track of the other skirmishers, who had either picked up fallen weapons and joined the fighters or dropped back to the rear. The only one of them still with him was the Morrisons kid who had laughed at him earlier for worrying too much. Ollie couldn't even remember his name. The two of them were firing off shot after shot, but the other kid was running low on ammo.

Arran and the others had moved forward, but Ollie could see that they'd gotten bogged down. The grown-ups would soon have them surrounded. There wasn't much more Ollie could do to help. He was doing his best, but it was like throwing pebbles into a raging river.

He wondered if this was the end. If they were all going to die here.

And then there was a roar, and a BMW thundered around the corner from Royal College Street. It plowed into the grown-ups, knocking them flying.

Ollie saw Blue at the wheel, grinning madly. He must have hot-wired the car. There was suddenly a rush of grown-ups blundering down the road, trying to get out of the way.

"Let them go!" he yelled, but the Morrisons kid was wound up for a fight. He grabbed a spear off the ground and waded into the stampede, stabbing at them. A short, stocky father with one eye was obviously also still up for a fight, though. He hit the kid hard with a lump of concrete. Ollie watched him fall and get trampled by the retreating grown-ups. He put a steel shot into his sling and kept an eye on the father.

He picked his moment, and the shot hit the father in the back of the neck. He too fell, and he too was trampled.

Lewis had been joined by the remnants of the skirmisher team and Jester. Jester had immediately ducked down the pathway to join the smaller kids. Lewis figured that was how he'd stayed alive when all his friends had died on the way up from the palace.

Lewis didn't blame him. Not all kids could fight. Sometimes hiding was a better option. The skirmishers were armed with an odd assortment of weapons, but it was enough to keep the grown-ups away. Lewis just had to hold out long enough for the front-rank fighters to come back and help.

If they lost the main battle, though, then all Lewis and the little ones could do was run.

A flood of grown-ups came down the road from the front. On the run. Maybe the tide had turned. Lewis pulled the rest of his fighters back into the pathway. It was more important to stay alive now than to kill the enemy.

He allowed himself a small smile of satisfaction.

He hadn't lost a single kid.

Blue kept in low gear, his foot hard on the accelerator, carving up the grown-ups, but careful to keep well clear of any kids.

He saw the girl, Maxie, working hard with her spear. She looked like some kind of warrior queen. He steered the car toward her, clearing the attackers out of the way. And there was Arran. That boy was tough. He was badly wounded but nothing could stop him. Blue smiled. He wished he had teamed up with the Waitrose kids before.

Arran knew how Freak had felt last night, when the

madness had taken hold of him. Anger burned like rocket fuel inside him. He was drunk with it. He waded in among the panicked grown-ups, swinging his club in vicious, punishing arcs. He was no longer tired or sick. His body felt nothing. It was as if he had left it behind and was watching it from somewhere else, like a film or a computer game. Yes. A first-person shooter. He kept pressing the X button and watching the club swing. It smashed into a skull. It shattered an arm. It snapped a spine.

He could see a long, blurry trail behind it as it moved through the air. And when a head exploded, there was no blood, just multicolored blobs of light.

They've turned off blood mode, he thought. They've made it suitable for under-fifteens. But this game was too easy. The enemy's AI was set too low. They were too slow, too stupid, too easy to kill.

Smack!

Look at them go down.

Slam!

He laughed. The kids were going to win this battle today.

Crack!

Sure enough, the grown-ups were falling back, trying to get away. He caught sight of the big father with the swollen head. He had a group of fathers around him and seemed to be surveying the carnage. He shook his head, which rolled backward and forward over the gold necklace at his chest, then he turned and retreated.

Yes. Run, you cowards.

Arran couldn't let them escape, though. Not after what they'd done. He ran after them.

Someone was shouting behind him.

"Leave it, Arran, they're finished."

"Let them go!"

"No!" He was a lion among wildebeests. A hunter. A killer. He ran with them; he would track down every last one of them and smash them into oblivion.

The grown-ups fell to left and right as he powered on. He funneled them onto a tree-lined side street, past a car wash. They scrambled clumsily, frightened and careless. And they fell. Silver bolts shot from his eyes, and they fell. He yelled with joy. He didn't even need a club. He threw it away. It was only slowing him down.

He had left the other kids behind. It was just him and the grown-ups. He saw them tumble, the silver bolts sprouting from their ugly broken bodies.

And then it was like he had been punched hard in the chest. He wasn't running anymore. He looked down. There was a silver bolt sticking out of him. No, that couldn't be. He couldn't have shot himself. He tried to laugh, but it hurt too much. What was going on? He had fallen. He was sitting down, his legs straight out in front of him. Dead grown-ups lay all around him.

Nothing moved.

He couldn't breathe. His lungs were full of liquid.

He looked up. The sky was flickering.

From far away he heard a shout.

"A-r-r-a-a-a-a-an!"

20

Small Sam was cycling like a demon. There were grown-ups everywhere. The roads were crawling with them. Where had they all come from? There was something going on. Every time he tried to get back toward Camden he'd come up against a group of them and had to turn around and cycle furiously the other way. He had gone in such a round-about route and taken so many side roads and turnings that he wasn't exactly sure where he was now. He was coming down a main road of grimy low buildings that looked like it hadn't been much even before the disaster. And then he saw something he recognized. Pizza Express. This must be Kentish Town, then. He remembered his mom and dad talking about which Pizza Express to go to. "Let's go to the one in Kentish Town." It was big and had a very high ceiling. There used to be a strange wire statue of a man standing in one corner. He'd found it a bit scary when he was younger.

How silly to be scared of a statue.

As far as he knew, Kentish Town was next to Camden. So

maybe he hadn't got as lost as he'd thought. All he needed to do was keep going downhill.

There was a cloud of black smoke filling the road ahead. A shop was on fire. He held his breath and zoomed through, screwing his face up. Luckily the road was clear on the other side. Grown-ups didn't like fire. They would keep away.

And there was the back of Sainsbury's, a funny-looking metal building on the canal, like something out of *Star Wars*. This was it. He'd made it. This was Camden. But with so many grown-ups out on the streets, he wondered where his friends might be. And Ella. He hoped she wasn't too scared without him.

He remembered the feeling he'd had when he'd first seen the mob of grown-ups marching down Camden Road, like an army. He knew what his fear was now. That the grown-ups were ganging up to attack his friends. Maybe the kids had also had to take another route to be safe?

He pedaled harder and soon came to where several roads met near the tube station. He stopped at a traffic island in the middle. In the past there would have been cars and trucks and buses rushing past in all directions, and the sidewalks would have been filled with kids going to the market. Now it wasn't like being in a city at all. The buildings might just as well have been rocks and cliffs. The abandoned, stationary cars were boulders. The road a dried-up riverbed.

There was even a sound, a rushing, swirling noise like water. He'd heard it before today. It wasn't water. It was the sound of massed grown-ups. Breathing, sighing, hissing, their feet scuffing on the asphalt. But where was it coming from?

He looked around.

There. In the direction of Holloway, up the road that led past the front of Sainsbury's. A great mob of grown-ups was moving toward him. Even from this distance he could smell them.

He would have to go faster.

Which way to go, though? Which route would the other kids have taken?

There were so many choices here. And now there were more grown-ups coming along the other roads. Maybe they were trying to see what was going on? The only clear route was the one heading back the way he had come, toward Kentish Town and the fire, which he could see now was spreading. The whole of the sky in that direction was hazy with a purple-gray smudge.

Come on. Which way was the center of London? The road signs were too confusing. They pointed to places whose names he didn't know.

The most obvious route was down the high street. It was the widest road. There were a few grown-ups wandering about on it, but if he went fast enough he could get around them. He shunted the bike forward, put his full weight on one pedal, then the other, and soon his feet were a blur as the pedals spun around and the chain rattled over the sprockets. He passed a knot of grown-ups, who made a feeble lunge at him, but as he glanced back at them, his front wheel hit a hole in the road. The whole bike jarred. He lost control and flew over the handlebars, landing in a painful heap on the asphalt. For a few seconds he was too stunned to move. His pants were ripped and his elbows and knees were bleeding. Then he sensed someone coming near and shook himself awake. He looked up just as a skinny young mother with no hair and dribble streaming down her chin made a grab for him. He rolled away from her groping hands and kicked out. He got her in the knee and she went down face-first.

Sam was up. He looked at his bike. The front wheel was bent out of shape and the tire had burst. All that work. Wasted. He would have to walk now. He might never be able to catch up with the others.

Actually, he would have to run. There were more grown-ups closing in on him.

He stumbled forward and felt his legs wobble. He was dizzy from the fall, and limping. He forced himself to move, though, watching his dirty sneakers as they slapped down on the road in front of him. He needed somewhere to hide. He passed some steps going down to a public toilet. No. He didn't want to get trapped. He remembered the tube station. Maybe if he could get in there, in the dark, he'd be all right. Just so long as he got safely off the streets. He broke into a run and dodged past some railings. Two fathers came lolloping behind him and smashed into the ironwork.

A car had driven into the side of the tube station, creating a gaping hole in the big steel shutters. A skeleton sat at the wheel. You normally never saw skeletons anywhere.

Sam ducked in and clambered over the ticket gates. He fumbled in his pocket for the flashlight he'd picked up at Waitrose. Pumped the handle and flicked the switch. He scribbled the blue-white beam over the walls. There was only one thing for it: he would have to go down toward the platforms. A shriek outside spurred him on, and in a few seconds he was rushing down the unmoving escalator two steps at a time, his flashlight beam zigzagging wildly, showing flashes of torn posters for vacations and televisions and shops and other useless things.

It was a mess at the bottom. Fallen bricks, tangles of wires, pools of yellow water—a dead body crawling with maggots. There had been a fire here recently, and he could smell smoke.

The grown-ups were still following him. They were on the escalator, their noisy progress echoing off the tiled walls.

Grunts and heavy breathing and clumsy feet. Sam looked quickly to right and left, and chose right.

He ran on through the passenger tunnels until he reached a platform. He quickly shone his beam along the rusting tracks. There was water and trash lying between the rails. He jumped down, pressed himself against the wall below the platform, and switched off his flashlight.

It was utterly dark. A darkness like he had never known before the disaster. There was no source of light anywhere. No winking safety bulbs. No glow of electricity. The world had ceased to exist. Sam suddenly became aware of his other senses. First the cuts and scrapes on his bruised body, then a metal bolt digging into his side. Next came the smells of dust and oil and damp and decay pressing into his nose. Then his hearing. Nearby some dripping water, and a small animal moving about, a mouse or rat. Farther away, but moving closer, the grown-ups. He could sense that they were unsure in the dark. Their footsteps uneven. There was a cough, a sneeze, chattering teeth. Long fingernails scraping on the tiles as they felt their way along.

He prayed that they would give up and return to the light. He was too small to bother with. They couldn't hope to find him.

Go away. Go away. Go away.

They arrived at the platform, and one came close. Sam could hear it sniffing, and smell its foul stink, like a blocked toilet. There was a rustle of clothing as it knelt down, and then it began to run its fingers along the edge of the platform. The dry skin sounded like paper.

Go away . . . Please go away.

Another one. He heard it flop onto the rails and begin to work its way toward him.

How quickly would they give up?

Could he risk trying to make a run for it, or was it safer to stay here?

If he ran he'd have to put the flashlight on, and that would tell the grown-ups where he was.

Then the one above him slithered over the wall, almost landing on him. He heard its feet slop into a puddle.

There were two of them down here on the tracks now, moving about. It would only be a matter of time before others followed. They knew he was here. They would feel about in the darkness for him. Eventually they would find him.

Sam's heart was racing, his whole body shaking. They would sense it. He was biting his shirt to stop from crying out in fear. It was no good. He couldn't stand it any longer. He pointed his flashlight toward where he thought the nearest one of them was, and snapped the beam on for half a second.

The light caught the grown-up full in the face; it gasped and put its hands up to cover its eyes, but not before Sam had gotten a good look at it. A father, his nose split almost in two, showing a nasty black hole in the gap. His lower jaw hanging loose. Sam quickly skimmed the beam both ways along the tracks, just long enough to get his bearings. Then he rolled over and dropped down into the gutter that ran between the rails. There were about four inches of water in the gutter. Sam hobbled along, somewhere between a crouch and a crawl, moving as fast as he dared in the dark toward one of the railway tunnels. His hands on the rails on either side. Behind him the grown-ups followed, grunting and panting. He had spotted at least six of them when his flashlight had been lit.

He gave another quick squirt of light. Just in time. Another second and he would have run into the end of the gutter. He clambered up and into the tunnel. It would be harder going now. He had to make his way over the cross ties without slipping. It was the same for the grown-ups, but they would be able to follow him by the noise he was making.

He stumbled on, every few seconds lighting the way ahead. The tunnel split in two and he made a quick decision, taking the left-hand branch. A little farther along he came to a stopped train. It fitted too tightly in the tunnel for him to squeeze past, so he would have to go underneath.

He dropped onto his belly and crawled under the front of the train, wriggling like a worm. It was hard work and difficult to move without making a noise. Were the grown-ups still following? He shone the flashlight back. There were three of them there, peering under the carriage, their eyes bulging, red and swollen, their tongues lolling. One of them flopped down and started to slither his way forward.

Sam switched off the flashlight.

Blackness again.

He crawled on. His knees stinging. The sound of his followers too close behind.

The one in front worked his way nearer and nearer, his rancid breath coming in short rasping gasps. He got hold of Sam's ankle. Sam kicked out and kept kicking. He felt something break like a twig, and he hoped it was at least a finger. No matter how hard he kicked it, though, the grown-up wouldn't let go. It was then that Sam remembered the butterfly pin. He had it stuck through a fold of cloth on the front of his sweatshirt. He pulled it loose, curled back around, and struck—jab, jab, jab, jab, jab—right where he thought the grown-up's face would be. It was like poking a watermelon. There was a shriek, and the grown-up let go and thrashed about like a wounded animal.

That might hold the others up. Sam crawled on. He risked another burst of light. The bottom of the train seemed to stretch away forever ahead of him, but off to one side was a dark hole in the tunnel wall. Maybe a way out?

He stuffed the flashlight back into his pocket, lay flat, and, making as little noise as he could, moved slowly sideways over the rail, past the wheels of the train, where there was a gap between two carriages. He couldn't risk the flashlight. It would show the grown-ups where he was. So he ran his hands over the wall until he found the opening and ducked into it. He heard the grown-ups move past him, still under the train. It wouldn't take them long to realize he wasn't ahead of them anymore, but would they be able to find this hiding place? Sam backed deeper into the hole; the ground sloped downward into shallow water. He soon came to a solid wall. Once more he used his hands to get the shape of his surroundings, and he discovered that he was at the bottom of a shaft of some sort. It was open above his head, and, what's more, there were metal rungs fixed to the wall. He hauled himself up and climbed into the darkness.

21

I didn't know. I'm so sorry. I didn't know . . . We couldn't tell . . ."

Arran was lying where he had fallen, surrounded by dead grown-ups, and Maxie, Blue, and a stunned circle of the rest of the Holloway kids. The girl was kneeling by him, her hand pressed to his chest where the steel shaft of the arrow stuck out. Her bow was lying next to his body.

Maxie didn't know her name. She didn't want to know. She was tall and thin and striking, with long dark hair and very white skin. She was wearing a battered black leather jacket and knee-high biker boots.

Standing in a small, wary knot behind her were her friends, five girls and seven boys. They were all lean and wiry and weather-beaten, as if they'd been living outdoors for some time. Their eyes moved like animals' eyes. Watchful, alert, unsure.

The Holloway crew outnumbered them easily.

And they had shot Arran.

"We'd been following the pack," said the girl. "The adults.

We didn't know what they were up to. We'd never seen them behave this way before. We know how to keep hidden. We were staying out of their way. And then they were charging down the street toward us. We thought they were coming for us. We started firing. We never saw the boy among them." She touched the feathers at the tip of the arrow. "This is mine," she said sadly. "I'm so sorry."

"Being sorry won't bring him back," said Maxie. "Being sorry never changed anything."

"It was an accident," said Ollie, and Maxie shot him a dirty look.

Maeve pushed her way to the front and knelt by Arran. She put her ear to his chest and a finger to the artery in his neck.

"He's not dead," she said.

"Oh, thank God," Maxie sobbed, and dropped to the road beside Maeve. She put her face to Arran's. It was wet with tears. She didn't care who saw it.

"Arran," she whispered in his ear. "Don't die."

Arran's lips parted and he spoke one word, in the quietest whisper they had ever heard. So deep was the silence, however, that there was no mistaking what he said.

"No."

Maxie smiled through her tears.

"He's not going to die. He's strong. He's our leader. He's going to get us to the palace. . . ."

"The palace?" said the girl, and now Jester stepped forward.

"I'm taking them to Buckingham Palace," he said. "It's safe there."

"It's not safe anywhere," said the girl. "We know. We've been all over."

"Have you been into the center of town?" asked Jester.

"Well, no . . ."

"Then you haven't been all over, have you?"

"She's not coming with us, anyway," said Maxie, standing up. "Not after what she's done to Arran."

"I didn't mean to."

"Yeah," said Blue. "It was an accident. If they want to come with us, then let them. We could use some more fighters. We lost seven kids in the battle."

"She's not coming!" Maxie shouted.

"If I say she's coming, she's coming," said Blue.

"Why?" said Maxie. "Because she's pretty?"

"What's that got to do with it?" Blue laughed dismissively. "I told you, she's a mad good fighter. We all need to stick together."

"Who put you in charge all of a sudden?" Maxie snorted.

"You said just now Arran was the leader," said Blue calmly, ignoring Maxie's outburst. "Well, that wasn't strictly speaking true, was it? We was both leaders. And now he's hurt bad, so, from here on, I'm in charge."

Maxie glared at Blue, her eyes defiant. "I'm Arran's second in command," she said. "I'll take his place until he's better."

"I'm in charge, girl," said Blue.

"It doesn't matter," said Ollie, stepping between them. "All that matters right now is we try to get Arran better. Then we can argue over who's in charge. Maeve, is there anything you can do?"

"I don't know," said Maeve, shaking her head. "The arrow's

in pretty deep. If we take it out he might bleed worse."

"Is it in his heart?"

"If it was in his heart he'd be dead already."

"His lung?"

"Maybe."

Maeve looked around at the girl who was still kneeling next to her. "What do you think? Do you know about arrows?"

"I think you're right. If you try to take it out you could make it worse."

"You can't leave him like that!" Maxie yelled. "You can't!"

Ollie nodded at the girl. "You," he said. "What's your name?"

"Sophie," said the girl.

"Tell me, Sophie," said Ollie, crouching down to inspect the wound. "Is it barbed? The arrow? Has it got a barbed tip?"

"No," said Sophie. "It's a sports arrow, designed for shooting at targets. It's probably gone right through him. It was very close range."

Maxie wailed and threw herself on Arran, cupping his face in her hands.

"He was already weak from the bite in his neck," she said. "What are we going to do?"

"Okay," said Jester, "as I see it, it's like this. He can't walk. So, whatever we do, we'll have to carry him. Maybe make a stretcher, or find a trolley, or something."

"We can't move him like that with an arrow sticking out of him," Blue objected.

"I know that," said Jester. "So we'll have to risk taking it out. We've no other choice. We'll have to bandage him up and just hope we can stop the bleeding."

"You'll only be able to stop the bleeding on the outside," said Maeve. "Not inside. He'll die."

"Well, what do you suggest?" said Jester. "We operate on him?"

"It would be the only way to save him," said Sophie.

"Don't be stupid," Maxie snapped. "We can't operate on him."

"I know," said Sophie sadly.

"If we can just get him to the palace, he might have a chance," said Jester. "But if we stay here he won't, and it'll be dangerous for the rest of us. We have to keep moving. I say we take the arrow out and see what happens."

"No," said Maxie.

"We ain't got time for this," said Achilleus, and he marched over to Arran, grabbed the arrow, and yanked it out. Maxie screamed. A gout of lumpy jellylike blood dribbled from the wound. Arran groaned and coughed. His body spasmed, and he was still.

"You've killed him!" screamed Maxie.

"No." It was Arran's voice.

22

Sam waited, perched on the metal rungs. There was no way out of the shaft. The top was blocked. He didn't know how much longer he could hold on, even though he had wedged his body across the gap. His muscles were sore and shaking. His back hurt.

He tried to concentrate on hanging on instead of imagining what the grown-ups were doing. Every time he thought they'd gone, he heard them again. Searching for him. Just be small, he told himself. Be small and still, and try to think of happier times. Of sunny days on the beach. Of playing with his Playmobil. Anything other than being stuck underground in this tiny space with the grown-ups sniffing around for him.

He heard one nearby. Snuffling like a pig. Its fingers raking the brickwork. He felt warm liquid trickling down his legs, and he realized he must have wet himself again. He prayed that they wouldn't be able to smell it. Then he heard the grown-up lapping at the water on the ground. A few seconds later it was sick. A fight broke out. The grown-ups snarling and whining at each other.

Why wouldn't they just go away?

He had had enough.

He was only nine.

A terrible voice inside tempted him to give up, to let go and drop down and make an end to it.

No more fear. No more pain.

But there was a stronger force making his hands grip tighter, tensing his legs, readying them to kick if needed.

He was Sam the Giant Slayer. Sam of the silver pin. He thought about his favorite film—*Time Bandits*—how the little people in it won in the end against the forces of evil.

And he remembered the story of Pandora's box that they'd read at school. After all the nasty things had come out of it, there was one thing left. Hope. And Pandora had let it out of the box.

He had to have hope.

The grown-ups would go. He would climb down. He would find his sister and his friends and walk to safety.

Callum pressed PLAY on the beat box and sat in his armchair. He smiled as the sound of ABBA filled the shop. "Dancing Queen." ABBA had been his mom's favorite band. She had taken him to see *Mamma Mia* live on stage, and although he'd complained, secretly he'd enjoyed it. He couldn't remember how many times they'd watched the DVD together. There were a lot of uncool things he liked but had to pretend to hate, like *High School Musical* and Harry Potter.

And ABBA . . .

Well, now he could listen to what he wanted, he could read what he wanted, he could do what he wanted without any other kids laughing at him. He opened a can of peaches and took a gulp of the sweet juice. The taste exploded inside his mouth and he closed his eyes. He couldn't remember when he had ever been happier.

Arran's mouth was dry and he felt hungry. God, he was hungry. He was hungry and he was thirsty, but there was no pain. He felt nothing. He was drifting in a warm sea. He struggled to keep his eyes open. Sometimes the sky looked black, sometimes a brilliant, blinding white.

And sometimes it was red as blood.

He slept for a while and dreamed of sitting at his Xbox.

When he woke, his mother was there, cradling him in her arms, and he felt an overwhelming happiness. He wanted to tell everyone. The nightmare was over. His mother looked down into his face and smiled the most beautiful smile. He knew that everything was all right if she smiled at him like that. There were no more monsters. She brushed his hair off his forehead and rested a cool hand on his face. Like she always did when he was sick. To see if he was hot. And all the while her eyes were smiling at him.

"I love you, baby," she said, and he smiled back. He opened his mouth to speak; he wanted to tell her something. It was hard to get the words out. They stuck in his dry throat.

They had bandaged the wound and wrapped Arran tightly around the chest. The white material was soon stained dark with blood, though. The wound was steadily leaking, and nobody dared catch Maxie's eye. They all knew the worst—Arran was dying—but Maxie wouldn't admit it. They hated themselves for it, but they wanted to move on, leave Arran behind. It wasn't safe here. The grown-ups had attacked once and they would attack again. The longer the kids stayed still, the more danger they were in. But Maxie sat by the body and wouldn't move. It was late. She'd been holding him for what seemed like hours. Talking quietly. Trying to give him water.

She could hear the others muttering. They were plotting. She knew they wanted to abandon Arran. She looked at his handsome face, so pale and tired looking. He hadn't moved for ages.

And then his lips parted and Maxie's heart leapt.

"Come over here," she cried. "Quick. It's all right, listen, he's trying to speak."

Ollie came back over with Maeve and Blue.

"Listen," said Maxie. "I'm sure he's trying to say something. He only needed a rest. He's getting stronger at last. If he can speak he's all right."

Arran's gray-blue eyes opened, and they were clear and bright. He smiled at Maxie.

"I love you, Mom," he said quietly, and he died in Maxie's arms.

23

They had ransacked the buildings and gardens nearby and collected everything they could find that would burn—fallen branches, tables, chairs, doors, mattresses, scaffolding planks, tires—and packed it around the BMW. It was no more use to them. Blue had driven it around, chasing off the last of the grown-ups after the battle, until the last of its gas had run out. Once they had a good-sized bonfire, they wrapped Arran and the other dead kids in sheets. They wanted to make sure their faces were hidden. Then they placed the bodies on top of the heap.

Maxie had insisted. There was no way she was going to leave them here to be eaten. Arran, with the others, would be given a hero's send-off.

The dead grown-ups they left where they had fallen.

Freak sprayed a message on to a nearby wall.

THIS IS WHERE ARRAN HARPER FELL. WE DON'T KNOW
THE DAY OR THE DATE, BUT WE'LL NEVER FORGET IT.
HE WAS THE BRAVEST OF US ALL.

Whitney and Josh gave him the names of the other kids who had died, and Freak added them to the mural, then finished it with a Freaky-Deaky tag.

When they were ready, Maxie lit a match and approached the car.

Freak called her back.

"Before you do that," he said, "can I say something?"

"Okay," said Blue, "but make it quick. We need to get going."

"I'll be quick," said Freak. He took a breath and looked at the faces of the kids.

"Arran talked to me this morning," he said. "Helped me to keep going. Now it's my turn. We all lost someone we loved today. But the thing is, we won. We beat them. I was going to write something different over there. I was going to write 'Arran Lives.' Cuz it's important we don't forget what he wanted. To get to the palace and have a better life. And we mustn't forget one other thing. Us kids are all in this together. We're all on the same side. The grown-ups are the enemy. It was an accident, what happened to Arran. And I don't want no one to blame Sophie. We work together, we survive together."

"Yeah, nice speech," said Achilleus with a touch of sarcasm. "Now light the fire."

Maxie stepped forward, and soon the great pile was sending flames several feet into the air. Maxie saw something lying on the ground and stooped to pick it up. It was Arran's club. It felt heavy in her hands. It was all that was left of him.

From now on it was hers.

Once the kids were sure that the fire wasn't going to go

out, they set off. They didn't want to stay and watch the bodies burn to ash. They said their farewells and marched away in battle formation, the fire at their backs.

The plan was to keep going and try to get to the palace that night, even though it was late and the sky had grown dark. The problem was not only that there was nowhere in Camden for such a large party of kids to shelter safely, there was also the danger of a blaze that was spreading down from Kentish Town, consuming every building in its path and sending up thick smoke that further darkened the sky.

Sophie and the archers walked at the front with Blue and Jester. Then came the other fighters, Big Mick, Achilleus, Freak, and the rest. Ollie and the skirmishers brought up the rear as ever. Lewis took up his position on the left flank. Maxie left Josh in charge of her group on the right flank, however, and joined the little kids in the center of the column. She wanted to be with them and take comfort from them. They were affectionate and caring and not afraid to show their emotions. They hugged Maxie and held her hand and told her it was all right and that they missed Arran, and they swapped stories about him, his great deeds. She nearly burst into tears again when little Joel gave her his puppy, Godzilla, to hold. The puppy felt warm and soft. He was very sleepy, but he managed to lick her face before snuggling down in her arms. She walked on with Joel staring up at her.

Whitney came over and tickled the dog behind his ear.

"Cute," she said, and Maxie smiled.

"Listen," Whitney went on, "I'm sorry about Arran. We all are."

"It's okay."

"I didn't really know him," said Whitney, "but I could tell he was all right. You had a thing for him, didn't you?"

"I don't know. We never spoke about it."

"Sometimes you don't have to, girl."

"It just seems so unfair," said Maxie angrily. "You wake up one morning with your whole life ahead of you. So many things to see and do, and then—bang! You're dead. There's nothing. I can't stop thinking about how his life has just stopped like that. He'll never grow up. Never have kids of his own. Never grow old."

"Just think of him like that, yeah?" said Whitney. "Forever young. Always the beautiful Arran you knew."

"Forever dead," said Maxie.

"Hey, come on, think positive," said Whitney. "That's an order."

Maxie gave a bitter, slightly hysterical laugh. "Think positive? Look at us, Whitney. Look at what's happened to us. What's to be positive about?"

"At least *Big Brother* ain't on TV no more."

"No." Maxie gave a snort of laughter that almost slid into tears.

"See, you can still laugh."

"I feel dead inside," said Maxie.

"It'll pass. We've all lost people."

"I know. I'm sorry. It's been a horrible day."

"Too many friends have been killed," said Whitney. "Too many."

"Yeah," said Maxie. "Arran's not the first and he won't be the last. Every time someone dies, I don't think I can take anymore."

"But somehow you do, don't you?" said Whitney. "You carry on."

"Yeah," said Maxie, and she wiped away a tear.

"I dunno," said Whitney. "Maybe, when this is all over, when we're safe and we can rest, that's the time to cry. Right now, like your man said, we gotta stick together and help each other."

"I know. Thanks, Whitney."

"And listen." Whitney held Maxie's arm. "Blue. He's all right, you know. He has to act tough cuz he's our leader. But he ain't stupid. You need to work with him."

"I'll try."

Whitney gripped Maxie's head in an affectionate arm-lock.

"You're strong. I know it, girl. Together we can be stronger."

It was a moonless night, and no stars shone in the clouded sky. Some kids had made flaming torches, but they were quickly burning out. Those that had them were using their flashlights. They had to keep in a huddled mass, though, or risk getting split up in the dark.

Freak was plodding along, lost in his thoughts. He felt someone nudge him in the side.

"You planning on going to the Oscars? Make some more cheesy speeches?"

It was Achilleus. Freak sighed and looked away. "Why do you always have to pretend to be so tough, Akkie?" he said.

"Who's pretending?"

"Don't you care about Arran?"

"Yeah. I care. He was all right. But you don't fool me. I know what that speech was really all about."

"Oh yeah, what?"

Achilleus put on a whiny voice, mocking Freak. "Don't blame Sophie, it was an accident, us kids have to stick together . . . Bullshit. You're just feeling guilty about what you did to Arran and don't want no one to blame you."

"What do you mean, what I did to Arran? I didn't do nothing to him."

"It was you got him killed, Freaky-Deaky."

"What are you talking about? I never shot that arrow."

"Didn't need to. He was already dying. And Deke was already dead. All because you wanted to go looking for a stupid vending machine."

Freak felt a lump in his throat. He fought hard not to sob. "Don't say that."

"It's the truth, Freaky-Deaky. You know it and I ain't never going to forget it. You nearly got us all killed. You think if Arran hadn't been bitten he would have gone crazy back there? No. And he wouldn't have gotten shot. All your fault."

Freak swore at Achilleus, who spat in the road and walked over to Mick. He said something to the big Morrisons kid, who looked at Freak and laughed.

Up at the front, Jester was talking to Blue, their flashlights raking the road in front of them.

"We should try to go faster," said Jester. "We've lost a lot of time. We should have arrived in daylight."

"We're safer at night," said Blue. "Less grown-ups around."

"I don't feel safe. Not after what happened today."

"Wasn't right," said Blue. "Grown-ups don't usually act like that. Clubbing together. They was an army. I've not seen that before."

"You still think that the park is the best way to go?" said Jester.

"Yeah," said Blue. "It's wide open—we can see anything that's coming. Grown-ups don't like wide-open spaces. I was thinking we could even set up camp for the night. Post sentries around the edges. Let the little ones rest."

"They've rested enough," said Jester. "We were hours in Camden waiting for Arran to die."

"That's cold, man," said Blue. "What do you think we should have done? Finished him off ourselves?"

"Of course not," said Jester. "But it was obvious he was going to die."

"We did what we did, man," said Blue. "Couldn't have done it no other way."

"I know," said Jester. "And I think it was good the way you took control. I think you should take overall charge."

"What do you mean?" Blue turned to Jester but couldn't clearly see his features in the dark.

"We don't need two leaders," said Jester. "Maxie can look after the little kids. She's a girl. She fell apart when Arran died."

"We'll see," said Blue. "The Waitrose crew ain't necessarily gonna accept me as their boss. We need Maxie."

"Maybe."

"And what about when we get there?" said Blue.

"How do you mean?"

"Presumably you got someone in charge at the palace."

"Yeah . . ."

"So what happens? Eh? I just sit down and do what I'm told?"

"Don't worry about that," said Jester. "We'll work something out."

"Yeah," said Blue. "We will."

24

They crossed the road at the top of Parkway and entered Regent's Park by Gloucester Gate.

The park had changed. The flower beds were overgrown. The short, well-kept grass was now waist high and tangled with weeds and wildflowers. Here and there young saplings pushed up through the undergrowth. Only a few inches tall now, but in time this would become a forest.

There was a playground near the gate. A relic from a forgotten age. And the little kids stared at it in wonder as they passed. Maxie gave Godzilla back to Joel and went to relieve Josh and join her team on the right flank.

Josh walked up front where Jester and the others were discussing the best route to take.

"Best stick to the path, I reckon," said Blue. "It'll be clearer and we'll have a better view. Who knows what might be hiding in the long grass."

"Like those raptors in *Jurassic Park*," Josh chipped in.

"There's a lot of things out to get us in London these days," said Blue, laughing. "But dinosaurs ain't one of them."

"You never know," said Josh. "The world's turned upside down. I wouldn't be surprised. Nothing surprises me anymore."

"Don't be scared of no dinosaurs," said Blue.

"Who said anything about being scared?" said Josh. "You know what they call me? Josh, the Boy without Fear. I'm gonna kill me a dinosaur."

"Don't nothing scare you, man?" said Blue, trying not to laugh.

"Nah. Grown-ups is stupid, and slow. And they got no weapons. Dogs is stupid too. Nothing scares me. Something tries to scare me, I just kill it, man. Dead."

"Well, I'm glad you're on our side," said Blue. "Now, let's get going."

They had to stretch out along the path, as it wasn't as wide as the roads they'd been traveling on. The flanking parties stayed close on either side, pushing through the grass.

The emos, Ben and Bernie, were helping the smaller kids along, listening to their chatter.

"That's the zoo over there," said Monkey Boy, pointing past a line of trees toward where some of the zoo's structures were just visible.

"I used to like the zoo," said Ella. "I had a birthday party there once. My favorites were the lions and tigers."

"What happened to all the animals, do you think?" asked Joel, clutching Godzilla tightly. "When all the keepers died?"

"Did the animals all starve to death?" said Ella. She sounded tearful.

"I don't think so," said Bernie comfortingly. "I expect the keepers moved them somewhere safe."

"They wouldn't have had time," said Curly Sam, one of those annoying small kids who thought they knew everything.

"I'm sure the keepers had time to make sure they were all right," said Bernie.

"Did they let them out, then, do you think?" said Ella.

"Yeah, 'spect so," said Ben, smiling at Bernie. "They would have set them free."

"Then they might be in the park," said Ella, suddenly fearful, and Ben immediately regretted saying anything.

"I thought you liked the lions and tigers," said Bernie quickly.

"I did when they were in cages," said Ella, "but not running free."

"Lions are dangerous," said Monkey Boy.

"Will we be eaten?" said Joel. "Like the Christians?"

"What Christians?"

"In the Colosseum. In Rome. They used to feed Christians to the lions."

"If any lions did get out," said Bernie, "then they'd be miles away from here by now. They'd be long gone. They'll have gone to the countryside to find cows and deers and things like that."

"I don't want to go to the countryside," said Ella. "I don't want to be eaten like a Christian."

"You're not going to be eaten by a lion," said Bernie.

"Yes," said Curly Sam. "The only thing that's going to eat you is a grown-up."

"That's not a very helpful thing to say," said Bernie.

"It's true, though," Curly Sam insisted. "They eat kids."

"What was that?" said Ella, her voice very high and thin.

"What was what?"

"I heard something moving in the grass."

"It'll be the bigger kids," said Bernie, trying to sound calm, even though she too thought she had seen something moving. "They're protecting our sides."

"No. It wasn't a big kid."

"Maybe a rabbit, then, or a cat."

"Like a lion?"

"Look," said Ben, trying not to lose his patience, "there's nothing there. Nothing's going to eat you. We won the battle, didn't we? We're strong. Nothing can get to us."

"We're safe, aren't we?" said Joel.

"Yeah," said Ben. "We've got Godzilla to look after us."

Joel hugged the puppy tighter. "Godzilla can't fight," he said. "He's too young."

"I was only joking," said Ben. "I just can't win with you lot, can I?"

They had come on to The Broad Walk, a much wider path that ran down the center of the park beneath rows of tall trees. There was enough room here for them to spread out a little. Bernie called Lewis over. He shambled up, scratching his untidy Afro.

"Did you see anything?" she asked.

"What you mean?" said Lewis.

"In the grass?"

"Nope."

"Did you hear anything?"

"There's nothing in the grass; we'd have seen any grown-ups."

"It's too dark to see anything properly."

"We've got flashlights."

"We heard something," said Ella. "Maybe a lion."

Josh came back from the front and looked at the frightened bunch of kids.

"Can't you keep them quiet?" he said. "They're getting spooked."

"They can't help it," said Bernie. "They're small. They've got overactive imaginations."

"I saw something again!" said Ella.

"No you didn't," Bernie snapped.

There came a rustle in the leaf canopy above their heads, and everyone stopped walking and fell silent.

A twig snapped.

Something was moving through the trees.

"What is it?"

"Grown-ups, maybe."

"They can't climb trees," said Lewis.

"How do you know?" said Josh. "Our problem is—we've been stuck inside those stupid supermarkets too long, and we've thought we knew what was going on in the world. I used to sit on that roof with Callum and thought I could see everything there was to see. Well, I couldn't see nothing. Except that tiny little bit of Holloway. For all we know there are grown-ups that've sprouted wings and learned to fly."

"They can't fly, can they?" asked a fearful Ella.

"Stop it, Josh," said Bernie. "You come back here and tell us not to spook the kids, and now you're terrifying them. It's bad enough as it is without having to worry about flying grown-ups."

"They can't fly, can they?" Ella repeated.

"Of course they can't fly," Bernie almost shouted. "Most of them can hardly walk."

"There's definitely something in the trees, though," said Lewis, looking up.

"Probably squirrels."

"Too big for a squirrel," said Maxie, who had also heard something and had come over to consult with Lewis.

"Well, I ain't climbing up there to find out," said Lewis.

"Look out, we're getting split up," said Ben, pointing to the front of the column where the fighters were walking on.

Maxie swore and ran after them, shouting to Blue to stop.

"What is it?"

"Wait for the others to catch up."

"Why have they stopped?"

"The little kids are getting scared. There's something in the trees."

"Yeah, we heard it. We reckon it's best to push on."

"Can you see anything up there?"

"Too many leaves. Whatever it is, it's good at hiding."

"Shouldn't we at least warn everyone to be careful?"

"We start shouting orders, the kids'll get even more scared," said Blue. "You go around and tell them. And get the others to hurry up."

Achilleus came over. "Why ain't we moving?"

"We need to look up, Akkie," said Maxie quietly. "There's something in the trees."

"I hate to say it, but there's something in the grass too," said Achilleus, peering into the darkness.

"What?"

"Something's crawling about in there. Not big enough to be grown-ups."

"What is it, then? Could it be other kids?"

"Dunno," said Achilleus, and before Maxie could stop him, he put a hand to his mouth and shouted, "Hey! Who's there? Show yourself."

Nothing. The grass was absolutely still.

"We need to press on," said Blue, and he started walking again.

"Wait," said Maxie, but it was no use.

Her heart was thumping as she made her way back to the huddled mass of smaller kids.

"You have to hurry up," she said, glad, in a way, to be doing something to take her mind off Arran.

"I don't like it under the trees," said Ella.

"Don't go in the grass," said Maxie. "Don't you dare go in the grass."

"Why not?"

"Just don't."

"Why? Is there something there? Is there something in the grass?"

"No. We just need to stick together, is all." Maxie sensed a mounting panic among the smaller kids.

Whitney had sensed it too, and was going around telling them not to be scared. Maxie looked to the front. Blue and Jester and the others were getting farther away. She felt like she was slowly losing control.

"Get going," she said, hustling kids forward.

Half the small kids walked on, the rest milled around

fearfully. Some were even heading back the way they had come.

"Hold still!" Maxie shouted, but at that moment something dropped from the trees and landed with the effect of a bomb going off among the children. In an instant they were running, screaming, in all directions.

Before Maxie could do anything, something else dropped from the trees. Then another. Gray blurs that shrieked as they came down. She gripped Arran's club.

It seemed that they were going to have to fight every step of the way into town.

25

It was chaos. The kids were running in all directions while more and more of the things—whatever they were—dropped down onto them from above. It was impossible in the dark to make out exactly what they looked like. They were just gray blurs as they plummeted, yelping and shrieking, through the air. They had to be animals of some sort. Too small to be grown-ups. Maxie shoved her way through the panicked crowd to where she saw one land. A girl was facedown on the ground with one of the things on her back. It was hairless, with mottled pinkish-gray skin studded with sores and boils. It had long arms and stumpy misshapen legs. Maxie ran to it and whacked it in the back with her club. It barely moved. It was a powerful, solid lump.

It let out a hideous high-pitched scream and lurched toward Maxie.

Maxie kicked out at it, and the thing grabbed her leg. She could feel the incredible strength in its arms. Before it could bite her, she quickly butted the end of the club into the top of its skull. It croaked and fell away with a pitiful whine. She struck it once more in the head, and it collapsed into a lifeless heap. At least the things could be killed. She helped the little girl up from the ground. Her back and neck were scratched and bleeding, and she was sobbing uncontrollably, her tiny body shuddering. Whitney scooped her up and cradled her in her arms.

"I'll look after the kids," she said to Maxie. "You rally the fighters."

Maxie yelled at the top of her voice. "They're attacking the little ones! Everyone help!"

She saw two of the beasts dragging Curly Sam into the long grass by the hair, and ran after them. She got there just as Lewis and his team arrived. The animals were swiftly dealt with, and Curly Sam was returned to his friends.

"What are they?" Lewis ran his flashlight beam over the dead animals. They had huge black eyes, great ragged ears, and long yellow fangs strung with saliva and spotted with blood. Like the grown-ups, their skin was covered with oozing pustules and ugly lumps.

"Gross," said Lewis, curling his lip with disgust. "They're some sort of mutated children."

Maxie didn't know what to think. Anything was possible. Before they had the chance for a proper look, though, they were called back into the fight. The beasts were everywhere, scurrying in and out of the legs of the kids, bowling them over, snatching the smallest ones. The fighters tried to get at them, but it was difficult in the dark with all the kids in the way.

Maxie switched on her flashlight and saw a group of little kids break off the path farther down on the other side.

"Stop them!" she shouted, but it was too late. She saw

them go into the grass, which came up almost to their shoulders, and one by one they went down.

Thank God Blue and the others had realized what was going on. They charged back from the front, weapons at the ready, and scattered a knot of marauding beasts. The noise was appalling. The animals screeched and squealed and bellowed, which terrified the kids even more.

Maxie saw a fighter run past with a creature on his back, its hands over his face, clawing at his eyes. She smashed it in the spine with her club, and the two of them fell over. The animal was quickly up, though. It ran at her on its knuckles, teeth bared into a ferocious grin. She butted it in the face but only succeeded in knocking it back for a moment and making it furious. It was soon up again and coming at her. She didn't have time to swing her club, and could only try to fend it off. Its skull seemed to be made of iron. Then it managed to get hold of the club and wrenched it out of her hands with tremendous force. Now she was unarmed. She didn't want to run, because she was terrified of it getting onto her back. It flung the club aside in a rage and lifted both hands above its head. She backed away and saw it preparing to charge. Then there was a flurry of activity as someone stepped in and stabbed it with a spear.

It was Josh.

"They don't scare me," he said as it ran off, dripping blood.

Maxie spotted Joel. He was sitting on the ground hugging Godzilla. She was glad that he was all right. As she watched, though, a fighter blundered into him and kicked him over. Godzilla was jogged from his arms, and he shot off into the grass, whimpering.

"Leave him!" Maxie shouted, but Joel ignored her and was soon lost from sight in the confusion.

Blue and Freak arrived.

"Get everyone together!" Blue yelled. "We need to make a run for it—get out from the trees and onto the road."

"Yeah, but some of the kids have gone off into the long grass," said Maxie, looking for Joel.

"Then go get 'em back," Blue ordered.

"Okay." Maxie turned to Josh. "You take the other side. Make sure you get any stragglers."

"Sure." Josh grinned. "You might need this," he said, handing Maxie Arran's club.

"Thanks."

Josh ran off.

"I'll take this side," said Maxie.

"I'm with you," said Freak.

They ran into the long grass and found Lewis and his team already bringing back a group of runaways.

"Is that all of them?" Maxie asked.

"Think so."

"What about Joel, the little kid with the puppy? Have you seen him?"

Lewis shook his head. "Nah."

Then Maxie heard a shout. Thin and high and far off.

"Come on!"

Maxie set off with Freak in the direction of the sound, swinging the club in front of her to clear a path. They hadn't gone far when two of the beasts suddenly reared up, clutching rocks.

"I'll deal with them," said Freak. "You get the kids."

Maxie ran on. Hoping she was heading in the right direction.

"Joel!" she called out. "Where are you?"

Again—a small piping cry.

Maxie sped up.

There was a big black sky above and a feeling of space such as she hadn't experienced in months. This had once been a cricket field, and it seemed to go on forever. If it hadn't been for the fear wrenching at her stomach, she might have enjoyed this exhilarating feeling.

At last she spotted something in the darkness. Two small figures running full tilt across open ground. She roared at them to stop. They were too scared, however, and kept on running. Maxie put on a burst of speed and finally caught up with them and grabbed hold of one. It was Ella.

"Stop," she said. "It's me, Maxie. You have to come back."

The other kid, Monkey Boy, now stopped, and Maxie held on to the two of them as they stood there sobbing and panting and babbling incoherently about monsters. But Maxie wasn't listening. She had seen something behind the little kids that they hadn't. It was approaching stealthily through the grass, bigger than the other animals. It came closer and reared up on its stubby legs, its arms out to either side like a wrestler. It had only one eye and a scarred, battered face. A crop of painful-looking boils nested in the crook of its neck. It stared at Maxie with its one big, black, glinting eye.

Maxie straightened up, the club raised ready to strike, never taking her eyes off the brute.

It tossed its head from side to side and quickly battered its chest with its fists, and at last Maxie understood what it was. A male chimpanzee, hairless and diseased, driven mad like the grown-ups. He pursed his huge lips and began to whoop. His call was taken up by the other apes. Maxie was sure he would strike, but a sad look settled over his face. He looked deflated, tired. He sighed, gave a last feeble whoop, then turned and walked off into the grass.

"It's just a monkey," said Maxie.

She picked up Ella, and they set off back to the others. On the way, they passed several more chimpanzees hurrying away through the grass.

Freak was standing where she'd left him. He picked up Monkey Boy and walked with Maxie.

A little farther along they heard something moving in the grass, and they froze.

Then Maxie smiled and knelt down. "It's only Godzilla."

But Godzilla was whimpering and shivering and nudging something with his nose. Maxie frowned and looked closer.

"Take the kids back," she said to Freak, and something in her voice told him not to question her.

"Come along," he said to the little ones, and walked off.

Joel was lying in the grass, bleeding from a wound in his head where he had been hit with a rock. His eyes were open and he had stopped breathing.

Maxie picked Godzilla up. He struggled and protested, whining quietly. He wanted to stay with Joel.

"I'm sorry, darling," Maxie said, and closed Joel's eyes.

She sniffed. Her throat was tight, but no tears came.

26

Small Sam woke with a start. At first he had no idea where he was. Suspended in a world of total, sightless night, he couldn't feel his body at all. For one crazy moment he thought he might be dead. He felt a small sense of relief. Nothing to worry about anymore. And then he was filled with the burning unfairness of it all. He was only a little kid, he didn't deserve to die, what had he ever done wrong? Okay, so there was the time he'd broken his mom's favorite mug and hidden it in the back of the cupboard without saying anything. And that other time when Ella had been to a party and gotten a fantastic face-painting of a jaguar. It had been beautiful. She'd come in with it and he'd been so jealous. He hadn't said anything, but when he was alone with her he'd thrown a cup of water in her face and ruined it.

All right. If he thought about it, there were lots of things he'd done wrong. But they were only little things. He'd been sorry enough about them at the time and still felt guilty when he pictured Ella with the paint running down her face mixed with tears.

Surely it didn't mean that he deserved to die, did it?

Then he felt awful pins and needles in his legs, and it came back to him. He wasn't dead. He was stuck up the shaft in the underground tunnel. The last thing he remembered doing was tying himself to the iron rungs of the ladder with his belt. He was still jammed there, half dangling, half wedged, half dead.

He held his breath and listened.

Nothing. The grown-ups had gone at last.

What time was it? He had no idea. He had no watch. He had no way of knowing if it was even day or night. He moved his stiff and painful shoulders, trying to get the blood circulating again, and then squeezed his legs with his tingling fingers. They were still numb. He couldn't move until he had some feeling back in them. He waited as the fizzing spread through his nerve endings. One moment it was a faint tickle, quite nice, then it was agony and he was kicking the walls and whimpering. After what felt like ages, he had enough feeling to risk undoing the belt, but as soon as he tried to climb down, his legs gave way and he tumbled to the bottom of the shaft, landing in a painful heap in a puddle of water.

All his cuts and scrapes from the day before had woken up. His body was a mess of stings and aches and painful throbbing.

It was time to stop feeling sorry for himself, though. He needed to get up, get out of here, and get back into the daylight. He switched on his flashlight and carefully emerged from the hole. He leaned over and flashed the beam up and down beneath the train. There was nothing moving in either direction. As he listened, though, he could hear distant sounds back the way he had come. Probably grown-ups at Camden station. That meant he would have to go the other way.

No matter. He could get out at the next station.

He crawled along under the train, pumping his flashlight as he went. Stopping every now and then in the dark to listen. There were odd underground sounds. Small animals moving about. The drip of water. Deep creaks and groans. But no human sounds.

He at last reached the end of the train and could stand up and move more quickly. He trotted along. Sometimes the water became quite deep, coming up past his knees. It was black and smelled bad, but he tried not to think about it. At least it was probably so toxic nothing could be living in it.

On and on he pushed, down the curving tunnel, until he saw a faint light up ahead. He hurried on with fresh energy, but as he got nearer he slowed down. What did the light mean? It couldn't be daylight, after all, because he was still underground. It couldn't be an electric light, because there was no electricity. It could only be one thing. Fire. He turned off his flashlight and studied the glow. It was flickering, all right.

As far as he knew grown-ups didn't light fires. Maybe it was a camp of kids then? Maybe kids lived down here? Or maybe it was just an accidental fire?

He walked slowly toward it. He could smell smoke in the air, like a barbecue. His mouth was watering. A pain in his gut reminded him how long it was since he'd last eaten anything. Why did he have to think about barbecues now? He remembered how whenever the sun had come out in the summer, you could smell them for miles around.

That had been the old days.

As he walked he gradually saw more of the way ahead. He made out wires and junction boxes on the walls, a stop sign for train drivers, and a sort of traffic light thing, then the edge of the tunnel mouth, and finally bits of the station platform.

He realized that the fire was pretty small. It had seemed bigger at first because it was the only light around. There were dancing lights and shifting shadows, but he could tell that they weren't being caused by a big blaze.

He reached the end of the tunnel and peered out. He could now see the full length of the platform. He saw some signs. He was at Euston. He was fairly sure he was going in the right direction.

And there was the fire. Just by the entrance where the passengers came onto the platform. A pile of trash was smoldering, and a man's legs were sticking out of it. Sitting on the platform nearby were five or six grown-ups. They were thin and dirty and feeble looking, little more than stick people. They stared at the fire and the man's burning legs but seemed too tired to move.

Sam swore to himself. If there were grown-ups on the platform, they had probably infested the whole of Euston. He would have to somehow get past them and continue on to the next station.

He figured that if he stayed down on the tracks and kept close to the wall nearest the platform, the grown-ups wouldn't be able to see him. He was short of breath and tried to fill his lungs with clean air. There wasn't a lot of oxygen down here. Smoke was drifting from the fire through the passenger entrance, but it was also hanging in the air above the platform.

No wonder the grown-ups looked half dead. If they stayed there long enough, the fumes would kill them.

Good riddance.

Sam ducked down and crawled out of the tunnel, hugging the wall, gasping for breath, praying that one of the stick people wouldn't get up and peer over the edge. As he passed below the fire he could hear it crackling and popping. A spark jumped through the air and a burning cinder dropped onto the far side of the tracks. Sam ignored it and pressed on.

His stomach rumbled, and he froze. Had they heard it? It had sounded like a bear growling. He was so hungry. When had he last eaten? How long ago had it been? No idea. He had a bottle of water in his backpack, but he'd finished off the stale biscuits and tinned fruit he'd brought from Waitrose while he was hiding in the shaft.

Now wasn't the time to be thinking about food. If he wasn't careful he'd wind up as somebody else's breakfast.

On he went. It must have taken him fifteen minutes of patient crawling to get to the end of the platform, but he made it safely and scurried into the comforting darkness of the next tunnel. He glanced back. The grown-ups were sitting exactly where they had been before. Not one of them had moved. Maybe they were already dead? He didn't want to find out.

He turned and pressed on toward the next station.

As he walked, the water on the tracks grew deeper and deeper. At one point it was up to his waist. It wasn't warm and it wasn't cold, but it was still unpleasant. Black as oil with scum floating on the surface. He held his hands and arms up above it, keeping his precious flashlight well clear. Without light he would be lost and might end up wandering around down here forever.

No. Not forever. Only until he starved to death. His stomach gurgled even more loudly. There were sharp pains in his guts. He had to keep moving, and somehow he had to find something to eat.

The journey to the next station was a repeat of his journey from Camden to Euston, except that at one point he came to a junction with two tunnels leading off it. He chose one at random and kept going, trusting to blind luck.

After a little way, however, he found the tunnel was blocked by a big pile of what he at first thought was sticks. As he passed his flashlight beam over it, he realized that it was bones. Human bones, some still wrapped in clothing. Not bleached and white like skeletons in films, but a dirty yellowish gray. There were hands and legs and arms and ribs and skulls, all jumbled up on top of each other, stretching away down the tunnel. Maybe someone had piled dead bodies down here out of the way, or maybe the grown-ups had crawled down here to die. Whatever the reason, he could go no farther in this direction, so he backtracked and went down the other tunnel.

He'd sometimes wondered where all the dead grown-ups had gone. At first the streets of London had stunk. A horrible rotting smell that made you cover your mouth and nose with your shirt; but slowly it had faded away.

He shuddered. What other secrets were buried down here in the tunnels?

He soldiered on, going as fast as he could. Time ticked past, and he got more and more tired and more and more hungry. He took sips of water, which helped. Every time he put his bottle back, though, the level was lower. Soon it would all be gone.

He almost didn't realize when he got to the next station. He was stumbling along in a daze, and as he shone his flashlight to the side, there was a platform. Pitch-dark like the tunnel he had just emerged from.

Good. If it was dark it meant that there was nobody around. He pulled himself up off the tracks and sat on one of the metal benches along the wall. He would wait here until he got his strength back.

Where was he?

He flashed his light over a sign.

King's Cross.

Was that good? Or had he taken the wrong branch after Euston? He wasn't sure. If he could only get up the stairs and back into sunlight, he could find his way. He was pretty sure that King's Cross was a normal overground station as well. That meant there would be maps on the wall.

Yes.

He remembered now. Didn't the Eurostar to Paris go from here?

Maybe he should go there. Get right out of London. Maybe everything was all right in France. He could go to Disneyland.

He laughed.

Imagine having Disneyland all to yourself.

No. He had to find his sister, and his friends. He didn't want to be alone. He wanted to be with them. Well, soon he would be. He'd made it this far, hadn't he?

Cheered by thoughts of sunlight and escape, he stood up and walked along to the foot tunnel. His flashlight beam dimmed with each step, until it died altogether.

He stopped and pumped the handle. He pumped and pumped and pumped until he was sure he had a good charge, then flicked on the beam.

It shone into the white faces of a group of grown-ups. They were packed into the foot tunnel, filling its width, standing there, waiting, their broken teeth showing yellow against their gray papery skin.

Sam was nearly sick with shock. The blood drained out of his head and he swayed on his feet, struggling not to pass out. And then a mother made a move, darting at him, and he turned and bolted. Sprinted along the platform, his flashlight beam dancing madly ahead of him. Leaped down onto the tracks. Fell and hurt his leg. He was up in an instant, and he limped on. Behind him he could hear the grown-ups, jumping and slithering onto the tracks.

He charged into the train tunnel, and something took hold of him from the side. He yelled and struggled, but a strong arm in a heavy overcoat was holding him still. A hand clamped over his mouth.

"Don't move," said a soft voice.

A kid? Grown-ups couldn't speak.

But the body connected to the arm felt huge and strong. Too big, surely, to be a kid.

Sam was turned around so that he was facing the way he had come.

"Shine your flashlight back that way," the voice commanded, and he did as he was told.

The grown-ups were hobbling and capering along the tracks.

The big figure raised its other arm. Sam caught sight of a sawed-off shotgun, just like he'd seen in the movies.

The shotgun blasted once, sending out a bright flash and harsh boom, then a second time.

The front ranks of the grown-ups fell away. The rest turned and fled.

"Come on," said the voice. "Time we were leaving, kiddo."

27

The kids woke at first light. Those that had slept. Many had simply lain on the grass or sat huddled together, too scared to sleep. They had spent the night in a fenced-off public garden at the top of Portland Place. It was semicircular and surrounded by roads, like one half of a giant traffic circle. There was grass and shrubs and large trees, but nothing could get close without being seen because of the road. The fence was black iron with a spearhead at the tip of each post. The kids had figured that it would be a safe place to spend the night. They had been too tired and scared and demoralized to go any farther after escaping from the park. Who knew what fresh horrors awaited them in the dark? So they had climbed the fence, lit a fire, and posted guards. There were small buildings in the corners, little more than fancy huts but tall enough for the kids to climb on the roofs and keep lookout. It was the best they could do, and thankfully nothing else happened in the night.

Now the sun was rising over London, painting the sky first purple then pink then gray. Soon it would be a vivid blue. It looked like it was going to be another sunny day. The kids stretched and yawned and hugged each other, glad to be alive.

Maxie had taken first watch, then swapped with Ollie and settled down under a bush in her sleeping bag. Too numb to feel frightened. She had instantly fallen into a deep and dreamless sleep, as if she had been knocked cold.

Now she felt sluggish and heavy, fighting to wake up properly. She hauled herself up into a seated position. Every muscle in her body was stiff. She ran her fingers through her short curly hair to try to untangle some knots, but it was a lost cause. She filled her lungs with clean fresh air. That was one small benefit from the disaster. No more cars pumping out poisonous fumes. No more factories and offices polluting the atmosphere. London couldn't have smelled this pure for at least two hundred years.

She saw Blue talking quietly to Jester by the remains of the fire. She stood up and went over to them, rubbing the sleep from her eyes.

"Hi."

"Morning," said Jester. "Did you sleep?"

"Think so," said Maxie.

"Good. Today should be a lot easier."

"We need to sort ourselves out," said Maxie, looking around at the kids sprawled everywhere. In the chaos of the previous evening they had arrived at the enclosure in an unruly rabble. Maxie had no idea how many kids had made it.

"Whitney's taking our attendance," said Blue.

"I'll find Josh," said Maxie. "I expect he's already done ours. He's always first up."

"Maxie . . ."

Maxie looked at Blue. He was trying to tell her something. But she was too tired and dazed to be able to work it out. Her brain wasn't really awake yet.

"What?"

"Josh never made it."

"What do you mean?"

"He was helping some little kids when four of them things, them apes, got him cornered. He went down fighting. He was a brave kid. Nothing scared him."

"No," said Maxie, shaking her head. "You're wrong. He's here somewhere. I know he is."

"Sorry. He wasn't the only one."

Maxie knew it was true. She slumped to the ground.

"And when exactly were you going to tell me?" she said.

"What you saying? I just did tell you."

"You didn't think to tell me last night?"

"Hey, cool it, girl," said Blue. "I was gonna tell you when the time was right."

"And when was that going to be?"

Blue looked exasperated. He rolled his eyes, then turned to Maxie with a sadder, more gentle look.

"You was tired last night, Maxie," he said. "I could see you was cut up over Arran and Joel. You was on your last legs. I thought it might break you if I told you about Josh right then. We lost some people as well. Okay? I liked Joel. He was a sweet kid. And there were two others from my crew. Both little ones."

"I'm sorry," said Maxie.

"Ain't no problem."

Ollie came over with a scrap of paper. He had dark rings around his eyes, and his red hair was all over the place. He looked like he hadn't slept at all.

"I've counted heads," he said to Maxie, "and made a list. You heard about Josh?"

"Yes," said Maxie. "Who else?"

"Katey and Louise and Curly Sam."

"But I saw him rescued."

"They came back for him. Josh tried to help, but . . ."

Maxie swore.

"They're not necessarily dead," said Ollie. "We left in a hurry. We didn't have time to check bodies."

"Then we should go back. We should look for them. We can't leave them all alone out there."

"No," said Jester, standing up. "We're not going back. We're lucky to have gotten this far."

"And who gave you a say in this?" Maxie jumped up and shoved Jester.

"He's right," said Blue, pulling Maxie away. "We've discussed it. We go back we could be attacked again, lose more kids."

"So we just leave them? Is that what you're saying?"

"Yeah," said Blue. "It is. We got to assume they're dead."

"And what if they're not? Put yourself in their position—wandering around out there. Lost and alone."

"Put yourself in the position of the other kids here," said Jester. "The ones we know for sure are still alive. The ones sitting all around us. You think they want to go back?"

"You can take a vote on it if you want," said Blue. "But I guarantee most kids will want to push on."

"How can you be so cold?"

"Cuz I want to survive, Maxie. Don't you?"

"At what cost?"

"Whatever it takes."

Maxie looked to Ollie for support.

"Blue's right," he said. "It'd be crazy to go back. It's not that we don't care, but there's fifty-three of us in the group now. Those fifty-three are more important than one or two kids we left behind. Who are probably dead anyway."

Maxie didn't know what to say, and was worried about bursting into tears in front of the boys, so she turned her back on the three of them and stalked off to a quiet corner. Ollie exchanged a look with Blue and Jester and walked over to join her.

"Maxie . . ."

"Go away. I want to be alone."

"I know you do, but I want you to listen to me."

"There's nothing you can say."

"Isn't there?"

Maxie spun around. "Go away."

"How do you think this looks?" said Ollie calmly.

"I don't care how it looks."

"Well, you should care. You're in charge now, Maxie. Now that Arran's gone. You've got to be strong. You've got to take charge. Our kids are looking to you for leadership. They want you to tell them what to do. They need you."

"What do I tell them, Ollie? What's the right thing to do?"

Ollie sat down. "They all think the same as you," he said. "They think the right thing to do, the good thing, would be to go back and check. See if we can find any of the others."

"Then why did you—"

Ollie cut her off. "That's what they think would be the right thing to do," he said. "But deep down, secretly, they would all much rather get out of here and put the park behind them. They'd rather not take any more risks. And as the leader you can make that harsh decision for them. You can order them not to go back. Then they won't feel so bad about it all."

"You mean I need to show them I'm tough?"

"Of course. Yeah. There are two types of leader in this world, Maxie. Wartime leaders and peacetime leaders. And they're totally different. They need different skills. A wartime leader needs to show no weakness. A wartime leader's got to show that one or two individuals don't really matter. What matters is the survival of the group. What matters is winning by whatever means, yeah? It doesn't matter how we do this, how we get to the palace, how we win this, just so long as we do. That's all that matters."

"What if I don't want to be in charge?"

"Who'd be better at it than you?"

"You, maybe, Ollie. You're smart enough. The kids listen to you. Arran listened to you."

"Yeah," said Ollie. "They listen to me, but they don't look up to me. I ain't a star. They look up to you."

"Do they? What do they think of me? Really?" said Maxie.

"Make them think what you want them to think," said Ollie. "You got what it takes. You're the best person for the job."

"But I don't know if I am."

"Listen," said Ollie, leaning closer and lowering his voice, "Blue and Jester are getting a bit too close for my liking. They could cut you out. And if they cut you out, they cut all us Waitrose kids out. We'll be second-class citizens. We need to stick up for ourselves. And I know you can do it, Maxie. Arran had faith in you. So I have faith in you."

"All right."

28

isten up, everyone," Maxie shouted. "We had a bad time of it last night, but it's not going to happen again. Right? We're going to push on. We're going to get to the palace this morning. From here on in it'll be safe. Okay?"

"But we're not all here."

"Yes we are. Some kids didn't make it last night. They're dead. There's no point in going back to look for them."

"But Katey was my friend."

"And Arran was my friend. He's dead. We burned him. I'm in charge now. And I'm telling you. Not asking. We move on. Anyone thinks different, they're welcome to go back and search for bodies. But you'll be doing it alone. There are fifty-three of us left, and we're going to the palace. Now let's move out!"

They left the semicircle and marched down Portland Place. Maxie at the front with Blue and Jester.

A few minutes later they arrived at Oxford Circus, the heart of the West End; once the busiest part of all London, now deserted and derelict. How quickly everything had fallen apart. How quiet it was now.

They stopped here, in the middle of the junction where Oxford Street met Regent Street, and looked down the long, empty roads.

"I used to come shopping here on Saturdays," said Blue.

"Me too," said Jester.

"Topshop," said Maxie.

"The Apple Store," said Jester. "HMV."

"Niketown," said Blue.

Many of the storefronts had been smashed, but some still had their windows intact, and in one or two there were still a few items.

"It's not all gone," said Whitney, grinning. "Think of it, yeah, if we scavenge around here, the things we'll find. And look—there's no grown-ups."

"I told you," said Jester. "It's peaceful here. There are still some Strangers lurking about the place, but it's nothing like it is out your way."

Whitney began to laugh. "We should go shopping," she said.

Now Maxie laughed.

"I'm serious, yeah," said Whitney. "Look at these rags we're wearing."

Maxie looked at Whitney. She looked immaculate as ever in her gleaming white tracksuit. Somehow she always managed to keep it clean.

"We're like a bunch of bums," Whitney went on. "Before everything kicked off I used to care about how I looked. We're arriving at Buckingham Palace, we deserve to turn up in clean clothes and new sneakers and stuff."

"We're not going to see the Queen," said Maxie.

"We're starting a new life," said Whitney. "I want to make a good impression."

"I can't argue with that," said Jester. "You guys are a mess."

"So we couldn't go back to look for lost friends," said Maxie, "but we have time to go shopping?"

"It wasn't safe back there in the park," said Blue. "This is different."

"How do you know? Just because we can't see any grown-ups doesn't mean there aren't any around."

"These streets are generally quiet," said Jester.

"And how often have you come up here, exactly?" asked Maxie.

"Once or twice."

"Once or twice?"

"Listen," said Blue. "It's no big deal. We'll just go a little way along Oxford Street. It's not out of our way none. We can come down to the palace from the north just as easy as coming in from the east. We can change our route."

"Arran worked out the best route," said Maxie.

"Arran's dead."

"Thanks for reminding me."

"If you're in charge," said Blue, "then you can change the route if you want. You don't need to stick to Arran's plan."

"It'll be okay," said Jester. "Going this way won't make any real difference. We can cut down via Bond Street or Grosvenor Square. If we see anything in the shops and there are no grown-ups around, we can grab some of it. Oxford Street's nice and wide, and I've learned from you lot that wide streets are good."

"Come on," said Blue, smiling at Maxie. "What harm can it do? It might lift everyone's spirits. And you know you'd like some clean clothes. Brand new. Fresh out of the box."

"All right," said Maxie. "But any sign of trouble and we get out."

"Cool," said Blue, and they walked on down Oxford Street, heading west toward Marble Arch.

Maxie felt okay. She had given in to Blue and Jester, but at least they had listened to her and discussed it sensibly. She felt sure that if she'd flatly refused they'd have respected her decision. Ollie had been right. She had to stand up for herself, and for the Waitrose crew.

And also . . .

She dearly wanted a change of clothes.

After a couple of minutes, Freak joined her on the flank.

"I don't like this," he said.

"We don't want to turn up at the palace like a bunch of dirt balls."

"We should keep going," said Freak. "This reminds me too much of the other day. When we went to the pool. We got greedy."

"Face it, Freak," said Maxie. "We could just as easily get attacked going the other way. The truth is we just don't know where the next danger's coming from. Besides," she added, sniffing the air and wrinkling her nose, "you stink."

"So do you," said Freak, and he smiled at her.

Some shops had been looted, some burned, some were

just empty, as if the stock had been taken away to a safe place before the collapse. They found a shoe shop that had racks and racks of shoes on display, but they were all singles—the other halves of the pairs were in a dark back room somewhere, and nobody wanted to go and look.

They found a discount store with a few T-shirts and track-suits hanging on racks, and they fought over who should get what. Blue picked up a New Era cap from a tourist shop, but on the whole the pickings were slim.

After a while they came to Selfridges, once London's biggest department store. Miraculously it was still standing and looked almost untouched. The front doors had been busted open, however, and the window displays were empty.

"What do you think?" asked Blue, with a certain amount of awe. "You can get anything in Selfridges. We should look inside."

"Wait," said Maxie. "First we send in a scouting party. If it's safe and if it's worth it, then we can all go in. But we check it out first."

"I'll go," said Lewis, and he was soon joined by Achilleus, Sophie, and Big Mick, the Morrisons fighter who looked like he was about eighteen.

"Be back here in ten minutes," said Maxie. "Don't mess around—even if you see something you want, leave it for now. Just make sure it's safe in there, that's all that's important."

"See you in ten minutes," said Achilleus with a smirk, and the four of them went into the gloom.

Everyone else stood in the road, gawking at the massive building.

Maxie went over to Ollie.

"Go with them," she said. "I need someone levelheaded in there."

"Sure." Ollie followed the others inside as Maxie clapped her hands and started shouting, moving among the kids.

"Okay. Let's not get soft. We should be in battle formation. Small kids in the middle, larger ones form a ring. Blue, you take the west side. I'll take the east. Come on, move it!"

Ollie smiled. This was good. Maxie was doing well. He only hoped that it wasn't a mistake sending the scouting party into the store. They were some of the best fighters. They couldn't afford to lose any of them.

Them? Surely he meant us. Ollie was in on this. It's funny, he thought as he slipped into the darkness. You always thought it was someone else who was going to die, not you.

It was dark in the store. There were no windows to the outside world. The flashlights of the scouting party scoured the murk of what used to be the perfume and makeup department. There were broken glass cabinets and display stands everywhere, draped with cobwebs. Some of the signs and logos were still in one piece, but there was a forlorn, deserted feel about the place, and smashed bottles lay all over the floor.

The lingering smell of perfume hung in the air, sickly and cloying. There was no evidence of any recent human activity, though. It was very still and quiet.

"If we can't find any clothes, we can always just swipe some perfume," said Achilleus. "It'll hide the stink at least."

"Yeah," said Lewis, sleepily scratching his head. "You can arrive at the palace smelling like a queen."

"That's right." Achilleus laughed.

Big Mick had been searching the debris on the floor with

his flashlight. "Look," he said, picking something up. "This one ain't broken."

"Show me that," said Lewis, and Mick passed it to him.

"Moisturizer," he said mockingly. "I know a few grown-ups could use some of this. They've really let themselves go since the disaster. Their skin care is appalling, bro."

"We should keep moving," said Sophie. "We've only got ten minutes. The clothing departments are upstairs, I think."

"Sure."

Sophie had to be very careful of what she said. She was well aware that at least half the kids hated her for killing Arran, even though it was an accident. She had to do all she could to get on their side.

They crossed the floor, glass crunching underfoot, and found the escalators. Lewis spotted a store map and ran his flashlight down it.

"Men's first floor, women's second floor."

"Let's quickly go up to the very top," said Achilleus. "Then work our way down."

They climbed the first escalator and found themselves on the men's fashion floor. There was a moment's panic as their flashlights settled on what looked like a pack of grown-ups, pale and naked and gray. But the kids laughed when they realized it was only a group of mannequins. It still made them jump, though, every time they came across other ones.

A quick scan of the area showed them that there were still some clothes here.

"Looking good," said Lewis as they walked around to the bottom of the next escalator.

As they went up, Ollie walked with Sophie.

"Listen, Sophie," he said, "I know you didn't mean to kill Arran. It could have happened anytime. To tell you the truth, he was badly wounded anyway. He got bitten. He was losing it a bit, sick. He'd gone crazy. Even without your arrow he might never have made it to the palace. Maybe you just saved him a lot of pain."

"Thank you," said Sophie. "But I feel awful about it."

"Don't."

The next floor was the same. In fact there were probably more clothes here than on the floor below. After a quick look around they continued on up to the top floor. Once again Ollie walked with Sophie.

"So where've you been living all this time?" he said. "Where've you been hiding out?"

"All over," said Sophie. "We'd find a house with food in it and stay there until it wasn't safe anymore. Always on the move, never in one place long. We started out in Highgate, came down through Dartmouth Park, tried Hampstead Heath, but it was way too dangerous and there was nothing to eat. Then we came up through Kentish Town and Camden. It was the same everywhere. Fighting just to survive. There were quite a lot of us to start with. We thought we'd be okay—safety in numbers, you know. But one by one they got us. I try to black it all out and just concentrate on getting through each day. That's why I feel so rotten about Arran. It's bad enough the adults killing us kids, but . . ."

Sophie fell silent and Ollie put his hand on her arm.

From the top they could look all the way down a central

well to the basement. Their flashlight beams made tiny pinpricks of light far below on the tables and chairs of the restaurant.

They poked around. It didn't look like anyone had been up here in ages. Dust covered everything. There was a bathroom department at the top, and a lot of the stuff was intact. In a time of crisis nobody was going to come all the way up here and loot fancy soap.

"What do you reckon, then?" said Lewis. His voice quiet and slow as ever.

"I reckon if there was anyone hiding here ready to jump out on us, they'd have tried it by now," said Achilleus. "I can sense it when they're about. When you find a nest of grown-ups, the smell is something else, man."

"Don't I know it, bro," said Lewis.

"It's getting late," said Ollie. "We should get back to the others."

"Yeah," said Lewis. "Then it's shopping time!"

29

Sam couldn't tell how long the man had been carrying him through the tunnels. He'd figured out it was a man, after a couple of minutes. Though he wasn't like any of the other grown-ups he'd seen since the disaster. He was clean shaven and had long hair knotted into untidy dreadlocks. He wore jeans and a baggy sweater under his heavy overcoat.

And he didn't smell.

He carried a flashlight. Not a hand-powered one like the kids had. A big battery-powered thing that cast a strong, wide beam.

When they had set off he had asked Sam who he was and whether he was alone, and after that he had said very little.

Sam wondered how it was the man could talk. None of the other grown-ups could say a word. Their brains had been destroyed by the illness. This man could talk and use tools and weapons. How had he avoided catching the illness? What was he doing down here? And where was he taking Sam?

Sam had so many questions to ask, but the man wasn't answering any. He hurried on through the tunnels, sure-footed, knowing exactly where he was going.

They had passed two stations—Angel and Old Street—and the man showed no signs of slowing down. He held Sam firmly under his arm, and it was getting more and more uncomfortable.

"It's all right," Sam said at last, fearing that his brains were going to be shaken loose. "I can walk, you know. You don't have to carry me."

"Quicker this way," said the man. "Soon be there."

"Be where?"

"You'll see."

The man's feet sloshed rhythmically through the groundwater, which had grown deeper and deeper after they'd left Angel. He'd had to wade up to his waist through one section. It shallowed a little after that, but when they finally got to the next station there was still about a foot of water along the tracks beneath the platform. They had come to Moorgate. Sam had no idea where that was.

The man stopped for a rest. Sat Sam on the platform edge.

"There used to be pumps," the man said.

"What?" said Sam, surprised that the man was talking to him.

"Pumps," the man repeated. He didn't have a London accent. It was a soft country accent, like a farmer. "All the tunnels underground used to have pumps in them, to keep the water out. With no one working them, the water's coming up. City's drowning, I reckon."

"Where are you taking me?" said Sam.

The man smiled. "You'll see."

He picked Sam up again and trotted off.

It wasn't far to the next station, but Sam still felt like he'd had enough. When they got there the man put Sam on the platform and climbed up after him. He took hold of Sam's hand.

"Stick with me, kiddo," he said, leading Sam along the platform. "We don't want you getting lost."

Sam looked at the station name. *Bank*. The tiles on either side of the sign made a shape of dragons. There were openings through to the platform on the other side, but they were barred by locked barriers. When they came to the last one, the man unlocked it and took Sam through, before locking it carefully behind him. This platform was identical to the other one, except there was a train standing at it. Small candles in glass jars on the ground gave a warm glow. There was the sound of a generator and the smell of gasoline fumes. The exit and way up to the station was at the end on the left, the opening crudely blocked with an old iron bed frame.

"Home sweet home," said the man, and he went over to the train and banged on the side of one of the cars.

Presently the doors slid open and a woman appeared in the doorway. She was round and jolly looking, with a big woolly sweater like the man's, and a long, wide skirt. She had a bush of graying reddish hair and a kindly face. She beamed at Sam when she saw him.

"And who have we got here, then?" she said.

"His name's Sam," said the man. "Found him up at King's Cross, and I reckon he's probably one hungry lad."

"Come on in, come in." The woman bustled back inside, and Sam followed.

The car had been fitted out as a living area, and it looked very cozy. There were flickering candles, curtains at the windows, rugs and cushions on the floor, and drapes over the seats. A makeshift double bed filled one part, and in the open area by two of the doors, the couple had even rigged up a stove. Sam noticed that there was a chimney above it that went up into the ventilation ducts in the station ceiling, exactly like the one Ben and Bernie had built at Waitrose.

"Now you sit yourself down, young man," said the woman, "and I'll get you some soup. How about that, eh? I'll just move Orion."

Sam looked. There was a big ginger cat lying on one of the seats. The woman scooped him up and tickled him behind his ear. He purred happily.

"You have a cat?" Sam said, sitting down. He couldn't quite believe any of this was really happening.

"That's right. Plenty of food for him down in these tunnels," said the woman. "I'm Rachel, by the way. Old grumpy face there is Nick. He don't say much, so I'm guessing he's not introduced himself. Am I right?"

"He hasn't," said Sam.

"Less of the 'grumpy face,' woman," said Nick.

"Oh, I know you're not really grumpy inside; it's just your manner. But the poor lad's probably terrified. You need to show him a bit of kindness."

"I'm all right," said Sam. "I'm glad Nick rescued me."

"So am I, my love," said Rachel. "So am I."

She tinkered about at the stove, stirring the contents of a

pan with a big wooden spoon. The smell was overpowering. Sam's mouth was filling with saliva, his stomach shouting for food.

"Be ready in a jiffy."

Sam felt warm and safe and sleepy. He was on the verge of crying. He looked across at Nick, who was sitting on the bed. Nick winked and his face creased into a smile. Sam smiled back.

"So what were you doing, all alone down there?" Nick asked, taking out a tobacco pouch and rolling a cigarette.

"I'd gone into the station to get away from some grown-ups," said Sam, yawning. "Then I got stuck down there. Every time I tried to get out, there were more of them."

"They're like big old rats," said Nick, making a sour face. "The sick ones. We're pretty safe around these parts, though. They've learned to leave us alone. They don't bother us none."

"Why didn't you two get sick?" asked Sam. "We thought everyone sixteen and over got ill."

Nick shrugged. "Dunno," he said. "There's probably others like us, somewhere. When we're ready I guess we'll go looking for answers. For now we're just glad to be alive and healthy." He tapped his head. "Knock on wood."

"So you were by yourself, young Sam, were you?" Rachel asked.

"We got split up," said Sam. "I was trying to find my friends. They were on their way into London to Buckingham Palace."

"What on earth for?"

"It's safe there."

"Yeah?" said Nick. "First I heard about it. Mind you, I ain't been over that way since this all started."

"So, these friends of yours?" said Rachel. "Are there many of them?"

"About fifty, I think."

"Fifty?" said Nick. "You're joking, aren't you? We never found that many kids together nowhere."

"You've found other kids, then?" said Sam. "Alive?"

"Yes, we have," said Rachel, bringing a bowl of soup over to Sam. "We look after 'em. We fix 'em up and we feed them and we make sure they're safe."

"So where are they all now?"

"Safe," said Rachel. "Now eat."

"Why do you stay down here?"

"We just do. We hid out here to start with and just sort of got stuck. That's enough questions now; you need some food inside you."

Sam scooped up a spoonful of soup and blew on it. It was thin and brown but smelled good.

"Just vegetables, I'm afraid," said Rachel, ruffling his hair. "Whatever we can find in cans."

Sam tasted the soup, which was watery but delicious. His whole body shuddered with the delight of it, and he instantly felt a warm glow in his stomach.

"You don't look too bad," said Nick, watching him eat. "You've been managing to survive all right?"

As he ate, Sam told them everything that had happened since he'd been captured.

"Shame you got split up," said Rachel, sitting down next to Nick and taking his hand.

"Is the palace a long way from here?" Sam asked, spooning up the last of the soup.

"Quite a journey," said Rachel. "All the way across London."

"When I've had a rest," said Sam, "will you show me the way?"

Rachel laughed. "What are you talking about? A little lad like you can't go traipsing off across London all on his own."

"Would you come with me, then?" said Sam. "To the palace?"

"I don't know about that," said Nick. "We're settled here."

"But they're growing food and everything," said Sam. "Adults like you would be really useful."

"It's a dangerous journey. I think it's best you stay here."

"Oh," said Sam, "but I can't stay. I mean, thanks and everything for the food. It's very nice, but I can't stay here. My sister—"

"We'll see." Rachel cut him off. "Don't you worry about that for now. You just eat your soup, and then you look like you could do with a nice little snooze. Am I right?"

"Yes," said Sam. "But I really must find my sister."

"All in good time," said Nick, and he got up to collect the soup bowl that Sam had licked clean.

Sam sat there, his stomach gurgling happily. His eyelids dropped down then flickered back up again.

"I'm very sleepy," he said.

"Why don't you lie on the bed?"

"Yes, I'd like that."

Rachel took him to the bed and settled him down, sitting

next to him, stroking his hair. Nick stood behind her, smiling. The cat, Orion, sat nearby, also watching him, with black shining eyes.

"When you wake up," Nick said, "we'll have a good old chat, eh? See what's to be done with you."

"Mmm . . ."

"My brave little soldier," said Rachel.

Sam was asleep.

30

The mannequins freaked Maxie out. She was on edge enough as it was, trying to keep the kids under control inside the store. They needed to stick together. The scouting party had given them the all clear, but she was still frightened. The last couple of days had reminded her that you were never safe; you could never know what was waiting for you around the corner. And if you let your guard down . . .

They'd been through the menswear on the floor below and picked it clean. And now as they searched through the women's casual wear section, there were squeals of delight. Blue had been right. It had certainly lifted everyone's spirits, but if they were attacked while they were vulnerable, it would soon wipe the smiles off their faces. And Maxie would get the blame for letting them come in here.

Although most of the stuff was too big for the smaller kids, they still grabbed anything they could. When they came across each fresh batch, the excitement rose as they snatched at the clothes and argued over them, running from one pile to another. Maxie tried to stay on top of things but kept on getting distracted herself when she saw something she liked. At least now the boys had calmed down and were more alert— they had no interest in the women's clothing. The main problem was that everyone kept ducking behind cabinets and shelves to change in the shadows and dump their old things. As many as stood guard were out of action.

Maxie found an Agnès b top and some pants that looked like they'd fit her. She slipped them into her backpack. She would change later, when she was sure it was safe. She was too anxious now. The thought of being ambushed when she was half naked didn't excite her. She pictured herself being chased around Selfridges with her pants around her knees.

She spotted a black leather jacket and was irresistibly drawn to it. She looked at the label—Belstaff. It was sturdy and well made, had several useful pockets, and would offer some protection. At least, that's what she told herself. In truth, she just liked the look of it. She put it on and tried to look at herself in a broken mirror. She couldn't see very well in the half-light. A little big, but it fit okay.

"That's nice. It's like mine."

Maxie turned to see Sophie watching her, her bow at the ready in her hands.

"You think I'm taking it so I can look like you?"

"That's not what I meant. I only meant I liked it."

"Why should I care whether you like it or not?"

"I'm sorry, I didn't mean anything by it."

"Didn't you? I know what you're doing. Trying to ingratiate yourself. Trying to make friends. Well, don't bother. We'll never be your friends, Sophie. Okay? Not after what you did."

"All right. I know how you feel, Maxie."

"No you don't."

"Just leave it. I'm sorry."

"You think you're so great, don't you?" said Maxie. "In your leather jacket with your bow and arrow. Well, you're nothing. The only person you've killed with that thing is Arran. Great. Well done."

"Listen, Maxie," said Sophie, and Maxie could sense the emotion in her voice, as if she was on the verge of tears. "I know we can't be friends. But we do have to find a way to get along."

"Why? I never wanted you with us in the first place."

"Fine. Be like that. I thought you were cleverer, though."

"What? What did you say?" Maxie advanced on Sophie. "Don't insult me."

"Why not?" said Sophie angrily. "You insulted me. I understand about Arran. He was your boyfriend, and—"

"He was not my boyfriend. Maybe if he'd lived he might have been. But we'll never know, will we?"

Sophie struggled to say something, then gave up. She turned her back on Maxie and walked away.

Maxie felt a brief moment of triumph, and then it was swamped by black despair. Why was she such a bitch?

She knew why.

She was tired and scared and miserable and still aching over Arran.

It wasn't Sophie's fault. She knew it wasn't, but when she saw her pretty face she just wanted to lash out at her.

She swore quietly and left the main group, returning to the central well. She needed to be alone for a minute. It was quieter here. There was no one around—and no one keeping watch. She looked over the low wall. Shone her flashlight down, searching the floors below.

She caught her breath.

There was something moving.

She called out.

"Hello? Anyone down there? Hey! We need to keep together."

Nothing. No sound. No movement. Maybe she'd imagined it? She was so jumpy she was seeing dangers everywhere. She raked the beam over the area. It was quiet now.

She sighed and turned to walk along the balcony.

Sophie was there, about four yards away, her bow up to her face. The string was drawn back, an arrow glinting, ready to be fired. Her face was set into a hard mask. Her eyes wide in the gloom.

Maxie swallowed. The blood throbbed in her head. She really didn't know this girl at all. Know what she was capable of.

"Don't move," said Sophie coldly, but Maxie couldn't have moved even if she'd wanted to. She was welded to the spot. Her legs felt like they were made of lead.

Why had she been so stupid? Pushing Sophie like that. They were living in a different world now with different rules.

What would the girl do?

Maxie let out her breath.

"Sophie," she said, "I . . ."

Sophie released the bowstring. The arrow sizzled through the air and swished barely an inch past Maxie's right arm.

She had missed.

Maxie heard a thud behind her and she spun around.

A grown-up was standing there, a father, the arrow in his chest. He staggered sideways, flapping at the arrow and whining, then he hit the wall and toppled over the balcony. Maxie twisted around to watch him fall. He dropped all the way down to the bottom, turning slowly in the air, and landed with an almighty crash, splintering a table.

The sound was followed by complete silence. All the kids froze where they were, listening hard. What was going on?

Achilleus ran up to Maxie. She hardly recognized him. He was wearing a shiny new silvery-gray suit over a dark blue T-shirt.

"What's going on?"

"Grown-ups," Maxie croaked, the words sticking in her dry throat.

31

Small Sam slept deeply. His chest rising and falling.
Rachel was still sitting by his side, stroking his forehead
and cooing to him.

"Don't he look peaceful?" she said.

Nick grunted, went over to a dresser, and pulled out a
drawer. He took a pair of handcuffs from it and walked back
to the bed. He gently lifted Sam's left hand and snapped the
cuffs tight around it.

"Almost seems a shame," said Rachel. "He's a nice kid."

"Don't get attached, Rachel, love. Remember how it was
with the pigs? You should never have named them. Once you
name them they become pets."

"It's all right," said Rachel, pushing a lock of hair off Sam's
face. "I won't get attached."

The kids had been called together, and a fighting party had
quickly assembled around Achilleus, but they could see no
sign of any more grown-ups.

"Maybe there was only one of them," said Lewis, who

was wearing a light blue V-necked cashmere sweater.

"No," said Freak, pointing. "Look."

"Oh, my days!"

Shambling down the frozen escalator from the floor above in complete silence were about fifteen grown-ups. They were all wearing new clothes, festooned with hats and jewelry and belts and scarves, and carrying expensive new luggage. But it was a mess, like some awful costume parade. They looked like children who had raided their parents' wardrobes. The clothes didn't match, or were the wrong size, or were simply being worn in the wrong way. One man was wearing two jackets but no pants, another wore a dress, some of the women had things on backward, and they had smeared their faces with makeup. One wore her underwear on the outside, like some freakish superhero, and had what looked like a lampshade on her head. An impossibly skinny old woman wore a flashy Nike track-suit, a fur coat, a long blond wig, and several strings of pearls. She carried a camera on a strap over one shoulder and had only one shoe. High heeled. Making her limp.

It was an eerie sight as they came down in a huddle, like a bunch of weird tourists.

"Kill them," said Achilleus, and he raised his spear.

"No, wait," said Maxie. "I don't think they're going to attack."

"Who cares?" said Achilleus. "They're grown-ups. Kill them."

"Look at them. They're harmless."

"We'll see about that." Achilleus walked over to the group, which had stopped at the bottom of the escalator. They cowered away from him. One father, who had several ties knotted around his shirtless neck, raised his hand defensively. Achilleus struck his spear into his chest and he fell back. The other grown-ups shrank farther away. Achilleus advanced on them, herding them across the floor. They stuck together like frightened ducklings. Utterly bewildered. Achilleus started to laugh.

"Look at the silly sods," he said. "They're pathetic." He grabbed the old woman and shook her until her wig came off.

"What do you look like? Eh?" he said, throwing her into the others. "The lot of you. You're freaks. Morons." He snatched a hat off one of the fathers and stuffed it on top of his own head.

"Come on, you sheep," said Achilleus, steering the little group between a row of columns. "Show us your stuff."

The other kids were starting to laugh now, and four of the older ones joined Achilleus, tormenting the grown-ups, chasing them around, tripping them up, until they were all crowded into a corner, shivering and gibbering.

The big kids prodded them with their weapons and pushed a couple over. Then Achilleus and Big Mick grabbed one of the fathers and dragged him across the floor.

Achilleus sniggered. "Come on," he said. "Let's see if you like heights."

Laughing, they took him to the balcony, and before Maxie could stop them, they'd taken hold of him by the ankles and hoisted him over the side. He dangled there, his arms clawing at the air.

"Look at him," said Achilleus. "He's trying to fly."

"Stop it!" Maxie shouted.

"Stop it? Why? These bastards have been making our lives hell. Killing us, eating us . . . well, now it's our turn."

"Not this lot," said Maxie. "They've never done anything to you. They're harmless. Look at them."

"They're all the same," said Achilleus. "All guilty. If it wasn't for grown-ups we wouldn't be in this mess. They mucked up our planet. They caused the disaster. Every one of them is to blame. We should wipe them off of the face of the earth."

"We don't know what caused the disaster," said Maxie.

"Oh yeah, I forgot, it was God, wasn't it?"

"Or spacemen," said Big Mick, and he sniggered.

"We don't know," said Maxie. "But we can't become animals. We'll be like them."

"No we won't. We'll be top dogs, and we'll hunt them down and slaughter them."

"Achilleus, this is not right."

Maxie looked around for support. Half of the kids were laughing, some looked worried, some were crying. She saw Blue staring at Achilleus, fascinated.

"Blue," said Maxie, "tell him."

"Let go of him," said Blue.

"All right."

Achilleus and Mick let go, and the father gave a little gasp as he plummeted to the basement floor.

"He couldn't fly after all," said Achilleus.

"You idiot," said Maxie with as much scorn as she could muster. Achilleus tried to look dismissive—but she saw in his eyes that he thought he'd maybe gone too far.

"Who's next?" he said, and strode over to the other grown-ups, but Blue put himself between Achilleus and them.

"C'mon, man," Blue said quietly, and nodded to the smaller kids. "I think there's been enough death lately. I don't think the little ones want to see any more. Okay?"

"So we just leave 'em?"

"They're not our business," said Blue. "They're certainly not dangerous. They just come in here like us. To get some new clothes. I guess old habits die hard. Now let's get out of here. They're waiting for us at the palace."

A couple of kids slapped Achilleus and Mick on their backs, but most avoided them, and Maxie felt disgusted. She caught Sophie's eye and Sophie looked away.

Now wasn't the time to thank her.

Someone put a hand on Maxie's shoulder. It was Blue.

"You done well, girl," he said. "You look after yourself now, yeah? We need people like you."

"Thanks. And thanks for sticking up for me."

32

Callum watched them from the crow's nest with his binoculars. They'd begun to arrive that morning in ones and twos, drifting in from the direction of Camden. They stood about aimlessly at first, now and then coming over to the shop and inspecting it. After a while they grew braver. They battered uselessly against the barricades or the windows, before wandering off and squabbling with each other.

Idiots.

He'd had a lovely morning. He had no idea what time it was when he got up. All he knew was that it was light outside. From now on he would get up when he wanted, and eat when he was hungry. He wasn't going to turn into a slob, though. He had made his bed and the place was clean and tidy. When he went to the toilet he took the bucket to the end of the Waitrose parking lot, climbed a ladder, and tipped it over the wall into a garden. It smelled a little, but it would decompose. Stuff would probably grow there.

He was going to look after himself. Clear away each meal when he was finished, wash regularly, and change and clean his clothes. He wasn't a savage. That was what his mom had used to say. "Callum, do the washing-up, we're not savages."

He thought of himself as being like someone stranded on a desert island. Marooned. Like Robinson Crusoe. Or the people on *Lost*. If he kept on top of things he would survive. He had calculated that his supply of food would last him at least a year if he was careful. And he was careful. After breakfast he'd done his exercises. Push-ups, sit-ups, jumping jacks, stretches, and a bit of work with an old set of weights that Achilleus had found one day and brought back to the shop. Then he'd run twenty laps around the circuit he'd made on the shop floor. He would be fitter than he'd ever been before.

He planned to spend most of his time up here on the roof, where he felt most at home. Of course it would be different when it got cold and wet, but for now it was glorious, sitting in the crow's nest, looking out over Holloway. He'd be able to stay up here as long as he liked today. The sky was blue and mostly clear. There was still a faint smoke haze from a big fire over Camden way, but it looked like it had stopped spreading.

Bliss. He had everything he needed. The stupid, meandering grown-ups below even provided him with entertainment. He liked to watch them fight, and he'd put imaginary bets on who would win.

He wondered where Arran and the others had got to. They must surely be at the palace by now.

He smiled. The last place he wanted to be was Buckingham Palace. Crammed in there with all those kids. No peace and quiet. Always someone telling you what to do. Waiting your turn for food. Lining up for the bathroom. Arguing all the time. No way. They could keep their palace. He was king of all he could see, and he aimed to keep it that way.

He felt something tickling his cheek. A fly, probably. He put a hand up to brush it away and it came back wet.

It was a tear. He was crying.

Why was he crying? He had no reason to cry. Even as he thought about it, though, his body heaved in a great sob, and the next moment there were tears flooding down his face, and he was wailing like a baby.

He shouldn't have thought about the others. He shouldn't have thought about them. He was so lonely. So bloody lonely.

33

The kids had reassembled on the sidewalk. Maxie couldn't help thinking they looked a little like the sad grown-ups they'd found inside, wearing clothes that didn't really suit them, or fit properly. But she had to admit that they were at least cleaner than they had been before. They wouldn't look so much like an army of tramps. Some, like her, had chosen to pack their clothes away for later, and she was determined not to be embarrassed or self-conscious about how she smelled. Besides, it was their bodies underneath that really reeked. No amount of clean clothes could hide that fact. You kind of got used to it when you were surrounded by it all the time, but if you ever stopped and thought about it—yeck. Maybe, if what Jester had told them was true, they could all get baths and showers at the palace.

The palace? The very idea of it sounded ridiculous. She didn't really quite believe it yet. She was taking every moment as it came, trying not to think too far ahead. Trying not to hope.

Blue was getting his crew together, checking with Whitney that they were all there. Maxie found Ollie, who was also counting heads. He reassured her that everyone was present.

"Okay," Maxie shouted at her kids, jumping up onto a street bench, "we're ready now. We won't stop again until we reach the palace. It's not far, half an hour at the most. Are you ready?"

Everyone gave a big cheer, and with a light feeling inside, Maxie went over to Blue.

"We're all set," she said. "Shall we go?"

"Yeah." Blue raised his arm, just as Arran had done the day before, then dropped it, and they marched across Oxford Street and down toward Grosvenor Square in perfect formation.

A group of little kids had adopted Godzilla. Monkey Boy, Ella, and Blu-Tack Bill. It gave them something to think about other than themselves, and stopped them from worrying too much. They took turns carrying him and they fussed over him like a little baby. They had some cans of dog food and fed it to him with a spoon.

It was Blu-Tack Bill's turn to hold Godzilla, and in his mind he spoke to him, and he imagined the dog's replies so vividly it was as if they were having a real conversation.

You're like me, Godzilla. You can't talk.

Doesn't mean I'm stupid.

Me neither. Talking don't make anything better. Maybe I should bark like a dog.

I don't think you should; people will think you're weird.

They already do. But I don't care. I'm never going to talk again.

The grown-ups don't talk anymore.

No. But you know what, Godzilla? They are stupid.

Will you really never talk again?

I think so. I'm happy like this. I'm safe. If nobody can hear your thoughts, they can't hurt you. You're the only one who knows me, Godzilla. And I'm the only one who knows you. We'll always be friends, won't we?

Yeah. Do you like any of the new kids?

I like Maxie, she's nice. And Maeve is kind. But Achilleus scares me.

Are you looking forward to getting to the palace?

Yeah. I've never been to a palace before. In fact, I've never left Holloway before. I wish I'd come here before everything went wrong.

"Can I hold him?"

Bill looked up. Ella was talking to him. He held Godzilla tighter. It wasn't her turn yet. He'd only had him a little while.

"Let her hold him," said Monkey Boy. "She's getting upset thinking about her brother again."

Bill held Godzilla even tighter. The dog squirmed in his arms and whimpered. Bill loosened his grip a little.

Don't worry. You can still talk to me if she's carrying me.

Bill shook his head.

Whitney came over. She was only thirteen, but to the small kids she was as big and imposing as an adult.

"What's the matter?" she said.

"Ella wants to hold the puppy," said Monkey Boy, "because she's sad thinking about her brother, but it's Bill's turn."

"What about Bill? Does he mind? Do you mind, Bill?"

Bill shook his head. He wasn't going to let go. Even if he was a little bit scared of Whitney.

"Come on." Whitney picked Ella up and put her on her shoulders. "When Bill's had his turn, you can carry the dog. It'll be something to look forward to, yeah?"

Ella nodded, swallowing her tears. She would never argue with Whitney. She looked sadly down at Godzilla. Sam would have liked him. Sam loved dogs. He'd always wanted one of his own.

She wondered if there would be other dogs at the palace. Jester said they had it all set up nice. Like a farm. Maybe there would be chickens and lambs. She'd like to see some lambs.

Maybe Godzilla would try to chase them.

No. They'd keep him on a leash.

"You all right?" Whitney looked up and squeezed Ella's knee.

"I think so."

Maxie left her team on the flank and moved among the kids, making sure they were okay. Joking about their clothes. She saw Ella on Whitney's shoulders, the two of them chatting away. Whitney was wearing a new white tracksuit that was slightly tight on her big body.

Ella looked like she'd been crying. Maxie asked if she was all right.

"She's okay," said Whitney. "She was just thinking about her brother, Sam. I told her he's gone to heaven, where he'll be happy."

"Yeah." Maxie patted Ella's leg. "Don't fret about him. He's gone somewhere where he can't be hurt anymore."

"I miss him."

"We all miss him. But when we get to the palace we can make new friends, meet new people. They'll never replace Sam, I know, but it'll be a new start for us."

"Will there be princesses at the palace?"

Maxie laughed. "I don't think so, darling. Just ordinary kids like us. So you stop your crying, okay? Just think happy thoughts."

"What about you?" said Whitney, fixing Maxie with a stare. "You thinking happy thoughts?"

"Trying to. Trying to keep busy."

"So, you're good?"

"I'm good," said Maxie.

Whitney studied her. "If you're lying I'll know."

"As good as can be expected," said Maxie.

"That's right," said Whitney. "Reckon that's the best any of us can say. Is that boy Blue behaving himself?"

Maxie nodded. "I guess so. We're sorting it out between us."

"He's cool, you know," said Whitney. "He helped all of us in Morrisons through some hard times, some really hard times, you better believe it. That's why he's in charge."

"I was wondering about that," said Maxie. "In the meeting, back at Waitrose, you seemed to be the one that everyone listened to."

"Blue runs around and shouts and waves his spear, but it's us sisters who really rule the roost. The kids, though, they felt safer with a man . . . well, a boy, in charge. A fighter. There was a lot of fighting in them days."

"You needed a wartime leader," said Maxie.

"War is right. And speaking of war, you should be out on the flank with your team. I can look after the little ones."

"Sure." Maxie smiled and rejoined her unit.

Lewis, on the other flank, was entertaining his team with a long story about a soccer match he'd played in where three kids had broken their legs. They were all laughing but keeping a watchful eye out at the same time.

"By the end of the game," said Lewis, "everyone was like, walking around wide-eyed and shivering, too scared to run. Nobody would tackle anyone, they was too scared to even like, kick the ball, man. I was the goalie, so I wasn't too bothered, and in the end they had to call the match off. Can you imagine. Three people! It was carnage, man."

This part of London couldn't have been more different from Holloway, where they had started their journey. There were expensive apartment buildings and houses, antique shops, art galleries, a Porsche dealership still with some cars in the showroom.

"Do you think there'll be a better class of zombies around here?" said Ollie.

Sophie was walking with him. Ollie was the Holloway kid who had shown her the most kindness. She noticed that he kept himself to himself. Didn't cozy up with any one particular group of kids. He was quiet and thoughtful, something of an outsider. Perhaps that was what he saw in her. She was an outsider too.

"They're not technically zombies, are they?" said Sophie.

"No," said Ollie. "They're not the living dead, as such. Thank God they can't come back to life after you whack them."

Ollie was almost walking backward, so often was he turning around to check behind. Sophie was seeing more of the back of his red head than of his face.

"You're making me nervous," she said.

"It's good to be nervous," said Ollie. "We don't want to end up as well-dressed corpses."

"You saw the grown-ups back at Selfridges," said Sophie. "I think you're right. The ones around here are different."

"Yeah, well, I'll bet you we have another fight on our hands before we get to the palace."

"You're on," said Sophie. "How much d'you want to put on it?"

"A million."

"A million? You haven't got a million."

"What if I did?" said Ollie. "What use would it be to me? There's nothing to spend it on. Money doesn't mean anything anymore. What if we were to break into one of these fancy banks around here? Get into the vault and take all the cash out. What would we ever use it for? Lighting fires?"

"Actually, I don't think bank notes burn that well," said Sophie. "But I take your point. So what do you want to bet with? How about my bow against your slingshot?"

"Are you serious?"

"No," said Sophie. "My bow is just about the most important thing in the world right now."

"Same goes for my slingshot."

"So the bet's off?"

"I've got a package of cookies," said Ollie. "You got any food?"

"Can of carrots."

"Okay—I'll bet my cookies against your carrots."

"These cookies?" said Sophie. "Are they stale?"

"What do you think?"

Sophie thought about it. "Okay," she said at last. "You're on."

They shook on it.

34

Ollie won his bet sooner than he expected. As the main body of kids was crossing Berkeley Square, Achilleus and Big Mick, who had been scouting ahead, came running back, out of breath.

"There's grown-ups. Up ahead," Achilleus panted.

"Can we go around them?" Maxie asked.

"They're attacking some kids," said Mick. "It don't look good."

"How many are there?" said Blue.

"About fifteen or twenty."

"Can we take them?"

"Yeah," said Achilleus. "We can take them."

"Okay," said Maxie. "I'll stay here with my squad. We'll guard the little kids and the non-fighters. Blue, you take everyone else down. Once it's safe, send someone back for us."

"You got it."

In less than a minute Maxie had the little kids safely in the center of the square, and Blue was hurrying off with Jester and the fighters. They turned a corner into a short straight street that ran down toward Green Park.

"They're just up ahead!" Achilleus yelled, and Blue slowed down.

"Lewis, take the left flank," he shouted. "Ollie and Sophie, keep your group on the right. Fire as soon as you can. The rest of us, wait for the missiles, then we go in hard and fast."

The street opened out on to the top of Piccadilly. Ahead was a wide four-lane highway, with the trees of Green Park on the far side. To the left was the Green Park tube station and the Ritz Hotel.

A bloody battle was taking place in the middle of the road between five kids and a much larger group of grown-ups. This was a mean-looking bunch, very different from the ones in Selfridges. They were half naked, lean and battle-hardened. Twelve fathers with no shirts, and five mothers in vests. They all looked like they'd been regulars at the gym before the disaster, and they'd somehow kept fit since. Fit but not healthy. They were studded with boils and sores and festering, weeping wounds. They were massacring the kids—three of whom were already down. The two kids left standing were a boy and a girl. The girl's face was covered in blood, but she was supporting the boy, who was on his last legs and clutching a sword. A ring of grown-ups was circling them, ready to finish them off.

So far they hadn't noticed the Holloway kids' arrival.

"Leave the ones in the circle," said Ollie, fitting a shot to his sling. "We might hit the kids. Take the others out first."

As he spoke, the grown-ups realized that they had company, and they turned almost as one, fresh bloodlust lighting up their faces, and charged across the road.

If they thought they were going to have an easy time of it, they were sadly mistaken. The battle was over almost before it began.

Ollie's team let loose a deadly volley. Six grown-ups went down straight away. Now Blue and Achilleus led the central group forward as Ollie's team fell back. The surviving grown-ups carried on, too stupid to pull out of their assault. They were met by the fighters, who punched into them, weapons held high. Most grown-ups fell to the asphalt, but three escaped and ran off to the sides. Lewis's team took down two. Ollie and Sophie got the other one. An arrow thudded into his back at the exact same moment a round from a slingshot got him in the head.

Achilleus and Mick finished off the wounded.

In a few seconds every one of the grown-ups lay dead on the ground.

Jester whistled. "That was well done," he said. "Very well done."

Ollie turned to Sophie. "You owe me some carrots," he said, but there was no joy in it. The sight of the dead kids was too upsetting.

Blue called Lewis's team over. "Go back for Maeve," he said. "Looks like we'll need her. Tell them it's all clear, but hold the others back out of the way until we've gotten rid of the bodies. I don't want the small ones to see this."

While Achilleus and Mick organized the removal of the dead grown-ups, dragging them across the road and dumping them down the steps to the tube, Blue checked the kids.

The three lying down were well dead.

"Better get these out of the way as well," said Blue. "No time for any fancy funerals."

The bloodied girl was sitting on the ground now, cradling the boy in her lap. She was staring into the distance, her eyes empty. Blue spoke to her, but she didn't respond. Her face was slashed, a flap of skin hanging down from her forehead.

"You'll be all right," said Blue. "You're safe now."

Again she didn't respond.

Jester's shadow fell across Blue.

Blue squinted up at him. "I thought you said there were no grown-ups around here."

Jester shrugged. "This isn't normal," he said.

"If you've been lying to us . . ." said Blue.

"This isn't normal," Jester repeated, and bent to pick up the sword that the boy had dropped.

Maeve arrived, her medical kit already out. She knelt down and checked the girl over.

"I'll need to disinfect that and put a bandage on it," she said, unscrewing a glass bottle. "What about the boy?"

Blue looked at the boy. He was lying very still. He tried to find his pulse. Shook his head. Gently he pried the girl's fingers apart where they were gripping her friend's jacket, and moved the body away.

Ollie and Sophie had broken into a nearby shop and quickly built a makeshift stretcher out of some clothes racks and a curtain. They came over and settled the wounded girl onto it. When the rest of the group finally emerged on the main road, there was little sign that any fight had ever taken place here. It was quiet and peaceful, apart from the flies that were already gathering by the tube station steps.

Maxie led the small kids across the road and into Green Park. The sunlight was dancing in the trees, birds were singing, but everyone was remembering the attack in Regent's Park and looking nervously around. So it was a shock when they realized they'd come to the edge of the park, and they glanced up to see Canada Gate, and there, beyond it, the great ugly bulk of Buckingham Palace.

35

They approached the building slowly, hardly able to believe that they'd arrived, let alone that they might spend their lives here. It was one of the most famous buildings in the world, and yet they were seeing it properly for the first time. Taking it in as a place to live rather than just another of London's many tourist attractions. In front of it was a massive expanse of pink-colored circular drive, on an island in the center of which sat the white marble block of the Victoria Memorial, with Queen Victoria herself sitting on her throne, looking off down the Mall. The still-gleaming gold statue of winged Victory stood over her.

Separating the palace from the public were tall black iron railings topped with gold spikes, and behind the railings was the parade ground where the famous Changing of the Guard used to take place. And then there was the building itself. This was no fairy-tale palace. It was a solid gray lump. Even though it was a good five stories high, its immense width made it look quite low and unimposing. The front was made up of three huge rectangular blocks linked by long sweeps of flat-fronted wall. Rows of neatly ordered windows ran from side to side with dull mathematical precision. The central block had an entrance at the base through an archway, above which sat the famous balcony where the Royal Family used to appear to cheering crowds on special occasions. Four pillars ran up from the balcony to the top of the building, supporting a wide triangle that could have come from a Greek temple.

In the dead center of the roof was a flagpole, from which a ragged Union Jack hung limply against the windless sky.

As the kids got nearer they saw that there were sentries in the sentry boxes. They hadn't been expecting this. They had presumed there would be kids keeping watch, but not in the sentry boxes where the soldiers in their bearskin hats had once stood. These sentries were only kids, but they were still in uniform. Red school blazers with black trousers and black baseball caps. They had rifles and had even been standing stiffly at attention. As they saw the war party approaching, however, they came alive. A couple ran back through the archway, the rest walked toward the railings, guns at the ready. Somebody on the balcony shouted something, and the next moment there were faces at the windows. Soon more kids began to trickle out through the arch onto the parade ground. They came over to the railings and peered out, just as tourists in the past had peered in from the other side.

They watched in silence. Hands up on the railings. Curious but watchful. There must have been about twenty of them, kids of all ages, clean and well dressed.

Jester waved and called out, "Hey. It's me. The Magic Man has returned. And look who I've brought with me!"

Some of the kids' faces lit up, and they smiled. They peeled away from the railings and followed the group as they walked along to one of the ornate gateways.

"Open up!" Jester called out, and a small boy ran from the archway, carrying a big set of keys. He rattled them in the lock and eventually the gates were opened. The war party trooped in, flanked by two lines of silent palace kids.

Lewis looked around at the staring faces. It reminded him of visiting another school for a soccer match. Everyone was checking everyone else out. Suspicious. Who were these strange new kids? Who were the ones to look out for? Who could be safely ignored? Who might be a friend? Who was a potential enemy?

More important: were there any nice-looking girls around?

There was a shout from the balcony, and everyone looked up. A boy who looked to be about seventeen was standing there, with six more of the kids in uniform on either side of him. He was tall and very pale-skinned, with a spray of freckles over his face and neat curly black hair. He was wearing a suit and tie, and he was beaming down at them, his arms spread wide.

"Magic Man!" he yelled. "Well done, Jester. We didn't think we were ever going to see you again."

"You didn't doubt me, did you, David?"

"Never! But where are the others?"

"They didn't make it," said Jester, and there were gasps

and groans from the assembled palace kids. "But these guys," Jester went on, trying to lighten the mood. "You should see them in action. They're skilled fighters, David. They're going to really make a difference."

David smiled. "Well, come on in!"

They passed through the archway into a large inner quadrangle. The newly arrived kids looked around, awed—they had never realized quite how big the palace was. It seemed to go on forever. Jester led them to a doorway on the far side of the quadrangle.

Inside they passed through a grand stateroom into a wide, glass-roofed corridor lined with old paintings. From there they entered another large room that overlooked the gardens. There were more kids outside, tending crops. It was just how it had looked in Jester's photographs, except the scale of it was more obvious. This wasn't a garden so much as a small park.

Maeve had a word with Jester, and he rounded up two boys. They took the stretcher with the wounded girl on it away. Maeve followed.

In a few minutes David appeared with his escort. He beamed at the newcomers and went around shaking hands and being introduced. He had a confident, friendly, but slightly aloof air about him, and had obviously been to a good private school. When he'd said hello to everyone, he took them all outside and showed them around the gardens. They were growing potatoes and carrots, cabbages, beans, onions, squash. You name it, they had planted it. The crops were laid out in neat rows and were well tended. There were also two enclosures, one for pigs and one for chickens.

They came across a serious-looking girl with glasses who was on her knees, weeding a patch of spinach.

"This is Franny," said David. "Our head gardener. Any questions about all this, she's the person to ask."

Franny got up. She rubbed her hands clean on her apron and said hello. A little shy. A little awkward around David.

As Franny chatted with the others, Maxie wandered away from the group and laughed, turning full circle on the lawn, trying to take it all in. The little kids were already running around and playing, all their cares forgotten.

Godzilla was gamboling on the grass while his little group of caretakers ran with him. Shouting happily.

Maxie closed her eyes for a moment and took a deep breath. When she opened them again she saw David strolling back toward the house, talking to a group of kids.

"The kitchens here were designed for feeding lots of people," he was explaining. "We've rigged up some of the stoves to work with wood. We can cook hot food. We even bake our own bread. We'll prepare a welcoming feast. We've plenty of food stored up."

Maxie marveled at how organized everything was, and how relaxed everybody appeared to be. It was such a different feeling from being cooped up in Waitrose, surrounded by grown-ups. To think that all this time these kids had been living this easy life when she'd had to spend every other day fighting to stay in one piece.

Arran would have been impressed with this.

Arran . . .

Maxie was overcome with a bittersweet feeling. Like when a small cloud drifts over the sun on a summer's day. She knew that elsewhere in London terrible scenes were being acted out. Kids were lost in a world of pain and misery. She wasn't sure she deserved this level of peace and contentment. She sat down on the grass and let herself go. Tears pouring down her face. She looked around. She wasn't alone. Other kids were sitting there, overwhelmed by it all. All the tension and fear of the last two days was coming out. Kids were hugging each other or sitting alone with their thoughts. Like her, many were crying.

She also spotted some of the palace kids in little teary huddles. They had lost friends too, from Jester's scouting party.

Maeve came out of the building. She saw Maxie and sat down next to her, putting her arms around her.

"Is this really happening?" she whispered.

"I hope so," said Maxie, and they laughed through their tears.

"I've just been upstairs, speaking to a girl called Rose," said Maeve. "They've got a proper sick bay and a sort of clinic. She's been telling me about the medicines they've got. She even wears a nurse's uniform. You should have seen how well they dealt with that poor girl we rescued. Oh, Maxie. It's amazing. I never thought I'd see anything like this ever again. For the first time since the disaster I really feel like we might have a future."

"I know," said Maxie. "And after what we've been through, I reckon we can cope with anything. We're going to survive, Maeve."

Ollie was walking alone by the lake. There were ducks on it, probably fish swimming down below. He felt neither happy nor sad. He was thoughtful. This all looked fantastic on the surface.

Franny had given him a small piece of lettuce to try. It had tasted delicious, but when he had pulled off one of the leaves he'd found a small slug on it.

There was always a slug on the lettuce.

This was too good to be true.

He had never trusted Jester, and he didn't trust David.

He wasn't going to let his guard down just yet.

Being careful had kept him alive this far.

There was no reason to stop being careful now.

36

David was true to his word. That evening the kids sat down to a five-star meal in the state dining room. The newcomers couldn't get over how fancy the room was, and how weird it was eating in here, like being in a lush film. The room, which was painted a deep red, was lit by countless candles in silver candlesticks. Along one side, tall glass doors looked out over the garden, and the wall opposite was hung with paintings of British monarchs. The kids sat around a massive polished wooden table piled with food. Three giant mirrors at one end of the room reflected the whole surreal scene.

The kids expected that at any moment a furious adult would come in and tell them they didn't belong here, and to get lost.

The food was simple but good, with a choice for everyone. Spaghetti, steamed vegetables, baked potatoes, and omelettes, with warm crusty bread. All washed down with jugs of cool, clear water. The bread was slightly heavy, but it was the first bread any of the Holloway crew had tasted in over a year.

They were all starting to relax and get to know each other. There was a noisy level of chatter around the long table.

Maxie found herself sitting with Franny, the gardener. She was very thin and jolly and well spoken. Rattling away between mouthfuls.

"I can honestly say I'm happier now than I have ever been in my life. I mean, of course I miss my family, but I'd been at boarding school so I hadn't seen that much of them lately anyway, no, that's not fair, I loved them dearly and I do miss them, but David's got everything so well organized here, he really is a genius, we worship him."

"Worship him?"

"It's just a figure of speech, I don't mean to say we throw ourselves to the ground in front of him and offer up thanks, though I think some of the younger children would like to, but he really is clever, things are a lot better all around than they were before."

"Are you joking, Franny?" said Maxie. "The world's fallen apart."

"No, I'm quite serious," said Franny. "Think about it, Maxine."

"It's Maxie."

"Sorry, yes." Franny giggled. "I used to know a Maxine at school, it's sort of stuck in my head, she was really into horses, she's probably dead now, poor girl, but what was I saying? Oh yes. The world. Think about it. The oceans are no longer being polluted, the fish aren't being wiped out, they're breeding now, multiplying like mad, in a couple of years there'll be more fish in the seas than there have been for centuries, and it's not just fish, there's whales, dolphins, turtles, wild animals everywhere. Think of the forests growing, the trees no longer being cut down. The world is going back to how it should be."

"But I'll never see any of those fish," said Maxie. "Or those whales. Or any lions or tigers. I'm never going to set foot in a rain forest now, am I? I won't even be able to watch any old DVDs of them without electricity. What does the future hold? It's like going back to the Middle Ages. Nobody knowing what was going on beyond their front doorsteps. All I'll ever know is this. This little bit of London."

"So?" said Franny. "As long as you are happy. And if the world is happy, we can be happy. The world will heal itself, the damage that man did will be repaired, future generations will maybe look after it better."

"Future generations?"

"Of course."

Ollie leaned over. "How do you know when we get old we won't all get the sickness?"

Franny made a face and shrugged. "David will think of something," she said.

"You reckon?"

"Let's not talk about gloomy things like that," said Franny. "Not tonight."

"Whatever."

Ollie looked around the room. He noticed that not every palace kid was eating with them. Some of the boys in uniform were sitting by the doors, still clutching their rifles. He didn't like the atmosphere it created. As if David and his friends were trying to recreate the days of royalty. The enemy was outside roaming the streets, not in here. What were they trying to prove with this display?

He could understand it if they were patroling the grounds—which he had no doubt they were, given the level of David's organization—it just about made sense to have sentries on duty out front, though even that had looked a bit much to him. They would have been a lot more useful watching from the roof. Whatever. They certainly didn't need these poor sad sacks in uniform watching them eat.

There was something military about the boys' behavior. They didn't speak. They stayed very still. It was creepy.

Ollie got up from the table and slipped out of the room. Kids had been coming and going all the time. Some using the toilet, some bringing in food or clearing away dirty dishes. Nobody noticed him leave.

He walked down the corridor as if he were heading for the toilet, checked that no one was looking, and kept on walking.

It was time for a little snooping.

Blue was at one end of the table with Jester and David. He was quizzing David. Anxious to find out how everything worked at the palace. "So are you in charge, then, Dave?" he asked, shoveling food into his mouth.

"He doesn't like 'Dave,'" said Jester. "He likes to be called David."

"Sorry. David." Blue took a sip of water. "David what?"

"Actually my name is David King."

Blue spluttered, spitting water onto his plate. "You are not serious, man?"

"I am."

"Well, remember. Just because you live in a palace it don't make you a real king."

"No?" David smiled.

"No way, man. We all used to live in a shop; didn't make me a shopkeeper."

"I never said I was a king anyway. It's just my name."

"Well, you certainly act like you're the big cheese."

"When we first got here it was chaos," said Jester. "We were all over the place. But if you want to survive you have to be organized. If you want to grow food, to drink clean water, to stay warm, to defend yourselves, all those things need organization. David arrived a little after the rest of us. He pulled us all together. He organized us."

Blue glanced at Jester. "Things are going to be very different from now on, man. Very different."

"How so?" said David.

"How so? Well, for one, you ain't gonna be organizing me, pal. Right? Ain't nobody gonna be organizing me. And that's a fact. You ain't my king. I never voted for you."

"You don't vote for a king."

"Listen—"

"We'll talk about it later," said David, smiling. "It's no big deal. We'll work out a way that we can all get along."

"Why can't we talk about it now?"

"Let's enjoy the food. You all need to settle in and find your feet. In the morning everything will seem so much simpler."

Ollie followed his nose toward the kitchens, making sure that he wasn't being followed. Most of the palace was eerily dark and empty, but it made it easy to stay hidden. A staircase near the state dining room led down to the service level. There was a lot of noise coming from the kitchen, and Ollie approached cautiously. Standing in the corridor was a large plastic bin on wheels. He looked inside. Empty tins of dog food.

That explained the spaghetti with meat sauce.

Oh well, he'd eaten worse.

He continued and found a spot where he could see into the kitchen without being seen. The room was packed. One group of kids was sweating away at the stoves, another clattering dishes at the sinks, immersed in clouds of steam and smoke. Yet more kids were crowded around a scrubbed wooden table. There looked to be about twenty of them, some in uniform, some still grubby from working in the garden. They weren't eating anything like what was being served upstairs. They had bowls of some kind of thin stew or soup. As Ollie watched, a boy stood up and shouted over to the cooks.

"Hey! Is there any bread to go with this?"

"You're joking, aren't you?" one of the cooks shouted back. "They're scarfing next month's supply upstairs."

"They're scarfing everything upstairs. We'll starve."

"We'll make do."

Ollie had seen enough. He slipped away. So David was lying to them, pretending they had more food than they really did. What was he up to? Showing off, probably. For now they would have to sit tight and see what happened. Ollie knew that he ought to be angry, but he was actually quite impressed. David was a clever boy, devious. He knew a bit of psychology. He understood about politics. About spin. He had achieved a hell of a lot here, obviously not quite as much as he was pretending, but it was still remarkable. Ollie would need to be

255

very careful—they all would—but David was a good person to be on the right side of.

Ella was eating her dinner slowly and quietly. Godzilla was under the table chewing on a piece of leather. Occasionally she would feel him bump reassuringly against her leg. She was thinking about Sam. He'd have liked it here. He'd have liked playing in the garden and running around the palace, looking at all the nice things. She'd seen a painting of a man in armor. Sam would have really liked that. He liked knights. He always loved dressing up in his play armor. She'd tried to play with him, as a princess, but he didn't like princesses. He only wanted other knights to fight with. She wasn't very good at fighting and always ended up getting hurt and crying.

Was he really in heaven like Whitney had said? Ella didn't exactly know what heaven was. She'd always imagined it looked a bit like this. A nice clean palace with pictures and a garden to play in and a nice man looking after you. And nice food.

She'd never liked vegetables before, but now they tasted lovely. So many things had changed. Too many. She'd always thought Sam would be there to look after her, even though he was only small. She was nearly as big as him.

Now he was gone.

She said a silent prayer. Sent it up to heaven.

Sam, if you can hear me, I hope you've got nice food
where you are. Some vegetables like these. They're meant
to be good for you. So eat them all up, like I'm doing.
When I die I'll come and see you, and we'll be together

*again. But for now I'm going to think of you safe and
happy and playing knights with a friend.*

Love from Ella. Your sister.

*P.S. I got a good long turn with Godzilla today after
we got here. Godzilla is very happy.*

*P.P.S. I forgot, you never met Godzilla. He is a
puppy and is very cute. He belonged to a boy called Joel
who got killed by monkeys. I think the monkeys were sick.
Monkeys are usually nice. At least in stories.*

*P.P.P.S. Maybe you'll meet Joel where you are. Say
hello. He is nice.*

*P.P.P.P.S. Good night, Sam. The others call you
Small Sam. To me you're just Sam—my brother.
I miss you. I wish I was with you.*

37

"They put something in the soup to make you sleep."

"What do you mean? Why would they do that?"

"Why do you think? They needed to chain you up. They're keeping us prisoner."

Sam had woken up in a different train car. There was no fancy furniture in here, no curtains or carpets. There was straw on the floor, a bucket at one end to use as a toilet, and the doors were jammed shut. Otherwise it was a normal car.

There were handcuffs around his wrists. A thin chain led from them up to the ceiling, where it was attached to the handrail. He had room to move around, but not far.

There were three other kids in here. Two were asleep. Twins. A boy and a girl, about Sam's age. They looked clean and well fed, but a little feeble, and their skin was very pale. The third kid was a girl, older than Sam, quite fat, but with withered, skinny legs. She sat on one of the seats and seemed to have some trouble breathing. Maybe it was asthma?

Her name was Rhiannon. She said she'd been here about three weeks. As far as she could tell.

"Why would they keep us prisoner?" said Sam. "They seemed nice."

"When I first came here," said Rhiannon, "there was another boy. His name was Mark Watkins. He'd been here a long time. He could hardly stand up. His muscles was all wasted away. They'd been feeding him canned vegetables and dog biscuits. Then one morning he wasn't here. I never saw him again. But I saw Rachel and Nick. They was stuffing their faces with meat. I saw them taking away garbage bags after. They're keeping us like cattle."

"They can't," Sam protested. "They're not like the other grown-ups. They're not diseased. They're not crazy."

"They still need to eat."

"They can scavenge . . ."

"They want meat," said Rhiannon. "I've asked them about it. They deny it. But why else would we be here? People will do anything to survive. I've read stories. People stranded at sea, or in plane crashes. They end up eating each other. Just to live."

"You're wrong," said Sam. "You've got no proof."

Rhiannon nodded at his handcuffs. "Ain't that proof enough for you?"

"But Nick saved my life," said Sam, close to tears.

"If a wolf attacks his sheep, the shepherd kills the wolf," said Rhiannon. "But he still eats the sheep when he's hungry."

"I'm not a sheep," said Sam. "I'm a boy."

"To them you're a sheep. Or a pig," said Rhiannon. "They feed us. They give us water. They check we're not sick. They won't eat us if we're sick. That's why I'm still alive, I reckon. They're waiting to see if my chest infection is serious. There was another kid, a girl, never even got to know her name. She kept throwing up. Was too ill even to speak. They took her out. Don't know what they did to her. Maybe they fed her to the rats or to their horrible fat cat. I call them Spiderman and Spiderwoman. It's like we're bugs caught in their web. They'll keep us here until we're ready to be eaten."

"We've got to escape," said Sam, jumping up and pulling at his chain.

Rhiannon snorted.

"I did it before," said Sam. "I escaped from a nest of grown-ups at Arsenal stadium. I'm Sam the Giant Slayer. I've come all the way here from Holloway by myself. I'm not going to let these buggers hurt me. We'll all get out."

"Don't you think I've tried?" said Rhiannon, shaking her head. "I've thought and I've thought, I've looked and looked, but there's no way out of here."

Sam sat down miserably. To have come all this way and end up like this was terrible, just terrible.

But he was Sam the Giant Slayer.

And he wasn't going to give up without a fight.

38

"This is ridiculous."

"Let's just go with the flow, yeah? We're their guests at the moment. If we want to live here permanently, we're going to have to learn to get along."

It was ten in the morning. The most senior kids from the Holloway crew had been brought to somewhere called the Green Drawing Room and were standing around on the plush carpet, waiting. It was a ridiculously ornate room with patterned green wallpaper and a huge crystal chandelier dangling from the middle of the over-decorated ceiling. Apparently the palace kids were organizing some kind of ceremony for them. But it was taking forever.

The newcomers had spent the night in their sleeping bags on cots in the ballroom, which had been made up as a huge dormitory. Most had slept well. Feeling secure and safe for the first time in a long while. They'd woken feeling excited, and eager to explore more of their new home.

Freak had announced that he was organizing a soccer match. He'd found a silver cup in a trophy cabinet and had renamed it the "Arran Memorial Cup." Now most of the kids were outside playing, but not this six. From Waitrose there were Maxie, Ollie, and Achilleus. From Morrisons, Blue, Whitney, and Lewis. They were alone except for two of the uniformed boys, who were standing guard on either side of the door through to the next room.

Blue was itchy about the whole thing. Convinced that David was trying to keep him down. He'd been wanting to talk to Jester about it since dinner last night, but hadn't seen anything of him. Now the six of them had been left standing around like fools for the better part of an hour. There had been rain in the night, but the day was fine and bright, and the thought of just sitting out in the sun unwinding was very enticing.

The Holloway kids were bored and restless and didn't like being made to feel second best, but Ollie was urging them to be cautious, and tried to calm them down, even though he knew all too well that David wasn't telling them the whole truth. Ollie wanted David to play all his cards before he played any of his own. He'd long ago learned that it was best to work behind the scenes. A quiet word here, a suggestion there, was always better than blundering in with all guns blazing. He recognized Jester as someone very similar to himself. Which was probably why he'd never trusted him.

"If nothing happens in the next five minutes, I'm outta here," said Blue. "They're pulling our chains."

"Yeah," drawled Lewis. "We don't want them to think we'll do whatever they say. We don't want to look like wusses."

"All the same," said Ollie, "don't you want to see what this is all about?"

"I'll tell you what it's all about," said Blue. "Respect."

"Blue's right," said Maxie. "I've had enough of this. Let's go."

"Remember, we're guests here," said Ollie. "They can kick us all out if they want."

"Why go to all the trouble of sending Jester to find other kids if they're just going to kick us out?" said Achilleus. "They want something from us. That's for sure."

"There's a couple of sweet-looking girls who want my body," said Lewis sleepily.

"Who'd want your scraggly body?" said Whitney. "There's some buff guys here. Guys that don't reek."

Some of the kids had had baths last night, but there hadn't been enough hot water for everyone, so they were using the bathroom on a rotating basis. They'd made up a schedule and the girls were going first.

"Come on," said Achilleus. "Nothing's happening here. Let's go."

"Yeah."

Just as they were turning to leave, the doors to the next room opened a crack and a boy came through.

"I'm really sorry, guys," he said. "Didn't mean to leave you hanging around so long. I'm Pod, by the way."

Pod was big and handsome with a thick thatch of fair hair streaked with blond highlights. He wore jeans with a rugby shirt, the collar turned up. He seemed like the type who went skiing and played rugby and met up with his friends in Cornwall every year to party and go surfing.

The others grumbled hellos, making sure he noticed how pissed off they all were.

"We wanted everything to be ready for you, yeah," said Pod. "It's taken us a smidgen longer than we thought. Our fault. Sorry, guys. Now, I didn't get the chance to say hello last night. I was out on patrol with the lads. I'm sort of in charge of security. Though I gather from my friend Jester that you lot could show me a thing or two about fighting. I'm really looking forward to working with you."

"What exactly are you getting ready in there?" Whitney asked. "You baking a cake or something?"

"You'll see. We wanted it to be a surprise."

"I don't like surprises," said Blue.

"It'll be worth it," said Pod. "Trust me."

"Don't know you," said Blue. "So don't trust you."

"Fair enough," said Pod. "Yeah, good philosophy, I like it. Now, listen, I know you've all been through a lot. But just remember—we're the good guys, yeah?"

The door opened again. This time it was Jester.

"Do you want to come on through?" he said, standing aside to clear the way.

"Why not?" said Achilleus.

None of them had known what to expect, but it certainly wasn't this.

The next room was long and red, with several massive chandeliers, though the only light was coming through floor-to-ceiling windows down one side. At the far end was a row of thrones set out on a dais beneath a long plush red drape that hung from a gold canopy.

Seated on the thrones were seven people in various stages of decay. The youngest looked to be about sixteen, the oldest at least sixty. They were dressed in formal clothing that included robes and sashes, tiaras and medals. Diamond jewelry sparkled on the women, while the men feebly held on to ceremonial swords. They looked like they didn't have a clue what was going on, and were very sick indeed. Their clothes hung loosely on them, and their scrawny necks poked out of their tops like vultures. They had sunken cheeks and waxy, sweaty skin marred by spreading sores and boils. But they were quiet; just sitting, staring with big blank, uncomprehending eyes.

Four boys in uniform stood near the thrones, rifles at their sides. David was standing off to one side with Franny and another girl in a white nurse's uniform. Maxie assumed this must be the Rose Maeve had told her about. Two more girls in nurse's uniforms stood a little behind her. Jester and Pod went over to join them.

"Welcome to the Throne Room," said David.

Maxie was staring at the grown-ups. "Who are they?" she said, her voice barely louder than a whisper.

"They're all that's left of the Royal Family," said Jester. "We found them here when we arrived. Hiding. None of the big names. Not the Queen or anything. But they're still royal."

"They're a mess," said Lewis.

"Well, they're sick, but not too sick," said David. "Who knows, maybe it's their royal blood, their blue blood. Maybe it's protected them from the worst."

An old lady lifted her hand; on it was a grubby white glove. She seemed to be trying to say something. She gave up.

"At first they weren't so bad," said Jester. "They could talk and move about. I must admit they've gotten worse, though. Now they just sit there, slowly rotting. Two of them have died. I guess this bunch won't live much longer."

"That's why we need to move quickly," said David. "We need to set ourselves up in London before it's too late. If I can say I'm putting the Royal Family back on the throne, it'll make everything easier."

"Whoa, hang on," said Maxie. "What are you talking about?"

"I'm talking about sorting London out. Putting everything right. We need to take control, and people will be much more likely to look up to us, to follow us, if we have some sort of authority."

"What people?" said Maxie. "I still don't get you."

"Ordinary people. They need things like this, things from the past, to reassure them."

"This lot wouldn't reassure anyone," said Whitney.

"This is the Royal Family," said David importantly. "Legitimate rulers of England."

"No way, man," said Blue. "It's a joke."

"The kids out there don't have to know how bad off they are."

"They're grown-ups," said Lewis. "Everyone knows how bad grown-ups are."

"We'll lie. Say they're special. Show them on the balcony now and then. From a distance they'll look fine."

A man flopped to the floor and started to crawl off the dais toward the kids, saliva dripping from his open mouth. Two of the guards picked him up and put him back on his throne.

"Don't worry, they're completely harmless," said David. "But in the right hands they could be a powerful weapon. Other children out there will—"

"Wait a minute," said Achilleus. "You keep talking about other kids. What other kids? I thought this was it."

"There are children all over the place," said David. "Children like you. We just have to find them. That's what Jester was trying to do. Our plan is to organize the whole of London."

"By organize, you mean rule?" said Blue.

"Call it what you like," said David. "But if we're to stand any chance of creating a secure and prosperous new world to live in, we all have to work together. And for that we need a figurehead."

"That lot of zombies?" said Blue scornfully, pointing to the grown-ups on the dais. "They're gonna look great on the stamps."

"They're a symbol," said David. "That's all. Before, when we had a queen on the throne, she had no real power."

"At least she could walk and talk," said Blue.

"As I say," David went on, "nobody needs to know just how sick they are."

"So if they're like, the Royal Family, what does that make you, then?" asked Whitney. "The prime minister?"

"I am a sort of lord chamberlain," said David.

"A lord what?"

"The person who puts the king's will into practice. When the king is weak, the chamberlain has the power. In times of crisis you need a strong person in control. But the Royal Family can unite everyone and provide a link to the past."

"We don't want no link to the past," said Whitney. "We don't want no new royal family. You think this is going to make things easier? This bunch of idiots on the throne? You're crazy."

At this, David stormed over to Whitney and shouted into her face.

"I am not crazy! I am the only person who can pull this country back together. I am your only hope for a secure future."

Whitney grabbed David by the throat and put her face very close to his.

"Don't you ever shout at me again, boy," she said, her voice cold and calm. David's face went scarlet.

The four guards leveled their guns at Whitney. She gave them a look of utter scorn.

"Do you even know how to use those things?"

"Do you want to risk finding out?" said David, his voice tight and high.

Whitney let him go.

"What you gonna do with us if we don't want to go along with this?" she said. "Execute us?"

"Wait, wait, wait," said Jester, putting up his hands. "Hold on a minute. This hasn't gotten off to a good start. We didn't expect you to get so upset about all this."

"Then why didn't you tell us about it before?" said Blue.

"The time wasn't right. We wanted to show you the palace first. All we've achieved."

"This is too weird," Maxie muttered.

"Look," said David, rubbing his throat, "all this arguing is getting us nowhere."

"I don't want no one telling me what to do," said Blue.

"Fine," said David. "Nobody's going to tell you what to do. If you'd only listen."

"I'm listening."

"Good. Okay. This is how it works. I don't order anyone about. I just organize things. Everyone has their own job. Franny's in charge of growing food, for instance, Rose is in charge of the medical facilities, and so on. What I'm proposing is that you, Blue, would be our commander in chief, our general. You would train the troops and lead them. Everyone else here would keep the job they have now. You'd still be in charge of your own people. Things wouldn't really be that different."

Blue grinned. "General Blue?" he said. "I like the sound of that."

"One thing?" said Ollie, who up until now had been silent.

"What?"

"This army? What's it for?"

"To fight grown-ups, of course," said Blue.

"Jester told us the grown-ups had all been driven out of the area."

"It's true," said David. "But there are other problems."

"Like what?" said Ollie.

"Like St. James's Park," said David.

"Where's that?" asked Achilleus.

"Just over the road," said Maxie. "It runs all the way down to Trafalgar Square."

"So what about it?"

"We want to expand our farming activities," said Jester,

"and turn the whole of St. James's into fields. But there's a group of squatters who've set up a sort of camp there, and they don't want anything to do with us. We need to sort them out."

"These are kids, right?" said Maxie. "Like us?"

"Kids, yes, but not like us. They're not organized. They just run wild. They're a real threat. If we can sort them out—"

"Sort them out?" Maxie interrupted. "What does that mean? You want us to attack them?"

"I don't think it'll come to that. I think a show of strength would be enough."

"We don't want to fight no other kids," said Whitney.

"We might have to," said David. "If we want to control all of London."

"No way," said Whitney.

"You should see them," said Franny angrily. "We had amazing stuff planted there, they just ripped it all up and then attacked us when we went to try and fix things. We're stuck here in the palace gardens now. And with all these extra mouths to feed . . ."

"You got us here as mercenaries, didn't you?" said Maxie, giving David a withering look.

"Jester tells me you're really good fighters."

"Yeah, what's the problem?" said Achilleus. "We've had to fight to survive. If these other kids are causing problems, we sort them out. It's what we do. I'm with you, David."

"What about the rest of you?" said David.

"I need to think," said Blue. "Maybe see these kids for myself. It's a lot to take in, man."

"We are not fighting other kids," said Whitney.

"I'll decide," Blue snapped. Jester suppressed a smile.

Maxie turned to Ollie.

"What do you think?"

"We need to talk."

39

Sam had had a bad time, slipping in and out of sleep and troubled by half-waking dreams. It didn't make it any easier having his hands locked together. Although he could just lie down on the seats, the handcuffs bit into him and rubbed his skin.

He was woken by a sound from outside. Something scraping along the roof of the car. It moved, and stopped and waited, then moved again. Little cautious movements like an animal would make. The car creaked slightly. Sam stared up with gritty, sore eyes. They were playing tricks on him in the half-light, and he kept thinking he could see something coming through the roof. Some dark and twisted animal unfolding out of the shadows. Then he would blink and it was gone.

He felt groggy and confused. Cold. Helpless.

After a while he became aware of another sound. Like some small creature whimpering. He eventually realized it was one of the twins crying.

It was the boy. Sam talked to him and tried to comfort him. His name was Jason. He was very weak and wanted his mom and dad. Sam didn't really know what to say. He wished he had someone to comfort *him*, but at least it took his mind off his own troubles for a moment.

Suddenly there was a roar and a thud, and Sam nearly jumped out of his skin as the door slid open. Nick came in, carrying a plastic basin. In the permanent nighttime world of the tube station, Sam had no idea what time it was.

Nick looked around at the four kids.

"Who needs the john?" he asked. Jason said very quietly that he did. Nick unlocked the end of his chain from the handrail above and led him to the bucket at the other end. Jason could hardly walk; his legs were flabby and weak. Nick almost had to carry him.

Nick stood over Jason as he went to the toilet. Sam didn't think he could go with someone watching him, and was determined to hold it as long as he could.

Afterward Nick slopped some food from the basin into four plastic bowls. It was porridge. Made with salt and water. Sam put his to the side to eat later.

"Best eat it now, kiddo," Nick commanded. "I need the bowls back."

Sam reluctantly did as he was told, shoveling the gloopy porridge into his dry mouth. When they finished eating, Nick passed around a bottle of water for them to drink and cleaned out some of the dirty straw where one of the twins had had an accident in the night.

Sam plucked up the courage to speak. "Why are you keeping us prisoner?"

"Prisoner? We're not keeping you prisoner, kiddo," Nick said, not unkindly.

"Then why are we chained up in here?"

"For your own safety. Don't want you wandering off out there and getting lost. Or caught by no nasties."

"You're lying."

"Listen," said Nick, ruffling Sam's hair, "we just want you to get fit and well and eat properly, then we'll see about what we're going to do with you. Now don't go worrying yourself. You need to rest."

He tidied the carriage, tested all the chains, and went out before closing the door behind him and wedging it fast. There were candles still burning on the platform, but inside the car it was dark. Sam sat there miserably, trying to keep bleak thoughts from his mind. Once again he heard the thing on the roof. Shuffling, scraping, sliding.

"What's that noise?" he said.

"Rats, probably," said Rhiannon. "Or the cat looking for rats."

"Do rats ever get in here?"

"No. Nothing gets in here except Nick and Rachel."

The shuffling noise seemed to shift to the side of the roof.

"I don't think it's rats," said Sam.

"Forget it," said Rhiannon. "You hear all sorts of things down here."

Sam stared at the side window for a long time. His eyesight was swimming with blurry dots that weaved themselves into random shapes and broke apart.

He blinked and saw a face at the window staring back at him.

It was floating there, seemingly without a neck or body.

Sam wasn't sure if it was even human. It was filthy. Covered in dirt. With a bald, pointy crown and a wild straggly beard sprouting from its chin. In the center of its face were two wide eyes, the whites showing around the pupils.

Sam realized with horror that it had no mouth or nose.

He tried to scream, but his throat was frozen, like in a dream.

Yes. A dream. It must be. Something like that couldn't be real.

It was still there, though.

Sam stared at it for half a second, and then it winked and disappeared.

"Did you see that?" Sam whispered.

"What?"

Sam thought for a while. The image of the inhuman face was seared in his memory. He couldn't dislodge it from his brain. The smooth stretch of skin where its mouth should have been upset him in a way he didn't really understand.

"Nothing," he said.

40

Ben and Bernie were sitting on a cot in the middle of the ballroom they were using as a dormitory, watching the other kids argue. Bernie shook her head and took hold of Ben's hand. Why did the fighters always get so pumped up about everything? She was glad Ben wasn't a fighter. He was clever and gentle and funny. She'd never liked macho guys. The two of them had been bullied at first, but when it became clear that they had some very useful talents, they'd been accepted. Bernie wasn't sure she fully understood what the argument was about, and even if she did have an opinion she doubted they'd listen to her right now. This was war talk.

On one side were Blue, Achilleus, Big Mick, and most of the best fighters. On the other were Whitney, Freak, and Maxie, with Sophie and her archers. In the middle were Ollie and Lewis, trying to keep the peace. The little kids and the other noncombatants, like Ben and Bernie, were watching in silence. None of the palace kids were present.

It was times like these that Bernie really missed Arran. He'd have sorted this mess out ages ago. The argument was going around in circles.

"Look, there isn't anything to discuss," said Freak, not for the first time. "The fact is, we shouldn't be fighting other kids. End of story."

"Exactly," said Maxie.

"Admit it, Freaky-Deaky," said Achilleus. "You're just scared."

Freak swore at Achilleus.

"Can't you two lovers keep your personal fight out of this?" said Whitney. "This is serious."

"It's boring," said Achilleus. "You're all just a bunch of wimps."

"The thing is," said Big Mick, "these other kids, these squatters, don't mean nothing to me. Us in here is all that matters."

"And what about the palace kids?" said Maxie.

"What about them?" said Mick. "I like it here."

Freak jumped up to make a point. He was getting very emotional. Bernie hoped for his sake he didn't start blubbering.

"Arran said something the night we found Jester, he said that every kid in London is one of our own."

"That's right," said Ben.

"Nobody asked your opinion, emo," said Achilleus.

Now it was Sophie's turn to speak. She'd stayed quiet up until now, but Bernie could tell she'd been listening very carefully and waiting for her moment.

"Can I say something?"

Maxie sighed. "This doesn't really have anything to do with you."

"She's one of us now," said Ollie.

"Is she?"

"Will you please let me speak, Maxie," said Sophie, a hard edge to her voice. Maxie looked embarrassed and stared at the floor.

"Go on," said Ollie.

"As far as I'm aware, I'm the only one here who knows what it's actually like to kill another kid. I wish I didn't know how that felt. But I do. It feels horrible. There isn't a minute goes by in any day when I don't regret it. Even though I didn't mean to do it. I'm not going to put myself in a position where it might happen again. Whatever you decide, I'm not going down there."

"The girl's right," said Whitney. "We don't kill no other kids."

"I can't believe you're even discussing it," said Maeve.

"Okay, okay, everyone just calm down," said Ollie. "Let's not get carried away here. Nobody's suggesting we go into the squatter camp and kill them all. David just wants a show of strength."

"We're just going to shake them up a little," said Mick.

"But why?" said Maxie. "What are they to us?"

"You know what?" said Lewis, which surprised Bernie, because she thought he'd dozed off. He'd been sitting back against a wall, eyes closed, his Afro bigger than ever since he'd washed it. "I think, in a way, maybe David's right. If we ever want to go back to any sort of normal life, we have to make everywhere safe. Not just this little part."

"Right, so we make London safe by attacking people, is that it?" Freak said sarcastically. "Don't sound safe to me, sounds like war."

"It's only war if they want to make it war," said Lewis.

"Oh, so it's their fault . . ."

"I agree with Lewis," said Ollie. "If these squatters listen to us—if they can work with us—then we've got allies. We expand, we take over this area properly, then we move farther out—"

"What do you mean, 'we'?" Maxie interrupted. "You mean David. He's the one wants to take over London."

"Why can't you accept, Maxie," said Ollie, "that David's got a good thing going on here? And we can help him build on it. If all the little scattered groups of kids in London can link up, before you know it we'll have civilization again."

"So we make peace by making war?" said Freak.

"I guess so," said Ollie. "If that's what it takes. Look at the ancient Greeks, the ancient Romans . . ."

"I don't know nothing about all that," said Freak. "I only know that the real enemy is the grown-ups."

"And we have to unite if we want to defeat them," said Ollie. "If we can't unite, then they win. It's as simple as that. I'm sure these squatter kids will see reason. I'm sure we won't have to fight them."

"Do you really believe that?" said Maxie. "You don't know them."

"I've made up my mind," said Blue. "I've listened to enough yak-yak-yak for one night. I'm going down there to-morrow to take a look. Check these squatter dudes out. I'll take anyone who wants to come with me. Anyone wants to stay here, that's cool. I'm not forcing no one. But let's see what these guys have got to say for themselves."

"And how do you think they're going to react when you go marching down there armed to the teeth?" said Whitney.

"We'll leave the heavy stuff behind," said Blue. "We won't take no spears or swords and knives. Only wooden tool handles—you know, ax handles, stuff like that. Just in case. If it does kick off we want to scare them, not kill them."

"That sounds like a good enough plan," said Ollie. "I'm with you."

"I still don't like it," said Maxie. "But okay. Let's at least check them out."

41

Callum was running around his track. A circuit of the supermarket floor, in and out of the aisles. He'd done sixteen laps and was going for twenty. He hadn't slept well, and even now it was barely light outside. He'd had a good day yesterday. He'd found a stash of old magazines he'd forgotten about, and leafing through them had helped take his mind off his loneliness. Before going to bed, he'd gone up to the crow's nest to watch the sunset and to see if the grown-ups were still hanging around.

They were.

Dumb jerks.

And then he'd seen a new grown-up arrive, and everything had changed.

He was a father. Fat and lumpy with boils. He wore shorts and an England vest with a cross of Saint George on it, and had little patches of hair sticking out from his huge bald head. So big it looked swollen. He had a pair of wire-framed glasses with no lenses in them and seemed more intelligent than the others, even having some sort of control over them. Callum had never known grown-ups to have a leader before; they usually just hunted in loose packs. This father seemed to be rallying them, organizing them. He had even turned up with a weapon. Just a club, but it was something else Callum hadn't seen before.

The boss grown-up was surrounded by a little gang, some of whom also carried weapons. They were a mismatched bunch, but they stuck together. One had a metal-shafted arrow through his shoulder, another had a Man. U. shirt, another had no shirt at all, only one arm, and his whole body was covered in blisters. The last one wore a filthy, pinstriped suit and appeared to have a Bluetooth earpiece embedded in his ear.

The worst thing was when the bald fat one looked up and met Callum's eye. He had seemed to smile.

Callum had worried about them all night. They looked dangerous. And as soon as there had been enough light he had crept out onto the balcony to see if they were still out there.

They were.

He still had two bombs and various missiles ready. If these new grown-ups made a concerted effort to smash their way in, he'd just have to use all his firepower. For the time being all he could do was watch and wait.

He told himself he was just tired. That's what his mother always used to say whenever he was cross or worried about something—"You're just tired" or "Have you had a glass of water?" or "Have some fruit, your blood sugar's probably low. . . ."

The fat ass in the Saint George vest would get bored

sooner or later and wander off. They always did. There was no point in getting worked up about it.

He'd run a bit longer. That would help.

Maybe thirty laps.

Maybe forty.

Maybe he'd just keep running forever.

42

Blue yawned and looked up at the sky. It was a gray morning with thickening clouds. It wasn't yet seven o'clock and it looked like one of those days that was going to turn nasty. There was a distant rumble of thunder, and he shivered. He'd rather have been in his bed right now, but there was work to be done.

They'd decided that the best time to go over to St. James's Park and check out the squatters was first thing, when they'd all still be asleep. Most of the fighters were going. Though Freak and Sophie's team and a few others had opted out, Pod and Jester had joined them, with a squad of fighters from the palace.

"So what's the deal with David?" Blue asked. "How come he ain't with us?"

"He's not really a fighter," said Pod. "He's more of a leader, yeah?"

Achilleus wandered over, swinging a sledgehammer handle.

"And what about all those nerds in uniform?" he said.

"With the cool guns? How come they ain't with us, neither?"

"If David wanted a show of strength, why didn't he send them down?"

"With six guns and only about twenty bullets between them?" said Pod. "They're really just for show. And besides, they need to stay behind and, you know, guard the palace," said Pod. "If anyone, like, attacked while we were all out, it'd be a total disaster."

"Tell us about the nerds," said Achilleus. "What's their story?"

"All the boys you see in uniform were from the same boarding school," said Jester. "Down in Surrey somewhere. When everything started to go wrong, David led them all up into town. We'd already set up here in the palace, but it was chaos. David sorted us all out. He was head boy before."

"We used to play them at cricket," said Pod. "Not me—I was a rugby player—but our school."

"I suppose as he'd been to boarding school he knew how to organize kids," said Jester. "Some of the boys he brought with him work in the gardens or the kitchens, but most stayed as the palace guard. I think they did army training and everything at school."

"I still don't think they're as good street fighters as you guys," said Pod. "I'm really looking forward to seeing you in action. I might pick up a few tips, yeah?"

"I'm hoping we won't be going into action," said Blue.

"No, of course not, not today at least," said Pod.

"We were kind of hoping the fighting was over."

"Come off of it," said Jester. "You'd be bored stiff. You love fighting."

Blue grunted. Could have been a yes or a no.

"Are we going, then?" asked Achilleus, anxious to be off.

"Guess so," said Jester.

"Let's move!" Blue shouted, and they tramped out through the gates.

As they passed the Victoria Memorial someone called out. "Look at that."

The memorial had been vandalized. The Queen's face had been sprayed yellow with two black eyes and a big smiley-face grin. And there, beautifully stenciled to the plinth below her, was a message. Two big words, multicolored and vivid. They simply said:

ARRAN LIVES

And under them the tag: FREAKY-DEAKY.

Maxie laughed when she saw it.

"How can Arran be alive, man?" said Achilleus. "I watched him burn."

"It's a message from Freak," said Maxie. "Not to forget what Arran believed in."

And there was Freak, standing at the top of the steps that led down from the statue, watching the kids troop past.

"Freak's an idiot," said Achilleus.

"Don't you believe in anything, Akkie?"

"Looking out for number one."

Maxie shook her head and broke away from the group. She ran up the steps to where Freak was waiting.

"Nice artwork."

Freak shrugged.

"You don't have to go, you know," he said.

"I know. But someone needs to make sure the fighters don't get carried away. It could easily become stupid."

"Well, good luck, and take care." Freak hugged her.

"You too," she said.

"I wish Arran was here," Freak said quietly into her ear.

"Yeah," said Maxie. "Now, I'd better go, or I'll be left behind."

Freak watched her jog over to the others and catch up with the last of them as they went down into St. James's Park.

He prayed they'd all come back.

Jester slapped Blue on the back. "You see?" he said. "This is where you belong, mate, at the head of an army. Not back in the palace doing all the boring crap. Watching vegetables grow. You're a born general."

"Maybe."

There was a lake running the length of the park. The water level had dropped, but it still contained a decent amount.

"Perfect for irrigating crops," Jester explained. "Did you know? During the Second World War most of the parkland in London was turned over to allotments. There's loads of space to grow stuff, easily enough to support the kids that are left. But you have to be secure or it won't happen. Without security you're reduced to scavenging, like you used to do, and like these squatters here have been doing."

"Who are they exactly?" asked Achilleus.

"They turned up a couple of months ago," said Jester. "Far as we know, they'd been wandering around London, taking stuff as they went. First thing they did when they got here was dig up all the crops we'd planted and eat them. If we try to go near and replant, they attack us. They don't want anything to do with us. I mean, they've tried to grow new crops, but they don't know what they're doing."

"They got someone in charge?" Blue asked.

"He's called John."

"John what?"

"Just John."

"Just John?"

"Yes. Just John."

"Well, this guy, Just John, what's he like?"

"He's hard to reason with," said Jester. "Harder even than you, Blue, if you can imagine."

"He'll reason with this," said Achilleus, slapping his sledgehammer handle into the palm of his hand.

"No fighting if we can avoid it," said Blue.

"Yeah, right."

The first drops of rain started to fall.

"God's policeman," said Jester.

"Say what?"

"The police always used to pray for rain before any big demonstration, because people wouldn't turn up. Nobody wants to riot in the streets if it's pouring. Who's going to want to fight in this?"

"Let's hope," said Blue.

Out on the right flank, Maxie put her hoodie up. It would keep some of the rain off, and her new leather jacket was reasonably waterproof. She glanced over at the main body of kids. Ollie had left his position at the back and was making his way to the front. She wondered if everything was all right. She watched as Ollie approached Achilleus and said something. The two of them then broke away to the side to talk to each other in private.

Maxie liked Ollie, but she never quite knew what he was thinking, what was going on in that scheming clever mind of his. Coming to the palace they'd had an aim, something to look forward to. It had kept them going. Kept them bound together. But since they'd arrived she wasn't sure of anything anymore.

The park opened out to their left into a larger patch of grass. There was evidence of cultivation, mostly trashed, but someone had obviously tried to grow some new stuff. A few scrawny plants were drooping under the downpour. Other plants lay flat and dying in the mud.

It was a sorry sight.

"Months of work wasted," said Jester. "This bunch don't know anything."

Blue looked around and spotted a bedraggled knot of kids sheltering under the awning of the old café. A modern structure of wood and glass. They appeared to be armed, and a couple of them sprinted off in the other direction.

"I guess they've seen us," said Blue.

"Let's keep going," said Jester. "Get this over with."

"Yeah." Achilleus spat into the rain.

They soon arrived at the outlying tents of the squatters. A mixed bag, large and small, expensive and cheap, flimsy and watertight. They clustered around the end of the park with no sense of order. A few sections of ramshackle barricade had been erected, and two boys were keeping watch from under a piece of plastic sheeting.

The party from the palace walked into the camp. There was litter everywhere, strewn all over the muddy ground, hanging in the trees, piled up in corners. There was an old stroller filled with scrap wood. Apart from the few sentries they had seen, there was nobody else around. They were all either asleep or sheltering in their tents.

Across the road at the end of the park was Horse Guards Parade, a large drill square enclosed on three sides by buildings. Behind the buildings the great circle of the London Eye was visible, rising up into the rain-heavy sky.

The squatters had built more permanent dwellings here: shacks and sheds and lean-tos knocked together from scavenged materials. More plastic sheeting covered many of the structures, but much of it was sagging under the force of the storm and simply pouring water onto the already sodden gravel of the square. It looked like a refugee camp.

The palace party trudged through puddles into the center of the square, where a welcoming party was coming out to meet them. They were a ragged bunch, tanned and raw-skinned from living outdoors.

At their head was a teenager armed with a thick staff that had three knives taped to the end of it. He was wearing a pair of long baggy shorts and nothing else. His bare chest was crudely tattooed, and his short hair had been shaved into patterns a little like Achilleus's. He had several teeth missing and a hard, bony face.

"Just John, I presume," said Blue. "He don't look like much."

"Don't trust him," said Jester.

"Man," said Blue, "I don't trust no one no more."

With Just John was an older kid who looked a little like a pirate, with a bandanna tied around his head, a shirt with the sleeves cut off, the same long shorts as John, and boots without socks. He was slapping a machete against his leg.

Behind them stood four big guys carrying baseball bats.

"That you, Jester?" Just John called out, squinting into the rain that was coming down fast and heavy now, battering the ground and sending up a misty spray.

"Yeah," said Jester. "We've come to talk."

"Picked a nice day for it," said the pirate.

"When are you going to learn?" said Just John. "We don't want to talk to you."

"And we're never gonna leave," added the pirate.

"We don't want you to leave," said Jester. "We want you to work with us."

"Or what?" said Just John.

"Or we trash all this. We make you leave."

"You've tried before."

"Things are different now. We've got help."

Just John looked over the ranks of newcomers with pity and contempt.

"Ooh. Am I supposed to be scared?" he said.

"Listen," said Jester. "This is stupid. Us kids have to stick together. You and us, we can make this whole area safe. You can live properly, eat proper food."

"We're happy as we are," said John. "We get by."

Maxie looked around at their camp. It was hard to tell in the rain, but it looked like a miserable, semipermanent affair. Could anyone really choose to live like this?

"What exactly is your argument with David?" she called out.

"Whassat?" John sneered. "Did the bitch say something?"

Maxie tried not to get angry. She knew it wouldn't help.

"I asked you what exactly your argument with David is."

"What's it to you? Who are you, anyway?"

"We've come to help David."

"He getting girls to do his fighting for him now? He must be desperate."

"Answer my question," said Maxie.

"Make me."

Maxie didn't know what to say. There was no reasoning with someone like this. She understood why David wanted a show of force.

Now the pirate spoke. "Our problem with David is that he's a jerk," he said. "We don't like him. We don't want him telling us what to do. Acting like he owns London."

"Well, can't you at least let them grow their food in the park?" said Maxie.

"Why should we?" said the pirate. "It's not his park." He twirled his machete around flashily. Showing off.

"Now, why don't you sorry bunch of losers eff off and leave us alone?" said Just John.

"We need to sort this out once and for all," said Jester.

"Go on, then," said Just John, and he laughed.

"All right," said Achilleus, stepping forward.

Before John knew what was happening, Achilleus let fly at his head. His sledgehammer handle made contact, and John went down heavily.

He didn't get up again.

Everyone from both sides looked at his still body in amazement.

"What you do that for?" said the pirate.

"I didn't like him," said Achilleus. "He was getting on my tits. Now—you—Captain Jack Sparrow, what's your name?"

"Carl," said the pirate.

"Well, Carl, you seem a little more reasonable. Are you going to talk to us, or do we trash your camp?"

A laugh went up from some of the palace crew. Carl looked around, unsure of himself. He was soon joined by several more of his friends, all armed and looking for a fight.

"What's there to talk about?" he said, readying his machete.

"Fair enough," said Achilleus.

"Stop it," said Maxie. "We don't want a fight."

"You shouldn't have started one, then, should you?" said Carl. "Cuz now you're going to have to finish it."

Pod and his team started up a chant. "Fight—fight—fight . . ."

Maxie felt the situation slipping away from her.

There was a bright flash, and a few seconds later a vicious clap of thunder. Maxie hadn't thought it could rain any harder, but it did. The rain came down as a steady solid force. It made it hard to think.

The chanting continued. More squatters appeared, carrying an odd assortment of weapons. They looked confused, the rain streaming down their faces.

"Back off," said Carl, seeing he had more support. "Someone's going to get hurt."

"Fight—fight—fight—fight—fight—fight—fight—fight . . ."

Achilleus stood there, sledgehammer handle at the ready, standing over Just John.

"Bring it on, pirate. . . ."

Carl advanced toward John, hoping to help him up.

"I guess you don't want to talk," said Achilleus. "That's good, cuz neither do I."

"Stop!" Maxie yelled. "Just stop!"

"Fight—fight—fight—fight—fight—fight—fight—fight . . ."

43

reak was sitting on the steps of the Victoria Memorial, his chin resting on his knees, getting soaked.

He had a bad feeling in his guts.

What if any of them got hurt? What if Maxie got hurt and he wasn't there to help?

They'd all been through so much together. He should be with his friends. Maxie needed support. With nutcases like Achilleus and Big Mick with them, anything could happen.

And Jester too. What did he have up his patchwork sleeve?

Freak got to his feet.

The sky flashed white with lightning. There was a long rippling crack and a deep boom. It sounded like World War bloody Three.

He started to walk.

He started to run.

"Fight—fight—fight—fight—fight—fight—fight—fight . . ."

It was on.

Achilleus ran at Carl, easily dodging a halfhearted swing from his machete. He ducked in and butted Carl in the guts with the end of his club. As Carl doubled over, Achilleus brought his knee up and connected with his face. Now Carl was down. Achilleus kept going, and soon two more of Carl's friends were also taken out.

This gave Pod confidence, and he and his gang charged forward with a shout. They grabbed a flimsy support holding up the roof of one of the shacks and pulled at it. It only took two or three heaves and the whole shack twisted and toppled sideways, spilling rainwater everywhere.

Pod's team cheered.

"Stop it!" Maxie screamed, but her voice was lost in the chaos.

The camp had come fully alive, and kids poured out of the shacks like angry wasps. The entire palace squad was forced into the fight now, and a messy brawl developed in the square. Fists and sticks were flying. The kids were kicking, gouging, wrestling. Not many of the squatters were armed, and Achilleus and his fighters concentrated on those that were, trying to get their weapons off them without getting hurt.

Freak was pounding along the walkway by the lake. He could hear the distant sounds of fighting.

"Shit!"

He kept his eyes open for something he could use as a weapon. He had nothing with him.

"Stupid!"

Some kid he didn't recognize stepped out of the café as he passed.

"Hey, what are you—"

Freak barged into him and sent him flying.

He raced on.

Blue was standing there, watching, not sure what to do.

"We've got to stop this," said Maxie, shaking him.

"How?" said Blue.

"Take charge," said Maxie. "Do something."

Before they could say anything else, a group of squatters ran at them, and Blue was forced to hack away at them with his ax handle. A hail of shot and small rocks from Ollie's squad rattled into the squatters' legs, and they fell back, hobbling and swearing.

Pod and his boys were moving from shack to shack, pushing them over. A fat girl ran out of one, shrieking.

"What are you doing? What are you doing?" she shouted. "There's kids in there!"

Pod wavered, and the wail of a distressed baby came clearly from inside the shack, which was rocking dangerously, ready to collapse. Pod's team tried to steady it.

"Idiots!" Blue ran forward and ducked inside. He emerged a second later with a baby in his arms and almost chucked it at the girl. He was instantly back inside, and reemerged with a second baby. He turned and went back in as the girl yelled that that was all of them.

He didn't hear, and the next moment the shack went down with a creaking, splintering sound. Pod and his team began to frantically pull aside sheets of plywood and corrugated metal, planks and boards, and bits of plastic.

While everyone was distracted, Maxie went to find Just

John. He was stirring, trying to sit up, his lethal spear held limply in his hand. If she could take him out, she might be able to stop this.

She had Arran's club in her backpack. She'd been hoping not to use it, but she needed it now. She reached back for it and felt a terrific blow in her side. It took all her breath away, and it felt like her ribs had been caved in. She staggered sideways, her vision blurred with the pain. Out of the corner of her eye she sensed a movement and turned to fend off another attack. The second blow caught her in the upper arm, and she lost all feeling in it.

It was a squatter with a baseball bat. He wasn't big, but he had two others with him. One of them swung at her, and she ducked, but it hurt like hell to move, and she thought she might pass out. There was no way she was going to avoid the next swing.

Suddenly the three squatters went down like bowling pins.

It was Freak. He had barreled into them full speed. As they struggled to get up, he grabbed a fallen bat and laid into them like a maniac.

Maxie was doubled over, fighting the pain and trying to draw some oxygen into her lungs.

Freak was making short work of his fight; one of the squatters ran off, another went down and didn't look like he was getting up again. Freak was just about to finish off the last one when he yelled and sat down on the gravel. He looked confused. A bubble of saliva formed on his lips. There was an ugly patch of blood spreading across his back.

Just John. He'd stabbed up at Freak from the ground with his horrible three-bladed spear.

"No!" Maxie's cry sounded like the snarl of a wild beast. All her pain forgotten, she moved quickly, with an inhuman strength fueled by rage and despair. Arran's club swung through the air in a blur of silver gray. It slammed into the shaft of John's spear and knocked it out of his hands.

He looked up at her, surprised. She raised the club above her head.

"Tell them to stop!" she shouted. "Now!"

"Make me, bitch."

Maxie swiped the club across John's face. It smashed into his nose and flattened it sideways. He howled. Maxie kicked him flat and picked up his spear.

"Now tell them!" she shouted, pressing the blades into the soft skin at his throat. "And don't ever call me a bitch again, you ugly piece of shit."

Just John mumbled something, blood streaming from his ruined nose into the gravel.

Maxie looked over and saw Carl, with a bunch of tough-looking squatters, grappling with Achilleus and his best fighters.

"Everybody stop now!" she screamed, finally making herself heard. Kids paused in what they were doing. Carl looked furious. All he could see was the blood pouring out of Just John, and Maxie standing there holding his spear. What had she done to him?

"I'll kill him!" Maxie yelled. "I swear it! Now stop! Throw down your weapons."

"You better do as she says," said Achilleus.

"Do it," Carl ordered, and the squatters gave up the fight.

Pod had finally gotten to Blue and was dragging him out of the ruins of the shack. His body was limp and lifeless. He'd been knocked cold by a falling beam. He was still alive, though. Pod ordered his team to make a stretcher out of bits of scrap.

Lewis watched them, his Afro flattened in the rain, his head looking two sizes smaller. "We're going to need another one of those," he said.

Pod gave him a quizzical look.

"Freak's hurt."

There was a sullen mood in the camp as the squatters surveyed the damage. Many of their shacks were completely trashed. Half of their tents trampled. They were getting thoroughly soaked. Younger kids were crying.

Achilleus and the fighters were standing in a ring around Just John, who still hadn't got his senses fully back. He was lying on the gravel, bewildered and bedraggled.

Another group was clustered around Freak, who was sitting where he had dropped. Ollie was pressing a piece of torn cloth over the wound in his back. Maxie was holding him in her arms.

"I don't want to die," Freak whispered.

"Then don't," said Maxie, trying not to sob. She looked at Ollie, who had a look of utter hopelessness on his face.

"I don't feel good," said Freak. "I wish my mom was here. How she was. Before she got sick. I wish everything was how it was before. I never asked for any of this. It was just me and Deke. Spraying our tag on the walls."

"Freaky-Deaky," said Maxie.

"Yeah . . . Is Deke here? Where's Deke?"

"He's not here."

"Neither am I," said Freak, and he closed his eyes.

"The bleeding's stopped," said Ollie.

"He's dead," said Maxie.

45

They wrapped Freak in a blanket and carried him gently to one of Pod's stretchers. They lifted Just John to his feet and tied his hands behind his back.

Maxie looked at the sky and then walked over to where the squatters were standing watching. She looked for Carl, the pirate, who seemed to be John's second in command.

"Here's the deal," she said, her voice cold and hard and clear. "We're going back to the palace and we're taking John with us. You have until this evening to decide what you want to do. But before it gets dark you send someone to the palace to talk to us, and we'll figure out what happens next."

"What do you mean what happens—"

"Shut up, Carl. I'm speaking. Two things can happen. One: you turn up and make peace, we figure out how we can all get along, and you take John home with you. Happy ending. Or two: no one shows up and we come back here with a bigger force, with all our weapons, and we don't hold back. We wipe you out. Kill you if we have to. You understand? It's your choice."

46

"On a Friday or Saturday night we'd get pizzas and watch DVDs."

"Me too . . . Only we used to get Indian takeout."

Sam and Rhiannon were sitting in the darkness of the car. The nightlights that Nick and Rachel kept burning twenty-four hours a day on the platform outside cast no light in here. All Sam could see was a vague yellow glow in the window, and Rhiannon's head silhouetted against it. They were sitting opposite each other, keeping the fear away by talking of old familiar things.

"I used to love chicken tikka," said Rhiannon.

"Me too," said Sam. "But we didn't get Indian food much. It was too spicy for my little sister, Ella."

"Don't she like chicken tikka? Everyone likes chicken tikka."

"She likes it a bit. But she's not very good with food. She's fussy. All she really likes is plain cheese pizza."

"Boring," said Rhiannon.

"I bet you wouldn't say no to one now, though," said Sam.

"Maybe we could call for a delivery," said Rhiannon, and she giggled.

"Domino's," said Sam. "Can I take your order?"

"Veggie Supreme."

"I don't think I ever had one of those."

"We'll rent a DVD and have pizza," said Rhiannon. "What shall we watch?"

"We used to watch TV series mostly," said Sam. "Sometimes three episodes in one night."

"Yeah," said Rhiannon. "I love box sets."

"*Star Trek*," said Sam. "And *Heroes*. But it was a bit gory."

"We were halfway through *Lost*," said Rhiannon.

"That was too scary for Ella," said Sam. "She liked *Ugly Betty*. She didn't really understand it, though."

"Did you have a Wii? We had a Wii."

"No," said Sam. "I used to play games on my computer. World of Warcraft."

"My favorite was The Sims."

"Yes, I sorta liked that. But I preferred World of Warcraft. I had a Tauran shaman called Dorkcrawler. I wanted to call him Darkcrawler, but that name was already taken. I also had a Night Elf Warrior called Deathbloooood, with four O's, and a gnome called Shortybottom. He was level sixty-two."

"Were you on Facebook or MySpace?"

"No. My mom wouldn't let me," said Sam. "I used to use MSN sometimes, but mostly I played World of Warcraft. Though I was getting a bit bored of it. My friend had Grand Theft Auto. I really wanted to get that, but Mom said no way."

There was a muffled thud from somewhere down the

train. Sam and Rhiannon fell silent. They were both asking themselves the same question.

What was that?

It was a sound they hadn't heard before. It could mean that Nick and Rachel were up to something in another car. Killing something. It could be other grown-ups attacking. It could be a brick falling from the roof.

Or it could be something to do with the nasty face at the window, and that posed as many questions as it answered.

Of all the things that had happened to him, the face freaked Sam out the most. The fact that it had no mouth.

Was it the mouthless creature that had made that sound? The truth was, it could be anything. But as the children lived a mind-rotting existence of boredom mixed with fear, their imaginations were working hard and fast.

There were no more clues. The thud was followed by a long period of quiet.

Sam and Rhiannon sat there in the darkness. Unmoving. For a brief moment they had been at home, with their families, snuggled up on the sofa on a Saturday night.

Now they were back in this cold comfortless train car.

They could hear the twins sleeping, their breathing shallow and feeble. Sam felt something touch his knee. He realized it was Rhiannon's fingers. She was reaching out for him. He took hold of her hand and squeezed. She was trembling. After a long while, which seemed like hours, there was another thud, nearer this time. Once again it was followed by nothing but deep silence.

Sam could stand it no longer. He went over to the window. Looked out at the platform. There was nothing moving out there. The sound hadn't come from the direction of Nick and Rachel's sleeping car, and he hadn't heard or seen anything of them, but it was possible that they could have gone down to one of the other cars without being noticed.

At last there came another bang, closer still but muffled again. Then a light appeared at the window in the door leading to the next car. A small flickering flame. Sam screwed up his eyes, straining to see what it was. He couldn't go any closer, as his chain prevented him from moving far.

Now a sheet of cardboard appeared at the window. It had been ripped from a computer box and there was writing on it. Seven words scrawled in marker pen. Whoever was there adjusted the cardboard so that the flame lit it from the side.

Sam read:

kip qwite I am her to help

It took him a few seconds to realize that it was meant to say "Keep quiet I am here to help." And no sooner had he figured it out than the cardboard disappeared and was replaced by a face.

Sam jumped.

It was the same face he had seen at the window.

Only it was different.

He smiled.

What an idiot he was.

When he had seen the face before, it had been upside down. Hanging from the roof of the car.

The bald crown had been its chin. Sam had been looking for a mouth where the forehead was.

Now that it was the right way up he could see that it was a boy's face. Black with dirt, eyes wide, small sharp teeth very white. There was a shock of dark, tangled hair sprouting from the top. The hair that Sam had thought was a beard when he had first seen it upside down outside the car.

The face grinned and then its owner raised a fist and gave a thumbs-up. The flame snapped off. A few seconds later there was a familiar dull thud and the sound of falling glass, tinkling onto the metal floor.

"If you hear the butchers, yell." It was the quietest whisper in the world.

Then silence.

Sam counted the seconds in his head. It was all he could think of to fill the time and ease the tension that was growing inside him like a balloon inflating.

He got up to sixty-five before the flame flickered back on. Startlingly close. Sam jerked back in fright. The boy had climbed through the window and come down into the car without them hearing or seeing anything. The flame was lit just long enough for them to get a proper look at him. He was about Sam's size, skinny and wiry looking, wearing shorts, sneakers, and a woman's leather jacket with the sleeves cut off halfway. He had a leather backpack slung over one shoulder, and he was carrying a cigarette lighter and a blanket.

He flicked the lighter and the flame died.

"Not safe," he whispered. "If the butchers see the light, they'll come running, mark my words."

"Who are you?" said Sam.

"Stay quiet," the boy hissed. "You're getting out of here pronto."

Sam felt the boy's hands groping along his arms to the handcuffs.

"Handy-cuffs," he breathed in Sam's ear. "Soon have these bracelets off. No more than a jiffy."

There was rattling and scraping as the boy poked around in the lock with some kind of tool. Then, finally, a snap and rattle and the cuffs came loose.

Sam now felt the boy slip the lighter into his hands.

"Light me, skipper," he said. "The Kid needs to see his surroundings."

Sam rolled the flint on the lighter, and the flame jumped and sparked. The boy was already at the end of the car, holding the blanket across the whole width.

"There's sticky-tape on my utility bat belt," he said, nodding downward.

Sam saw a roll of strong black tape hanging from a piece of string at the boy's waist. He gave the lighter to Rhiannon, and in a minute had managed to roughly tape the blanket up. Now if Nick and Rachel happened to look along the length of the train from inside their car, the blanket would block some of the light.

The boy grinned at Sam.

"Nice work," he said, and pushed Sam against the blanket. "Press your ear against blankie. Tell me if you hear anything moving, anything speaking, squeaking, or meandering, even a mouse's fart, so to speak. Get it? Got it? Good."

The kid scuttled over to Rhiannon and inspected her wrists. Instead of handcuffs she was secured with plastic bindings.

"Naughty," he said. "I'm going to need to cut." His hand

darted into his pocket and came out with a little folding knife with a wide blade. He pulled it open with his teeth and smiled at Sam.

"This should do the trick, eh, Jeeves?" he said. "It's a wicked little snickersnee. Not half."

He took the lighter from Rhiannon, gave it back to Sam, and set to work. The blade was razor sharp and it sliced through the plastic in no time. As soon as Rhiannon's hands came apart, he blew out the flame.

"Lights out, boys and girls."

He drew Rhiannon and Sam into a huddle.

"We have to go careful and quiet as spies. Can't risk too much light. It's like this. If I'd tried to get on the train from the platter-form, those beastly butchers would have spotted me, no sweat. So I've gone right to the end and I've bonked and bashed my way all the way down the cars, cuz Mr. and Mrs. Lovely have fixed all the doors and windows shut. So we go back and out that same way. Once we get to the end, we drop down on to the tracks and slither back along under-the-neath of the train to where we can get up on to the platter-form and thence to the stairway to heaven. It's the best way. Safe as milk. You follow?"

"I'm not sure I can walk," said Rhiannon.

"You can walk. When they have to, your legs will do as you say. Just speak to them firm."

"I can't."

"No such word as *can't*. No such word as *babagoozle* neither!"

Rhiannon laughed, trying to stifle the sound.

"You talk funny," she said.

"That's just the way it is," said the boy. "Now let's get these two snoozing muckers out of here. Match me, Sidney!"

Sam figured out what he meant and quickly lit the flame again.

The boy hopped over to the two sleeping twins, unlocked them, and shook them awake. They were groggy and feeble, with no idea of what was going on.

"This is going to be tricky, captain," the boy whispered. "These ones are weak as kitties." He glanced up at Sam. "You strong enough to help carry 'em, squirt?"

"I don't know," said Sam. "I'll try. I don't feel too good myself."

"You don't look it, skipper."

Jason looked up at the boy, fear pulling at his face.

"Who are you?"

"I'm the Miracle Kid," said the boy. "The lizard boy, something of a worm and something of a cat. King of the tunnels. I'll have you out of here in a thrice, I do declare."

Jason opened his mouth wide to say something, and the Kid put a finger to his lips and shushed him. He winked.

"I'm your ticket outta here, buster-balloon. Hoick your bones up and let's get shifted."

"I'm not leaving," said Jason.

"Are you joking me?"

"I can't leave here," said Jason anxiously. "Where will I go? Nick and Rachel are looking after me until I'm well."

The Kid looked around at Sam and Rhiannon. "He really believe that?"

Sam shrugged. "We're all confused," he said.

"I've seen the rest of this train, my old china," said the

Kid. "I've seen what they're up to. Had my peepers on them for some long time. I found my way down here looking for food, skulking like a blind mouse, running up their clocks, so to speak. You get me?"

"No, not really," said Sam.

"Half of what I say is rubbish," said the Kid. "But listen to this bit. I could smell food. You get me? Mm-hmm—finger-licking good. But I don't want to eat what those two ghouls are serving up. Wish upon a star, squire, that you are gone from here soonish, before they get their teeth into you. Trust me, young man, you do not want to stay for dinner."

"I'm not leaving," said Jason. "I don't know you. Nick and Rachel are looking after me. I can't walk. I'm sick."

The Kid hefted Jason onto his shoulder and tried to walk; he went about five steps before he stumbled, and Sam just caught them as they fell. The commotion woke up Claire, the other twin. She was even more feeble than her brother, and spent most of her time sleeping.

"What's going on?" she said.

"It's all right," said Rhiannon. "We're getting out of here."

"I don't want to go," Claire whimpered. "I'm tired."

"She can't stand up," said Jason. "Leave us alone."

The Kid looked at Sam. "It's beyond me," he said. "I'm quick and slick and well nifty, but I ain't strong enough to lug no dead weights."

"We'll never do it," said Sam. "We won't get them through the windows."

"We'll have to leave them," said Rhiannon, struggling to her feet. "We don't have a choice."

The Kid sat down cross-legged on the floor and looked glum.

"Had me heart set on it," he said. "Was gonna get you all out of here. Was gonna be a hero for the first time."

"You *are* a hero," said Sam. "But you're not Hercules. You can't do the impossible."

"You want to leave them too?"

"If they don't want to come, we can't force them."

The Kid jumped up and grabbed Sam. "Persuade them, small fry. The gift of the gab, the wagging tongue. Only we can't waste too long here. The more noise, the more light, the more chance that the butchers will stir from their slumber and come sniffling after us."

Sam knelt by the twins, who were sitting huddled together with wide, scared faces.

"We're used to it here," said Jason. "It's safe from strangers. We get food. We don't have to worry about anything."

"But they're going to kill you," said Sam.

"You don't know that."

"What happened to Mark?" said Rhiannon. "And that other girl?"

"They got well," said Claire. "Nick helped them to go up into the light. When we're well, when we're strong, they'll help us too."

"You're idiots," hissed Rhiannon, and Claire began to cry.

"Just keep it quiet," Rhiannon whispered, and then moaned in pain as she tried to walk, biting her lip to stop from crying out.

"My legs are so stiff," she said.

"Unstiff them," said the Kid. "We have a good deal of climbing to get done before we're home free."

"Okay. I'll try."

"So," said the Kid. "Do we leave them or take them with?"

"Let's go," said Sam.

"We're gone."

47

The Kid scampered down the length of the car, almost on all fours, keeping low. Sam followed. The Kid had broken the window in the door at the end. The glass in the door of the next car was also broken. Sam looked at the gap between the cars—he thought he might just be able to squeeze down there. He caught the Kid's eye. The Kid glanced at Rhiannon and shook his head.

There was no way she'd fit.

Instead, the Kid laid his piece of cardboard over the jagged lower edges of both windows, and wriggled through.

He turned in the opening and grinned back at the others, beckoning them to follow.

Sam helped Rhiannon along the car, leaving Jason and Claire crying behind them. Rhiannon was struggling to catch her breath, and wheezing horribly. They made it to the window, though, and Rhiannon climbed up onto the cardboard.

It took forever to get her across. Bravely, she didn't make a sound, though Sam could see that it was agony for her, with her infected lungs and her wasted legs. But she struggled on, and, with the Kid pulling and Sam pushing, she at last got through both windows and into the next car.

Sam jumped up after her and wriggled through without any trouble. He was so intent on helping Rhiannon that he barely noticed his own aches and pains.

As soon as Sam put his feet down, the Kid was off and moving.

This car, which Sam had caught glimpses of when Nick had let him go to the toilet, was used as a storeroom. All the pathetic bits and pieces that Nick and Rachel had collected from underground were in here. Chairs and tables with the tube logo on them, some tools, crates filled with bits of scrap metal and wood, coils of wire, piles of old newspapers and magazines.

The children hurried down the central aisle, half dragging Rhiannon, until they got to the doors at the far end, where there was more broken glass strewn on the floor. The Kid scraped it aside with his sneakers and once again laid the cardboard across the sharp edges of the window frames.

They repeated the same maneuver as before, but it was even harder this time. Rhiannon seemed weaker and more breathless. Sam remembered helping his mom put his duvet back in its cover after it had been washed, how the duvet was big and floppy and wouldn't go where you wanted it to. It was the same with Rhiannon, trying to somehow shove her up and through the narrow gap.

Sam was sweating and tired out when they finally got her through, and she landed with a nasty thump on the other side. He quickly hopped up after her, though, and clambered across.

They settled Rhiannon on a seat, and she rested. Sam looked around. This car was where Nick and Rachel kept spare food. Cans mostly, filled with fruit, vegetables, meat, pudding, fruit juice, and soup. There was even a separate stack of dog and cat food.

"Where'd they get it all?" asked Sam.

"Some of the under-the-ground stations, they got shops in them, gyms, clubs, all sorts, you poke about down here, baby, you'd be amazed at what you turn up. Mark my words."

"So much stuff," said Sam. "Surely they don't need any more. Maybe you were both wrong. Maybe they weren't going to eat us."

"They were looking through a telescope," said the Kid. "Looking ahead. And they has a plan. Fatten you up on the stuff they don't want to eat, then eat you when you're ripe and juicy."

"I feel sick," said Rhiannon.

"Don't sit there like a lazy lump feeling all sorry for yourself," said the Kid, and he pulled her to her feet. "We've got work to do."

He hurried her along the car, Rhiannon grumbling every step of the way.

"This next one's not so pretty," said the Kid as they approached the window.

Sam could smell it before he got there. The sickly sweetness of decay, mixed with a salty, meaty pong.

"We're nearly out," said the Kid. "Next car is the last. I've opened the doors at the end. We can get off the train, so we can."

This time Sam honestly didn't think they were going to make it. He was sure Rhiannon was going to get stuck halfway, and they'd all be trapped down here. The poor girl was weeping, and every movement made her gasp. But they at last managed it. She was through to the last car. Sam struggled after her. Slower this time, feeling the tiredness in his bones and muscles.

Flies buzzed around, and the smell was stronger in here.

"Hold your hooter," said the Kid, flicking on his lighter. "And try not to look."

But of course that was the worst thing he could have said. Sam couldn't help taking glimpses on either side as they went along toward the car door.

He got brief flashes.

Something hanging from a hook on the handrail. A bucket catching drips of fat. A box with three small brown skulls in it. A pile of bones on the sawdust-covered floor.

He felt vomit rising in his throat and he fought to hold it back. Rhiannon wasn't so lucky; she fell in a messy heap to the floor, puking and sobbing.

"We have to go back for the others," she said. "Tell them what we've seen."

"No way, holy ghost," said the Kid. "We got to keep moving and save our own bacon, else we'll end up swinging from a hook."

"I can't stand it," wept Rhiannon.

Sam knelt by her and gently put an arm around her.

"It's all right, Rhiannon," he said. "You'll be all right. We'll soon be out of here. Maybe we can get help and come back to rescue the others."

"Yes." Rhiannon sniffed and wiped her nose. "Okay. Yes. I'll be all right."

Sam helped her up. In the center of the car was a huge block of wood, a chopping block, scarred from much use, stained black. A meat cleaver was embedded in it. Sam wrenched it free.

"Leave it, shrimp," said the Kid. "I already thought of that. Too heavy. No use to you."

"I'll use it if I have to," said Sam. "I'll kill the both of them."

"Not with that, you won't. It's for a grown man, not a pipsqueak like you. You need a skinky like mine. I looked, there ain't nothing else here of use to a desperado. That great chopper will only slow you down."

Sam tried to lift it, but the Kid was right. He'd barely be able to swing it in a fight. He dropped it to the floor with a clatter.

And then he saw something else. Lying in a box of skewers.

His butterfly pin.

He snatched it up. He felt strong again.

"I've got my own skinky now," he said. "Let's go."

"Please," said Rhiannon. "I need to rest. I can't go on."

"In here?" said the Kid. "You gotta be pulling my plonker. Up and at 'em, Tiger Lil."

The Kid took them to the door, opened it, and dropped down to the tracks. Rhiannon sighed and grumbled, but she followed him while Sam brought up the rear, his heart racing.

"Why do we need to go back to the platform?" he said.

"We can't go no farther this way," said the Kid. "Tunnel's blocked. All we got to do is go back under-the-neath of the train, to the join between the cars. There's space to get out there."

"I know," said Sam. "I've done it before."

"Then let's do it." The Kid gripped Rhiannon by the shoulders. "Do you feel up to some Olympic sneaking, my girl?"

Rhiannon swallowed. She was breathing heavily and could barely nod her head.

They scrambled along in the gulley underneath the train. The Kid didn't dare use the lighter anymore, so they had to feel their way, just as Sam had done when he'd first escaped from the grown-ups in Camden Town.

How long ago was that?

He had no idea.

It didn't take them long to get to the gap, and Sam peered out.

The nightlights still bathed the area with a yellow glow.

He looked along the platform to the right. It wasn't far to the way out at the end. The length of one car. But they would be exposed all the way and would have to climb over the bed frame that was blocking the exit.

"This is the hard part," whispered the Kid, poking his head out next to Sam's. "Open ground. There's no way around it."

The boys ducked back under the train.

"We got to dash across there like froggers," the Kid told Rhiannon. "If we make it unseen, we're home free. We'll slimper up topside and be gone. If they spot us, it's a different

319

story, morning glory. Curtains I reckon, and blinds and shutters as well, maybe, probably carpets too. What do you say, girl?"

"Her name's Rhiannon," said Sam. "I'm called Sam."

"Nice name. Nice girl. Pleased to meet you. I shoulda brought flowers or chocolates or a dead mouse."

Rhiannon giggled, and it lifted Sam's spirits. There was always hope.

Rhiannon put her hand on Sam's shoulder. "You go first," she said. "If I see you can make it, it'll make me braver."

"You sure?"

"Go on. Good luck."

Sam looked out. As far as he could tell it was all clear. He squeezed through the narrow opening and shuffled on his belly onto the platform. A quick glance to left and right, then he sprinted to the end in a low crouch and gave the bed frame a quick once-over. It was secured in place with a chain and padlock. He would need the Kid's help.

His heart was hammering, the blood pulsed tight in his head, and he felt sick again. He looked back. The train was still. There was no movement in Nick and Rachel's livingcar. The doors were shut.

Rhiannon was slowly groping her way onto the platform; the Kid was obviously pushing her from below. Helping her up. Sam knew how hard that was. Once up she lay there on her stomach, catching her breath. The Kid quickly whispered something in her ear, and Sam waved him over.

Somehow the Kid seemed to blend in with the surroundings and almost disappear, moving like a rat and sliding into the shadows next to Sam.

"Nothing to it," he whispered, his teeth very white in the darkness. "Piece of Coca-Cola."

Sam showed the padlock to the Kid, who made short work of it, wriggling his tool in the lock until it clicked open.

It was a nightmare trying to unthread the chain without making a sound, but between them they managed it and were able to slide the bed frame back just far enough to squeeze past.

"Let's get the babe, chicken legs." The Kid signaled to Rhiannon.

"Don't call me that," said Sam crossly. "I don't have chicken legs."

"They sure are skinny."

"You're not exactly fat."

"Not exactly, no—"

"Shhh." Sam clamped a hand over the Kid's mouth.

Rhiannon had gotten to her feet and started to come across. She was limping and fighting for oxygen. Moving painfully slowly.

"Come on," said Sam. "Come on, you can make it."

He could just see the expression on her face. Desperate, scared, yet determined. Nothing was going to stop her.

"She's gonna make it," said the Kid. "Come on, girl. Come on, my Rhiannon."

Then Rhiannon staggered and fell to her knees. She couldn't stop herself from grunting, and Sam held his breath.

"Get up, girl," said the Kid, but Rhiannon couldn't.

"Come on," said Sam, and the two of them left their cover and went over to her. They hooked an arm under each shoulder and wrenched her up.

They hadn't gone three steps when there was a movement. Something darted out of the shadows and skidded to an alarmed halt in front of them. It was Orion, Nick and Rachel's ginger cat. It put its back up, fur on end, and gave a hideous squalling shriek.

Sam jumped back in shock and then swallowed hard as the door to Nick and Rachel's car slid open with a harsh scrape of metal, and there was Nick with a face like fury.

"Hey!" he called out. "Where do you think you're going?"

"Does that hurt?"

"Yes!"

"Does that?"

"Yes—everything hurts!"

Maeve sat back in her chair and tried to give Maxie a reassuring smile.

"Well, I don't think your arm's broken," she said. "It could have a small fracture, but I don't think so. It's very badly bruised."

"I don't need you to tell me that."

"You're a terrible patient, you know."

"I don't want to be a patient. What about my ribs?"

"They could well be broken. But there's no bones sticking out or anything. You can't do much for cracked ribs. You just have to be careful. And try not to laugh."

"That'll be easy."

Maxie stared up at the ornate ceiling of the ballroom. All wedding-cake plasterwork with gold leaf and fancy bits and pieces. Dusty chandeliers dangling down all over the place. Funny how quickly you got used to all this.

"Maybe you should go up to the sick bay with Blue," said Maeve. "Let Rose and her nurses look after you. They're pretty organized up there."

"No," said Maxie. "I'm not putting myself in their hands. I'll be all right."

She didn't feel all right. Her side was one big bruise, and she could barely move her arm.

And she couldn't stop thinking about Freak.

They'd buried him in the palace gardens that morning, as soon as they'd got back from the fight. Standing in the rain, everyone silent and miserable. Maxie had wanted to say a few words, like Freak had done when they'd burned Arran's body, but she had nothing to say.

"I'll get you some more painkillers," said Maeve.

"Thanks."

"And try to think positive thoughts. You'll get better much quicker."

"Positive thoughts . . . ? Right."

"I know it's hard."

"The idea was, Maeve, that when we got here everything was going to be all right. But it isn't. Everything's crap."

"Come on," said Maeve. "Don't forget so soon what it was really like back at Waitrose. It was hell. There was one less of us nearly every week."

"At least before, we knew where we were. We were friends. We stuck together. Now there are too many of us. We're falling apart. Losing touch with each other. It's too complicated."

Before Maeve could say anything, the doors opened and Ollie came in.

"I've just been up to see Blue," he said. "He's in the sick bay with that girl we rescued near Green Park."

"I'd forgotten about her," said Maxie. "How is she?"

"Pretty bad, I think."

"And Blue?"

"He's conscious, at least, but being sick everywhere. Puked up this stuff that looked like egg yolk."

"Bile," said Maeve. "Often happens if you get concussed."

"Is anyone with him?" asked Maxie.

"Whitney was up there, but Rose got rid of us. Says he needs to rest. How are you doing?"

"I'm fine."

Ollie sat down. "David wants to talk to you about what happened this morning."

"I've got nothing to say to him."

"We owe it to him to—"

"We don't owe him anything!" Maxie exploded, then winced and clutched her aching ribs.

"We do, actually," said Ollie. "They've given us their food. They've let us stay here. David may be a dick, but he's smart and he's organized. We don't want to screw things up."

"I'm not going to spend the rest of my life fighting his fights for him," said Maxie. "What kind of a life is that?"

"Right now it's the only life we've got," said Ollie. "Wherever we go in London it's going to be the same. We're going to have to fight. That's how the world is now. Better that we fight for something that's worth it. Better that we stick with the strongest bunch around. With whoever looks like they're coming out on top."

"Okay, so what if those bastards we fought today look like they're coming out on top? Would you join them?"

Ollie sighed and ran the fingers of both hands through his red hair.

He thought for a while, but said nothing.

49

Sam and the Kid were holding Rhiannon's hands and dragging her through the station as fast as they dared. It was dark and they couldn't risk using the lighter. None of them was sure of the way out; they only knew that they had to keep going up. That was easier said than done. The station was a maze of tunnels and hallways with openings going off in all directions to other platforms and other tube lines. It would have been confusing enough with the lights on—Sam had never really got the hang of the underground system—but in the dark it was a nightmare.

After spotting them, Nick had ducked back inside the car to get something, and the children had bolted. It would only be a matter of time before he caught up with them, though. He knew his way around and he was faster.

"We need to hide," said the Kid.

"Where?" said Rhiannon.

"Search me," said the Kid.

They heard pounding footsteps behind them and looked back to see a flashlight beam scouring the darkness, bouncing off the walls. The Kid whipped his lighter out and lit it one-handed. They saw an exit sign and followed it. They ran down a short tunnel, turned to the right, and spotted some escalators. Two of them, going up, with stairs between them.

"That way," the Kid hissed, and they darted up the middle. It was easier taking the stairs than the stationary escalators, which had taller steps.

When they got to the top, Rhiannon was wheezing and panting, doubled over in pain. It was obvious they'd need to stop soon. But when the Kid flicked on the lighter, they saw that they were faced with more stairs and an exit sign pointing to the right.

"We've got to keep going," Sam said to Rhiannon, who couldn't speak.

"We must," said Sam, and he shook her.

Rhiannon gulped. Nodded. The boys took her arms and dragged her along again.

Another tunnel. Another escalator. Dim light filtering down from above.

"We must be nearly there," said Sam. "Once we're outside it'll be easier."

"I-won't-make-it-up-there. . . ." said Rhiannon, every word hurting her.

Sam looked around. There would have been two escalators here, but one of them had evidently been under repair. It was boarded off. There was only the one way up and down. There was a pile of trash dumped at the foot of the out-of-order escalator. Bits of plywood and wire and sheets of cardboard.

The footsteps were getting nearer. The flashlight beam was shining along the tunnel they had just come through.

Sam nodded to the pile of trash, not daring to speak.

The three of them climbed behind some cardboard and ducked down, huddled together, trying to make themselves small. Rhiannon was still fighting for breath.

"I can't go on," she wheezed. "I feel like I'm going to explode. I'm so dizzy. Don't make me. Please . . ."

"Shhh," said the Kid. "Be quiet now."

Sam made sure he could see what was going on, peeking from behind a flap of cardboard. He watched Nick come charging down the tunnel, his flashlight in one hand, his sawed-off shotgun in the other. Behind him came Rachel, also carrying a flashlight. They both shone their beams quickly up the escalator.

Rachel swore. "Did they go up?"

"Dunno. Couldn't hear anything," said Nick.

"Have they gotten away?"

"They can't have," said Nick. "They was only just ahead of us."

"Did they go the other way, then?"

"Could have. Could be anywhere."

Rachel looked back up the escalator. Something was making her nervous.

"Maybe we should let them go, lover?"

"Let them go?" said Nick. "After all the food we've wasted on them?"

"I don't want to go up top."

"Maybe they're not up there," said Nick. "Maybe they never made it this far."

"You think maybe they're still down in the tunnels?" said Rachel.

"Must be. I'll go back down and look."

"I'll keep going up to the ticket hall," said Rachel. "I'll holler if I hear anything."

"All right," said Nick. "But be careful."

"Ah, they're only kids," said Rachel, and she started up the escalator.

Nick ran off back the way he had come.

Rhiannon had been trying to hold her breath, to stop from making a sound, but it was too hard for her—she took a long rasping gasp of air that rattled in her throat, and Rachel's flashlight beam swiveled around.

She came back down the stairs.

"Who's that I hear?" she said softly. "Is that you, kids? Are you there? Don't be scared, it's only me. It's Rachel. I know you must be terrified as anything, all alone up here in the dark. Don't worry, I'll look after you."

As she spoke she reappeared at the bottom of the stairs and edged closer to the pile of trash, her voice soft and reassuring, like someone talking to a kitten or a frightened bird that had gotten into the house.

Now her flashlight beam fell on the three of them, and she smiled, tilting her head to one side.

"There you are, my lambs," she cooed. "Don't be frightened, now. Just look at you. You shouldn't be out, should you?"

Sam could feel Rhiannon next to him trembling, and he could hear her breath scraping at her lungs. He gripped his butterfly pin tight.

"Come on. Come to Mommy. I'll look after you. Haven't we kept you warm and well fed? Hmm? Haven't we kept you safe from harm, kept the bad ones away? Hmm? You don't want to go out there into the big world, now, do you? Whatever would you do? All those crazies out there. You're much safer with Rachel and Nick, now, aren't you?"

She got herself into a position that blocked their escape, then straightened up and bellowed at the top of her voice.

"Ni-ick! I found 'em! They're up here, love!"

"Get her!" shouted Sam, and he charged at her, butting her in the stomach with his head. She grunted and staggered back, but she was strong and Sam was small. It reminded him of play fights with his dad. His dad had pretended to be beaten, to be hurt, when Sam knew all along he could have picked him up and tossed him across the room.

"Now, now," said Rachel, holding her temper in. "That's enough of that." She cuffed Sam to the floor, and he went down hard. But now the Kid was up and out, beating Rachel with his fists. Even Rhiannon joined in. They had all seen the meat wagon. They knew what Rachel was capable of. Between the three of them they tripped her and sent her tumbling to the ground. Sam lunged at her with the pin, but only managed to scratch her neck.

"Where did you get that?" Rachel roared, finally letting her anger show as she struggled back onto her feet. "Give that back!"

"It's mine," said Sam. "You should never have taken it."

"Give it to me!" Rachel snapped, and as she made a snatch for it, Sam stabbed it into the palm of her hand. She shrieked and jerked her hand back. Almost immediately she batted him to the ground again, using the flashlight that she was holding in her other hand, smashing the bulb. She tried to stamp on Sam, but he rolled out of the way and jabbed the pin into her leg. Her shriek this time was terrible. Loud and piercing, it echoed off the tiles. Sam scrambled up, grabbed Rhiannon and the Kid, and they started up the escalator.

It was agony for Rhiannon, and halfway up, Sam knew they were never going to make it to the top. He was just about to say something to the Kid when there came an almighty bang and a flash, and Rhiannon screamed.

The three of them stumbled and fell over in shock. Sam was stunned; the noise and the light had completely disorientated him. It was a few seconds before he realized he was unhurt, but Rhiannon was crying. She was three steps below him. He sat up and put his hand out to her. Her top was wet. He could see it stained black in the dim light. She was bleeding. Some of the shot from the cartridge had hit her.

It was clear she wasn't going to go any farther.

"Go on," she croaked. "You'll never make it with me."

"No," said Sam, but then Nick's voice rang out in the half-light.

"Don't move, none of you, I'll aim the next shot straight at you."

"Keep down," said the Kid, "and run like mad. He can't shoot and point his flashlight at the same time."

"We can't leave Rhiannon," Sam wailed.

"Just go!" said Rhiannon.

Sam didn't know what to do, but the Kid decided for him—he pulled Sam up by his shirt, and the two of them darted up the stairs.

Nick was running up after them, but when he got to Rhiannon she threw her arms around his knees and they went crashing down to the bottom. It was all the two boys needed to get away.

They were in the ticket hall at last, a pale light showing them the way out to street level. There were shouts and screams behind them. Sam tried not to imagine what was happening, but he silently thanked Rhiannon. He would owe her for the rest of his life.

They vaulted the ticket gates and headed for the stairs.

They ran up three steps at a time.

The daylight hit Sam like a blow. He was blinded. He staggered along, shielding his eyes from the glare. It was physically painful, and he had an instant headache. He was vaguely aware of a church and tall old buildings.

He felt the Kid grab him.

"Move it, slowpoke," he said. Sam squinted at him— the Kid had produced a pair of sunglasses from somewhere, a big pink pair in the shape of love hearts. Sam resisted the urge to laugh. It was the Kid who should be laughing; at least he could see what he was doing. He dragged Sam down the wet pavement. Sam could just make out, through the narrowed slits of his eyelids, where he was. This was the City of London—where old and new London butted up against each other, modern skyscrapers shouldering up through Victorian buildings on a higgledy-piggledy medieval street layout. "We need to hurry, dog," said the Kid.

Sam stumbled on, feeling the Kid tug him across the road. They came to a paved area in front of a massive building that looked like a Greek temple. Sam's eyes were getting a little better. They weren't hurting so much. He looked up at the statue of a man on a horse. Then something jerked him back, and he was thrown against a wooden bench.

It was Nick.

"I'm going to slaughter you, little pigs," he snarled. His dreadlocks were flapping around his head like the rays of the sun in a child's drawing. His face, though, was twisted into a picture of rage. There was no sign of Rachel.

He held his shotgun in one hand, but before he could bring it around on Sam, the Kid threw himself at his arm, knocking it sideways and smashing the gun into the base of the statue. The gun exploded in Nick's hand, and he dropped it, the barrel bent out of shape.

Nick didn't waste any time, and pulled a knife out from inside his coat. He glanced at the Kid. He'd fallen heavily, the gun going off very close to his face. He looked stunned. Winded.

Nick turned his attention back to Sam, who was struggling to open his eyes properly, squinting in the bright light. He saw that Nick was having trouble, too; his eyes were red and tears streamed down his face. He wiped them away and blinked at Sam, raising his knife. It was old and well used, with a wide, curved blade, worn thin from constant sharpening. He took a swipe at Sam, who ducked. He felt the knife swish across the back of his head, ruffling his hair. Nick immediately brought the knife back again, and as Sam dodged to the side, he felt a sting in his neck. He backed away, down some steps, toward the road. He splashed through a puddle. It had been raining. He realized that the sun wasn't even out. Though the clouds were beginning to break up in the sky.

He was breathing fast. He knew he couldn't keep this up

for long. Nick was too big, too fit. Sam was just a kid.

"Hold still, you little pig," Nick hissed. "I'll make it quick and painless for you. If you muck me about, though, I'll string you upside down and bleed you slowly, just you see that I do. You'll feel every minute of it. I promise you that. Now, hold still."

"Go to hell!" Sam shouted, his voice a hoarse croak.

"I'm already there," said Nick, and he chuckled, so sure was he of success. "Didn't you know I was Satan, hisself? Old Nick. That's me."

Sam swore at him, using all the dirty words he'd ever heard, and some he'd made up. Nick just laughed louder.

Sam scrambled under a van, and for a moment felt safe, until he realized he was trapped now.

Idiot.

He should have run.

The ground here was oily, and he was soon black with filth. He saw Nick's lower legs as he stalked around the van, banging on the sides and calling out in a high-pitched voice.

"Here, piggy-piggy-piggy, come to Nick." Then he stopped and ducked down. Sam saw his grinning face appear below the edge of the van. He reached out a hand for Sam, who just managed to slither back from it. But it was a bluff. Nick quickly dodged around the van and made another grab for him. As Sam tried to shift again, his shirt caught on something and he was stuck. Then he felt Nick's hand take hold of him, and he was dragged out, kicking and yelling.

Sam looked for the Kid and saw him struggling groggily to his feet over by the statue. The Kid then bent double and vomited. Nick tucked Sam under his arm, clamping him tight, and strode back over to the Kid. Nick aimed a kick at his backside and pitched him into the street.

The Kid wasn't going to be any help.

Nick set Sam down and held him upright with one hand. He raised his other hand above his head. The sun came out from behind a cloud and shone onto the blade, the sharpened edge glinting like liquid fire.

"I'm going to cut your little pig's head off," Nick said with relish.

He paused. Licked his dry lips. He didn't want to rush this.

This boy had caused him a lot of trouble. He wanted to see the fear and pain in his eyes before he finished it. He wanted the brat to know full well what was about to happen to him.

The boy's eyes were satisfyingly wide. There was a look of horror in them that pleased Nick. They were fixed on his knife, as they should be.

No. Wait a second. Something was wrong. The boy wasn't looking at the knife at all. He was looking at something else. His eyes had flicked down and appeared to be looking at Nick's hand.

Nick frowned and looked up.

A rash of spots was spreading across his skin; already one or two had swollen into fat blisters. His throat went tight. He could do nothing but stare, mesmerized.

He should never have come out into the sunlight.

Sam couldn't tear his eyes away, either. It was like watching a piece of food in a microwave. Nick seemed to be cooking in front of him. Another crop of blisters and boils blossomed from the knuckles, as his fingers swelled up like bloated slugs.

Nick moaned. The knife was wobbling in his grip, his puffed-up hand no longer able to keep hold of it. He dropped it, and it fell to the pavement with a clatter.

"Look what you've done," he said in a strangled voice, and Sam looked at his face. The skin there was erupting too. Pearly boils were spreading from one ear across his cheek. His lips were growing fat, like sausages in a frying pan, the skin tightening then bursting.

It was as if all the evil inside Nick were erupting, forcing its way out of his body. The boils began to pop one by one, leaking blood and pus down his face. His eyes were swelling too, the blood vessels showing dark red. They bulged out of his face. Sam could imagine that someone had stuck a bicycle pump in Nick's ear and was inflating his whole head.

Then Sam had to look away as the eyes burst.

Nick let go of Sam and put his hands up to cover the wounds. He opened his mouth wide to scream, but Sam saw that it was filled with swellings and lumps and ulcers, his tongue a fat warty toad-thing, forcing its way out from between his teeth. His throat was completely blocked, so that he could neither breathe nor speak.

He no longer looked human. His whole body was bulging and writhing. He dropped to his knees. Blind. His hands groping the air. They looked like two udders and were still filling with liquid so that in a few moments the fingers had all but disappeared, the blackened stubs of the fingernails all that remained.

Sam saw the knife lying on the ground and picked it up, ignoring the stickiness on the handle. He felt almost sorry for the thing that had once been Nick. He wondered if he should put him out of his misery. But before he could bring himself to do anything, Nick's skin split and he seemed to disintegrate completely. He collapsed to the pavement, a mass of putrefying, liquefying flesh and steaming entrails that bubbled and hissed in the sunlight.

Sam retched, and then felt the Kid's hand on his arm.

He sang a little ditty.

"TV highlight of the week . . ."

"What happened to him?" said Sam.

"Blame it on the sunshine. That's why Mrs. Spiderlady wouldn't come out. She's going to be so angered, but what can she do about it? Now let's get gone from here."

"Shouldn't we go back for Rhiannon?" said Sam.

"Can't," said the Kid. "Look . . ."

He nodded to where a group of grown-ups was lumbering along the road toward them.

"We need to get out of here sharpish, skipper. Poor girl's probably dead as a dormouse already. Just thank her in your prayers."

"I don't pray," said Sam. "I don't believe in God."

"Well, somebody up there's looking after you, titch. Now let's motor."

They ran off down the road, hand in hand, Sam glad of the human contact.

50

They arrived at sunset. Carl, the pirate, had brought ten of the meanest, toughest-looking squatters with him, plus a couple of smaller kids. Wiry little bruisers with even more attitude than their larger friends. They were escorted to the Throne Room and came in intending to be unimpressed, to play it cool, to show the stone face, but now they were all standing there with eyes wide, mouths hanging open.

"Oh, my days," said Carl. "This is unreal."

Everything about the scene was unreal. The decrepit Royal Family were slumped in their thrones, drooling. Just John was standing to one side, his hands tied behind his back, his feet loosely roped together so that he could walk but not run. There was a wad of cotton wool taped across his nose, and his eyes were ringed with purple bruising. He looked uglier than ever.

David and Jester stood on the other side, arms folded. David's suit was clean and pressed, his tie immaculate. The palace guards were at attention in front of the thrones, wearing their red-and-black uniforms, their rifles at the ready, trying their hardest to look like professionals.

Pod and his team of fighters were along one wall. Maxie and the chief Holloway kids were along the other wall. Maxie thought it was like some ridiculous school play, like Shakespeare or something, with kids pretending to be kings and queens and soldiers. But she was interested to see how the scene would play out. She could see a faint smile curling David's lip. For the moment he had the upper hand. The squatters were thrown, their guard was down.

He raised his hand for silence and started to speak.

"This morning my ambassador spoke to you."

Maxie bit her lip. Since when was she David's ambassador?

Just John obviously didn't like the idea of an ambassador any more than Maxie did.

"Ambassador?" he said, his voice sounding choked and nasal. "What you talking about, moron?"

"The girl, Maxie, was speaking on my behalf. Now I will speak for myself."

"Listen, mate," said Carl. "We didn't come here to talk, we came to get John."

"That wasn't the deal, though, was it?" said David. "The deal was—if you wanted John back you'd have to talk."

"There's nothing to talk about," said Carl. "As I see it we won the fight."

"But we've got John," said David.

"This doesn't need to get heavy," said Jester. "We don't have to be enemies."

"Who says?"

"We have food here," said Jester. "We have security. We also have many more kids than you do. We have weapons as well, good weapons, and a well-organized army. All we're saying is—why not join us? Together we can be strong. We can take on any other gang of kids. We can rule London."

Again Maxie winced. She had no desire to rule London. She just wanted a roof over her head, food on her plate, and to be able to sleep at night without waking every half hour in a sweat of fear and anxiety. But maybe this was the only language the squatters would understand.

"We don't want you to change," said David.

"That's big of you," said Just John.

"You can keep your camp," said David, ignoring the interruption. "You can still be in charge, John. But we make peace. We grow food together. We share everything. If there is an outside threat, we stand shoulder to shoulder against it."

A couple of the squatters sniggered at David's fancy language. But Carl was looking at Just John quizzically.

"You say you won this morning," Pod chipped in. "But we could have destroyed your whole camp if we wanted."

"You didn't fight fair," said John. "You cheated."

Now it was the turn of some of the palace kids to snigger. The idea of someone like Just John complaining about fair play was more than faintly ridiculous.

"I could have beaten you with a blindfold on, man," said Achilleus. "You are sad."

"Oh, tough guy, aren't you?" said John, and Achilleus shrugged. "I was trying to talk to you and you whacked me.

If I'd've been ready for you, you wouldn't be standing there now."

"If you was any good you'd have been ready," said Achilleus. "But you ain't nothing."

"All right, all right," said David, raising his hands again. "That's enough of that. We don't need to start an argument. This isn't about fighting each other; it's about becoming allies."

"This is boring," Achilleus muttered. "It's too much like politics."

"All I'm asking for is a truce," said David.

"There's unfinished business," said John darkly.

"What unfinished business?" said Jester.

"Me and him." John pointed at Achilleus.

"You want another fight, I'm ready," said Achilleus.

John spat on the carpet and shuffled over to Carl. The two of them had a quick quiet chat, which ended with Carl slapping John on the shoulder.

"We're ready to make a deal," he said.

"As long as you understand that we might not accept it," said David. "As I see it, we have the upper hand. We have John prisoner, and—"

"You gonna listen to our deal or are you gonna blab, fancy boy?" said John.

"I'll listen," said David. "But it better be good."

"It's good," said John. "It's the best you'll ever get."

"Go on then."

"It's like this. We'll do everything you say. We'll help you grow food; we'll join up with you if anyone attacks. All that you said. We'll make a truce. On one condition."

"Which is?"

"Him there." John was pointing at Achilleus. "If he can beat me in a fair fight."

"It's a deal," said Achilleus without any hesitation.

"Wait," said Maxie. "That's just stupid."

"Yeah?" said Carl. "Well, it's our deal. Take it or leave it."

"What do you say, David?" asked John, his chin raised cockily.

"What if we lose?"

"If you lose you can forget any kind of truce, and if you want to start a war, that's fine with us. We'll be ready for you."

"Wait a moment."

David and Jester went over to Achilleus. It was their turn for a quiet chat.

"Can you beat him?" David asked.

Achilleus smiled. "No problem. I took him before. I can take him again. He's all talk."

"Are you sure? A lot rests on this."

"You don't think I can do it?"

"He can do it," said Jester.

"All right." David broke away from the huddle. "You've got a deal."

"Wait a moment," said Maxie, pushing between David and Jester. "We need to think about this."

"I *have* thought about it," said David. "It's agreed."

"Wait . . ." said Maxie, and Achilleus put his hand on her arm.

"Don't you want revenge?" he said. "For what he did to Freak? Don't you want to see him dead?"

"If I'd wanted that, I could have killed him myself this morning."

"Revenge, Maxie."

"I don't want revenge. And I don't want any more fighting."

"It's not your decision," said David, and he walked over toward John.

"The two of you will fight for it," he said. "Our champion against yours."

"All right." John smiled, showing his small, jagged, yellow teeth, and shook hands with David. He didn't let go. Instead he leaned closer until their faces were only about an inch apart. "The winner decides what happens between us. The loser gets buried with a nice ceremony and some flowers."

David laughed, trying to pull his hand free. "I don't think we have to go quite that far," he said. "We're not talking about a fight to the death."

"Oh yes we are," said John, and he grinned wider. "It's the only way to decide it. A fight to the death. We've shook on it."

A great hubbub broke out in the room. There were cries of protest, and angry accusations. John stood there, smiling his smile, clutching David's hand in an iron grip. David looked unsure of himself. Once again he turned to Achilleus for reassurance.

Achilleus was unfazed.

"What's the problem?" he said once the noise had died down. "That's my kind of fight."

He walked over to Carl and the other squatters. "Better

get your shovels ready, chaps. You're gonna have some digging to do."

"No!" Maxie shouted. "This is horrible. We're not animals."

"Speak for yourself, bitch," said John, and the room erupted into a chaotic frenzy of shouting and shoving.

John stood there in the middle of it all with his broken-toothed grin, his hard bony head nodding slowly on his long neck.

51

Sam and the Kid were sitting at the bottom of the Gherkin. The weird skyscraper that looked like a huge vegetable. They were finishing off the last of the provisions from the Kid's leather backpack. Some murky water in an old plastic bottle and a can of peas.

They'd been wandering, lost, through the empty canyons of the City of London for the last hour. The street plan made no sense. There were no straight lines; roads twisted and turned and came to sudden stops. The boys were trying to reach the river so that they could get their bearings, but it was proving impossible. Every direction they tried seemed wrong, or took them back to where they'd started. So time and again they made their way back to the Gherkin as the chief landmark in the area.

And now it was growing dark.

Paper fluttered in the air. Sam looked up to see that it was spilling from a broken window high up in the Gherkin.

He didn't like it here. The glass walls of the towers that loomed on either side reflected each other back at themselves.

It was like a city designed by a madman. The scale was all wrong and none of the buildings matched. There would be an old church right next to an office block made of metal that looked like a giant engine. Everywhere there were abandoned building sites, some little more than deep holes in the ground, others home to the steel skeletons of office blocks that would now never be finished. Cranes stood over them, and the boys had seen three that had fallen, smashing into the buildings next to them.

"Shall we try again?" said the Kid.

"Okay."

They got up stiffly and set off, trying a new route.

"We need to keep our eyes peeled like spuds, Frodo," said the Kid.

"It's Sam," said Sam testily.

"Oh yeah, sorry, I knew it was one of them hobbits."

"And besides," said Sam. "You don't have to tell me to look out. I can look after myself. I've survived on the streets all by myself."

"Not these streets," said the Kid.

"They're all the same," said Sam.

"Not so," said the Kid. "You never know what you're going to find around here. This part of London is way weird. Things happened differently here to how they did everywhere elsewhere, I reckon. That's why your bully-butcher friends down below didn't become sickos. This is an old place. There's some kind of special magic here. Some old power, from the dark days, the storybook time, maybe even before Caesar and his Romans came, eh?"

"I don't believe in magic," said Sam.

"I believe in everything, titch," said the Kid.

"Don't call me 'titch.' You're not much bigger than me."

"I know I ain't, but you're still small, buster boy. You're a right tiddler."

"I'm a giant killer."

"I can believe it. As I say, I believe everything, shrimp."

"Don't call me that," said Sam. "Or I'll call you rat boy."

"Midget."

"Tree frog."

"Crumb."

"Scab."

"Plankton."

"Poop head."

"Poop head?"

"Yeah," said Sam, giggling. "That's what you are. You stink."

"Not as bad as you, pip-squeak."

"No, you smell worse, you smelly sock."

"Don't you call me a smelly sock, you hairy yellow vetch."

"Rat boy, rat boy!"

"Squirt."

"Ass."

"Hold up." The Kid tensed and went into a crouch. He was looking intently down the street, like a hunting dog. Sam looked in the same direction.

It was another group of grown-ups. The third they'd seen since they'd been up here.

"We need to be somewhere else, microbe," said the Kid.

"You're a microbe, you punk," Sam muttered wearily as they turned and ran.

52

Achilleus was sitting alone in the palace kitchen, eating a big bowl of spaghetti with tomato sauce. It was warm in here and quiet. He wanted a little time to himself before the fight, to get his act together. He was loading up on carbs, like a runner before a marathon. He'd put on a tough front upstairs, put on his macho hat, but he knew it wasn't going to be easy. Just John was one mean bugger.

There was a knock on the door and he glanced up from his bowl.

It was Jester. He was carrying a small round shield.

"I've been looking for you," he said, coming into the kitchen.

"You've found me."

"Yeah." Jester dropped the shield on the table with a clatter.

"Thought this might be useful," he said. "It's ceremonial, really, but it'll be better than nothing."

Achilleus got up from the table and picked up the shield. It was made of lightweight steel, backed with wood and leather. He slipped his arm through the strap and held on to the grip.

"Yeah," he said, experimenting, moving his arm, raising and lowering the shield. "Feels good. Coulda used one of these before."

Jester sat down. "You really think you can win?"

"I gotta think that, dog, or I ain't got no chance."

"I could see if I could find you a piece of armor, or something," said Jester.

"Nah," said Achilleus, taking the shield off and returning to his dinner. "It'd only slow me down. Wouldn't be used to it. I'm all right like this."

He had changed into a fighting outfit. Sweatshirt and pants. Sneakers. A marked contrast to Jester in his patchwork coat. What was with that coat, anyway? Achilleus had been meaning to ask, and now might be his last chance to find out.

"Tell me something, Mister Magic," he said.

"What?"

"David goes around in that nasty suit, everyone else here is kind of preppy, like they're all at private school or something. But not you, you wear that tatty old coat. What's that all about?"

"I used to live in Notting Hill," said Jester. "West London."

"Ritzy."

"I suppose so. Anyway, when it happened, what you call the disaster—"

"Ain't it that? What do you call it?"

"I don't call it anything," said Jester. "It's what it is. It happened. So, as I was saying, I ended up in this big house. Massive place. With a load of other kids. Mostly friends to start with, but more and more joined us. It was easy back then. There were loads of big houses around there. A lot of rich people. They'd hoarded stuff like you wouldn't believe. It was rich pickings at first. We thought we had it made. But then . . ."

"Grown-ups."

"Grown-ups. Bad ones. And a lot of them. We didn't have anyone like you, Akkie. We didn't stand a chance. There was a girl with us, Persephone."

"Greek name."

"I suppose so. But anyway, the first of us to get it was her sister. We divided her things up among us. But Persephone, she took one of her sister's party dresses, her favorite, and cut a patch from it. Sewed it onto a piece of cloth. To remember her. Then every time another kid died, Persephone made a patch from their clothes. Made a sort of quilt. She showed me how to do it. You know what it was like, there wasn't much to do to pass the time. And when Persephone was killed, I added her patch. Kept the cloth. In the end we had to leave Notting Hill, it got too bad. Headed into town, where it was quieter. Some of us died on the way. But not everyone. Rose was with us. One or two others in the palace. And when we got here I made the quilt into this coat. To carry those dead kids with me. You know how many patches there are on here?"

"How many?"

"Forty-three. No, forty-four. I added Freak today."

He showed Achilleus a fresh patch.

"And this one here is Arran."

"You took his shirt?"

"He didn't need it anymore."

"You're deep, man," said Achilleus. "Really deep. You happy to let David boss you around?"

"Are you?" said Jester.

"As long as I got something to eat, somewhere dry to sleep, I'm okay. I don't want to be no boss. Too much to think about. But you . . . do you even like David?"

"He's bonkers," said Jester. "Gets nuttier every day. But it kind of works. For now. He's sixteen, you know? Quite old."

"Yeah?"

"Yeah. I sometimes wonder if that's what's making him the way he is. I watch him all the time for any signs—you know, boils and that. Nothing yet. None of us knows what's going to happen as we get older. . . ."

"Don't like to think about that stuff, man," said Achilleus. "Don't like to talk about it."

"No. I'm sorry." Jester paused. Studied Achilleus. Then went on. "If you win tonight, Akkie, you're going to be in a very strong position, you know. I don't know if David understands that. You could topple him if you wanted."

"Told you, Magic Man, don't want to be no boss."

"No," said Jester. "But you and me. We'd make a very good team."

"Excepting I couldn't never trust you, man. I'd fear to turn my back on you. You're a backstabber."

"I'm a survivor, Akkie, a winner like you. There are forty-four kids on this coat that didn't make it. And I'm the one wearing it."

"You gonna add another patch tonight? After I've fought John?"

Jester shrugged and stood up. "Let's hope it's not your patch."

"Yeah. Well, with this shield you've given me, I reckon I'm safe. It'll give me the edge over Johnny boy."

"You do realize I had to give him one as well."

"You what?"

"We can't have them crying foul."

"You're one slippery bastard, Jester, you know that? I suppose you've had this exact same chat with Just John, haven't you?"

Jester laughed and went out.

53

The quadrangle, the large central courtyard of Buckingham Palace, was crowded. Kids hung out of the windows, waiting. Others stood around the edges of the space, looking toward the center, where flaming torches had been set up to make a ring.

Not all the kids were here. The younger ones and the more squeamish had been kept away. Some hadn't even been told what was happening. Many of the smaller kids still woke from nightmares, screaming in the dark hours. They had had a very traumatic time. They didn't need to be exposed to any fresh violence.

Maxie wished she wasn't here either, but she couldn't bear to leave Achilleus to fight alone. She had to know who was going to win. She still couldn't really believe that this was happening. It was like some awful barbaric Roman gladiatorial contest. She had never exactly liked Achilleus. He was a typical boy—a bully, used to throwing his weight around, lazy and rude and full of himself—but she nevertheless respected him as a fighter. Valued him. He had saved them all on many occasions. Before the disaster she never would have hung out with someone like him. In these tough times, though, he was a good person to have on your side. They'd been through a lot together. The thought that he might die today was too terrible to contemplate.

And what was the alternative? That Just John would die. Another kid.

Yes. He was a truly horrible person. Like Achilleus ten times over. And he had killed Freak.

That morning, she would gladly have seen him dead. She'd almost killed him herself. But not anymore. And not like this.

She didn't want to ever see anyone die again.

She'd had enough. Holding Freak as he'd slowly slipped away had been awful. And what had made it worse was that afterward she hadn't felt anything. Just a numbness. A blankness.

Maybe there were no more tears left inside her.

She looked around at the faces of the assembled kids. Some were keyed up, some slightly glazed and shocked like herself, some sitting on the ground, nervous and quiet. The thirteen kids from the squatter camp stayed together in a huddle. The younger ones at the front, like they were about to watch a show, shoving each other, jostling for position, chatting excitedly.

And there was David with Jester and his uniformed guards clustered around him. David looking all high and mighty. An emperor. His champion ready to fight the barbarian champion. She noticed that Ollie was with them. She wondered sadly if he'd gone over to the other side.

There was no one for Maxie to talk to anymore. Ollie was with David. Arran was dead. There was always Whitney, but she was in the ballroom with the little ones, trying to distract them from what was going down.

In a funny way she missed Blue. Even if he had been somewhat condescending. At least he understood what she was going through. He knew how hard it was to be a leader.

Was she still a leader? She didn't know anymore. Everything had changed since they'd come here. Things were slipping out of her control.

She felt a tap on her shoulder.

Sophie. Standing there with her archers.

Maxie was torn. Under different circumstances they would have been friends. Sophie was someone Maxie could talk to. She would understand. But Maxie couldn't tear down that wall between them.

"What do you want?"

"I've come to tell you we're leaving," said Sophie.

"What?"

"We just can't stay. If it hadn't been for Arran maybe it might have been different. As it is—we don't like David, and you don't like us. We've never fit in. And then the fight today. We've made up our minds, we're going to get away while everyone's here. But I didn't want to go without saying anything."

"Where will you go?"

"Don't know, but we survived on the streets for a year, and it does seem to be safer around here, so . . ."

"Good luck . . ."

Sophie gave her a quick hug.

"I wish things had been different," she said, and she slipped off into the shadows.

Maxie stood there stunned. Had she driven Sophie out. . . ?

Before she could get things straight in her mind, a great shout went up as Achilleus walked into the center of the ring.

Maxie looked around.

There were Pod and his fighters, like schoolboys at a soccer match, cheering their side on. Couldn't they see how obscene this was? How disgusting? Had they really come to this? Was a human life worth so little now? She supposed this must have been what it was like in a coliseum. No different than a cup final. Cheer on your favorite; boo the losers.

No matter that they were going to be slaughtered.

She winced. The pain in her side was worse than ever. It hurt just breathing. She'd give anything to be able to rewind the events of the last day.

Achilleus did a circuit of the ring, pacing it out, then took his sweatshirt off and went over to Big Mick, who was standing with Lewis. Achilleus gave Mick the shirt and nodded as his friends urgently talked at him from either side. They seemed to be giving him advice. Meanwhile, Just John emerged carrying a shield and his spear. He strutted backward and forward in front of his crew like a caged lion, bouncing up and down on his toes, flexing his arms, throwing challenging glances over to Achilleus.

Achilleus ignored him. He looked to be slowly withdrawing into himself. Gathering his strength, sharpening his concentration, holding himself in.

"Come on, then, Gaylord!" John shouted over to him, spinning his vicious three-bladed spear around his head. "Kiss your boyfriends good-bye and come over here. Or are you going to roll over?"

Lewis handed Achilleus his spear. Maxie noticed that it had been freshly sharpened, the tip glinted silver, honed to a needle point. It was made from a long steel spike, with a pommel at the blunt end and thick leather bindings just behind the head to stop another weapon from sliding down it. Achilleus was always working on it, getting the balance just right. It was lethal, but John's looked more lethal, with the three knives strapped to the end of its sturdy wooden shaft. One jab from that would cause a terrible wound, and he handled it expertly. He must have practiced for hours every day, twirling it around from hand to hand.

Lewis scratched his head. He looked half asleep as usual, but he was nervous.

"That's an evil spear he's got there," he drawled.

"It's clumsy," said Achilleus. "It looks nasty, but it's not aerodynamic, not with them stupid knives stuck on the end. It's not weighted right."

"Don't matter," said Lewis. "It's a killer. And he looks like he's killed some."

"And I haven't?" said Achilleus.

Lewis shrugged. "This is different, bro," he said. "This is another kid. He's fit, man, and strong. He ain't no shuffling zombie like the grown-ups."

"He's flesh and blood like anyone else," said Achilleus.

"Don't he scare you?"

"'Course he scares me," said Achilleus. "You think I'm

nuts? He's a hard-nosed son of a bitch. So I'm gonna keep on my toes."

"Not so hard-nosed now," said Big Mick. "You land him one in the middle of his face, he's gonna feel it." He handed Achilleus his shield.

"Thanks," said Achilleus, shoving his arm through the strap. "Shame John's got one of these too. But them knife blades of his aren't going to be as strong as my spear. If I can get him to keep knocking them against my shield, they're gonna bust."

"Just make it quick," said Mick. "He's taller than you, with a longer reach. He'll be hard to get at."

"He's full of it," said Achilleus.

"Hey!" John was yelling again. "Gay boy? You coming out to play?"

Achilleus sniffed, stepped away from the crowd, and swung his own spear through a couple of gentle arcs.

"Ready," he said, and strolled casually into the center of the yard. He moved gracefully, like an athlete. Still holding it back. Unlike John, who was pulsating with wired-up energy, his head bobbing, his muscles jittery.

"I've never fought a gay before," he said, and spat at Achilleus's feet.

"What's with all the insults?" said Achilleus.

"Oh, sorry," said John. "Am I upsetting you, darling?"

"If you fancy me, why don't you just say?" said Achilleus affably.

"That the best you got?" said John.

"It's all you deserve, loser. Now, are you going to talk, or are you gonna fight?"

David pushed forward from behind his line of guards, chin up, a snooty expression on his pale freckled face.

"When I give the word, the fight will begin," he said. "And let's not forget that this contest will decide what—"

But Achilleus and John weren't listening. Before David had finished speaking, they ran at each other, roaring, spears at the ready.

Wait!" David shouted. He was wasting his breath. John and Achilleus clashed together, their spears thudding into one another's shields.

Achilleus looked at John's spear. It was undamaged. The tip of his own weapon, however, had broken off. He had sharpened it too much. He wasn't used to fighting someone with a shield. No matter. It would still do some damage if he made contact.

One – nothing to John, though.

He didn't have long to think about this as John launched a furious attack; evidently he had the same idea as Mick—go in hard and get it over quick.

He ran at Achilleus, driving him back with a series of short, powerful thrusts. Achilleus used his shield to block the assault. He soon found that he didn't have the muscles for it. Holding it up used a lot of energy. He held on, and in the end he saw a gap and managed to get in a counterstrike. Jabbing beneath John's shield at his legs. John saw it coming and skipped out of the way, but it broke his rhythm, and he stopped his assault. Achilleus grabbed the breathing space and moved away, dancing around the ring, loosening his muscles. He had tensed up under John's attack and needed to work off any cramps before they took hold.

The attack had given John some encouragement. He strutted around the ring with a sneer on his face.

"Had enough, batty boy?"

In reply, Achilleus suddenly lunged at John with an overhand downward stab that took John completely by surprise. He got his shield up only just in time and managed to knock the blow aside. Achilleus was left wide open, and John came straight back at him, slicing his spear upward. The triple blades slashed across Achilleus's chest, ripping his T-shirt and drawing blood. Achilleus swore and spun away, but John didn't leave him alone for one moment, following in hard with a wild low sweep that took Achilleus in the side of his shin and sent him tumbling to the gravel. John was on to him, thrusting quickly down again and again, like someone trying to spear fish in a barrel. Achilleus rolled and squirmed on the ground so that the blades dug harmlessly into the dirt.

It wasn't going well for Achilleus. John was good. He was constantly getting the upper hand. Achilleus was looking like a fool. Wriggling on the ground at John's feet.

At last John came too close and Achilleus smashed the rim of his shield into his lower legs so that he too fell over. Landing heavily on his face. The two of them scrambled up. John's bandage had come loose, and there was blood dripping from his nose, but he barely seemed to notice it. For a while nobody had the upper hand, and they circled each other, panting and sweating. There was a wicked glint in John's bruised eyes, however. He was enjoying himself. He had rattled Achilleus, and they both knew it.

The crowd had become deathly quiet. Intent on the battle. Willing their champion to victory.

Achilleus's T-shirt was drenched with blood, and although John's mouth was bloody and he was limping slightly, there wasn't a fresh scratch on him. Achilleus was wary. Not wanting to let John inside his defenses again.

There began a long stretch of cautious fighting, as first one, then the other, would lunge forward and the blow would be blocked. Their grotesque distorted shadows fought around the walls of the palace like some violent puppet show. They were taking stock of each other, checking out their fighting styles, their strengths and weaknesses. If they had wanted it to be over quickly, they were disappointed.

There was no doubting that John's reach was longer. Both his spear and his arm were longer than Achilleus's, and he was taller by a good three or four inches. More of his strikes were getting through. True, most of them clattered harmlessly off Achilleus's shield, but one or two found their mark. Achilleus had a gash in his scalp and another on his shoulder. It was looking more and more like John's size was going to win the day.

And he knew it. He just had to work away at Achilleus, wear him down, weaken him, then move in for the kill.

He nudged his assault up to the next level, attacking with such force that Achilleus's shield rang out like a cracked bell.

Then John swore as one of his blades shattered and broke in half.

Achilleus smiled. Seeing that John was distracted, he

seized the moment, barged into him, pushing his shield aside and bringing his own shield up with a straight left punch to the side of John's head.

John was tough.

He barely flinched, and shoved Achilleus away with his spear arm, too close to use the blades. He was wounded, though. His right eye was bleeding and swelling shut.

Lewis nudged Mick. "That's good," he said. "John can't see so well now; he can't judge distance with one eye. He's blind on that side. Akkie needs to concentrate on his left. Keep on hitting him from there."

That was easier said than done, though. The injury had made John furious, and he was advancing on Achilleus like a berserker, knocking him back with a series of spear thrusts and smashes with his shield. Achilleus tried to hold his own, but he was tired. Finally John cracked him on the jaw with the shaft of his spear, and Achilleus staggered across the yard, stunned.

"He's faking it," Lewis drawled.

"You think so?" said Mick, unconvinced.

"Yeah," said Lewis. "He's my dog! He's leading him on, man, hoping John gets cocky and makes a mistake."

If Achilleus was faking, he was doing a very good job of it. He looked dazed, cross-eyed, unsteady on his feet. His spear wavered in the air and his shield was low.

"Here it comes, gay boy," said John, and he lifted his spear and drove it downward from shoulder height, aiming above Achilleus's lowered shield.

Achilleus just managed to jerk his head to the side in time. One of the knives raked his cheek, though, and cut his ear half off. Then some instinct told him to lift his shield, and in the tangle, another of John's blades broke.

He was down to one now.

But one was still enough to kill.

Achilleus shook his head and blinked. His eyes were red and burning. Feverish. He was losing a lot of blood. His ear was hanging off.

He was a wreck.

John was grinning, showing his little jagged teeth.

"Had enough?" he asked. "You want to surrender? You want to give in?"

Achilleus smiled back at him. John didn't know it, but he had shown his first hint of weakness. To offer Achilleus surrender meant that somewhere in the back of his mind he maybe didn't want to take this fight all the way. There was something making him hold back just that tiny bit.

He didn't want to kill Achilleus.

Filled with a fresh burst of energy, Achilleus gripped his spear under his arm halfway down the shaft so that it was perfectly in balance, the point toward John. He arced it up from his knees toward John's heart. John blocked it, but the momentum of Achilleus's swing brought the point back and around so that the blunt end of his spear was now toward John. Achilleus swung the spear quickly back in the same arc as his initial thrust, sweeping in toward John from his blind right side. The side that was unprotected by his shield. The pommel punched into John's shoulder, and he cursed. It wasn't enough to make him drop his spear, but he was rattled.

Achilleus now set up a regular attacking rhythm. A slice up with the point, a punch down with the pommel on the return swing. Steady and solid like a machine. Not giving John time to gather himself and respond properly. At first he was thrown, blocking, ducking and weaving, always on the back foot. It gradually dawned on him, however, that Achilleus's attack was the same each time. His swing the same length. Holding the spear halfway along the shaft meant that his reach wasn't too great. John only had to step back each time and the spear swished harmlessly past in front of him. Achilleus could keep it up for as long as he wanted. He'd get exhausted long before John. John let him come on, swinging away. Then he would step lightly back to keep out of reach. He had always known that he had the longer arms.

He didn't smile now. He didn't want Achilleus to know that he had the measure of him, that Achilleus's strikes were useless.

"What's he doing?" said Mick. "He can't get near to John. He's just walking out of the way."

"That blow to the head must have shaken his brain loose, man," said Lewis. "I can't watch. It's embarrassing."

Still Achilleus plodded on. Slicing up and clubbing down. Like a nerd with a playground bully, goaded to fight, and swinging his arms in useless silly punches. John was growing more relaxed with each swing. More sure of himself.

Sure of victory.

Even Maxie could see that Achilleus's plan wasn't working. John was playing with him, letting Achilleus wear himself out, hardly even bothering to counterattack, just offering the odd contemptuous poke with his longer spear. Maxie closed her eyes. She couldn't watch any more. She knew it now. Achilleus was going to get killed.

Still Achilleus swung away—up down up down. He stumbled, blood pouring down his face, his ruined ear flapping.

John smiled at last as his cockiness got the better of him. He lowered his shield and spear, mocking Achilleus, exposing himself, as if to say, "Look at me. You can't get anywhere near me." He sneered at Achilleus and gave a dismissive click of his tongue.

Achilleus was ready. It was time to finish it. On the upswing, as the point of his spear lanced back over his shoulder, he loosened his grip, letting the shaft run through his fingers. As it slid to the end and he felt the pommel, he gripped tight again. He now had the full length of the spear in his grasp and he swung it around in a wide circle.

Instead of Achilleus's reach being a yard, it was now nearer to two, and the sharp end of the spear easily reached John's head.

It happened too fast for John to react. He had no idea what Achilleus had done. He stood there, casually expecting the spear to be out of range. And then the spear slammed into the side of his head. He staggered drunkenly, shocked and stunned, with no idea where the blow had come from. Achilleus quickly choked up on his spear and moved in for the kill. He knocked John's shield and spear out to either side with his own weapons, stepped in, and brought a knee up sharply between John's legs. John grunted and buckled, bent double. Achilleus raised his shield and brought it crashing down on the back of John's head. John went down fast and heavy, his face smashing into the dirt.

"That was for Freak," said Achilleus.

John lay there without moving.

A great cheer went up from the palace kids, and a groan of disappointment came from the little knot of squatters. It was over so quickly in the end.

Achilleus stood over John, sucking in oxygen, his chest heaving. He rolled the body over with his foot.

John was conscious, but his black eyes were swollen shut. The bandage had fallen completely off his nose, which was a horrible flattened mess.

Achilleus put the point of his spear to John's stomach, pushing it into the soft flesh.

John winced.

"Do it, then," he said. "Kill me."

"Nah," said Achilleus. "You're already dead. Nobody remembers a loser."

"Kill me!" John yelled.

Achilleus gave his spear a little push, and John gasped.

"You really want me to? You know how slowly you'll die if I stick you in the stomach? You really want me to shove my spear into you and spill your crappy guts all over the ground? Hmm? Do you? You really want that, big man?"

"No," John said quietly. "No, I don't. Please don't. I don't want to die."

"Who does?" Achilleus knelt down. He put his face very close to John's. Dripping blood onto it.

"And this is for me," he said, and kissed John full on the lips.

The palace kids laughed as Achilleus stood up. Carl the pirate went over to John and helped him to his feet. His legs were like rubber.

Achilleus looked at David.

"You got what you wanted, David. They ain't backing out of this."

David shouted at the squatters.

"Do we have a deal?"

"Guess so," said Carl.

"Yeah," said John. "You've got your bloody deal."

Achilleus faltered and nearly fell. Maeve and Maxie ran to him and steadied him on either side. Maeve already had a bandage ready, and she began to wind it around Achilleus's head. Achilleus tried to push her away, but he was too weak.

"I'm all right," he slurred. And he once again looked at David and the palace kids.

"Remember what I done for you here today," he shouted, and passed out.

55

Are you satisfied? Freak dead, Achilleus nearly killed as well. Are you so damned keen to become emperor of bloody London that you don't care one bit about our kids at all?"

"Your kids?"

"Yes, our kids."

Maxie and David were standing on the balcony above the parade ground at the front of the palace. A bright moon was shining through a break in the clouds. The streets and roof-tops and trees, still wet from the earlier rain, were streaked with silver.

"We're all in this together now, Maxie," said David, in that annoyingly unruffled and patronizing manner of his. "You mustn't keep thinking about us and them. We're all playing on the same team."

"I'm not sure I want to be on your team, David."

"Then what are you doing here, Maxie? Living under my roof? Eating my food?"

"I'm sorry? Your roof? Your food? I thought we were all playing on the same team."

"We are. But if you prefer not to, then why don't you just leave?"

Maxie looked out over London. From up here there was a view clear down across St. James's Park to Admiralty Arch and Trafalgar Square beyond. There was a whole world out there.

She wondered where Sophie and her archers might be now. It took guts to leave somewhere safe like this and go back out onto the streets.

Did Maxie have the guts to do it?

"What do you think you'll find out there?" said David. "Other wandering bands of kids, living like savages, scavenging for food. Is that what you want? Because that's what it's like."

"I know, David, I'm not stupid. I've seen more of all that than you have."

"I don't think so," said David, a cold edge to his voice. "You don't know half of what I saw on my way to the palace. I saw things you couldn't even dream of. I've done my fair share of killing. It's different here in the center, but I fought my way through a total nightmare to get to where I am now. And I don't want to go back to all that. I want to build on what we've achieved."

"Killing grown-ups is one thing," said Maxie. "They're diseased. They're crazy. No longer human. We have to defend ourselves from them. But killing other kids. That's wrong."

"I agree," said David. "But with some kids it's the only language they understand."

"Maybe you're one of those kids, David."

"As I say, if you don't like it here, why don't you leave?" The smug, superior tone had come back into David's voice.

"Maybe I will," said Maxie quietly. "And maybe I'll take my crew with me."

"Maybe they won't want to go," said David, his voice flat and bland and irritating. "I don't know if you've noticed, Maxie, but your kids like it here."

"If I say we're going, they'll come with me," said Maxie.

"Are you so sure of that?"

"Stop trying to undermine me, David," Maxie snapped. "I know my kids."

"And what about Blue's crew? The kids from Morrisons?"

"What about them?"

"Can you speak for them as well? Maybe you'd better go and see Blue, see what he thinks about all this."

"He's sick. Your nurse, Rose, won't let anyone up to see him."

"Nonsense. You can go and talk to him anytime you want. He's well enough now. You're seeing plots and conspiracies everywhere. I'm not an evil person."

Maxie shook her head slowly. She suddenly felt dog tired. The day had been very stressful.

"I know you're not evil, David. But we're all so young. We can't always know the best thing to do."

David put a hand on her shoulder and squeezed it. The action felt clumsy and calculated.

"You do what you think's best, Maxie," he said. "I'll respect your decision. Now, shall we go in? I think it's going to start raining again."

56

"This would be so much easier if you'd come up to the sick-bay clinic. I've got all my proper equipment up there."

"No way, man, it's too much like a hospital."

Achilleus was slouched in one of the big chairs up on the dais in the Throne Room with his shirt off. Rose was inspecting his damaged ear. She'd given him some painkillers and was trying to clean his wounds with disinfectant. Achilleus was wincing and flinching and complaining and generally making her job difficult.

It hurt like hell.

"Don't you like hospitals?" Rose asked, dabbing at the wound.

"Nope," said Achilleus. "Spent too much time in them when I was a kid."

"You were ill?"

"Not me, my mom. She had MS. Multiple sclerosis. Bad news, man. That's how I remember her, as a sick person. Hated hospitals ever since. The only good thing about Mom being ill, she died before everything went bad. I never had to see her go crazy. Ow! What you doing there?"

"Sorry. It's your ear."

"What about it?"

"I'm going to have to try and stitch it," said Rose.

"You done stitching before?"

"No, not really."

"You know what to do?"

"No, not really."

"What are the chances you'll make a good job of it?"

"No chance at all," said Rose. "But at least it won't fall off. Urgh. It looks really nasty. It's going to be ugly no matter what I do."

John's blade had cut through the top of the ear, so that it was only attached by the bottom inch or so of skin.

"I shoulda killed Just John."

"I'm glad you didn't."

"I'm not. I've got a enemy now."

"You had an enemy before."

"That's true enough."

There was a knock at the door, and they looked over to see two of David's guards escorting a boy into the room. A stocky little lad with cropped black hair. He looked shy and nervous, but was masking it with a macho swagger.

"Sorry to bother you," said one of the guards. "But this squatter kid's been hanging around, we can't get rid of him, says he wants to talk to you."

"I'll come back in a minute if you want," said Rose, putting down her equipment.

"No. You stay," said Achilleus. "Get stitching."

Achilleus turned his attention to the squatter. "What d'you want?"

"Can I shake your hand?" said the boy, with a broad Irish accent.

Achilleus gave a snort of laughter. "What you want to shake my hand for?"

"I think you're cool."

"Yeah?" Achilleus laughed again and held out his hand. "This ain't a trick?"

"Nope."

The little lad came up onto the dais and pumped Achilleus's hand up and down.

"That was awesome out there," he said, his eyes transfixed by Rose as she started to push a needle and thread through Achilleus's ear.

"Shouldn't you have gone on with the others?" said Achilleus. He was determined to show no pain in front of the boy, even though it was agony.

"Nah," said the lad. "You were right, what you said. John's a loser. I'm coming over to your side. Jeez, that must hurt. . . ."

"Meh." Achilleus gave a dismissive shrug.

"Don't move," Rose warned.

"Just keep stitching," said Achilleus.

"I think I'd faint," said the boy.

"What's your name?" Achilleus asked.

"Pat. Patrick. Don't care what you call me. I want you to teach me everything you know. How to fight like that. I'll help you. I'd be like your servant. I'll look after your weapons for you. Sharpen them. Carry them into battle. You know, like when you look after a knight, like a . . . What do you call it? A caddy."

"Paddy the caddy?" said Achilleus. "All right. You got yourself a job, soldier."

57

Callum pressed PLAY on his boogie box and ABBA came on. "The Winner Takes It All." His mom's favorite song when she was feeling sad.

"Dancing Queen" when she was happy. "The Winner Takes It All" when she was sad.

She always said that you needed sad music when you were feeling down. "Last thing you want is someone trying to cheer you up. You want to know that someone else is as miserable as you are and knows how you're feeling. Lets you know you're not alone."

Callum wasn't exactly feeling sad. Inside he felt quite calm and peaceful, really. But he didn't want to listen to happy music. He remembered how his mom would sit on the sofa and put her arms around him and not say anything. Just the two of them sitting there.

His mom was often sad. Sometimes she'd stay indoors for weeks on end with the curtains drawn. Not wanting to see anyone. Not even answering the phone. Callum had to be the man of the house then. He had to look after her. So they'd sit and listen to ABBA together. He supposed that's where he'd got his fear of going outside from. From his mom.

Her friend Marion had told him that his mom suffered from depression.

He wasn't sure it really helped giving names to things. His mom was just his mom. And he was just himself. Callum.

The piano intro ran around and around, and then the blond one started to sing. He could never remember if it was Agnetha or Frida. His mom had the videos. Callum could picture them clearly. Thinking about them now made him smile. He turned the volume on full and sat back in his chair as they sang about the winner getting everything and the loser feeling small.

He pictured that bit in the film *Mamma Mia* when the mother—what was her name? The actress? Something weird. She sang the song by the sea.

Greece looked nice.

Callum had never been abroad. Not with his mom being how she was.

Meryl Streep. That was it. Definitely a weird name.

He picked up his Coke from the floor and popped the top. His last can. He'd been saving it for a special day. Well, there would be no more special days after this.

The Coke was warm, but it didn't matter. If it'd been winter he could have left the can outside, but otherwise there was no way of keeping things cold. He took a sip. The sugar hit him instantly. He gave a satisfied smack of his lips and went "Aaaaaaah," just like they did in the commercials.

Next he unwrapped his chocolate bar. Cadbury's Dairy Milk. It was a little white and hard, but that was all right. He took a bite. Oh, that taste. He closed his eyes to better appreciate it. This was heaven.

ABBA sang about the gods. Not caring. Everything being ruled by chance, a throw of the dice.

There came another crash from outside. The crack of something big breaking. A window maybe?

He hadn't gone away—the father in the cross-of-Saint-George vest. He and his little gang had stayed. And they'd been busy out there. Steadily smashing their way in. They were very nearly through. If not tonight, then tomorrow. He'd always known it, really, in the back of his mind, that sooner or later the grown-ups would come for him. He just hadn't thought it would be this soon.

The fat father and his cronies were different. They were clever. Callum had hurled things down on them, bombed them, but he'd missed the ringleaders every time. He'd taken out a couple of the normal grown-ups. The stupid ones. That was all. And the others—they wouldn't give up. They were working away at the defenses.

He remembered seeing a wildlife documentary about a pack of wild dogs. They trapped some animal in its lair. A badger or a lizard or something. And they dug it out. Took them ages. More than a day. They just kept on digging and digging, until they found it.

And then they ate it.

A huge bang followed by a thud. Something had fallen over.

He could hear them coming in now. They'd made it into the mall. There was only the shutter between him and them. He supposed he could run, but where would he go? It was too long since he'd been outside. That scared him worse than the grown-ups.

Another track came on. Another of his mom's favorites when she was feeling "blue," as she called it. "I Have a Dream." They'd sung this one together a million times. On the karaoke version. With the words on the screen. It was only now, though, that Callum really paid attention to what the words meant. No wonder his mom liked it. It was all about believing in your fantasies to help you forget reality.

It would be over quickly, at least, when they got inside. For now he would enjoy the chocolate and the Coke and the music. He wished he wasn't alone. He wished he had someone to share his last moments with. He'd been slowly dying of loneliness since his friends had left.

He'd gotten what he'd wished for, but, like in the fairy tales, he'd discovered that what he wished for wasn't what he really wanted.

He leaned over and plugged in his headphones, turned the volume up so that he wouldn't hear the grown-ups scrabbling at the shutters. He slipped the headphones over his ears. ABBA was still singing away. They reckoned if you had a song to sing, you could cope with anything.

Yeah, right . . .

He stuffed half the chocolate bar into his mouth. The taste of it was overwhelming. It seemed to fill his whole body. He sighed with delight. When he'd licked all the chocolate from his teeth he took a swig of Coke to wash it down.

He'd killed his mom in the end. Smothered her with a pillow while she was asleep. Not that she was really his mom anymore by that time.

There was an almighty crash and a rush of cool air from outside. He could sense movement.

They'd broken a window.

He tried to keep his eyes clamped shut, to lose himself in the music. But he couldn't bear it. He had to look. He had to.

He opened his eyes. For half a second. Less. Saw grown-ups running toward him. The bald man with the huge lolling head at the front. He was grinning, his arms raised, clutching his club.

Callum closed his eyes.

He sent a silent hello out to his mom, and they were upon him.

58

Achilleus had been patched up, but he still felt like crap. His muscles were stiff and bruised, the whole left-hand side of his head throbbed, the cuts across his chest where John's blades had raked him stung like a bastard. He was covered with a patchwork of tapes and bandages and had been liberally painted with disinfectant. He prayed that the wounds were clean. He saw what had happened to Arran after he'd been bitten. What were the chances that a filthy animal like John would keep his weapons clean?

The one thing that gave Achilleus hope was that after his mom died, his dad had been surprisingly good at looking after him. He'd learned to cook, he'd gotten involved with Achilleus's schoolwork, he'd made sure he always had clean clothes, and he'd taken him regularly to the doctor for his injections. He'd been obsessive about it. His dad had moved to England from Cyprus when he was twelve. He still had stories about the little village he'd come from. Achilleus was sure he exaggerated the backward nature of the place. But his dad loved the British health system. And he had horror stories to tell about all the diseases that had been stamped out by vaccinations.

So Achilleus was pretty sure he was up to date with tetanus. The kids here were organized. They had a well-stocked first-aid center, but they weren't up to giving injections for things like tetanus.

Rose had given him some antibiotics, though, and had done her best with his ear. He wondered how it would come out. He'd never been particularly vain about his appearance. He knew he wasn't pinup material. But he still didn't want to look like a monster. True—a little scarring would increase his status. Looking hard was halfway to winning a fight. Right now, though, he didn't so much look hard as a mess. His head was wrapped up like a mummy.

Could have been worse. Much worse.

He'd been lucky with John. The guy was thick. Couldn't see when he was being suckered. But if Achilleus's trick hadn't worked, that would have been the end of it. He'd have been wide open to John's counterattack.

No problem. He'd won. That was all that mattered.

He'd moved to the Music Room at the back of the palace and was sitting looking at the rain as it ran down the windows. He was waiting for his dinner. He was hungry again. Probably from losing so much blood.

He was settled in a big fancy armchair, wearing tracksuit pants and a bathrobe. It hurt too much to put a shirt on over the bandages. Every now and then a palace kid would come through and compliment him. Want to shake his hand, hoping for some of his star status to rub off on them.

He could get used to this.

Paddy the Caddy came in with a cup of tea and a plate of food on a tray.

"You took your time."

"It's not my fault," said Paddy, in his thick Irish accent. "They was busy in the kitchens."

"I don't want excuses, PC, I want results. Yeah?"

"Yeah, sorry. Plus I had to look for the other thing for you."

"Did you find it?"

"Yeah."

Paddy put the tray down and unslung a pack from his back.

"Open it up."

Paddy unzipped it. There were a few bits of clothes, a toothbrush, a flashlight, and three cans of spray paint.

Achilleus sat looking at it all in silence for a long while. Then he picked up one of the cans.

"Was he a friend of yours?" said Paddy.

"Freak? Nah. Not really." He tossed the can to Paddy. "Look after this for me. And the others. The rest you can dump."

"Okay. I'm not supposed to be your slave, though," said Paddy. "More of a servant, I thought. I do things for you and you do things for me. Like teaching me to fight."

"We'll see."

"You said . . ."

"Don't bug me, little man."

"Sorry."

Achilleus took a sip of tea. It was too hot. He put it back down.

"Blow on that for me, will you?"

"I will not."

"You want me to teach you to fight, you blow on my tea."

"You teach me, I'll blow on it."

Achilleus stood up and stretched. Looked at Paddy.

"You really want to learn bad, don't you?"

"I sure do. So can we start?"

"What, now?"

Paddy shrugged. Achilleus waited a moment, then pushed him down on the carpet and laughed. Paddy looked angry and hurt.

"What did you do that for?"

"First lesson," said Achilleus, holding out his hand to pull Paddy up, "be ready for anything. At any time. The best fighter in the world can be taken out if he ain't ready. Look at what happened to Just John. Twice now I've had him. Once back at the camp, once out there. He was a better fighter than me, mos' def, but he's none too smart, and both times I caught him napping."

Paddy grinned. "I'll be ready next time."

Achilleus hauled him to his feet, but halfway up he let go and Paddy fell back down with a thump. Achilleus laughed at him, and the little boy looked even more pissed off this time.

"Thought you said you was ready," said Achilleus.

"That was just stupid," said Paddy.

"Ah, but you're learning, padawan. Don't trust no one."

"So how do you know you can trust me?" said Paddy, getting up by himself this time. "Maybe I'm a spy in your camp."

"You think I haven't considered that?" said Achilleus.

"I ain't, though," Paddy said quickly, throwing a pleading

look at Achilleus like a cute puppy. "Don't chuck me out. Please. I don't want to go back to the camp. It's cold there and wet. I kept asking John why we couldn't just live in the houses like everyone else, but he said we was different. Special. I never understood half of what he used to go on about. He said we was like gypsies. But we never went anywhere. We never did nothing, neither. It was boring there."

"You think it's gonna be any better here?" said Achilleus.

"Hope so," said Paddy. "When you start giving me my lessons. Real ones. Not like that. Not like a kid's game."

"What, you want me to come at you with a pointed stick?"

"No. There's more to giving lessons than just attacking someone."

"Wouldn't know," said Achilleus. "Never given a lesson before. Not sure I'll be much use as a teacher. You'll just have to watch and learn, I guess. Pick up what you can on the job. It's not nothing I ever usually think about."

"I'm a quick learner," said Paddy.

Achilleus smiled at him, then shoved him down on the floor again. Paddy looked like he was going to burst into tears, but Achilleus just laughed at him. He was still laughing when Maxie came in.

"I'm going up to see Blue," she said.

"Give him my love," said Achilleus.

"Will you come with me?"

"What for?"

"I want to talk to him about whether we stay here."

"Why would you want to leave?"

"You could have died today, Akkie."

"That was my choice."

"And Freak did die."

"Could have happened any time."

"We're just doing David's dirty work for him."

"So? I like doing dirty work."

"Be serious."

"I am being serious, Maxie. I mean, look at me, I'm a fighter. What do you expect me to do? Sit around all day counting potatoes? I'm not like you, Maxie, I'm not interested in politics. So long as I have a bit of excitement in my life, get some food at the end of the day, I'm cool."

"Like an animal."

"Jeez, calm down, Maxie. Look around you! We're living in Buckingham Palace, for God's sake, not the zoo. Before— how we used to live—that was living like animals. This is living like a queen."

"I thought you'd rather live like a king," said Maxie.

"Same difference," said Achilleus. "Bottom line: I like it here. I don't know why you'd want to leave."

"Because if we stay here we'll become like David. All he really wants is power."

"That's fine with me," said Achilleus. "As long as I'm on the winning side. Don't want to hang with no losers."

"Will you come anyway?" said Maxie. "To see Blue?"

"I get bored of too much yakking."

"Fine. Don't come, then."

"I won't."

Achilleus winked at Paddy, who laughed. Maxie blushed

and headed for the door before she lost her temper and made a fool of herself. Her side was throbbing badly enough to make her cry. Jester was waiting in the corridor outside, carrying a candelabra with five lit candles. She wondered how much he had heard of their conversation.

What the hell. It was no secret how she felt about David.

Damn Achilleus. Damn him! At least Ollie was meeting her up there, so she had some support.

As she left the room Achilleus called out to her. "Where would you go?"

"I don't know," she called back angrily. "Anywhere away from here."

Jester took her to the grand staircase, where they climbed one of the twin stairways. At the top was a statue of Perseus holding the Gorgon's severed head. Maxie was struck by how young Perseus looked, and how old Medusa looked. Maybe that was what the story was about. A boy killing an adult. The new world killing off the old.

Jester took her through the upper floors of the building, his candlelight flickering along the walls. It was less grand up here, more like a normal house, albeit a huge one.

The sick bay was tucked away in a corner of the top floor. It was off a short corridor reached by a small back staircase. Two of David's guards sat outside, with rifles by their sides.

Maxie turned to Jester with a questioning look.

"I thought this was a sick bay, not a prison."

"Lighten up," said Jester. "They're not keeping guard. They're just there if anyone needs anything."

"So why the guns?"

Jester leaned over and spoke quietly in Maxie's ear. "They won't go anywhere without them. They love their toys."

He chuckled as they went inside.

There were six beds in here. Each with a little night-light burning by its side. Four of the beds were empty. The other two held Blue and the girl they had rescued. She was lying there, staring at the ceiling, her face covered with bandages.

Blue was sitting up, naked above the sheets, reading a book, which he put down as Maxie came in.

Rose sat by the window with her own candle, leafing through a magazine. Another girl in a nurse's uniform was filling a glass with water from a jug. There was an air of peace and calm. Maxie wondered what she'd been so worried about.

Blue gave her a wide smile, genuinely pleased to see her. He looked fine. Well fed and rested. Maxie was struck for the first time by how fit his body was. Since the disaster they had all been eating a lot less; their bodies were mostly lean with little fat. Their active lives kept their muscles in shape.

"How you doing?" she asked.

"Better," said Blue. "Couldn't stop being sick for ages. Kept falling asleep. But when I woke up this evening I felt almost normal. Mother of all headaches, though. How you doing?"

"I'll leave you two alone," said Jester, and he slipped out.

Maxie sat down by the bed and told Blue everything that had happened since the battle at the camp. Rose and the nurse fussed about the room, trying to keep busy and giving them space.

When she'd finished, Blue was silent for a long while.

"I'm sorry about Freak," he said at last.

"Yeah," said Maxie. "To have gotten all the way here from Holloway and then die in a stupid squabble with some other kids."

Blue took her hand and squeezed it. Maxie frowned. Taken by surprise. She didn't pull away, though. It felt comforting.

Presently there was a knock, and Ollie came in. Blue let go of Maxie's hand.

"Have I missed anything?" Ollie asked, sitting on the other side of the bed.

"Maxie's told me everything," said Blue.

"You should have seen her," said Ollie. "A proper wartime leader."

"I'd rather be a peacetime leader," said Maxie.

"It's all sorted out now," said Ollie. "We won."

Maxie shook her head. "You must admit that it sucked, what went down back there. A fight to the bloody death."

"No one died," said Ollie. "And the squatters are on our side now. I don't see how we could have done that without some kind of fight."

"It wasn't our fight, though," said Maxie.

"If we're going to stay here, then yes, it was our fight."

"*If* we're going to stay."

"What are you saying?"

"I'm saying I think we should all leave."

"Wait a minute, Max," said Ollie. "David's—"

"Oh, shut up about David!" Maxie interrupted. "I know how palsy you two are, but I want nothing more to do with him."

"Listen," said Blue. "Before you two start getting into a

fight. While I been lying here I been thinking. About me and David. On the way to the palace I talked to Jester, asked him who was gonna be in charge when we got here. He said we'd talk about it. It hasn't really happened, except for all that crap about being a general and stuff."

"It's not about who's in charge," said Maxie. "It's about what David represents."

"That's too deep for me, girl. Far as I'm concerned it comes down to the fact that we've got too many bosses."

"He's never going to let you take charge, Blue."

"Then what are we talking about? We either fight David for top job, or we get out."

"That's one way of looking at it. . . ."

"It's the only way I know, girl."

"Well, we're not fighting," said Maxie. "Whatever I think of David, I don't want to fight him and the other kids here."

"So we go, then?" said Blue.

"Hold on a minute," said Ollie. "We need to talk about this properly."

"Whose side you on, man?" said Blue.

"I'm not on anybody's side."

"Then you ain't on our side."

"There don't need to be sides."

"Well, there are," said Blue. "You gotta choose."

"No, no, no," said Ollie, standing up and pacing the room. "David's got a good thing going on here. I don't like him much. But I respect him. He's our best bet in all the chaos of London."

"That's your opinion," said Maxie. "My opinion is that

we'd all be a lot happier if we got out of this place."

They watched Rose take her candle to the window and stand there looking out at the night. She blew the candle out and went over to straighten the sheets for the girl with the bandaged face, who lay there unmoving, though she appeared to be awake.

Ollie sat back down again and leaned toward Maxie and Blue, speaking more quietly now.

"Listen, Maxie," he said. "The little kids aren't going to want to leave. They're happier and safer than they have been for months. This is crazy."

"We can't lose all we believe in. Our sense of right and wrong," said Maxie. "Just to survive."

"Just to survive? There's no *just* about it. Survival is everything."

"Me and Blue both want to go," said Maxie. "So there's nothing more to talk about. I'll go down and tell the others. They'll do what I say. Me and Blue are in charge. That's what you wanted."

Ollie sighed and sank his head in his hands. He could think of nothing more to say.

Maxie walked over to the door and opened it.

She paused.

David was standing outside. His two guards on either side of him.

"What's this?" said Maxie.

"I can't let you leave, I'm afraid," said David. "I need your fighters. I was hoping Blue would talk sense into you, but it seems he's a problem as well."

"How do you know what we've been talking about? You got spies in here?"

David's eyes flicked toward Rose. She looked down at the carpet.

The candle. At the window. It had been a signal.

Maxie laughed without any humor. "So what? You're going to take me and Blue hostage?"

"If that's what it takes. I reckon if we lock away the ring-leaders, the others will do as they're told."

"Don't be ridiculous, David. You can't hold us here. We're leaving."

"You are not leaving," said David, and the two guards leveled their rifles at her.

Blue jumped out of bed, shouting angrily, and took a couple of paces toward David, but he was still weak. He faltered, clutching his head and moaning. Maxie had to catch him before he fell.

David now looked at Ollie, challenging him.

"I'm with you," Ollie said wearily. "I never wanted to leave in the first place."

David looked over to Rose, and she nodded that Ollie was telling the truth.

"Maxie's a fool," said Ollie. "And Blue's just ticked off that he's not in charge."

Ollie walked over to the door, pushing past Maxie and Blue, and went out.

"It looks like you two are alone, then," said David.

"The others won't go for this," said Maxie.

"Who's going to help you? Achilleus? I think not. He's

with me now. He knows a good thing when he sees it."

Rose and the nurse left, looking rather sheepish. Not catching anyone's eye.

Maxie and Blue were alone in the room with the silent bandaged girl.

"You can stay up here as long as you like," said David. "When you see sense, you can join the others. In the meantime, I'm taking charge of all your kids. Good night."

59

Sam didn't think he could walk another step. He was leaning against the Kid, not sure exactly which of them was holding the other up. They hadn't spoken for ages; they were too tired and hungry and scared. The steady thin drizzle was making them cold, sapping their spirits. They'd been wandering aimlessly, trying to find food and avoid the marauding gangs of grown-ups who seemed to be very thick on the ground. The Kid's lighter had eventually run out of fuel, and in the dark they were even more confused. They'd passed among the towers of the City and got lost in the tangle of streets that clustered at their feet, backtracking, running, hiding, going in circles. They'd tried to shelter in several different buildings, but nowhere was safe, and there was nothing to eat and the darkness grew ever deeper.

The river had to be close, and once they hit it they'd know where they were and could get away, but they were losing hope of ever finding it. They knew that if they didn't stumble across it soon they'd have to find somewhere to spend the night, but the thought of that frightened them. This was an alien place. There were no houses, only offices and bars and shops. They wanted to get away from these gigantic glass-faced blocks that hid nameless secrets.

They were trying a new direction. Into a very run-down area that had looked too scary before. They trudged toward a railway bridge.

As Sam grew more and more delirious—exhausted, soaked, hungry, and thirsty, sucking rainwater from his shirt-sleeves, his head throbbing—he began to see things. Flitting shapes in the corners of his eyes, dancing spots of light, moving shadows. Whenever he turned his head to look, though, there was nothing there. He had a powerful urge to lie down in the street, curl up into a ball, and fall asleep. Hardly caring if he woke up again. How nice to just go to sleep forever.

As always, that little voice in the back of his mind told him to keep going. He owed it to Rhiannon. She had sacrificed her own life to help him get away. He had to keep going. Her death had to count for something.

And what about Ella? His little sister needed him. He had to find her. Help her. Look after her.

It was like the two girls were at his side, urging him on, one foot after the other. Rhiannon on the right, Ella on the left.

Without warning, the Kid stopped. Sam tensed.

What was it? What had he seen? More grown-ups? Would they have to fight this time? Sam gripped his butterfly pin. Maybe this night would never end.

"Look," said the Kid, his voice a croak. And he pointed.

Sam squinted into the murky gloom.

"What is it?" he said. "What am I looking for?"

"There," said the Kid. "Up ahead. Flames."

Sam saw them now—a row of what looked like flaming torches along the top of a wall. And he realized, with a little jolt of hope, that he recognized the building. He smiled. He had been here on a school trip.

It was the Tower of London. The castle by the Thames, originally built by the Normans after the Battle of Hastings. How reassuring it was to see something familiar.

And someone must have lit those torches along the outer wall.

"There are people there," he whispered.

"Adult people?"

"I don't know," said Sam. "They don't usually light fires, do they? But nothing's normal around here."

"We should go careful," said the Kid, but almost as he said it, a voice called out from the darkness behind them.

"Stand still. Don't move."

A boy's voice. Not an adult.

"We're kids," Sam cried. "Only kids."

"I can see that," said the voice. "Where have you come from?"

"Waitrose," said Sam.

"Waitrose?" There was the hint of a suppressed laugh in the voice.

Sam slowly turned around.

"In Holloway."

"Where's that?"

"North London. Past Camden Town."

"You've come all the way from there?"

"Yes—I'm trying to get to Buckingham Palace."

"Well, you're more than a little lost."

"I know. Please, we're very tired and hungry. We've been running from grown-ups all day."

"Is it just the two of you?"

"Yes."

Four figures appeared out of the darkness, and Sam felt like he'd somehow slipped back in time hundreds of years.

The figures, all boys, were dressed in medieval outfits. Tunics and boots with pieces of armor, swords, shields, and helmets. One carried a crossbow.

"Will you help us?" said the Kid. "We can't go on. These are our last legs."

The two tallest boys talked quietly to each other before one of them broke away and came over. He took off his helmet. He had a face that would have been handsome if it weren't for a long scar down one cheek that pulled his face out of shape. He smiled and the scar twisted his mouth into a grimace. His eyes were kind, though. Soft and brown.

He knelt down in front of Sam and the Kid. "How old are you two?"

"Nine," they both said together.

"And you've made it all the way here from north London?"

"The shrimp did," said the Kid. "I been living around about Spitalfields, but I got into the tunnels and I was sore lost and—"

"Whoa, hold on, not so fast," said the older boy. "So you've been in Spitalfields? Who's been looking after you?"

The Kid shrugged. "No one. There was some other kids with me one time, but they're all dead now, you can count on it. It was only me. But then I found the hobbit. We been help-ing each other. We're pals."

The boy with the scar shook his head and let out a snort of laughter through his nose.

"And here we were thinking we were pretty clever living in the Tower, pretty tough. You two kids have shown us up as a bunch of wimps."

"Is it safe there?" said Sam.

"In the Tower?" The boy nodded slowly. "Safe enough."

"You sure?" said Sam.

"You've been through a lot, haven't you?"

Sam nodded.

"Well, it's as safe as anywhere, I guess. Safer than out here on the streets. Safer than down in the tube tunnels, that's for sure."

"Will you take us there?"

"Sure. Why not?"

"And we'll really be safe? It's just you? Just kids?"

"There's sixty-seven of us living there," said the older boy. "All kids. All ages. It's not the greatest life in the world. But it's a life. You're safe now, mate."

Sam burst into tears, and the Kid joined him. The boy opened his arms and pulled them to his chest, holding them there until they stopped sobbing. Then he picked them up so that they sat against his hips, and carried them toward the Tower.

60

Ben and Bernie were eating a late supper in the Dining Room. Most of the other kids had eaten earlier, and the food was cold. They'd been out of the way all evening, tinkering with a gas generator they'd discovered in a storeroom in the utility area of the palace. They hadn't wanted to watch the fight, and had kept as far away as possible.

Since arriving they'd been spending their time exploring and scavenging. They'd tried to get David interested in engineering plans. A pump and filtration system to get clean water from the lake, a plan to get some heating set up for the winter using the gas bottles they'd found in a shed, even a plan to generate electricity, but David wasn't interested. His sights were firmly set outside the palace. He even said that it would make the kids tougher if they didn't have too many luxuries. Ben and Bernie realized that the big welcome of the first-night feast, the show of abundance and opulence, had been just that—a show—to impress the newcomers. Since that night the food had been steadily getting worse. Tonight it was boiled potatoes with cabbage, and canned peaches for dessert. Ben and Bernie weren't complaining—they weren't that bothered about food, and at least this bland stuff filled them up. They'd noticed it, though. How the portions were getting smaller. How they never had any meat.

They'd had such high hopes when they arrived. A new life with new opportunities. But David had set the palace up to be little more than functional. They could survive here, and that was about it. The two of them often talked about how they'd been more appreciated at Waitrose, and how much they'd enjoyed inventing things. They even missed all the stuff they'd left behind. They felt part of things there, an important part. Now what were they? They couldn't fight and they didn't look forward to spending the rest of their lives as farmers. But food and fighting were all that David cared about.

They looked up from their plates as Achilleus came in, wearing a bathrobe. He was a mess. Limping. His face and chest bruised and bandaged. A young boy they didn't recognize was with him, a stocky, bullet-headed kid carrying a shield and a collection of weapons in a golf bag slung across his back.

"There you are," said Achilleus. "Been looking all over for you."

"What's up?" said Ben.

"Nothing. I just need to know where everybody is. Can you make sure you're in the dormitory by eleven o'clock with everyone else?"

"Why?" Bernie asked. She'd never much liked Achilleus, and resented his bossy manner.

"Why? Because I say so. I need everyone to stay together."

"What is it, like a curfew?" said Ben.

"Dunno," said Achilleus. "What's a curfew?"

"Doesn't matter."

"We're busy anyway," said Bernie. "Might not be able to make it by eleven."

"You will be able to make it," said Achilleus. "I'm not asking you—I'm telling you. If you're not there, things'll go bad for you."

"What about Maxie?" said Bernie. "She gonna be there?"

"She's in the sick bay," said Achilleus.

"She all right?"

"Yeah. She's looking after Blue."

"Good job in the fight, by the way," said Ben, trying to stop the situation from getting heavy. Achilleus merely shrugged.

"*You* look like you should be in the sick bay," Ben went on. "I heard your ear got messed up."

"That loser nearly cut it off."

"So when's Blue coming out?"

"Do I look like a doctor?" said Achilleus.

"No," said Bernie. "You look like a patient."

"I ain't neither, darling. I'm a fighter, and right now that's the most important type of person around. You got it?"

"If you say so, big man," said Bernie with a slight mocking sneer. Ben flashed her a warning look. Bernie was one of those girls who didn't watch what they said to people, which meant that the boys with her quite often got beaten up.

Luckily, Achilleus only grinned.

"If you two losers hadn't made life bearable back at Waitrose I'd have given you both a good slap a long time ago."

"Yes, well, I think you'll find that you need losers to make the world go 'round," said Bernie.

"You said it."

"So you concede that we might be of some small use as well as a big tough fighting man like you?"

"Small is right," said Achilleus. "Now just make sure you're in the ballroom by eleven. We're going to be checking everyone. Got it?"

"Sir, yes, sir!" said Bernie, standing up and saluting, and Achilleus laughed before sweeping out with his caddy and leaving them to their cold potatoes.

61

Maxie lay on her bed and stared up at the patterns of light that the candles were making on the ceiling of the sick bay. She felt flat. Physically flat, like a sheet of paper, with no room inside for any emotions. She'd exhausted herself worrying about David and how Ollie and Achilleus had betrayed her. She'd gone through anger, shame, fear . . . She'd felt stupid and abused and mocked. There was nothing left to feel anymore except the oddly comforting ache in her side. She'd even gone beyond tiredness. Resigned herself to whatever lay in store for her.

A blank sheet of paper.

"I'm sick and tired of feeling sick and tired," she said.

"I know how that feels," said Blue, who was also lying on his bed staring at the ceiling.

"I think some pharaoh had that carved on his tomb," Maxie added.

"Yeah? Times don't change much, do they?"

"I don't know about that," said Maxie. "I can't think of any other time in history when most of the population of the world was wiped out by some unknown illness."

"What about the Black Death?" said Blue. "The plague. I think about half the people in Europe died during that one. We still made it through, though. We've done it before. We can do it again."

"You're optimistic, aren't you?"

"Why not?"

"It's just that life's been pretty crappy lately, in case you hadn't noticed."

"Yeah. I noticed."

Maxie looked over at Blue just as he looked over at her. He smiled.

"Don't worry," he said. "We'll get outta this jam. We'll be okay."

"You know," said Maxie, still looking at Blue, "you're much nicer when you're away from everyone else. You don't try to keep up such a front."

"You gotta be tough to survive, girl. Don't show no weakness to no one."

"Yeah, well, it's easy for you. You've been tough all your life. I was just an ordinary girl before. Nothing special. I wasn't even that athletic."

"You don't know me at all, girl."

"Oh yes I do. I knew loads of boys like you before the disaster," said Maxie. "They used to strut around, intimidating people."

"You know what my nickname was before all this?" said Blue.

"I dunno," said Maxie. "Killer? King Dude? The Boss?"

"Bookface."

"Bookface?"

"Yeah."

"That's a crappy nickname."

"Don't I know it."

"What does it mean anyway?"

"A lot. Not a lot."

"No, come on, what does it mean? Like you always had your face in a book, or that your face looked like a book?"

Blue sighed. "Everything that happened, you know, it changed people. It's changed me. I had another nickname as well."

"Surprise me."

"Fat Boy."

Maxie laughed. "You're not fat."

"I used to be. I was a fat nerd."

"No!" Maxie came up on her elbow and leaned toward Blue with a shocked smile on her face.

"Straight up." Blue laughed. "I had two brothers and two sisters. You know how families are, everyone finds their space. My oldest brother, Akim, he was trouble. My next brother, Felix, was into sports. My big sister, Lulu, was obsessed with fashion, looking good and all that. My other sister, Sissy, she was into boys. My thing, I was the brainy one of the family. I was always good at school. Didn't really try, just came easy to me. Because I was good at it, I really liked it, homework and all, though I couldn't tell anyone back then. They found out that I read lots of books, though. Gave me a hard time for it. I didn't much care. I didn't get out much. I spent hours on my computer, and not just playing games. My mom used to go on about me not getting enough exercise, but at the same time, she liked the fact that I was learning stuff. She wanted me to go to college. I didn't know about all that. Akim, he was into gangs. Mom didn't want me having nothing to do with that way of life. Some kid from our school was stabbed. It was big news, Mom was scared. But I was never part of that world. Never got in a fight or nothing. When it all kicked off I had to learn fast, man. You know what? The first to die were the tough kids. They went out there on the streets. No more cops. No more adults telling them what to do. No more rules. All the gangs just went crazy and fought each other. Killed each other. Stupid jerks. For a little while it was like a war zone out there. Soon those that didn't kill each other began to realize who the real enemy was. So then the gangs went up against the grown-ups. Most of them died early on. Not all, though. Me, I kept my head down. I watched, I learned, it was what I was good at. Who lived and who died. Was a lottery. Just raw luck. Like in a war, the first to get it are the regular army, the trained soldiers. After that the army takes whoever they can get. I'm who they got. The disaster made me tough, Maxie, and that's why I have to try hard when there's people around. Because it don't come easy for me."

"Aren't I a person?" said Maxie.

"You're different. You understand all this stuff."

"Sometimes I think I do, sometimes I think I don't."

"It's funny," said Blue. "Lying here, I feel I can talk to you about anything. It don't matter no more."

"I'm glad you told me all that," said Maxie.

Blue rolled onto his back and looked away. "Maybe I just want you to like me," he said.

"Oh yeah?"

"I know we haven't always agreed on stuff, Max. But you know what it's like. With no adults around to tell you what to do all the time, you'd think we'd all just want to stay up late and drink and smoke and take drugs and make out. And I know a lot of kids did do that at first. But when you're scared, struggling just to stay alive, those thoughts go right out the window. Sometimes, though, you get feelings."

"What are you trying to say, Blue?"

"I like you, Max. Always did. That's why I act the way I do. I know you liked Arran. I didn't think I had a chance at first. I'm Fat Boy, remember. Bookface, the computer nerd. Girls never used to go for me. Well, not in that way."

Maxie looked over at Blue. He was staring fixedly at the ceiling. Might even have been blushing.

"Are you saying you *like*-like me, Blue?"

Now Blue looked embarrassed.

"No. Yes. No. Not like that."

"Like what, then?"

"I don't know like what. I shouldn't have said anything."

"It's all right. I'm confused right now, Blue. I don't know what to think. About Arran, about you, about me. Until we can get out of this mess and I can get my head together and think about things, then I can't think about anything. Does that sound dumb?"

"No more than anything I said." Blue sat up. Smiled. "You didn't yell at me. Does that mean that if we get out of here I might have a chance?"

Maxie laughed. "Let's get out of here and we'll see."

"But say we did get out, yeah? Where would we go?"

"We've got the whole of London to choose from."

"But we don't know it around here, we don't know where's safe."

"There must be other kids," said Maxie. "This can't be it."

"Nowhere else is going to be as well set up as this," said Blue. "Nowhere else is gonna be as safe. David's the only one around here who's organized."

They both jumped as a voice came from across the room. "David's a liar."

They had forgotten all about the girl with the bandaged face in the other bed. The one they'd rescued at Green Park.

They both sat up and looked over at her. Her eyes were glinting in the half-light.

"What did you say?" Blue asked, even though he had heard her quite clearly.

"David's a liar," she repeated. "He's been lying to you all along. Why do you think he's been keeping me out of the way up here?"

"Because of your injuries?" said Blue. Wasn't it obvious?

"They're not as bad as they look," said the girl. "When you cut your face there's a lot of blood. Rose fixed me up pretty well. I'm going to look like hell, but it's only skin. David didn't want me mixing with you all, though. He didn't want me talking. Once it was clear they were keeping me prisoner, I made sure I didn't speak, hardly even moved. Just listened."

"I don't get it," said Blue. "Where are you from?"

"The museum."

"Museum?" said Blue. "What museum?"

"Natural History Museum," said the girl. "Loads of us live there. It's better than here, there're more houses around, more places to find food. Though we do grow stuff as well."

"Just like David?" said Blue.

"Just like David," said the girl. "But he didn't want you to know that."

"For sure," said Blue.

"And it's not just us," said the girl. "There's kids all over London, set up, in safe places. Surviving. We've tried talking to David before, about all linking up and sharing, but he wasn't interested. He wants it all for himself."

"King David," said Maxie.

"Me and my friends from the museum," the girl went on, "we were searching for some friends of mine who I'd split off from last year. We'd heard they might be on the other side of town. We thought it was going to be easy. We got careless. It's mostly safe around here now. There's a few adults, but it's not like it used to be. Or so we thought. We hadn't been going more than an hour . . . and then . . . we came across those ones . . . hunting . . ."

The girl broke off. Stared at something a thousand miles away.

"It's all right," said Maxie.

"I just want to go home."

"To the museum?" said Blue.

"Yeah. If you get me out of here, I'll take you with me."

"If there's kids everywhere," said Blue, "nicely set up, why should we come with you?"

"Because . . . well, just because . . . I can't give you a reason other than a selfish one, other than I just want to get home."

"That's good enough reason for me," said Maxie. "If you'd given us a load of bull I wouldn't have trusted you."

"We'll do it on one condition," said Blue.

"Which is?"

"That you don't never tell anyone anything about what I was talking to Maxie about just now."

"It's a deal."

"Okay," said Blue. "We're on our way."

"The only problem is," said Maxie, "we do have to actually get out of here first."

62

On the other side of London, Sam was standing on the battlements of the Tower of London, staring out at the great swollen River Thames, a wide strip of silver in the moonlight. It had risen a few feet since the disaster, and the Tower once more had a water-filled moat around it, just as it had hundreds of years ago. Sam felt as if he were living inside a medieval story. When they'd arrived, he and the Kid had eaten some hot food and drunk some clean water and rested in soft beds. Sam still couldn't quite believe they were here. Living in a castle, safe at last from all the dangers of London.

The Kid was standing next to him. His chin resting on his arms on top of the wall.

"What are you thinking about?" said Sam.

"Cheese."

"Cheese?"

"The Kid used to like cheese. Hasn't eaten any for a wicked long time. Tasty cheese. Cheese, cheese, cheese, cheese, cheese . . . Did you spot it? Down there?"

"What?"

"They got a genuine hundred percent cow. A living breathing lawn mooer."

"I saw it, yeah," said Sam. "And chickens and pigs and a goat."

"Well, if there's a cow, there's milk, ain't there?" said the Kid. "And if there's milk, there's possible cheese."

"Could be," said Sam. He didn't want to disappoint the Kid, but he was pretty sure you needed a bull if you wanted a cow to make milk, though he wasn't quite sure exactly how it all worked. Who knows? Maybe they had a bull as well.

"What you thinking about, over there yourself, Babybel?" the Kid asked. "If not cheese."

"My sister, Ella."

"You think she's all right?"

"I hope she's still alive somewhere," said Sam. "I hope she made it to the palace and they're looking after her like we're being looked after here. I mean, if I can make it. Me. Small Sam. All the way across London all by myself—"

"Hey! Don't I count?"

"You know what I mean," said Sam. "If midges like us can do it, then surely Ella, with all those other kids—Akkie and Freak and Josh and Arran and everyone—surely she can do it too."

"I'm sure she's hunky-dory," said the Kid, and he put an arm around Sam.

"Is that a good thing?" said Sam.

"The best."

"You're quite weird, you know?" said Sam.

"I'm different," said the Kid. "My gran always said I was half clever, half stupid, and half crazy."

"That's three halves," said Sam.

"Yeah. I told you I was different."

"When we're strong enough," said Sam, "will you come with me?"

"Where? To Bucko Palace?"

"Yes. To find Ella."

"'Course I will," said the Kid. "It'll be a new grand adventure of the old school. They'll write books about us. Long books. Nothing's gonna split us up, small fry. We're a team. Like Batman and Robin Hood." And he sang. "Ner-ner-ner-ner-ner-ner-ner-Batman!"

63

Blu-Tack Bill was sitting on his bed, playing with his lump of Blu Tack, molding it into shapes. One moment it was a horse, then it was a house, then it had become a tree, then a little man, then a bomb. He was playing a game and the Blu Tack became anything he wanted it to, any toy he could imagine. Sometimes he would pull it apart and turn it into two figures, or more. He was never alone as long as he had his Blu Tack. It spoke to him in the voices of the characters in his story. He could sit like this for hours, lost in his own little world.

It was late, and all around him the other kids were settling down for the night. Even though the ballroom they were using as a dormitory was huge, it smelled of dirty clothes and sweaty feet and bad breath. Bill tried to shut out the smells by concentrating on his game. But a short sharp bark distracted him, and he looked over to the next bed, where Alice and Ella were playing with Godzilla. The puppy was tired; Bill could tell he wanted to sleep. He was irritable, so he snapped at them, but they didn't know when to stop. When Godzilla got bigger they'd have to be careful. He'd bite their hands off.

Bill saw Ollie go past. He was counting each kid, muttering the numbers out loud to himself. Blu-Tack watched him move along the row of beds, and when he got to Whitney, who was also counting, they had a quiet chat. Whitney nodded. They looked very serious. Blu-Tack could have saved Ollie the bother. He could have told him how many kids were in the room without counting, just by looking. He had a good head for numbers and his memory was perfect. His brain didn't work like other kids. He'd always known that. He could tell just by glancing around the room that everyone was there—forty-eight kids in all. Everyone except Maxie, Blue, Lewis, and Achilleus.

Bill looked down at his hands—he had shaped the number forty-eight without even thinking about it. He scrunched the stringy figures into a ball before anyone noticed, and kneaded it between his fingers.

Blu-Tack never said anything, but he never missed anything either. Something was going on. A group of big kids, the most important ones, had been having lots of whispered conversations all evening. Ollie and Achilleus, Whitney and Lewis.

Something was going to happen tonight. Bill tried to stop feeling worried. Slowly the ball of Blu Tack in his hands changed shape and became a smiling face.

Bill looked at the face.

"Don't be scared," it said.

There were shouts from outside, the sound of running feet.

Bill tensed; his hand squashed the face into a flattened

mess. That was the only visible sign that he was concerned. His expression gave nothing away. He had lived so long now on edge, waiting for something awful to happen, reacting to it when it did, that he was like a small wild animal. Constantly alert. All his senses tingling.

The footsteps passed by. Ollie and Whitney exchanged glances. It all went quiet again.

The face had reappeared in the Blu Tack.

"It's okay," it said. "You're safe now."

64

The royals sat in their bedroom in the dark, staring into space. It smelled in here. They had long since forgotten how to use the bathroom. Every now and then they were herded downstairs to sit on their thrones, but otherwise nothing happened in their world.

A cockroach crawled across the leg of a young man who was sitting on the floor. The young man's face was so bloated with swellings that his eyes were two tiny holes, and his nose had disappeared. He picked the bug up and put it in his mouth.

They were always hungry.

There was a noise in the corridor outside. Something scraped the door. All the heads in the room turned as one and looked in the direction of the noise.

There was a bang, the crunch of splintering wood. A second bang . . .

The door opened.

The corridor was empty.

Still chewing the cockroach, the young man got up and shambled to the door.

The others followed.

David's two guards had been sitting outside the sick bay for five hours straight. They were bored stiff. David had promised them that somebody would come to relieve them after three hours. No one had come.

This wasn't fair. It wasn't as if anything was going to happen anyway. The heavy wooden door was locked. There were only three kids in there. Two girls, one of whom was injured, and a boy with a concussion. What were they supposed to do? Batter the door down and overwhelm the two of them?

Fat chance. They had guns, after all.

"They've forgotten about us," said the taller of the two. He had short brown curly hair and a bad case of acne.

"They always do," said the other one, a fair-haired boy with a big nose. "Everyone thinks that just because we're in David's guard, our lives must be great. But this sucks."

"We do get a bit more food than the others," said Spotty.

"Oh whoop-di-doo," said Big Nose. "If I could, I'd trade this in and do farming or something. This is just tedious."

"We're the elite."

"So what?"

"When we take over London," said Spotty, "we'll be in a really strong position. It'll be like in the Middle Ages. When the king invaded another country he'd divide up all the lands and all the wealth to his favorite dukes and barons, the ones who'd helped him."

"When we take over London?" Big Nose mocked. "You mean *if* we take over London, don't you? All we ever do is sit around the palace with these bloody guns, trying to look important. We weren't even allowed to go on the raid to the squatter camp."

There was a clatter on the stairs, and they tried to look alert as Pod appeared, red-faced and flustered.

"Everything okay here?" he asked.

"Yeah." The boys shrugged.

"You haven't seen anything? Heard anything?"

"Like what?" said Spotty.

"The royals have escaped," said Pod, sounding ticked off and harassed.

"Say what?"

"They got out somehow, yeah? David's gone absolutely ballistic. It's crazy down there—everyone's, like, running around, trying to catch them."

"We should go and help," said Spotty, standing up.

"No, you need to stay up here and guard the prisoners."

"They're not going anywhere."

"Even so. If the prisoners got out too, David would go off the scale."

"One of us could stay here, the other could come with you," said Spotty.

Pod thought about this for a moment.

"All right." He looked at Spotty. "You come with me."

"What about me?" said Big Nose.

"Stay put until further orders," said Pod.

Big Nose watched sadly as the two of them hurried off down the narrow staircase.

Now, with no one to talk to, it would be even more tedious sitting here. Big Nose spat. Feeling a guilty pleasure as the gob of saliva sat there on the patterned carpet.

He swore loudly and colorfully, and for a moment it lifted the boredom.

65

Godzilla was asleep in Ella's lap. She was gently stroking his head and talking to him about Sam.

"I wish he was here, Godzilla. I really miss him. I don't like to think that I might never see him again, but every day I forget a little bit more about him. What he looked like. How he spoke. It's like he's slowly disappearing. What I remember most is that he was small. I'd do anything to make him come back."

Godzilla yelped and wriggled out of her arms. He jumped off the bed, and Ella chased him over to where Whitney was standing at the open ballroom door, looking off down the East Gallery.

Whitney saw Godzilla and grabbed him. She looked angry.

"Who's supposed to be looking after this dog?" she asked.

Ella looked like she was about to cry. "I'm sorry," she said.

Whitney's expression softened. She handed the puppy to Ella.

"Just keep him with you, darling," she said kindly. "All right?"

"All right."

As Ella went back to her bed, Maeve came over to join Whitney.

"See anything?" she said.

"Not a lot. No, wait a minute, here comes Pod."

In a moment Pod came bustling into the dormitory with two of David's guards.

"What's going on?" said Maeve. "There's people running everywhere."

"It's nothing to worry about," said Pod. "Some royals have escaped, that's all. It's a bit of a drag. We need some of your group to, like, come and help round them up, yeah?"

"Nothing to worry about?" Whitney exploded. "With grown-ups on the loose?"

"They're harmless," said Pod.

"No grown-up is harmless," said Whitney.

"So why don't you come and help look for them?"

"No way. I'm taking the kids somewhere safe, man."

"Listen." Pod offered Whitney a big cheesy grin. "It's no big deal. Nothing to get upset about, yeah?"

"I'm taking everyone outside the building. Now. Into the yard."

"You won't be safe out there," said Pod. "We've called all the guards in to look for the royals."

"We can look after ourselves, thank you very much," said Whitney.

"No—you should stay here," said Pod, trying to sound

like he was in control. "If you keep the doors closed you'll be fine."

"You don't tell us what to do, rich boy," said Whitney. "We're going to the parade ground until this is all over. End of story."

"Actually, I really do think you'll be a lot better off in here." Pod's smile was slipping.

"Like I care what you think," said Whitney. "With Blue and Maxie not around, I'm in charge. And if I say we go outside, we go outside. When you've found your precious royals we'll come back in."

Pod planted his feet wide apart and folded his arms. The smile had become a superior smirk now.

"You are not in charge here, actually, babes," he said. "I am."

"Who you calling 'babes'?" said Whitney, and she belted Pod hard in the stomach. He gasped and doubled over in pain. The two guards sprang to life, raising their rifles, but Big Mick and another of the Morrisons fighters had been standing ready. They seized the guns and wrenched them out of the boys' hands.

"We're going outside," Whitney said coldly to the two guards. "You stay here and look after Pod."

Pod had collapsed on to the floor and was sitting with his back against the wall, clutching his belly.

"It's all right," he groaned. "Let them go."

66

hree royals shuffled down a long corridor lined with paintings of past British kings and queens. They looked bewildered. David was waiting for them, one of his guards at his side. Apart from his freckles and a red flush across his cheekbones, David's skin was bone white. He was absolutely livid.

He held up his hand.

"Stop!" he shouted, his voice firm and clear.

One of the royals moaned. It was the young man with the bloated face. He was the son of a duke. He'd once been something of a party animal. Now he was a shambling wreck whose brain was so riddled with disease you could hardly even call it a brain anymore. It was just a tangle of damaged nerve endings, randomly firing off, as if someone had poured water into a fuse box.

He walked on.

"I command you," David said, louder this time, "to stop."

Still the royals staggered down the corridor. Whining, stiff-legged, red-eyed.

The guard turned to David. Scared. "They're not going to stop," he said.

"They will stop," David snapped, and he stepped forward.

The young royal sped up, his arms stretched out. Drool was pouring from his open mouth and had soaked his filthy shirt.

There was a deafening bang, and the corridor filled with smoke. The royal went down, a bullet in his skull.

"You idiot!" David yelled, wrenching the gun from the guard's grasp. "That was the Marquess of Tavistock!"

He battered the guard to the floor with the butt of his rifle.

"You can't go shooting them, you moron," he said. "We need them alive. They're no bloody danger."

Another royal, a middle-aged duchess, grabbed hold of David's sleeve, and he angrily shoved her away. She hit the wall and gulped with surprise.

David hauled his shaking guard to his feet. "Grab hold of them and drag them back to their room, for God's sake," he commanded. "Just don't let them bite you."

Jester appeared, running down the corridor with Rose.

"Any sign of the rest of them?" he called out.

"Not yet," said David. "It's only a matter of time, though. They won't have gotten far. They're too stupid. But how the hell did they get out?"

"The door was forced," said Jester.

"Was anybody guarding them?"

"Not as far as I know. We don't always keep a guard on them. And with two of your boys tied up at the sick bay . . ."

"So someone let them out?"

"Looks like it."

"Could it be the squatters?"

Jester shrugged. "It could be the Holloway kids. Maybe they're up to something."

"I want you to find whoever did this, Jester, and I want them punished. Properly punished."

"Okay."

"And where the bloody hell's Pod?"

"Last I saw him he was heading for the ballroom."

"Right. Come with me." David strode off down the corridor.

"Where are we going?" said Jester, hurrying after him.

"To the ballroom."

67

Big Nose was falling asleep. His head kept nodding forward and jerking him back awake. He could hear people moving around in the palace below and wished he could join them. It was very quiet up here. No sound came from behind the door. The murmur of voices from the sick bay had died away. He was utterly, utterly fed up.

He closed his eyes for a moment. The sound of hurrying footsteps died away. He was drifting off again. Dark fizzy milk filled his head. Bubbles swam and burst. He had a brief flash of a memory. Being on vacation in Florida. A giant Mickey Mouse.

Mickey called out his name. His head jerked forward; he opened his eyes with a grunt.

There were two boys standing there.

Two of the newcomers.

He recognized one. It was Achilleus, the one who'd been in the fight with the squatter. He'd missed that as well. The other one was tall and skinny with a messy Afro.

"What are you doing up here?" he said, struggling to look like he was on top of things.

"The royals have gotten out," said Achilleus.

"I know."

"They need your help. It's wild down there, man."

"I'm not allowed to leave my post."

"We'll take over," said Achilleus. He and his friend were casually edging closer as they talked. But casually enough for Big Nose not to notice.

"You can't," he said, standing up and leveling his gun. "You're newcomers, you might try to—"

The boy had been concentrating on Achilleus; he knew his reputation. The other boy looked too laid back to be much of a threat. Suddenly, though, he moved. And with startling strength and speed. Before the guard knew it, the newcomer had him pinned to the wall his rifle trapped, uselessly, between their bodies.

"Don't make a sound, cowboy," said Lewis, and he grinned at him. "Or I'll bust your face."

Big Nose nodded.

"We're not very good at this sneaking-up business," said Achilleus. "We should have just rushed him."

"Take his gun," said Lewis, "before he shoots me in the foot."

Inside the room, Maxie and Blue had silently forced the window open and were seeing if there was any way they could remove the bars that blocked it.

They turned together as the door swung open.

One of the guards from outside, the one with the big

nose, stumbled into the room. Behind him came Lewis and Achilleus, who was carrying the guard's rifle.

Maxie set her face into a cold mask. "What do you want?"

"It's like that scene in *Star Wars*," said Lewis. "We've come to rescue you."

Maxie laughed without much humor.

"Straight up," said Achilleus. "And you'd better hurry, we ain't got much time before David realizes what's going on."

"I don't get it," said Maxie. "I thought you were on his side."

"That prick?" said Achilleus. "You got to be kidding me. The only side I'm on is *my* side. And as I see it, that's your side too, Maxie. And yours, Blue."

"You can count me in," said the girl from the museum.

"Who's she?" said Achilleus.

"I'll explain later," said Maxie. "All you need to know for now is that she's coming with us."

"Fair enough."

"Where's everyone else?" said Maxie.

"If it's all gone according to plan, Whitney should be waiting for us outside on the parade ground with the other kids. We're all going over the fence. We've had to keep it quiet in case David found anything out. So far so good."

"But David's bound to find out what's going on," said Maxie. "He'll try and stop us."

"We created a diversion," said Lewis. "Let out his pets. With any luck the palace bozos are going to be way too busy to notice we've gone until it's too late."

"My man," said Blue, and he gave Lewis a hug.

Achilleus looked at Maxie. "You want a hug?"

"Nope."

"Didn't think so."

They went to the door and checked that the coast was clear.

"Wait!" Big Nose shouted, and they turned around, ready for anything.

"Take me with you."

"What?"

"I've had enough of David's crap. Please. Take me with you. He'll only punish me if I stay."

"Fine with me," said Achilleus. "But if you try any funny stuff, Big Nose, you're sausage meat."

Five minutes later the six of them burst out through the front arch onto the parade ground, where they found the entire Holloway crew assembled in battle formation, ready to leave. Maxie laughed and whooped and tilted her face up into the rain to shout "Yes!" at the top of her voice.

Paddy the Caddy hobbled over to Achilleus, struggling beneath the weight of his golf bag and Achilleus's shield.

"You need your spear yet, Akkie?"

"Not yet, caddy boy. Give me one of them cans, though."

Whitney gave the order, and the whole group marched toward the already open gates. Maxie could hardly believe it. Ten minutes ago everything had looked hopeless. And now they were walking to freedom.

It wasn't over yet, though.

As they were trooping out onto the road, there came a shout from the balcony.

"Where do you think you're going?"

It was David. He had Jester and five guards with him. The guards were training their rifles down toward the block of kids.

"We're off," said Maxie. "You blew it. That's all you need to know."

"I don't think so!" David shouted. "You go any farther and I'll order my guards to open fire. And don't think I won't, because—"

There was a sharp crack and one of the guards fell back with a cry.

He'd been hit by a slingshot. From this distance it wouldn't kill him, but it sure would hurt. Maxie looked around. Ollie was already fitting another steel ball into its pouch and pulling back the rubber band. His skirmishers were with him. The next moment a hailstorm of shot was rattling up onto the balcony. David's guards ducked down and cowered behind the parapet, Jester ran back indoors, and David was left crouching behind a pillar.

The Holloway kids laughed and jeered, and with Ollie's missile unit watching their backs, they safely left the palace grounds.

As they regrouped on the road, one of the little kids pointed to the Victoria Memorial and shouted. "Look at that!"

Achilleus was standing there. He had added his own message to Freak's. Big clumsy red letters spelled out two words.

FREAK LIVES.

And under them the tag—AKKIE DEAKY.

Maxie smiled and ran over to Achilleus. This time she hugged him.

"I finally figured out what Freak's original message meant," said Achilleus. "I was wrong about him. Blamed him for what went down with Deke and Arran. Wasn't his fault, any more than it was mine. Should have listened to him more. He was all right. He believed in what Arran believed in. For us to be together and strong and to do the right thing. In the end, all the bad stuff that happened to us, as well as all the good stuff, we got to share."

"I thought you'd gone over to David's side," said Maxie. "I thought you liked it here."

Achilleus shrugged. "Once I found out David had locked you up, that was it. You're one of us, Maxie. You're our leader. And besides, it's like I said, I wasn't gonna sit around here counting potatoes. I go where the action is."

"And what about Ollie?"

"You best ask him yourself. That boy is way too complex for me."

As the kids tramped off down the road, singing a selection of TV themes, Maxie went to find Ollie.

"I thought you'd sold me out," she said.

"It did cross my mind," he said with a grin. "I genuinely thought David had a good setup here. I didn't want to leave. But at the same time, I never really trusted him, and I needed to find out how far he'd take things."

"All that stuff you gave him in the sick bay . . ."

"By then I'd found out. He'd played his hand. And the last thing I wanted was to get locked up in there with you and Blue. Someone had to tell the others what was going on."

"You're a devious little red-haired rat," said Maxie. "But I love you."

"Steady, girl," said Ollie.

Maxie went to take her place at the front, and Ollie was left with his thoughts.

He looked at his watch. Quarter to eleven. Not long until midnight.

He hadn't told anybody about tomorrow. The others may have forgotten what date it was, even what day it was, but not Ollie. He had it all logged.

Tomorrow was his birthday.

Ollie knew a lot of things, but he had no idea what was going to happen to him as he got older. None of them did. If you made it to the end of the day, then it was a good day. You didn't think any further ahead than that. The future was a mystery.

How could Ollie know if he'd get sick or not? He was only a kid after all.

Everything was going to be all right.

He would just have to wait and see.

They marched down the middle of the road. Maxie, Blue, Achilleus, Paddy the Caddy, and the girl from the museum at the front with a fighting crew. Whitney in the middle with Maeve, Ben and Bernie, all the non-fighters, and the little kids. Blu-Tack Bill, Monkey Boy, and Ella fussing over Godzilla. Big Nose walking with them, not sure if he'd made the right decision. Lewis and his fighters were on one flank, Big Mick on the other with the gun he'd taken from the guard. Ollie at the back with the other skirmishers.

The little kids weren't scared. They'd been through too much together for that. They knew that the big kids would look after them. They trusted that they'd find a safe place to sleep, and food and water.

They headed west away from the palace. And as they entered Belgrave Square they came across a group of ten grown-ups who were eating a dead dog. When they lifted their heads from their filthy meal and saw the resolute army of kids approaching, they were like rabbits caught in the headlights.

Weapons bristled from the front rank of kids.

"You want to try and take us on?" Maxie shouted. "Come and get it, you sad old losers!"

The grown-ups took one look at each other, then turned and bolted, leaving their dinner behind.

Maxie laughed; Achilleus joined her. Blue put his arm around her waist. The other kids joined in, and soon their laughter was bouncing around the square and echoing off the empty houses, filling the night, chasing away the demons.

The fog inside his head was strong tonight. There was a red sheet in front of his eyes. And the pain was worse than ever. It was a living thing in his veins, like battery acid running through him, making him itchy and scratchy. His whole head throbbed. With the red mist and the hurting and the voices screaming in his skull, it was hard to think straight. He had to try to sneak up on his thoughts, take them by surprise before they slipped away from him. Like rats.

Or kids.

The kids were fast; you had to be clever to catch 'em. But he was clever. Somewhere inside his seething brain he knew that. He was learning that if he snatched hold of one of his thoughts, he had to act fast before it slipped away again and he was lost in the fog of confusion and pain.

He looked over at the buildings and saw someone looking back at him. No. Not allowed. Anger rose inside him, more powerful than the pain.

Who are you looking at?

A man in a white vest with a red cross on it.

He closed his eyes and clamped his hands over his mouth and rocked backward on his aching feet as a fresh agony clawed at him. Needles were sprouting from his brain and piercing outward, breaking the skin of his face. He growled in his throat and was comforted by the sound, the feel of the vibrations in his neck. He growled again. Enjoying it. It took his mind off everything else.

He opened his eyes.

He was surrounded by people. Why were they looking at him? All their bloody eyes on him. He snarled at them, and some of them backed away. God, that was good. He had power over them.

Yes.

It came back to him now. He was their boss. They were his army.

He'd been doing something.

What was it?

He shook his head. Growled again. Spat on the ground and looked at his spit. Maybe the shape of it would give him a clue. The spit was thick and yellow, flecked with red. He was momentarily hypnotized by it.

A thought was there. Circling. He pounced.

The car.

That was it. He turned around and clambered onto the hood. Then up onto the roof. He could see all the people now. Spread out around him, filling the road.

What was this road? He'd known its name once. He'd known the names of everything around here. It had been his manor. All gone now. All the words. All the difficult ones. Only a few remained.

Car. Road. Shop. Kid. Blood. Eat.

Look at them. His people. They worshipped him.

Scum. Boss. Kill . . .

Those sneaky kids. They tried to run. They tried to hide. Like words. Like thoughts. They were clever. But he was strong. And strong beat clever. He would kill them, every one of them. He would eat them. Like the one that had been in the shop.

He remembered that. Him sitting there. The kid. That boy.

They had his head. On a pole. It was their battle standard.

He roared. He was a lion. The top lion. He could choose the best bits from a kill. He looked over at what had once been the shop.

Fire.

That was another good word. Well, there it was. All on fire. He would move on now, take his army with him. Find every kid. Burn them, eat them, smash them. All the clever ones.

A memory came back to him. Clever kids at that place. With all the other kids. Laughing at him.

What was that word? A powerful one. One he didn't like.

School.

All the other kids laughing.

Well, look at me now. Boss. King. Lion. Killer . . .

He spread his arms wide, opened his mouth for a shout of triumph, but as usual nothing came out, just a low strangled growl.

They understood, though. His army. They raised their arms, shook their fists. The smarter ones, they shook weapons.

He looked over and saw that same man again, looking back at him. He hadn't moved.

Fat man. Bald. White vest with a red cross on it. He knew the words.

Saint George.

Then he smiled. The man was him. It was a . . . What was it? A mirror? A window? Yes. He was Saint George. A crusader. That made him happy. To remember hard words like that.

You see. If he was sneaky . . . If he came around the side. The words were there, just hiding.

He had a plan. Crusade. He would go into the lands of the enemy and burn and kill and break. And his people would follow him.

He began to stamp up and down on the roof of the car, hammering out a rhythm with his big feet. *Bang-bang-bang-bang-bang-bang*, one two, one two . . . Come dance with me.

Bang-bang-bang-bang-bang-bang, one two, one two . . .

His people joined in. Stamping up and down in the road. Their feet hammering the asphalt. *Thud-thud-thud-thud . . .*

The sound of an army marching. And that was what they were. They would march and they would kill and they would smash everything in their path.

He climbed down off the car and broke all its windows with his club. All the while stamping, one-two-one-two . . . And the more he stamped, the more he smashed, the more words came back to him, the more thoughts he could hold on to.

Everything he broke made him stronger.

He went into a frenzy, attacking every car in the road. Still stamping. It was the comforting sound of a machine.

Then he led them on. Back toward the battleground. The battle they had lost against the kids. They wouldn't lose any more battles. They were too many now. They were too strong.

He was Saint George.

This city belonged to him.

THE DISEASE SEPARATED THEM.
THE ADULTS TURNED ON THEM.

THE FIGHT
FOR SURVIVAL
BEGINS NOW.

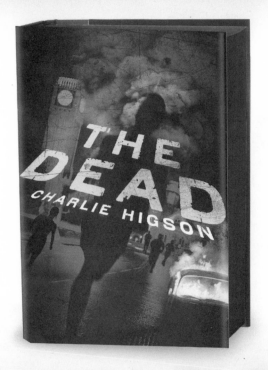

The terrifying prequel to **THE ENEMY**

from **Charlie Higson**

HYPERION | www.hyperionteens.com

DATE DUE